DESCENT: LEGENDS *of the* DARK

Terrinoth: an ancient realm of forgotten greatness and faded legacies, of magic and monsters, heroes, and tyrants. Its cities were ruined and their secrets lost as terrifying dragons, undead armies, and demon-possessed hordes ravaged the land. Over centuries, the realm slipped into gloom…

Now, the world is reawakening – the Baronies of Daqan rebuild their domains, wizards master lapsed arts, and champions test their mettle. Banding together to explore the dangerous caves, ancient ruins, dark dungeons, and cursed forests of Terrinoth, they unearth priceless treasures and terrible foes.

Yet time is running out, for in the shadows a malevolent force has grown, preparing to spread evil across the world. Now, when the land needs them most, is the moment for its heroes to rise.

ALSO AVAILABLE

ARKHAM HORROR

Wrath of N'kai by Josh Reynolds
The Last Ritual by S A Sidor
Mask of Silver by Rosemary Jones
Litany of Dreams by Ari Marmell
The Devourer Below edited by Charlotte Llewelyn-Wells
Dark Origins: The Collected Novellas Vol 1
Cult of the Spider Queen by S A Sidor
Grim Investigations: The Collected Novellas Vol 2
The Deadly Grimoire by Rosemary Jones

DESCENT: LEGENDS OF THE DARK

The Doom of Fallowhearth by Robbie MacNiven
The Shield of Daqan by David Guymer
The Gates of Thelgrim by Robbie MacNiven

KEYFORGE

Tales From the Crucible edited by Charlotte Llewelyn-Wells
The Qubit Zirconium by M Darusha Wehm

LEGEND OF THE FIVE RINGS

Curse of Honor by David Annandale
Poison River by Josh Reynolds
The Night Parade of 100 Demons by Marie Brennan
Death's Kiss by Josh Reynolds
The Great Clans of Rokugan: The Collected Novellas Vol 1
To Chart the Clouds by Evan Dicken

PANDEMIC

Patient Zero by Amanda Bridgeman

TERRAFORMING MARS

In the Shadow of Deimos by Jane Killick

TWILIGHT IMPERIUM

The Fractured Void by Tim Pratt
The Necropolis Empire by Tim Pratt

ZOMBICIDE

Last Resort by Josh Reynolds
Planet Havoc by Tim Waggoner

ZACHARETH

ROBBIE MacNIVEN

First published by Aconyte Books in 2022

ISBN 978 1 83908 144 6

Ebook ISBN 978 1 83908 145 3

Cover art by Joshua Cairós.

Map by Francesca Baerald.

Distributed in North America by Simon & Schuster Inc, New York, USA

Printed in the United States of America

9 8 7 6 5 4 3 2 1

ACONYTE BOOKS

An imprint of Asmodee Entertainment Ltd

Mercury House, Shipstones Business Centre

North Gate, Nottingham NG7 7FN, UK

aconytebooks.com // twitter.com/aconytebooks

To Dad, as ever with all my love.

PART ONE

CASTLE TALON

CHAPTER ONE
Highsummer, 1822

The first punch didn't draw blood, but the second did.

Zachareth felt it across his lips and in his mouth, warm and bitter. He spat, smattering Mikael's face with red.

The heir to the Barony of Cailn had been astride Zachareth in the dirt, but he recoiled. Zachareth seized the advantage, heaving against him with both hands and kicking out with his feet. The boy was thrown off, sprawling in the dust.

The surrounding stable hands jeered and shrieked. Zachareth was only half aware of them as he scrambled back to his feet. His ears were full of a dull ringing sound, and his cheeks burned. He spat more blood, cuffing it from his lips.

"Is that the best Cailn can do?" he demanded.

Mikael was back on his feet as well, his blond hair unkempt, his jerkin dusty and askew. He bared his teeth and flung himself at Zachareth.

As was so often the case, it had all happened fast. Castle Talon was hosting the Silver Tourney, a contest of arms held every four years between the northwestern baronies of Carthridge, Cailn, and Rhynn. Mikael, Cailn's heir, had arrived with his father's entourage the day before and had quickly sought out Zachareth along with several of his squires. Sharp words had been exchanged, Zachareth's own father insulted, and the honor of Carthridge questioned.

Zachareth couldn't actually remember who had struck the first blow, but just then he didn't much care. He tumbled in the dust with Mikael, grappling furiously, his long, dark hair half blinding him as he tried to rip himself free from the other boy's hold and land a blow of his own.

Mikael was a year older and quite a bit taller, but Golfang, the lieutenant of Baron Zelmar's guard, often told Zachareth that he was broad and strong for a thirteen year-old. He used that, trying to bear Mikael back down into the dirt, his teeth bared, pink with blood. Slowly, agonizingly, he overcame his rival's resistance, his limbs shaking with the strain as he pressed him against the ground. He managed to throw a leg over to straddle him and poised one fist, his thoughts keening with vengeance.

Something struck him in the ribs below his raised arm, not painfully so but sharp enough to make him yelp. He twisted astride Mikael, expecting to find one of the Cailn squires intervening. Instead, he was confronted by Bernard.

"Don't make me bloody your nose as well as your lip, boy," the heavy old tutor exclaimed, ruddy faced and brandishing his walking stave like a spear. Zachareth glared at him, cursing the fact that he had found him and was, predictably, now interfering. The cursed tutor was always interfering.

"You wouldn't dare hit me," he said.

"I just did, and I will again," Bernard replied, jabbing the stave threateningly.

Zachareth didn't get a chance to respond. Mikael heaved

against him, throwing him off. Once again, the two boys sprawled, and Zachareth cursed the loss of his advantage.

Bernard waded in, rapping the tip of his stave across Mikael's knuckles as he grabbed the front of Zachareth's doublet before physically wrapping one forearm around Zachareth's throat and hauling him up and away. The baronial heir struggled and choked on the musty wool of Bernard's long robe sleeve, finding his feet but remaining clamped in the tutor's grasp. Despite his age, Bernard possessed a fearsome strength.

"Cease your squirming, you accursed worm," he exclaimed irritably, keeping hold of Zachareth with one arm.

"That's quite enough from you too, Master Cailn," he added, using the stave in the other hand to ward off Mikael as the boy made to lunge at the pinned Zachareth. "Another twitch from either of you and I'll call for Captain Travas and have you both dragged before your parents. I'm sure they'd appreciate hearing that you've been fighting in public again just two days before the start of the tournament!"

Thoughts of parental chastisement took the edge off the furious energy coursing through Zachareth. He had no wish to stir his father's anger. He forced himself to be still and was rewarded with a loosening of Bernard's grip. He pulled himself free, glaring at Mikael, who glared right back.

"Be gone to your chambers," Bernard snapped, pointing the stave at the Cailn contingent before addressing the gawking pages and serving boys surrounding them. "And the rest of you, back to work! You should know better than to indulge these highborn dolts!"

As they scattered, Bernard grabbed Zachareth's shoulder and steered him firmly into the nearby stable block, the smell of both horses and straw hitting him. The beasts loomed on either side, snorting and stamping, seeming to tower over him. Bernard marched him between their pens to the trough at the far end of the outbuilding, wheezing and muttering under his breath, stave clacking against the straw-scattered cobbles.

"Avoiding your lessons is one thing, but scrapping like a feral street dog? For shame! By the flames of Kellos, if I could still travel, I would have taken up that posting at Greyhaven. At least there my students would wish to attend my classroom of their own volition!"

Zachareth didn't respond. He was still angry, but he knew better than to test Bernard any further. Right now, the tutor's goodwill was all that was stopping him from reporting Zachareth's misdemeanors to his father and, worse, to the baron's advisor, Leanna. That was a conversation he wanted to avoid at all costs.

Bernard stood him before the trough and planted a hand against the back of his head. Zachareth began to protest, then was forced to seal his mouth shut as he was plunged into the tepid water. The shock slammed through him, and it was an effort not to instinctively exhale the air he'd trapped in his lungs.

Bernard held him under for a few heartbeats, then hauled him back up. Zachareth gasped as water poured from him, drenching his doublet and running from his lank hair. His lip stung.

The tutor turned him around and snatched his jaw, angling his head left then right.

"It's stopped bleeding at least," he said, squinting at Zachareth's lip. "If you're lucky, the swelling will be gone by the time you're called to the hall for supper."

He let go. Zachareth scowled up at him and swept his sopping hair back out of his eyes.

"You look just like your father when you do that," Bernard said, his tone finally losing its hard edge.

"I know," Zachareth replied. Bernard often said such things, and he was never sure if it was meant as a compliment or not. He had no wish to turn out like his father, not now anyway.

"You're late for today's lessons," Bernard continued, pulling Zachareth's doublet straight. "I'll avoid telling Zelmar why, but in exchange, you have to make an effort with your readings this time. Do we have a deal?"

Zachareth knew he didn't have much of a choice. He nodded.

"We have a deal."

In the end, Zachareth didn't get far with the day's assigned text. They had just settled into Bernard's makeshift classroom – a cluttered, dusty garret in the north tower – when a sharp rap sounded at the door. Zachareth paused halfway through a ponderous recitation of the epic poem *The Foxes of Kell* and looked at Bernard, seated across the scroll-scattered lectern from him.

Had the old man betrayed him after all? Zachareth's expression clearly made the accusation for him because Bernard held his gaze for a moment before shaking his head. He picked up his stave and headed for the door.

Golfang was waiting beyond it, his craggy face unreadable. Like the rest of the baronial guard, the massive orc had been fully armed and armored since the arrival of the Cailn and Rhynn delegations, and he had to stoop slightly just to look in through the crooked attic door. Zachareth doubted he'd actually be able to fit through it, certainly not with the heavy-bladed falchion hanging at his hip.

"The baron wishes to see him," Golfang said to Bernard, nodding at Zachareth.

"He's in the middle of his studies," Bernard protested, even his heavyset bulk appearing tiny before the hulking warrior. Golfang wore a battered breastplate and a chainmail skirt over leather breeches, but his arms were bare above the vambraces that clad his wrists. To Zachareth, his arms appeared like mighty tree trunks, gnarled and axe-hewn, each ringed by dozens of white tattoo bands. The orc had once told Zachareth they represented every enemy's skull that he had crushed with his bare hands, though Bernard had confided that the more prosaic truth was that each band represented a year's service on the baronial guard.

"Still, the baron wants him," Golfang reiterated, his expression stoic as he looked past Bernard at Zachareth. Despite himself, he felt his heart quail at the thought of what awaited him.

"Is it actually the baron who wants him, or Leanna?" Bernard asked, seemingly unwilling to give up his charge. Golfang offered the merest of shrugs.

"You would have to ask the baron that yourself. Now, am I going to have to come in and take him myself?"

"No, you are not," Zachareth said before Bernard could answer. He forced himself to get down from behind the lectern, pausing to pointedly close the heavy cover of *The Foxes of Kell*. He wasn't going to let Golfang see he was afraid. He valued the guard's opinion more than he feared his father's summons.

Golfang nodded and moved aside for Zachareth to descend

the creaking wooden staircase beyond the garret's door. He heard Bernard calling out behind him.

"Don't think this means you're done with your studies. I'm leaving this book in your bedchamber, and I expect the next three chapters read by the time we meet again tomorrow!"

"Then I pray to Kellos that my father's punishment involves making me wear a blindfold," Zachareth called back, ignoring Bernard's irate response. Golfang chuckled as he followed him down the stairs, his chainmail clinking heavily.

"You are wise to only bait the word teacher when out of reach of his stave," he said. "If you had not come quietly, I fear I would not have been able to wrestle you from him."

"You never had to learn letters," Zachareth complained, disgusted at life's unfairness. "And look what you've achieved! You're second-in-command of the baronial guard of Carthridge!"

"True," Golfang admitted. "But I am not a tiny little raven-haired human pup like you."

Zachareth half turned to lash out at Golfang, but the orc simply swatted him away, laughing.

"Enough," he said. "It is not for idle merriment that your father summons you."

They passed through the echoing corridor that ran around the inside of the keep's western wall, evening sunlight streaming through the arrowslits to dapple the smooth stonework. As they went, Zachareth tried to gauge how bad things were.

"You might be in the hot stew this time, pup," Golfang admitted. "Your father knows about your scrapping."

Zachareth looked up at the guard as they walked, a frown crossing his face. "Did Bernard tell him?"

"No," Golfang responded. "Who do you think?"

"Leanna," Zachareth growled. It made sense. She seemed to know everything, her presence within the baronial court of Castle Talon all encompassing. She was a Latari elf but had advised Zelmar Carth for almost a decade. She was also a sorceress. Zachareth hated her for how she had wormed her way into his father's life, for how she now seemed to rule the barony more assuredly than he did. The emotion was so raw it momentarily came close to eclipsing his fear.

They descended the next set of spiral stairs and passed along the guest chamber corridor, pausing to let a pair of serving maids hurry by with bundles of used linen. This part of the castle was usually quiet, but now it bustled with the presence of the Rhynn and Cailn entourages. They encountered more chattering chambermaids, a scurrying errand boy, and a member of Greigory of Rhynn's household, bearing the Grandmother Oak on the chest of his jerkin. There were also retinue guards posted outside the bedchamber doors, who stiffened to attention as Zachareth and Golfang went by. Zachareth half hoped he would run into Mikael leaving his room. They'd see how that Cailn whelp fared with Golfang to back him up.

Their route took them to the antechamber outside Castle Talon's great hall. A taperer was lighting the braziers bolted to the walls, their kindling flames illuminating the graven expressions of Zachareth's grandparents and great-grandparents, rendered in Carthmount stone in alcoves on either side. He always looked at them whenever he passed, trying to imagine his own likeness alongside them some day. It was difficult because he so rarely felt that he wanted to become baron like his father. He wanted more than a lifetime of duty and leadership. He avoided the hard, stony eyes.

They halted outside the oaken doors that led into the hall. Golfang placed one massive hand on them, but before opening them, he paused and looked down at Zachareth.

"You are afraid," he said.

"I'm not," Zachareth replied, scowling. The guard was too perceptive for his own good. His heart was racing.

"You are a poor liar too," Golfang continued. "Which does not bode well for what is about to unfold. Have courage, little pup. There are worse things in this world than a father's scorn."

"If that's so, I have yet to encounter them," Zachareth said heavily, steeling himself and staring straight ahead. Golfang let out a short laugh and opened the doors.

CHAPTER TWO

"Don't just stand there, boy," Zelmar Carth barked, his voice ringing from the timber rafters. "Come here where I can see you."

Zachareth stepped across the threshold and into the great hall. It was a high, wide space, the finest of its kind in northern Terrinoth. Though the arching ceiling and its rafters were built from timber, the walls and floor were fashioned from stone, great slabs that had been set in place centuries before. Tapestries decorated the flanks of the long room, massive lengths of woven cloth depicting moments in time from both Carthridge and from wider Terrinoth. There were hunting scenes with loping hounds and boars and soaring hawks as well as representations of the marriages and deaths of the noble line of Carth, interwoven alongside the construction of Castle Talon upon its crag, the defeat of terrible dragons wreathed in flame, and silver knights driving into the legions of Waiqar's undead. Zachareth loved to sit and stare at them and imagine himself in the midst of each depiction in turn, but right now, he was too afraid to even glance at them.

The floor underfoot was covered by a wide red and gold rug, worn and faded but still soft underfoot. Zachareth's great-great-grandmother had, according to the chronicles Bernard made him read, been a princess from far-off Al-Kalim. The rug had been part of her dowry. A section of it had been removed so it didn't rest up against the vast fireplace that dominated one wall, its blackened bowels freshly rekindled. A heavy timber feasting table, each leg carved with the likeness of one of the Carthridge barons of yore, sat unoccupied along the opposite wall. Zachareth passed by it on the way to the room's far end.

It felt like a long walk. Golfang didn't go with him but remained by the doors. Zachareth suddenly felt very alone as he passed beneath the gallery of beasts and ancestors adorning the walls.

Zelmar waited. He was reclining on his baronial throne, clad in a white gown with silver trim, one leg raised and planted on a footstool. His face hinted at the fact that it had once been like Zachareth's, the features formerly strong and well defined, but it had long lost the freshness of youth. His eyes were hooded and sunken, his jaw fattened, his long, black hair thinning and rooted in gray. He was not yet forty Highsummers old, but he seemed older. Again, as he approached, Zachareth found himself wondering when and why his father's love for him had turned so bitter.

Leanna was with him, as ever. She sat on the consort's throne beside Zelmar, the place Zachareth knew would once have been occupied by his mother before her death. She wore a dress of silver scales that shimmered in the firelight, its skirts widening into great folds of black silk. A staff rested in one hand, designed like a twisting length of root knots and enameled black. Her hair, a dusky red, was piled high upon her crown. Her face always left Zachareth feeling cold. It was beautiful, in a deadly sort of way, high-boned and sharp-eared, her elven heritage unmistakable. She reminded him of one of the hawks woven into the hall's tapestries, cruel and keen and deadly. Her golden-yellow eyes rarely seemed to blink.

Zachareth's step almost faltered. He managed to make himself look at Leanna and noticed the small smile on her lips. It sent fresh anger burning through him, momentarily scorching away his fear. He carried on until he was standing before the pair.

"Your lip is swollen, boy," Zelmar said. "Who hit you?"

Caught somewhere between fear and defiance, Zachareth said nothing.

"Answer me," Zelmar demanded.

"Mikael."

"Did you hit him back?"

"I tried."

Zelmar's expression darkened further.

"Once again, you embarrass me," he said. "Brawling like a street urchin with the heir of one of our closest allies. The Silver Tournament begins in less than two days, and I have to apologize to Wilem and Maria because their son was set upon in my own castle's bailey!"

"Mikael insulted you," Zachareth blurted, his cheeks beginning to burn with anger and shame. "He called you an old, weak fool who couldn't even mount a horse anymore. He said Carthridge was tarnished, and its might spent. That I would inherit nothing that wasn't rotten or crumbling!"

"And I'm sure you said much the same in turn," Zelmar sneered, his voice rising to fill the hall, making Zachareth flinch. "You think I am so hopeless, so weak that I need a scrawny youth like you to defend my honor? You offer me greater insult with your pathetic lack of control!"

Zachareth choked up. He desperately didn't want to cry, but his eyes were stinging. He had been dreading this. He screwed them shut, trying to master himself. Zelmar let him suffer for what, to Zachareth, felt like an age before carrying on.

"Fortunately for you, I have already apologized to Baron Cailn, and he has accepted it. I have yet to decide on your punishment. I've a mind to give you the rod."

"Perhaps a practical redress might prove more beneficial," Leanna said. It was the first sound she had uttered since Zachareth had entered the hall. He managed to cuff his eyes dry, glowering at her. Every time she spoke, he feared the worst.

"I believe Master Carth got into his dispute while avoiding the tutelage of Bookkeeper Bernard," she continued. "Perhaps extra lessons are in order to make up for lost time?"

"Bernard's lessons hardly seem to be having an effect," Zelmar pointed out, shifting uncomfortably in his seat. "I pay the old fool too much as it is."

"Nevertheless, Zachareth needs an education," Leanna urged, placing a hand lightly upon Zelmar's. "Maybe while the tournament is on? I would call that punishment both fitting and sufficient."

Zelmar grunted noncommittally, waving his free hand. "If you think it's for the best, Leanna, then let it be so." He fixed his eyes once more on Zachareth.

"I will inform Bernard, and you will report to him at the second dawnsbell tomorrow. He'll keep you as long as he wishes. Your swordplay with Golfang is also canceled for the foreseeable future, and you'll not dine with us tonight. Nor will you attend any of the jousts or contests-at-arms over the coming days. You can consider all this a mercy. Were it solely my decision, I would have you confined to the western tower until the tournament has ended."

"It should be solely your decision," Zachareth declared,

managing to find his voice. He felt a small sense of satisfaction as he saw Zelmar's eyes widen with shock.

"I will take the master to his chambers," Golfang said. Despite the orc's size, he had approached Zachareth from the doors without him noticing. He placed one massive hand on the boy's shoulder, an act that might have appeared threatening but from which Zachareth took silent comfort.

"That might be for the best," Leanna said, a warning note in her voice. Zelmar was gripping the arms of his throne now, on the verge of a fresh tirade.

Holding him firmly, Golfang steered Zachareth out of his father's hall.

It turned out Bernard was as good as his word. Zachareth returned to his room to find the weighty text of *The Foxes of Kell* resting on the table beside his bed.

He was tempted to throw it from the tower window, but it was so large he realized he would have struggled to fit it through. Instead, he ignored it, slumping on his bed.

He felt miserable, and even worse, he was frustrated by what had passed in the hall. Braced for his father's wrath, he'd instead been offered a degree of clemency thanks to Leanna, which somehow seemed even worse – it felt as though it had put him in her debt. Even without using her magic, she was too powerful, too influential. He was certain she was poisoning Zelmar against him. The fact that he was going to have to spend the duration of the Silver Tournament in Bernard's musty garret was the final blow.

As the sun set outside, he wallowed in his unhappiness, trying to ignore his hunger, until a soft knock at the door dredged up his thoughts from where they had sunk. He ignored the first summons but at the second got up and freed the latch.

Leanna was outside. Zachareth immediately tried to close the door again, but she planted her lacquered staff between it and the frame. Zachareth heaved on it, but despite the elf's painfully slender build, the door showed no hint of budging.

"We should talk," she said.

"You should leave," Zachareth replied.

"If only it were that easy," Leanna said. Zachareth frowned, not understanding.

"What do you want?" he asked acidly.

"To be friends," Leanna replied. "Or at least to stop being enemies. A truce, if you will, with an eye to a lasting peace. May I come in?"

Zachareth considered his options. Leanna rarely spoke to him directly, especially in private. As much as his anger still simmered, a part of him was curious about why she had sought him out after having him banished.

"Leave your staff at the door," he told her. She arched one wicked eyebrow.

"You have nothing to fear from me, Master Carth," she said. "I am your family's most loyal servant."

"Then, as my family's most loyal servant, I'm telling you to leave your staff at the door," Zachareth repeated. Leanna offered a terse smile, clearly stung by his stubbornness, but she released her staff, propping it against the inside of the doorframe. Zachareth stepped back, allowing her in.

"If you want to be friends, you could start by releasing my father from the spell you have him under," Zachareth said, backing up to sit on the end of his bed without taking his eyes off Leanna. She laughed, the sound cold and clear as a Deepwinter morning in the Carthmounts.

"The arrangement between your father and I involves no spell," she said, easing the door so it stood only slightly ajar before facing Zachareth, smiling down at him. "I told you, I am your family's servant. I fulfill my duties by advising him."

"You weaken him so he relies on you more and more," Zachareth said accusingly. "You think I am too young to remember a time before you came to Carthridge, but you are wrong. He was strong once and kind. He did not stay in his chambers day and night, never leaving Castle Talon. Now he can do nothing unless you first suggest it."

"Even my people are not immune to the passage of time," Leanna said, speaking slowly as though he were still a small child. "And humankind most certainly is not. Your father is not an evergreen ironbark that stands unbowed through the ages. Ruling this barony is a weight he has borne since he was your age. That he still conducts his duties, despite the lance injury he suffered as a youth and his ailments, is a credit to him and to his forebearers."

Zachareth was hardly listening. He'd heard the sorceress defend his father, along with her own presence at his court, before.

"One day he will stop listening to you," he told Leanna. "And I pray to all the gods that day is soon."

She smiled her cold, condescending smile.

"I did not come here to spar with you, Master Zachareth," she said. "In truth, I came to advise you."

"Advise me?" Zachareth repeated incredulously. Leanna moved across the chamber to the chair beside the window, lowering herself onto it and pausing a moment to rearrange the heavy black folds of her dress. The last of the evening sunlight was shining in through the window's small, cloudy panes. It made her red hair look like fire and left her angular face half shadowed. The silver scales of her dress glittered.

"I told you, I serve the Carths," she said, her tone serious. "That includes not only your father but you as well. Someday I will advise you in your role as ruler of this barony."

"You seem very sure that day will come," Zachareth said.

"Fates willing," Leanna replied. "It occurred to me recently that part of our antagonism might spring from the fact that you have never really witnessed just how effective my advice can be. Take today's… unfortunate events for example. You attacked Mikael outside the stables."

"He attacked me," Zachareth responded sharply, though in truth he still couldn't remember who had struck first.

"Who began it has little relevance," Leanna said. "The story that has spread is that you attacked Mikael of Cailn in a rage and had to be restrained. You are now experiencing the consequences of those actions.

"You have your own version of events," she went on before Zachareth's outrage had a chance to vent. "You were attacked in your own home by a larger, older rival who insulted both your honor and your family's. You defended yourself and, by extension, Carthridge. In such an account, your actions appear wholly understandable, possibly even laudable. Such a story would have reaped different consequences."

Zachareth tried to make sense of what she was suggesting. He felt as though he was being lectured in Bernard's classroom.

"Why has your account lost out to the other?" she said. "Perhaps it fits the perceptions others hold of you? More importantly, though, no one has backed your claims. What do you think might have happened in the great hall if I had spoken up in your favor? If I had told your father that what you had done was bold and brave? Do you think he would still have punished you so?"

"You want to prove to me the power you hold over him," Zachareth said, trying to get to the heart of the matter. He didn't trust the sorceress's words, and he didn't want to be drawn into a verbal game with her.

"No," Leanna replied. "I want to show you that people's opinions matter. Even more so than the truth. That is the first thing I might teach you. The next is how you could have avoided your current censure."

Zachareth found himself listening. The elf's words flowed so easily, so precisely. For a moment, he did want to know more. It was tempting to let go of his reservations, to just sit and allow her to speak.

"You and Mikael have shared your disputes for as long as either of you can remember," she said. "Whenever the Silver Tournament takes place, you fight. Such a thing is hardly unusual. But I would caution you to be more aware of when and how you come to blows with him. If you must clash – and sometimes, in your future role, you will indeed be left with no choice other than to resort to strength of arms – you should do so wisely."

A furtive note had entered the conversation, Zachareth realized. It felt underhanded yet ever more intoxicating. He leaned forward slightly on the edge of the bed.

"Go on," he said carefully.

"If you fight Mikael again, do not do so in the middle of the castle courtyard," Leanna said. "Far too many will see. Strike instead when it is dark, and quiet, and when only those whose loyalty you are sure of stand nearby."

"There is no honor in that," Zachareth pointed out, trying not to admit that a part of him was intrigued by the idea.

"Honor is an abstract notion, Master Carth," Leanna said, her tone steady and patient. "It has its uses, but a ruler who is hidebound by it will soon come undone. Honor does not have an answer to many of the situations you will face when you are Baron of Carthridge. It will not gather the harvest, or raise taxes, or mine the Carthmounts for silver."

Zachareth said nothing, considering her words carefully. For once, what she said seemed true enough. With the ease of hindsight, he could see that his attack against Mikael had been foolish. He could still remember the fury that had gripped him, the unreasoning heat of it. His father had blamed his lack of control. He resolved not to be so weak in the future.

"Now, on to the final reason I am here," Leanna said, her hawkish smile returning. The sun had almost faded behind her, the shadows within the room deepening. "It does involve matters of honor, I suppose. Mikael insulted you and, through you, your father, and this very barony. You sought redress, but it was clumsy and ill considered. It is my duty to offer more effective solutions."

"Speak plainly," Zachareth said, repeating a phrase he'd heard his father use in council. He still wasn't entirely certain the sorceress wasn't mocking him.

"Mikael of Cailn is due some form of misfortune," Leanna said. "A minor one, of course. Perhaps a trip near the bottom of the stairs leading to his chamber corridor or a jammed entrance to the garderobe privy."

"You could make that happen?" Zachareth asked with a note of incredulity. He was listening intently, his thoughts turning over the possibilities. All his life, he'd viewed Leanna's presence as a threat, her abilities a challenge to be overcome. He had never once considered utilizing them for his own benefit.

"Say it, and it will be done," Leanna said. "I told you, I am your family's servant."

Zachareth frowned again, pondering what was being offered. The temptation to strike back at Mikael was overwhelming, but other thoughts troubled him.

"He wouldn't know I was the one who caused his misery," he pointed out.

"Which is for the best," Leanna said. "If you wish to avoid the likelihood of further punishment."

"Then it loses its point," Zachareth said. "Cailn must know it cannot challenge Carth."

"Now you are speaking like the future ruler of this barony," Leanna said.

"You would put me in your debt as you have done with my father," Zachareth replied, realizing abruptly how close he was to falling into the sorceress's trap. "With little deeds, you would control me as you control him."

"You are perceptive," Leanna said. "But still mistaken. A lord cannot owe his servant a debt."

"How did my father find out about the fight?" Zachareth asked her, deliberately changing tack. It was now too dark to clearly make out whether Leanna's expression changed when he asked the question.

"Perhaps your tutor told him?" she said.

"I do not think Bernard would have betrayed me. Either way, I wish to know. Were your sorceries responsible?"

Leanna leaned forward so the light from the door caught her face. Zachareth saw that she was smirking.

"Indeed," she said. "I sacrificed one of the stable boys and anointed myself with his blood, then used my enchanted mirror to scry your whereabouts."

Zachareth recoiled in horror before realizing that she was jesting. She laughed, and he glowered.

"I saw you from my chamber window," she said. "There is nothing more to it than that. Magic has many uses, but it does not make me omnipotent. Not yet, anyway."

Zachareth stood up, making a mental note to ask Bernard what *omnipotent* meant when he was next caught by him. He thought he knew, but if the tutor was angry at the time, then asking an educational question would probably help distract him.

"It has grown late," he said, using an excuse he had heard his father employ with unwanted company. "Time for you to leave."

Leanna rose, brushing down her skirts. She stood wholly in darkness now, only the torchlight coming through the crack in the chamber door offering any sort of illumination, spilling across Zachareth and his bed.

"Consider again the fate of Master Mikael," she said, moving past him to the door, momentarily blocking off its light before she opened it wider. "Let me know before the feast tomorrow. And, oh, I almost forgot…"

She reached into one of the pockets of her voluminous skirts and drew out something bound in a square of linen. She unwrapped it to reveal a slice of bread and cheese. She left it on the stool by the door. The sight of it sent a pulse of hunger, unbidden, through Zachareth.

"I wouldn't want you to starve, Master Carth," she said, before picking up her staff and easing the door shut behind her.

CHAPTER THREE

The Highsummer sun was beating down on Castle Talon, making the stone bake and turning the rolling valley the citadel guarded into a patchwork of green, gold, and purple.

Zachareth had spent his morning hiding from Bernard in one of the turrets in the castle's northeastern tower. He'd paid the guard who was supposed to be on watch, Skerrif, a silver half star to take an hour off, promising to keep a good eye on the approaches to the citadel's crag. Alone, he had instead contemplated life's miseries. His father cared nothing for him. He was too busy drinking the poison Leanna dripped into his mind, day by day. That was what Zachareth told himself, though he was afraid that, in truth, even if Leanna hadn't been a part of the court, Zelmar would still have hated his only son. He just wished he understood why.

Bitter thoughts coiled through his mind as he leaned against the turret wall, gazing out over the valley. Its flanks were mottled with northern heather, just coming into full bloom, while the stream that coiled around the base of the castle's rocky outcrop stretched away like a glittering blue ribbon along the valley floor, fading eventually into the haze. In the distance, the Dunwarrs stood out against the azure, a craggy parapet of far-off white peaks.

He watched the mountains for a while, his mind finding refuge as he conjured up epic fantasies of travel and adventure. He wished he could go there, could go anywhere really, anywhere that wasn't Castle Talon. Bernard and Zelmar spoke only of his duties, of how important it was that he became a strong ruler when he was baron. He didn't want any of that, though. Right now, he just wanted a life beyond cold stone walls and musty old books.

His fantasies were banished by a flurry of feathers, making him yelp. A pigeon had just tried to enter through the turret's arrowslit, veering off at the last moment as it spotted Zachareth within. Judging by the twigs and droppings on the stonework around him, he realized the creature probably used the tower as a refuge just as frequently as he did.

Growing bored, he wandered down through the keep toward the bailey, no longer caring if he was apprehended. As he stepped out the main doors and into the sunlight, he caught the ring of steel and the flash of bared swords.

Two men were fighting in the castle courtyard. One was in his forties or fifties with a bushy beard, edged with white. He was dressed in a leather smock bearing the oak of Rhynn and carried a longsword, his weathered face creased with concentration as he used it to defend himself.

His opponent was younger, perhaps in his late twenties. He wore blue hose but was naked from the waist up, his lean musculature glistening with sweat. His hair was long, thick, and blond, and it flew as he swept his own longsword in a series of scything motions toward his opponent, the wide blows driving the older man back. He fought with a grin on his face, and Zachareth suspected he knew why.

The heir of Carthridge slunk into the shade of the castle's curtain wall and planted himself on one of the barrels being loaded into the kitchen. The cook's assistants hefting the produce had paused to watch the clash, as had an increasingly large number of the citadel's servants, keepers, and staff.

A gasp went up as the topless combatant appeared to overextend with one of his arrogant, sweeping blows, leaving himself exposed. The older man lunged in for the kill.

Zachareth had been expecting as much, and so had the other fighter. Golfang had always taught him that the most important parts of the body during single combat were the feet. Zachareth had already noted that the younger fighter had been moving his lower half conservatively, even while making a great show with his lunges. He wanted to appear overly aggressive and lacking in control, but he had kept his balance, his center. As his rival sought to take his chance, the other fighter twisted his toned form and, with only a small flick of his wrist, brought his sword back in, scraping along the lunging blade and diverting it off to one side. At the same time, he stamped his foot in close, meeting the attacking thrust and snatching the wrist of the bearded man's sword arm with his other hand, pinioning it away from his body.

"Almost, uncle," the younger man panted, his grin staying fixed as he released his bested rival and shook his blond hair from his eyes.

Zachareth had seen him fight before. He knew them both. The bearded one was Augen Rhynn, and his smiling rival was his nephew, Greigory, Baron of Rhynn. Zachareth had been introduced to them on several occasions, including at the last

Silver Tourney, when Rhynn had hosted the competition. This was the first time that Zachareth had encountered Greigory since he had taken on the mantle of baron, however. His father had died of the flux the year before.

Augen stepped away from his nephew, switching his sword to his other hand and flexing his fingers. Greigory stretched nonchalantly, gazing around at the onlookers as though only just noticing them. His eyes swept through the crowd before coming to rest on where Zachareth was perched.

He beckoned him with one finger. Childish instinct made Zachareth want to ignore the direct summons, but the bared steel still in Greigory's fist had caught his interest, gleaming brilliantly in the noonday sun. He hopped down off the barrel and approached.

"Bring me a gourd from the well, stable boy," Greigory said, stretching once more.

"I'm not a stable boy," Zachareth said indignantly. "You know full well who I am."

"If you're Zelmar's son, you've grown a fierce amount since I saw you last," Greigory said, laughing. "Did your father send you down from the keep to spy on me before the start of the tournament?"

"I doubt my father would trust me to spy on anyone," Zachareth responded, unable to keep the ice from his tone. Greigory looked down at him thoughtfully for a few moments, then gestured to Augen, who had been standing by, watching the exchange.

"Give him your sword, uncle," he said. Augen seemed about to argue, then thought better of it. He turned his weapon so the blade was resting against his left forearm and the grip was extended beyond it, offering it down to Zachareth.

He took the handle, body tense as he fought to control its weight. He was able to hold it with both hands, but the grip was uncomfortable, a far cry from the sparring sticks he normally used with Golfang whenever they trained.

"Child's too small for a longsword," Augen said to Greigory, smiling. Zachareth glared at him.

"I am no child," he said. Greigory's own grin returned.

"No indeed, Lord Carth! How old are you now? Ten summers? Eleven?"

"Thirteen," Zachareth said, trying and failing not to sound surly as he focused on keeping the sword's tip raised. He knew Greigory was making fun of him. It stirred his anger, triggering that childish desire to lash out.

"Old enough to defend the honor of Baron Zelmar of Carth then," Greigory said. "Or so I hear." Zachareth felt an unexpected pang of embarrassment.

"You know about the fight with Mikael?" he asked.

"Mikael is a little rodent," Greigory said in a low, conspiratorial tone. "His father indulges him too much while yours indulges you too little, I think."

"He is preparing me for my role," Zachareth said, becoming defensive, sensing Greigory's judgment about his father. "To rule a barony, especially one as large and as powerful as Carthridge, requires strength."

"Your familial loyalty does you credit," Greigory said. "Now let's see if we can take your mind off such matters for a while, shall we?"

He raised his sword to salute Zachareth. Face tight with concentration, the heir of Carthridge returned the gesture, immediately adopting a low guard. His heart was pounding, and sweat was starting to bead his scalp. The sun felt infernally hot, amplified by the high stone walls surrounding them. He tried to remember everything Golfang had ever taught him all at once.

Greigory adopted a high guard and stamped his front foot forward. Zachareth recoiled, then glared when he realized Greigory hadn't actually swung into the attack. He was taunting him.

The anger returned. He lunged in at the Baron of Rhynn, yelling, all lessons forgotten in an instant.

Greigory swept his blade downward, knocking the point of Zachareth's longsword into the dirt. The clanging impact hurt his hands and seemed to shudder right through his body. He snarled and threw himself into Greigory's legs and stomach, ignoring both guard and posture. The fact that he had been disarmed so easily frustrated him, his earlier desire to maintain his self-control evaporating.

The sudden charge caught the baron by surprise. They both went down together, Zachareth losing his grip on the heavy longsword. He was the first back up, about to leap on his opponent as he had done with Mikael, but Greigory lashed out a foot, kicking a cloud of dust up into Zachareth's face. He recoiled, coughing and hissing, rubbing furiously at his stinging eyes. By the time he'd recovered, Greigory was back on his feet, sword in hand.

Zachareth's fury redoubled. He scrambled in the dirt to retrieve his own sword as Greigory watched, heaving it back up and lunging once more in an uncontrolled stab toward Greigory's guts. The baron sidestepped and deftly trapped the blade against his torso with his left arm as it slid past, twisting his body so it was wrenched from Zachareth's grip.

Disarmed, Zachareth was about to start swinging with his

fists when Greigory's theatrical cry made him stop. The ruler of Rhynn dropped his sword and, with Zachareth's weapon still lodged under his arm, stumbled a few paces.

"I am slain," he announced to the onlooking crowd before collapsing in the dirt to a spate of laughter. One of the kitchen hands started applauding.

Zachareth stood over Greigory, fists balled, unsure whether he was still angry or not. The baron lay prone for a few moments, his eyes glazed, then he looked at Zachareth and winked.

"You play games," Zachareth said tersely, part embarrassed, part annoyed. Greigory pretended to be shocked as he jumped lithely back to his feet and released the sword, catching it.

"The murder of the Baron of Rhynn is but a game to this boy," he said to Augen, who was now grinning as broadly as his nephew. "Do the ambitions of Carthridge know no bounds?"

"You mock me in front of my people," Zachareth pointed out, remembering his father's anger over fighting publicly with Mikael. Greigory looked about at the dispersing crowd and leaned down to Zachareth's level, speaking in a stage whisper.

"In truth, I wanted to end this before you ran me through, little master."

"There is still time for that," Zachareth said. Greigory chuckled and tossed Augen's sword back to him.

"You have spirit, Lord Carth," he said. "Which is more than can be said of some at this tournament. I hope you will be in attendance at the feast tonight."

"My father will make sure of it," Zachareth said. Just then he caught the sound of his name, ringing out from somewhere within the keep. He froze, looking up at the towering fastness. It was Bernard, hunting for him.

"Is that your tutor?" Greigory asked, noting Zachareth's

expression. "Best make yourself scarce. I'll tell him I've seen neither hide nor hair of you."

"Then I'll consider us even," Zachareth said, already making for the bailey's outhouses.

Bernard finally cornered him hiding in the pantry beside the kitchen block.

"Class," the tutor snarled, snatching Zachareth by the ear and twisting. Hissing with pain, Zachareth allowed himself to be led to the foot of the north tower before shaking Bernard off.

"It's almost time for the feast," he declared indignantly. "I'm banned from the tournament, not from the great hall! Zelmar will want me to be seen by the guests."

"I've no intention of attending the feast tonight," Bernard said, herding Zachareth up the tower stairs. "I've no time for sycophants and clowning and bad venison. And since you've wasted so much of my time looking for you today, I shall waste a little of your time in turn, Master Carth. Your father has put you at my disposal, feast or not."

Back in the garret, Bernard attempted to apply Zachareth's thoughts to his spelling and lettering before eventually giving up.

"You are quite the most ungracious, ungraceful boy I have ever had the misfortune to teach," he said as Zachareth botched another word, throwing his hands up in despair. "Don't you want to achieve anything in your life?"

"You think I want to be like my father," Zachareth responded, tossing down his quill in exasperation. "Or like Leanna or like you. Always talking about prestige or power or learning. But I don't want to be like any of you. I want to be like Baron

Greigory. I want to be a strong warrior. I want to be respected. I want a life beyond this place."

Bernard looked surprised for a moment, then scoffed.

"That knave. More concerned with his swordplay and his handsome face than with his duties. He inherited his role too young, I say."

"He is a good man," Zachareth replied, instinctively rallying to the Baron of Rhynn's defense. "He treats me like an equal. That's more than anyone else does. All you do is talk down to me and scold me! I am forbidden from playing with the servants, forbidden from sparring with Golfang, forbidden from leaving the castle on my own. Now I cannot even attend the jousting tomorrow! My only enjoyment is hiding from you!"

Zachareth expected an angry response to the outburst. Instead, Bernard pursed his lips, looking at him. Zachareth narrowed his eyes, wondering just what the tutor was planning, whether it was going to be some further form of punishment.

"You know I take my duties seriously," Bernard said eventually. Zachareth was surprised by the hint of remorse in his voice. For a few moments, it seemed as though the stern tutor had withdrawn, leaving behind someone altogether less fearsome, less sure of himself.

"I owe the Carths a great deal," he carried on. "I was but a young kitchen hand when I became friends with your grandfather. He funded my entry into Greyhaven. I found I had no aptitude for the runes, but I learned my letters and learned them well. When your father asked me to teach you, I thought of it as helping to repay the debt I owe your household. It is a serious matter, and I have always handled it as such. But perhaps in doing so, I have not treated you as you deserve."

Zachareth didn't know what to say. He vaguely knew the story of how Bernard had ended up employed at Castle Talon, but he had never had it delivered firsthand and not with such contrition. He found himself unsure of how to respond.

"I have something for you," the tutor continued. He rummaged through several of the untidy mounds of books piled around the loft, then approached Zachareth's lectern with one of the texts he'd unearthed.

Zachareth tried not to feel too disappointed. Another book, albeit one far smaller looking than the tomes he was usually assigned to read.

"This is *The Canticle of Rufus the Bold*," Bernard said, placing the book down carefully in front of Zachareth. "Written by Malrond the Younger, one of the most celebrated storytellers in Terrinoth. You have heard of Rufus?"

"Yes," Zachareth said, looking down at the book. He recalled the name from the lineages Bernard had made him memorize. "He is one of my forebearers. A baron of Carthridge in the 1500s. He helped turn back the unliving armies of Waiqar, the dread necromancer."

"He did," Bernard agreed, opening the leather cover for Zachareth. The first page was a magnificent illustration of a mounted knight in silver armor, trampling over skeletal reanimates. Zachareth had seen its likeness before on the tapestries in the great hall. It shimmered on the page, almost mesmerizing in its color and detail.

"Rufus Carth was one of this barony's greatest rulers," Bernard said. "His story is a grand one, full of heroism and desperate daring, and it is well told by Malrond."

"It is a chronicle, a historical account?" Zachareth asked, a little confused.

"Not entirely," Bernard said. "The tale it tells is true, but it is conveyed with wit and passion. It is not one of the more... ponderous texts I have set you."

"And I suppose you want me to read the first three chapters by tomorrow?" Zachareth asked, his heart sinking further.

"No," Bernard replied. Zachareth looked up at him in surprise, wondering what sort of new trick this was. The tutor offered him a smile.

"You do not need to read it at all," he said lightly. "I believe, if you give it a chance, you might enjoy it, though. But if it sits untouched, it is no great loss. Consider it a gift, yours to keep and do with as you please."

Zachareth had never been gifted a book before. He looked at the image page a little longer, drinking in its detail, fascinated by it. He noticed he was staring and hastily closed the cover, some instinctive part of him not wanting Bernard to see he was so intrigued.

"Thank you," he said. "Does this mean I can go now?"

CHAPTER FOUR

Zachareth returned to his chamber and left *The Canticle of Rufus the Bold* on top of *The Foxes of Kell*.

It was almost evening. While he had been gone, someone had laid out his formal attire on the bed – leather shoes with silver buckles, silk stockings, breeches, and a fiery red tunic with the black talon of Carthridge embroidered in its center. A black felt roundlet cap with a long pair of blue and green peacock feathers sat atop the other garments.

He was tempted to avoid the feast altogether, just to spite his father, but after missing a proper meal yesterday, his stomach ached. He'd filched bread from the castle bakery and bribed one of the cooks for a few strips of ham during the afternoon, but the scents of the impending dinner had been wafting through the keep all evening. That overcame his desire to annoy Zelmar.

He got dressed in everything but the cap, which he thought made him look foolish and childish. He heard voices rising up from the great hall below and decided it had grown late enough. He walked down into the antechamber, steeling himself for another encounter with Zelmar and Leanna.

The hall was bustling. Guests were still entering, and maids and serving boys were hurrying to and fro. The fireplace had been lit and was blazing away, illuminating the changes made to the space. The great table had been joined by two other, smaller ones while a fourth had been set before the thrones at the far end, raised up on a short wooden dais that Zachareth had seen being carried in plank by plank and assembled earlier that day. Each place at the banquet had been set with fine silver utensils, bowls, platters, and goblets, a collection that Zachareth had heard described as the finest in all Terrinoth and the pride of the Carths.

Most of the feast's attendees were already seated, the combined entourages of Carthridge, Cailn, and Rhynn intermixed. Women wore dresses of silk and fine wool, red and white, yellow and blue and green, the seams lined with silver or gold trim, their hair bound up under escoffions and tall steeple hats. The men were garbed in surcoats or jerkins and hose or breeches with stockings, most with chaperone hats or feathered caps. The place was loud and merry with conversation.

Zachareth almost collided with Golfang as he stepped into the hall.

"You're just in time," the orc said, towering over him. "Your father was about to send me to hunt for you, and you know there's no duty I enjoy more."

Zachareth smiled, enjoying Golfang's deadpan sarcasm.

"Imagine, when you become the captain of the guard, you can let your lieutenant be the one who worries about me," he said.

"I could never place such a burden upon anyone," Golfang said, ushering Zachareth into the hall. "Go, pup. The feast is about to begin."

Zachareth made his way through the guests to the high table.

The rest of its occupants were already seated, overlooking the hall from the dais – Zelmar at the center, flanked by Leanna on one side and Zachareth's empty seat on the other. Arrayed with them were Zachareth's uncle Marchant and aunt Elise, his cousin Welf, and the two other court advisors, Ragasta and Amalie.

Behind them all hung the Silver Banner, the baronial standard of Carthridge. Unlike the flags of most of Terrinoth's other baronies, it didn't bear upon it any device or crest, but was woven from uniform silver thread. It shone and glimmered brilliantly behind the throne.

Zelmar pointedly ignored Zachareth as he took his seat beside him, though Leanna gave him a smile. He looked away without responding.

The feast began with the clowning. Zelmar's two court jesters, Leggit and Hogg, entertained the tournament's guests with bouts of juggling, sword eating, and crude japes. They wove acrobatically around the tables and benches set up throughout the hall, picking out targets at will. At one point, Leggit, the heavyset one, played the lute while Hogg, the skinny one, danced a jig on one of the tables, miraculously managing to avoid disturbing a knife or spilling a drop of wine across the loaded setting.

Zachareth had once enjoyed the antics of the two knaves, giggling as they made privy jokes or impersonated chickens, but as he had grown, the pair had lost their shine. He sat sullenly as they performed the same tricks he had seen dozens of times before to the gasps and table-slamming approval of the visiting entourages.

The finale of the display was the fire taming. The mismatched duo produced torches and called upon Leanna.

The elf pretended to demur for a while before caving to the pleading of the knaves and the boisterous encouragement of the crowd.

"If I must," she declared to cheers as she rose from behind the table, resplendent in a gown of purple velvet trimmed with mottled white ermine, a string of rubies around her neck glittering darkly in the firelight. An expectant hush fell as she paced around in front of the table and raised her knotted black staff.

She spoke in a language none present understood. The words of the Aymhelin seemed to cut the atmosphere in the hall open, scything through the smoky, warm fug. Zachareth felt his hairs stand on end as he watched the flames that were dancing around the heads of Leggit's and Hogg's torches rise and respond to the arcane litany.

There was a gasp as the fire surged. It physically ripped itself free from the torches, leaving them smoldering as it snarled and surged through the air, coiling like a living being to crackle just beneath the rafters.

Leanna flicked her staff as though she were scribing words into the air with it. The flames responded once more, dancing and coiling into a flurry of different shapes – a hissing serpent, a soaring phoenix, a racing horse, its mane a plume of black smoke. The crowd responded with equal parts shock and delight, every eye fixed on the display. Despite his own desire to remain detached and disdainful, Zachareth found his attention locked to what was unfolding. This was more impressive than usual.

The sorceress grasped her staff over her head with both hands. The fire surged one last time, coalescing into an orb of pure, white heat. Zachareth felt it prickling at his skin as it roared over his head, twisting with the rest of the high table to see it sear into the Silver Banner, engulfing it in flames.

The hall was on the brink of tumult. Several revelers had risen to their feet, faces contorted with fear, ready to run for the door if, as now seemed certain, the whole chamber was engulfed in a sorcerous conflagration.

But instead of catching, the fire died. It flared down to the edges of the Silver Banner where it flickered and smoldered before, in a wisp of smoke, it vanished completely. The standard remained, completely unmarred, its surface showing no evidence of having been touched by the flames.

"See how the majesty of Carthridge remains untarnished?" Leanna exclaimed, bringing her staff down from over her head with a flourish.

There was a moment of stunned silence before a storm of cheering and applause swept through the hall.

Zachareth refused to join in. He had seen Leanna perform similar feats before – transforming kits into frogs, calling forth frost in midsummer and blooms of flowers in midwinter, snuffing out every torch and fireplace in the castle at once with a click of her fingers. Where others felt wonder and amazement when they witnessed such abilities, Zachareth felt only fear. Small magics were hardly unusual in Terrinoth, but he had no doubt her powers extended far beyond feast trickery. He had no idea how anyone would go about overcoming them unless they were a master sorcerer too. Perhaps, he realized, that was what he would have to do, even if he'd never sensed he had any particular aptitude for magic. There had to be a way to tame the energies of the arcane, to bind them to him.

Leanna returned to her place at the high table. As the acclaim died away, the minstrels in the gallery took their cue and struck up, beginning a rendition of "The Rhynns and the Raven".

The food was brought forth to more cheers. Liveried serving staff processed into the hall hefting great platters that they arrayed in unison first upon the high table and then upon the others. The initial course consisted of thin pottage, followed by venison, leeks, and cabbages, then a full, roasted swan for each table. Lastly, there was a selection of sweet pastries, rounded off with boards of thick Allerfeldt cheeses.

Zachareth took up his silver cutlery and devoured each course relentlessly, paying no heed whatsoever to his neighbors at the table. It was only as he was tucking into his third pastry twist that a noise disturbed him, making him look up from his shining platter.

He did so just in time to see Mikael throw up all over the remnants of his table's half-devoured swan. Ugly retching sounds filled the hall, followed by a cry of disgust from those seated near the heir of Cailn.

Mikael managed to struggle to his feet, both hands clamped over his mouth and a look of horror in his eyes. Knocking his chair back, he ran for the hall's doors. His father, Wilem, snapped something, and one of the Cailn squires hurried after the boy as servants swooped in from all sides to clear and rearrange the table. Zachareth's surprise turned to amusement and then annoyance.

As most of the hall stared in revulsion at the mess Mikael had left behind, he leaned forward and pointedly glared past his father at Leanna. She looked as shocked as everyone else, but as she turned to look back at him, he caught the lie in her eyes.

"I didn't tell you to do anything," Zachareth said, not caring if his father heard. Leanna gave him a raised eyebrow.

"It seems Master Mikael has had a bad cut of venison," she

said. "But I'm not sure how you thought I could prevent that? His Cailn stomach probably isn't used to such rich meat."

That made Zelmar laugh. Zachareth sat sharply back, fuming. He felt no joy at Mikael's embarrassment – after all, he had had no hand in it, which made it worthless. What was the point? Even worse, he now felt as though he was in her debt. It only made him more determined to have nothing to do with the sorceress.

He finished up all the cheese on the nearest platter. As the feast drew to a close, various distant relatives and minor nobles began to rise from their seats and approach the high table, seeking short, informal audiences with Zelmar. Zachareth was listening in to their stilted conversations about the health of family members, withheld rents, boundary stone disputes, and the projected size of the summer's harvest, all of it leaving him thoroughly bored, when he caught the eye of Greigory.

The young Baron of Rhynn was reclining in his chair at the table set up nearest the blazing fire, backlit by it. His uncle was next to him, speaking to him, but he didn't seem to be listening. He was looking at Zachareth, and as their eyes met, he smiled and gestured.

Zachareth glanced at Zelmar, who was deep in conversation with the latest supplicant, a cousin of the Baron of Rhynn.

"May I be excused?" he asked. Zelmar shot him a glance, clearly annoyed but unwilling to be distracted. He waved him away.

That was sufficient. Zachareth slipped from his chair and padded through the hall, weaving his way around the servants gathering up the remaining scraps of the feast.

Greigory pushed away his own empty silver plate and offered him his infectious smile as he arrived at his side.

"Ah, Lord Carth graces our own humble table," the Baron of Rhynn exclaimed. "I have a proposition for you, my friend."

"I'm listening," Zachareth replied, secretly pleased that Greigory seemed willing to talk to him as an equal.

"Word has it you won't be attending the joust tomorrow," Greigory said, lowering his voice so it was only just audible over the crackling fire. "By edict of your father. Now, old Uncle Augen and I have been discussing things, and we're in agreement that missing out on such a contest is no way to punish a good, strong lad like yourself. Thankfully, we might have a solution."

"What kind of solution?" Zachareth asked carefully, looking back up at the high table. Leanna, he noticed, was watching him.

"Oh, don't worry," Greigory said in his low voice. "She won't find out until it's far too late."

With a crack of shattering wood, the lance impacted Sir Ralland's shield.

The knight was slammed from his mount in a hail of splinters, landing so hard that his armored body bounced twice across the trampled dirt of the lists.

Greigory galloped onwards, nonchalantly tossing the split haft of his lance away. The crowd roared their approval, cheering and jeering. Watching through the flap of one of the adjacent green and black Rhynn tents, Zachareth punched the air with delight. He had relished seeing Greigory unhorse every opponent he had ridden against all day, including Zachareth's older cousin, Welf. He forced himself not to burst from the tent's shelter and cheer as the Baron of Rhynn steered his horse around the liveried boards and raised a mailed fist in salute toward the main stand.

Zelmar, seated in the shade beneath the platform's crimson

awning, didn't return the gesture. Leanna and most of the other dignitaries clapped politely, a stark contrast to the unbridled reactions from the crowd of servants, staff, and retinue members who crowded the makeshift terraces on either side.

The jousting arena had been erected at the foot of the southern side of Castle Talon's crag. The citadel towered above the temporary arena, a monolithic block of turrets and parapets and the many sightless eyes of its arrowslits. It was one of the great fastnesses of northern Terrinoth, built by the first Baron of Carthridge and then expanded and strengthened by successive lords until it now occupied the entirety of its perch at the head of the valley. It was difficult to discern just where the cliff face ended and the curtain walls began.

It made a fine backdrop for the day's contest. Besides the jousting circuit itself and the attendant stand, a small forest of brightly colored tents and pavilions had sprung up around the temporary arena, demarcated by fluttering standards and housing the squires, armorers, and equerries responsible for tending to the contestants. Four warriors were competing in the name, and for the honor, of each of the three baronies. Cailn and Rhynn were both led by their rulers directly, but the leader of Zelmar's baronial guard, Captain Travas, was the foremost of the Carthridge contingent. Zelmar had been grievously wounded in the thigh by a splintering lance during a Silver Tourney twelve years before, not long after Zachareth had been born. The injury had never properly healed, often swelling or becoming infected. It was difficult for Zelmar to walk now, let alone mount a horse.

The tournament was held over three days, and the first was nearing its end. Wilem of Cailn had already been knocked out by Lady Jan of Rhynn, a fact that Zachareth had particularly relished. He had seen no sight of Mikael in the stands or behind the hoardings. One of the cook's assistants, selling platters of sweetmeats to the watching crowd, had claimed that he was laid up in bed ill, a fact that had apparently infuriated the castle's head cook, who was adamant that none of the food he had served the night before was spoiled or noxious.

It was turning out to be an almost perfect day, dampened only by the fact that Zachareth had to stay under cover. As far as Zelmar was aware, he was confined to his chambers, locked away with Bernard's books.

Greigory had helped make sure that wasn't the case. Zachareth had bribed the guard posted on his door to look the other way while one of Greigory's squires had furnished him with a suitable disguise. Dressed up in a long jerkin bearing the green oak heraldry of Rhynn and with his hair piled up beneath a cap he kept pulled low, he had looked like just another attendant belonging to Greigory's retinue, unnoticed in the bustle at the start of the day. It wasn't the first time he had disguised himself as a serving boy either – he had learned quickly that those in positions of power tended not to look too hard at the lower orders, especially if they kept their eyes averted.

Greigory's assistance hadn't stopped at smuggling him out of the castle. In between bouts, he'd enlisted his aid in changing his armor and weapons, making much of the fact that Zachareth was familiar with whichever piece of equipment he demanded and jovially chastising his other squires for their supposed laxness. They in turn had joked about making Zachareth a Rhynn squire on a full-time basis. Zachareth's answer – that he would consider their applications to join his own retinue when he was tilting at the next Silver Tourney – had drawn good-natured cheers.

It had all been a thrilling change of pace. Even if he hadn't been banished to his rooms, attendance at the tourney would doubtless have seen him sat beside his father in the stands, far from the immediacy of the action. He had always wanted to be down among the armor and horses and knights. And he was certainly now a world away from the joyless day Zachareth had anticipated, sequestered away in his chambers. He'd become caught up in the excitement of it all and now felt as though he was in the very heart of the contest. His only regret was that he couldn't venture outside for fear of being recognized. It was one thing to slip through a busy castle hallway, hurrying as though on some errand, and quite another to step onto the edge of the lists before the eyes of hundreds of onlookers.

"I thought Ralland would offer me some challenge," Greigory declared as he swept into the pavilion tent, hauling his great helm off and casting it to the ground. He was grinning even more than usual, his face ruddy with sweat. The crowd was still cheering audibly outside.

"His years are starting to tell," Selwin, Greigory's chief shield-bearer and knight-errant, declared, moving to unbuckle the baron's pauldrons so he could flex his arms.

"So you're saying that I did not in fact just win a great victory for House Rhynn?" Greigory admonished, a knowing glint in his eye. Behind him, Selwin shook his head with a smirk, well used to his lord's humor.

"The final duel of the day is next," Zachareth said, trying and failing not to sound excited. "You must face the captain of my father's guard, Travas, on foot."

"And you think he will offer a better fight than Wilem's cousin?" Greigory demanded as though he was not perfectly aware of who Travas was.

"He will," Zachareth said solemnly.

"Any words of advice?"

Zachareth tried to think, but in the rush of the moment, he couldn't come up with anything coherent to say.

"It is the guard's lieutenant, Golfang, who trains me in swordcraft," he admitted. "I do not often see Travas fight."

"Well, you will today," Greigory said, pacing over to sit in the chair set at the back of the tent. He mopped at his brow with a rag, casting his eye over the rack holding his weapons.

"Time for the longsword then," he said. "I'll trust nothing else in a true contest of arms."

"Which one?" Selwin asked, as another squire offered Greigory a gourd to drink from. He took a swig, then gestured at the second blade from the left, flanked by a mace and a warhammer.

"Bring me Keenheart, Zachareth," he said.

Zachareth obeyed, hefting the sword and passing it pommel first to the reclining knight. Greigory took it in one fist, gazing up at its tip.

"This will do," he said. "You know, I've never lost a duel with this sword in my hand, Zachareth."

"One day you will," Zachareth said, grinning. "To me."

Greigory feigned outrage for a moment, then passed the sword back to him and stood up.

"Enough idle chatter," he said, beckoning for his retainers to attend him. "I have a tournament to win."

CHAPTER FIVE

From the tent's shadow, Zachareth watched Greigory stride out into the arena. The crowd bellowed and jeered. Travas was already waiting, the sun shining brilliantly on his silver plate mail. The pair saluted the main stand, their swords drawn, and then faced one another across a patch of scuffed dirt before the lists.

Zelmar passed a silken handkerchief to Leanna. Zachareth glared at her, unseen from his prime position within the list-side tent, as she dropped it from the edge of the stand. The moment it fluttered to the ground, Travas launched himself at Greigory.

Clearly the champion of Carth intended to show his opponent that he wasn't in Rhynn anymore, and that his status as a fully-fledged baron wouldn't protect him. Travas moved with the sort of speed that spoke of a man who was just as accustomed to being in heavy armor as he was out of it. He kept a longpoint guard, driving at Greigory, who met him with the ox guard, sword held high and horizontal before his face.

Steel clashed, competing with the renewed uproar of the crowd. Zachareth realized how sharply he was conflicted. Up until now, he had delighted in Greigory's victories, in the easy confidence with which he had become master of the lists. But Travas was a different matter. As Carthridge's chosen champion, this contest was, more than any of the others that day, a direct competition between Zachareth's barony and that of Rhynn. As much as he wanted to see Zelmar's and Leanna's moods ruined, he was still loyal to his house. The Silver Barony was his own, after all.

Greigory gave ground initially before switching to the plow guard – sword held at waist height, tip angled upward – and counterattacking. Zachareth suspected he'd been gauging Travas's skill, just as Travas had no doubt been waiting to see how Greigory would respond to his attack. The two knights met, swords locked, the sun reflecting from their burnished plate.

Travas threw Greigory back, using his superior strength. The crowd cheered all the harder. Zachareth understood that, regardless of baronial loyalty, his instincts were crying out for Greigory to win. He had shown kindness to him, and his humor and wit were infectious. He held his breath as the Baron of Rhynn stumbled, pushed back almost onto the list boardings.

Travas redoubled his efforts, raining blows on Greigory as he fought to keep his balance. Zachareth expected the baron to respond in a flash, to reveal that he had only been drawing Travas in for the finishing strike. He looked at his feet, but Greigory's stance was planted, defensive, in no position to lash out. He had been physically pushed up against the list and was parrying desperately, seconds away from coming undone.

Travas raised his sword high and brought it slamming down, all finesse gone now as he sought to break the faltering rearguard. Greigory managed to block the first strike, then the second, the crowd gasping with each shuddering impact. The baron had been driven right back against the boardings, retreat and maneuver impossible.

Travas swung high for the third, and surely final, stroke. At that moment, Greigory dropped his guard.

Zachareth, like most of the crowd, cried out in horror, certain the baron was about to have his helmet cleaved in two. But Greigory followed the motion, moving to the right, a desperate lunge designed to throw himself out of Travas's way.

It would only have bought him a few heartbeats of time. Even given the strength Travas had committed to his strike, he would have been able to recover faster than Greigory might have found his footing and raised his guard. But that was without factoring in the list.

Travas's longsword, missing Greigory, slammed down into the wooden boarding that separated charging knights during the joust. Even partially blunted for the tourney, it bit so deep it almost cleaved the timber in half.

Instantly realizing his mistake, Travas attempted to heave his blade free, but it was stuck fast.

Greigory seized his chance. Still only half recovered from his wild lunge to escape Travas's sword, he delivered a huge, ringing blow of his own against Travas's weapon, just above the hilt. It knocked it from both the Carthridge champion's grasp and the list where it had been wedged, leaving it in the dust at their feet. Before Travas could react, Greigory whipped Keenheart up and lightly tapped the crown of Travas's helm with the flat of the blade, indicating his defeat.

The crowd became uproarious. Zachareth couldn't help but cheer as well, exultation and relief surging through him. As

Travas stepped back, seemingly stunned by the sudden turn of events, a liveried herald rushed forward from beside the main stand and interposed himself between the two combatants, facing the spectators and raising his arms for quiet.

"The contest-at-arms is ended," he cried out. "Baron Greigory of Rhynn has defeated Sir Travas of Carthridge and has won the first day's bout!"

The herald stepped aside for Greigory and Travas to briefly grasp one another's forearms in congratulations. Greigory then stooped and retrieved the captain's fallen longsword, returning it to him. The pair once more saluted the roaring crowd.

Zachareth could help himself no more. Buzzing with so much excitement he momentarily forgot to hide, he rushed from the Rhynn pavilion just as Greigory was striding back toward it. The baron caught him in his arms and lifted him back inside before he'd made it a dozen paces. He was laughing as he removed his helmet.

"Your captain almost had me," he admitted as he clapped Zachareth on the shoulder. "He's relentless. But the gods favored me today, huh?"

He ruffled Zachareth's hair. The impropriety was lost on Zachareth. He was too caught up in the moment.

"Did you know he was going to trap his own sword?" he asked. "Did you do that on purpose?"

"Now, I wouldn't want to give away my secrets to a future rival," Greigory said. "As I said, the gods were with me!"

He gave Zachareth Keenheart to return to the rack. Selwin was handing his master his ceremonial great helm, bearing atop it a rendering of Rhynn's Grandmother Oak and a great crest of green and black feathers. Greigory took it before looking down at Zachareth.

"You should accompany me out there when I receive my prize," he said.

Zachareth wondered if the baron was being serious. He had already resigned himself to watching the ceremony from the tent.

"I will be recognized for sure," he protested, not daring to raise his hopes too high. "I cannot risk it. If Zelmar discovers I am here…" He trailed off, not willing to consider the punishment that might await him.

"Don't you want him to know how you defied him?" Greigory asked. "That you've gotten the better of him?"

Zachareth supposed that was true. The only thing he hadn't enjoyed about the day was remaining hidden. It took the sting out of his defiance. He considered seeing Zelmar's and Leanna's faces when he revealed himself at Greigory's side. It was outrageously bold to reveal that he had flaunted their orders and assisted a tourney rival, and that fact alone was enough to thrill him.

"Lead my horse out for the victory lap," the Baron of Rhynn urged with a mischievous expression. "Do not fear your father's wrath. I will see you protected. Do you trust me?"

"I do," Zachareth said without thinking. It was true. He had come to trust Greigory over the past few days, more so than almost anyone else he knew. Perhaps, he realized, that was naivety on his part, but he couldn't deny it. He had made him happy.

"You won't need that anymore," Greigory said, plucking the cap from Zachareth's brow and letting his long, dark hair fall down around his shoulders. He looked at Selwin.

"Ready Thomas," he told the squire. "Lord Zachareth will take him out."

Zachareth found his excitement turning rapidly to nervousness. Was he making a mistake? He knew he should be thinking about this from a mature angle. What were the political ramifications? Would what he was about to do harm Carthridge? Those were the sorts of questions Leanna and his father would have demanded of him.

That gave him the anger necessary to ignore them. Greigory was buckling another sword to his hip. With his great helm cradled under one arm, he placed his heavy gauntlet on Zachareth's shoulder and, as the other squires fell in behind, led him out of the tent.

At first nothing happened. The crowd's excitement had ebbed to a busy chatter. There were few exclamations as Selwin helped Greigory up into the saddle of his mighty gray destrier, Thomas. Zachareth took the leather lead strapped to the bit.

"Fear not," Selwin said, smiling casually. "He is tame so long as Greigory is astride him."

Zachareth was far more concerned about his father's reaction than he was leading the large warhorse. He tugged lightly on the leather strap and, in concert with Greigory's mild urging, the horse began to walk across the arena to the stands. As they went, Zachareth fixed his eyes on where his father sat in the shade of the crimson awning. He was too far away to make out his expression, but he saw him gesture and twist in his chair to speak to Leanna. A ripple of motion seemed to go through the dignitaries in the high seats, heads turning, fingers pointing. The noise of the crowd began to build.

Zachareth forced himself to hold his course, defiant now in the face of all before him. Greigory would protect him, of that he was sure.

"Baron Greigory of Rhynn, champion of the first day of the

Silver Tourney," the herald announced to the stands. Zachareth saw the man glance his way and hesitate as though uncertain whether he should be declaring his presence as well. Wisely, he said nothing more.

"What in the gods' names is this?" Zelmar demanded from the stand as quiet fell once again upon the crowd. "Zachareth, is that you?"

"It is, father," Zachareth called out as Thomas came to a halt. He looked up at Zelmar, holding his gaze as the baron clutched the stand's barrier, leaning as far forward as his unresponsive leg would allow.

"Why are you bearing that damned oak upon your chest, boy?" he demanded. "I ordered you confined to your chamber!"

"Don't be too harsh on Zachareth, noble lord," Greigory called. "His presence here is no fault of his own. I awoke this morning to find one of my squires laid low by a sickness of the stomach. It seems not uncommon around these parts."

A few people in the crowd on either side of the stands laughed.

"I was reminded that your son would not be required by you today," Greigory continued. "And I had no doubt he was familiar with lance and sword, pauldron and helm. I sent for him and begged that he would replace my fallen squire. He was good enough to agree to the task."

"You helped the Baron of Rhynn vanquish our own champion?" Zelmar asked, ignoring Greigory and addressing Zachareth, obviously struggling not to unleash his wrath in public. "Have you any idea what a fool you've made of me?"

"On the contrary, my lord." Greigory spoke up as Zachareth looked toward him, trying not to cringe before his father's mounting fury. He felt frozen to the spot, locked in place by the hundreds of eyes upon him. Were it not for Greigory and the bulk of Thomas beside him, he was afraid he would have already fled, cursing the decision he'd made to leave his room.

"Your son was well aware that I am ranged against the great and the good of Carthridge and Cailn this day," Greigory said. "He spoke to me earnestly of his hope that Captain Travas would emerge victorious, and that he was only assisting me as a favor. In that regard, I fear House Rhynn finds itself indebted to House Carth. You and I shall have to discuss how I might pay that debt, my lord Zelmar."

Zachareth understood Greigory's strategy. By making the most of the help Zachareth had given him, he was hoping to take the sting out of Zelmar's anger, pointing out that, in a way, Carthridge now held an advantage over Rhynn. Zachareth watched his father carefully, not daring to hope that he might escape without punishment, wondering if Greigory's plan would be enough.

Zelmar glared down at Greigory and Zachareth, his eyes narrowed. Leanna leaned over to whisper in his ear, a sight that caused Zachareth's fists to clench. The baron listened for a while, the redness gradually draining from his cheeks. Eventually he waved her away, repositioning himself so he was sitting upright on his throne rather than bent forward.

"I am… glad Carthridge was able to offer assistance to Rhynn in their time of need," Zelmar declared. "It would have been a poor tourney were you not able to compete. My son, as ever, is quick to help a worthy ally. Though I might suggest that, as of tomorrow, one of my own squires takes his place."

"Of course," Greigory said humbly, clearly playing along with the charade that had been hastily constructed to cover the possibility of a public spat between Carth and Rhynn. "I simply did not wish to inconvenience your noble house at such short notice."

"We thank you for that concern," Leanna said, taking over from Zelmar, who appeared no longer able to maintain the dignified aura that Leanna was clearly demanding of him.

"I believe congratulations are in order," the elf said, moving on before the situation became even more of a spectacle for the gawking onlookers. "Baron Greigory of Rhynn, you have vanquished all comers! By the laws of the Silver Tourney, the first day belongs to you. As a token of your victory, tradition demands that this be bestowed upon you."

She rose out of her seat and held forth a leather belt bound with silver clasps and etched with silver leaf. It was the belt of Jura Carth, one of the tokens of success used at the tournament for the better part of a century.

Greigory held out a hand, and Selwin hurried to his side, hefting his lance into his grip. The Baron of Rhynn lowered it so that the tip was just below the stand's edge. Leanna leaned forward and tied the belt around the lance's head.

"Rhynn victorious," she called out. A great shout went up from the Rhynn contingent and those among the castle staff who had backed Greigory. Despite his best efforts, Zachareth couldn't keep the smile off his face. It had all worked out, and the joy of the moment banished any further fears of punishment.

Greigory acknowledged the crowd and spoke a few respectful words toward the other contestants before once again thanking Zelmar. At Selwin's direction, Zachareth helped him steer Thomas around and back toward the Rhynn tents. As they went, the crowd's acclaim still ringing out, Greigory bent down in the saddle to speak with Zachareth.

"I would return to your room now," he advised. "Quickly. And think about how you can always use diplomacy to turn an advantage. Not all fights are won with a longsword."

"Just the fun ones," Selwin added from the other side of Thomas. Zachareth let go of the destrier, struggling for the words to thank Greigory. The baron waved him away.

"Go, boy, go," he urged.

Zachareth turned and, still grinning, ran toward the castle.

CHAPTER SIX
Harvesthorn, 1824

Zachareth settled cross-legged atop the boulder and laid the book open in his lap.

He had discovered the large stone, perched precariously near the eastern crest of the valley, six months before. He'd taken to visiting it whenever he wanted time and space to read. At Castle Talon, he always felt one sharp rap at his chamber door away from being disturbed. The fastness was always busy, always bustling. There were eyes everywhere. Leanna had taught him that.

Up on the valley sides, though, there was no fear of interruption or of being observed. Castle Talon was a small, proud block upon its rock at the far end of the cleft in the hills. There were no squires and inquiries, no visiting cousins and uncles or dignitaries, no Bernard or Golfang, and definitely no Zelmar and Leanna. There was only the sun and the clouds and the wind that made the heather nod and sway. That, and his occasional companions – sometimes a soaring hawk high above or rabbit flitting through the undergrowth along the slope or, during Highsummer and Suntide, buzzing flies and crawling ants, thriving in the heat.

Sometimes he would slip out of the castle using the water gate or the sally port in the northern curtain wall. He'd run all the way from the crag's base to his boulder until his heart was slamming and his limbs and lungs were burning, and he'd arrive at the welcoming stone sweating and grinning to himself. He'd cool off for an hour up on the rock, reading, then run back to the citadel.

The past week had seen him going to the spot on a daily basis. It had been ten days since Captain Travas had left with a large contingent of the baronial guard, and he wanted to be the first to spot their return. There had been all sorts of rumors circulating for months about the presence of the walking dead on the barony's border with the Mistlands. Travas had been dispatched to find out the truth of such accounts, and Zachareth wanted to be the first to hear his report.

The valley stretched away from him on either side, dappled in half-light as heavy gray clouds fought to keep the sun at bay. The wind, often sharp, had a particular bite to it today, the herald of the changing seasons. It was the reaping time, the close of Harvesthorn, near to Turning. One or two more weeks of sun, and the days would begin to shorten, and the weather would change to rain and then snow. He doubted he would come often to the boulder then, not until the sun returned.

Zachareth found where he had left off in *The Canticle of Rufus the Bold*, just before his favorite section where the silver baron clashed with Waiqar's dread lieutenant, Ardus Ix'Erebus. In the two years since Bernard had given it to him, it was the fifth time he had read it from cover to cover, though he often dipped into passages and chapters when he found the time. Ironically, he had forgotten about it initially until weeks after he had first been given it – Bernard had demanded the return of *The Foxes of Kell*, and Zachareth had found *The Canticle* on top, the pair hidden under old clothes and platters scattered across his chamber. Interminably bored, he'd read the first page and ended up missing Golfang's lesson in the tiltyard the next morning because he'd finished the whole book in one night. He immediately reread it again the next day.

He had never known anything quite like it. The story was nothing like the chronicles and the grand, weighty histories Bernard prescribed. Those were dry and dusty and dead things while the narrative of Rufus and his exploits felt quick and alive, fresh like the air in the valley after a summer thunderstorm. He read again and again Rufus's speech to his knights before the battle of Sorrow Glade or the daring escape through the hordes of the undead that had surrounded Castle Stonespire. The chapters that spoke of Rufus's strong kinship with the Baron of Rhynn, Talward, made him long for the same form of brotherly camaraderie. When he wasn't reading, he spent hours staring out his chamber's window or wandering the keep's corridors, oblivious to those around him as he fantasized about being part of Rufus's adventures, one of his squires or knights at the great battle of Bogmound.

The experience had opened up other books to Zachareth. He particularly enjoyed the tale of Selwyn, a human adopted by the Latari elves, and the account of Dalamar the Great, a runemaster who had actually succeeded in binding the power of one of his shards permanently to his body, acquiring its power forever. But it was to *The Canticle* that he returned again and again. He'd resolved to do another full reread the day before, trying for once to take his time with it.

He bent forward, the boulder warm beneath him, and picked up where he had left off. He was so lost in the book that it wasn't until he heard a shout, accompanied by a horse's whinny, that he noticed the riders approaching down the valley.

He looked up from the page, startled, to see the lead horseman waving up at him. He was a few hundred yards down the slope, following the track that ran along the banks of the stream winding through the valley floor. There were more horsemen behind him, nine in total, but they were strung out.

Zachareth recognized them immediately as members of the baronial guard. He slammed *The Canticle*'s dog-eared pages shut and leapt to his feet, bounding down through the brown heather to the pathway.

"Master Carth," the lead rider said. His name was Fulwen, and he looked exhausted. His armor was scarred and muddy, and both his helmet and shield were gone. His mount was lathered white with sweat, its legs trembling.

"Fulwen," Zachareth said, running up and grabbing the horse's bridle as it struggled to a halt. "What happened? You came from the border?"

"Reanimates," Fulwen said, his voice grim. "And worse. An army from the Mistlands. Death itself."

"Are you all that's left?" Zachareth asked disbelievingly, feeling a surge of horror as he contemplated the fate of the two hundred guards and men-at-arms who had departed Castle Talon.

"A few dozen more," Fulwen said. "On foot. We went ahead with the more grievously injured, doubling up on our mounts."

"What of Captain Travas?" Zachareth asked, looking back along the track at the other riders making their weary approach.

"He fell," Fulwen said simply.

There was a shout and a clatter of armor as one of the

horsemen further back down the track fell from his mount. He'd been sharing it with another, who shouted for help as she tried to dismount.

Zachareth let go of Fulwen's bridle and dashed along the path to crouch beside the fallen man. It was Skerrif, and he had a brutal-looking wound to his scalp. Zachareth tossed down his book and crouched beside the guard, then froze up as he found himself with no idea what to do.

Skerrif's mounted partner, Marwand, had clambered down and now knelt to support him by the shoulders, holding a water gourd to his lips. He groaned, his eyes half-lidded.

"Run ahead, lad," Marwand said urgently, looking at Zachareth. "Bring help."

Zachareth stayed still for a few seconds, panicking, overwhelmed by the situation. Then the reality of what was happening kicked in. He leapt back to his feet and set off toward the distant bulk of Castle Talon, running harder than he ever had before.

Golfang stood and stepped back from Zelmar's throne. Even kneeling, it had been difficult for the baron to touch his sword upon the orc's shoulders. He'd managed it eventually, though, reciting the formal words that inducted him as the captain of Carthridge's baronial guard.

"You are now the commander of this garrison," Zelmar announced. "And I will defer to you in all military matters."

Golfang muttered his thanks, retreating further from the throne. He knew what Zelmar had said was far from true. Privately, he had dreaded this day. He had hoped never to have to take Travas's place in command of the barony's household troops. He was a fighter, a warrior, as his mother and his father had both been and their mothers and fathers before them. He was not fond of clever speeches or careful politicking, both things that, in his years of experience serving under Travas, he had witnessed the captain having to engage in all too often. At times, fighting seemed like the last, least relevant duty of the captain of the guard.

But Travas was dead, and Carthridge was in crisis, and so Golfang had knelt and been anointed.

"We must respond," Ragasta, one of Zelmar's advisors, said, the ceremonial niceties already dispensed with. "These raids on our border cannot be allowed to continue."

"Raids implies some form of planning, of coordination," Leanna said from Zelmar's side. "You see agency where there is none. The border peoples disturb the dead from time to time. The Mistlands are cursed. We all know that. The evil there bleeds over, but it always recedes again."

"It has been bleeding over with increasing regularity," Ragasta pointed out. All three of Zelmar's advisors had been summoned in the wake of the return of the border expedition. Golfang had wanted to speak to the survivors, to find out who else had perished and just how such a disastrous defeat had occurred, but his presence had been demanded in the great hall. The guard needed a captain, and his promotion had been considered a priority.

"The attacks coming from the Mistlands are resulting in more than just a few torched border hamlets," Ragasta pressed. "People are fleeing deeper into the barony. I have heard reports of refugees growing in number in Strangehaven and along Korinna's Tears, even in Greyhaven. The harvest along the edge of the Mistlands is going uncollected. Food will soon start to run short. That is how a crisis starts."

"Then we ask for further supplies from Rhynn and Cailn," Leanna said brusquely. "They will always honor our alliance."

"For the third year running?" Amalie, Zelmar's other advisor, asked incredulously. "My Lord Carth, this is unsustainable. With the rise in bandits operating from the Carthmounts and striking into Rhynn, we risk stretching our neighbors' goodwill as it is."

"Then perhaps we should have sent Travas's expedition to the mountains, rather than the border," Leanna said before Zelmar could respond to Amalie directly. "As it is, we have suffered a grievous loss of men and arms. We must look to our immediate defense in the short term."

"My lord, might I be excused?" Golfang asked, interrupting the war of words in midflow. Zelmar hesitated as though unused to responding personally, even to such a direct request.

"I wish to see to the survivors and establish the cause of this defeat," he added, avoiding the fact that the last thing he wanted was to be dragged into yet another spat between the baron's advisors. He knew it was only a matter of time before one demanded his opinion or tried to curry his favor in front of the others.

"Yes, go," Zelmar said, gesturing airily.

Golfang withdrew faster than he ever would have done from a battle. On the way out into the antechamber, however, he paused, spotting a figure sitting cross-legged by one of the old statues. It was Zachareth. The youth scrambled to his feet as the hall doors closed behind Golfang, looking sheepish.

"Listening in, pup?" Golfang asked. The young Carth looked as though he was about to deny it, but he shrugged and smiled.

"How can I rule this barony if I don't understand the problems besetting it?" he asked. "Zelmar still does not permit me to attend the council meetings."

"Then count yourself blessed by all the gods," Golfang said.

"I shall, captain," Zachareth said, his smile growing. "And congratulations on your new post. It is long deserved."

"I'm not sure about that," Golfang said. It was striking, seeing Carthridge's heir standing beneath the idols of his ancestors. It didn't seem like so long ago that the dark-haired youth had barely reached up to their stone-carved waists, yet now he was nearly as tall as them. His shoulders were filling out as well, and his face was taking on the same firmness visible in the stony visages behind him. Golfang experienced a moment that might have been conflated with parental pride, an emotion he quickly quashed. Regardless of whether or not he had watched over him since he was a babe, Zachareth was his future ruler.

"Captain of the guard bears many responsibilities," Golfang continued. "Few of which involve actual combat. Regrettably."

"I would not worry too much, Golfang," Zachareth said, his smile fading, his face even better matching the grim expressions of the statues. "From the sound of it, we shall have plenty of fighting soon enough."

"Tell me more of Waiqar," Zachareth said.

Bernard looked up from his book in surprise. They had been sitting, reading in companionable silence in the garret. He had spent the afternoon teaching Zachareth the foundations of the elements and the nature of the three realms of power – the Empyrean, the Aenlong, and the Ynfernael – but he could tell the teenager was distracted. He'd opted instead to let him pick one of his manuscripts from among the scattered piles. Zachareth had chosen Prentice's *Histories of the Thirteen Baronies Since the First Darkness*, a book Bernard was certain would have resulted in Zachareth physically fleeing from the classroom if he had demanded he read it a few years previously. Still, it didn't take long for Zachareth to be once more distracted by his thoughts. Bernard found himself wondering what specifically had made him think about the great necromancer.

"I'm sure you know nearly as much about Waiqar as I do," Bernard said in response to his question.

"The living dead assail us from the Mistlands, burning our villages and slaying our warriors," Zachareth responded. "Surely it is Waiqar who leads them? He is the master of all necromancers, after all."

"Waiqar has been dead for three centuries," Bernard replied, injecting a dose of well-practiced reproval into his tone. He knew better than to indulge such legends. "Fully dead. The restless spirits of the Mistlands obey him no longer."

"What if it's one of his champions then?" Zachareth pressed. "Lord Farrenghast or Ardus Ix'Erebus! It was Ardus that Rufus defeated in *The Canticle*."

"Again, dead," Bernard said. "Or mythical, or both. The revenants that haunt our northern border know no master any longer, or if they do, it is some petty hedge necromancer or misguided devotee of Nordros, turned to corruption."

Zachareth lapsed back into silence, looking down at the histories, but Bernard could tell he wasn't really reading. He found himself wondering if he needed to reiterate the fine line between history and fable.

The change since he had given Zachareth *The Canticle of Rufus the Bold* had been incredible, and he chided himself for not thinking of it sooner. Zachareth was a sharp youth, but he could not see the use for dusty, dry old tomes, not while he was surrounded by the realities of swords and sorcery. He had needed to unlock the enjoyment of reading, and that was just what the pithy tale of Rufus, champion of Carthridge, had done.

It had opened a whole realm of new possibilities for Zachareth. Seeing him devouring fictional texts was one form of delight to Bernard, but watching him tentatively start reading – sometimes wholly of his own volition – the drier chronicles and chronologies Bernard had once tried to force upon him was particularly special. From being a scrappy, angry youth, he'd become almost scholarly, and he often asked Bernard for stories of when he'd been a student himself at Greyhaven. He did his best to regale him with accounts of the great university, telling him of evenings spent with fellow students in Makari's tavern or of days spent reading quietly in the university's yard of Nordros beneath the yew trees. It seemed to bring a degree of calm to the youth, a sight which in turn brought Bernard a private joy. In the past few years, the frustration he had felt toward the child had changed into something approaching pride.

Zachareth was troubled today, though, that much was clear. Bernard had heard the reports of the bedraggled band of survivors that had arrived back at the citadel that morning. It was clear it had affected Zachareth.

"If the Mistlands are so accursed, why can we not seal ourselves away with a wall?" he wondered out loud, just as Bernard had picked up where he had left off in Jayson's *Voyages*. He lowered the book once more.

"Such a project, if undertaken, would require leagues upon leagues of construction work," he pointed out patiently. "It would be quite easily the largest construction in all of Terrinoth. Carthridge is not in a position to afford such an expense."

"But we are the Silver Barony," Zachareth exclaimed.

Bernard sighed and closed *Voyages*. Lately, Zachareth had been asking more and more questions about Carthridge and his father's reign, questions Bernard rarely felt comfortable answering. It wasn't his place to discuss Zelmar's rulership, and he had no wish to spread stories, true or not. Still, there was only so much that could be hidden from the boy.

"Carthridge's silver mines are not what they once were," he admitted carefully. Zachareth frowned.

"Have they run out?"

"No, not entirely. But they have long been the target for the bandits and malcontents that infest the Carthmounts. Many have fallen to them."

"Then we should drive them out," Zachareth exclaimed with all the fierceness of youth. "How dare they steal from the barony!"

"They are numerous and know the mountains well," Bernard said, trying to lead Zachareth to the answers that might serve him when his time to rule came. "It would take a substantial force just to drive them off, let alone pursue them to their camps deep in the valleys. It would take a substantial part of the baronial guard and likely a band of mercenaries, not to mention local guides. Only one thing can bring all of that together."

"Silver," Zachareth said after a moment's thought.

"Indeed," Bernard replied. "Silver that we don't have because the bandits control most of it."

"Surely it can't be that simple," Zachareth wondered. "There must be something that can be done!"

"We could forge ahead," Bernard agreed. "Incur debts to pay off later. But it is a great risk, especially with the dead stirring so often on our northern border. As it stands, your father has an arrangement that solves much of the problem without the attendant dangers."

"What arrangement?" Zachareth asked suspiciously.

Bernard hesitated. It was not his place to speak of such matters. Zachareth was clever, though. It surprised Bernard that Zachareth had not gleaned the truth already, even if Zelmar refused to include him in any aspect relating to the running of the barony.

"There is a treaty between us and the bandits," he said eventually, trying to be political. "What we might call confidence and supply. They provide us with a portion of the silver from the mines they control, and in exchange, we let them take the rest and do not otherwise trouble them."

Zachareth looked shocked. Bernard didn't blame him. The specifics of the deal Zelmar had struck with the Carthmount banditry were known only to a few, but gossip abounded. It was a source of shame, but then Zelmar didn't seem much concerned with what was and wasn't shameful these days. Bernard had overheard it discussed by the baron's advisors on several occasions – the scheme seemed to have originated with Leanna. Privately, he saw no good coming from the influence she wielded, but he considered himself too wise to speak up about it. What could he, an aging tutor, do about the state of Carthridge?

"That is outrageous," Zachareth said.

"It is statecraft, albeit of a low kind," Bernard corrected, knowing he should do something to at least seem to defend Zachareth's father. "Zelmar makes the best of a bad situation."

Zachareth said nothing more, clearly giving thought to the new information. Bernard had noticed he'd grown far more considerate of late – once he would have reacted with outrage and thrown a tantrum. Now he was starting to internalize more. Bernard considered that progress.

There was a knock at the garret door. Bernard nodded to Zachareth, who was closer. He slipped from behind the lectern and opened it.

"Marwand," he said to the woman outside, sounding surprised.

"My apologies, Master Zachareth," she replied. Bernard shifted so he could see through the doorway and recognized one of the baronial guards. She was clearly one of the survivors of the expedition to the border – she was still clad in muddied armor, bar her left arm, which had been stripped off and bound up.

"Captain Golfang said I'd find you up here," she went on. "I wanted to return this. You left it up in the valley."

Marwand handed Zachareth a book. Bernard recognized it as *The Canticle*. Zachareth stared at it, then nodded to her.

"You have my thanks," he said. "I had quite forgotten it. Skerrif... does he live?"

"He is still with the surgeon," Marwand said heavily. "More wounded are still coming in."

"If you speak with him, give him my regards," Zachareth said.

Marwand gave a short bow and withdrew back down the tower stairs. Zachareth closed the door and returned to the lectern, placing the book upon it. He opened the front page and couldn't hide a grimace.

Bernard pulled himself up from his seat and maneuvered across the room to Zachareth's side. The boy was looking down at the title page with its beautiful rendering of Rufus locked in battle with the undead. Blood – Skerrif's, Bernard assumed – had soaked the lower right-hand corner of the page a dark russet shade, staining the skeletal figures of the reanimates and spreading to Rufus's horse and armored thighs. It was still slightly damp.

"I have another copy," Bernard said, sensing Zachareth's unspoken distress. "It doesn't have the pictures, and the paper is coarser, but the tale is one and the same."

Zachareth was still staring at the bloody page. He shook his head.

"No," he said. "I'll keep this one."

He turned through the other pages, all of them marred to steadily lesser degrees.

"Rufus fought and bled against the undead," he said, his tone becoming determined. "This is simply a continuation of that same story."

CHAPTER SEVEN
Greentide, 1827

"What did you say the place is called?" Zachareth asked, shifting in his saddle as he gazed out over the miserable homesteads.

"Mirefield," Skerrif replied. Zachareth smiled humorlessly.

"They choose their names well on the borders," he said. "Or are starkly lacking in imagination. Perhaps both."

"Who can blame them, living in a place like this?" Skerrif said morosely.

Zachareth could see what he meant. The hamlet of Mirefield was a collection of eight farmer's cottages, three barns, a stable, and a few outhouses and pens. It lay hard upon the old border between Carthridge and what had once been the thirteenth barony of Terrinoth. Now it was known as the Mistlands, an accursed place blighted since the fall of Waiqar many centuries before.

Carthridge's soil was rich and, until lately, often yielded a good crop, but Mirefield teetered on the brink of that tillable land. Its farming acres straddled the vast expanse of marshland that stretched north to the Dunwarrs, unworkable even were it not for the dark stories that surrounded it. Zachareth had never heard of the tiny hamlet before last week, and he doubted any of its destitute population had ever set eyes on Castle Talon or even much beyond the hall of their local lord, Eckwain. He knew he wouldn't get a chance to ask any of them though because one Moonday's night, ten days before, the entire population of Mirefield had vanished.

It hadn't been a prominent story until Zachareth had insisted on making it so. The vanishing of a farming hamlet's small population was hardly news nowadays with reports of walking dead and unquiet spirits reaching as far south as Morrowglade and the Ruby Gate. Zachareth had heard of Mirefield's fate from a castle porter helping a merchant unload fresh stock. The merchant bought grain directly from the border communities, something he'd been reduced to doing as supplies grew ever scarcer. He had arrived at Mirefield to find it deserted. Despite the fact that the barns were well stocked with grain, he'd left immediately.

The story had stayed with Zachareth, in part because he knew that Mirefield lay close to the site of the battle of Bogmound, described in *The Canticle of Rufus the Bold*. The hamlet hadn't been there at the time, but it had sprung up in the years after when dredging had driven the marshes back and it had seemed that even the deathless curse that plagued the land might be lifted.

Zachareth had demanded that he be allowed to go and investigate the village's disappearance. Zelmar had refused in no uncertain terms, but Zachareth had threatened not to attend his banner hold, his eighteenth birthday. In the past few years, he had bowed to his father's demands less and less, finding a self-confidence that had only enhanced his determination. Zelmar had relented eventually, even in the face of Leanna's disapproval, telling him that he was damned if he cared what happened to his son if he went north. He'd denied him the use of the baronial guard, but Zachareth had chosen six to go with him anyway. None had refused.

"This is an inopportune time for you to go seeking adventure," Bernard had told him sternly before he'd set off. "Your banner hold is in eight days!"

"All the more reason for me to go now," Zachareth had said. Bernard had pursed his lips, and for a second, Zachareth had thought he was going to menace him with his walking stave. That would have been ludicrous, of course. Zachareth was far taller and broader than Bernard now. Instead, and to Zachareth's surprise, he had embraced him.

"Keep your wits about you up there," he had said. "And don't tarry. Set double watches at night." Zachareth had promised to do so, finding himself touched by the tutor's concern. He had come to not only trust his advice but value his counsel. It was a bond his younger self would never have envisaged.

"The mist is lifting," Skerrif said. "I think."

Zachareth's small expedition had taken up post on a little grassy mound just east of the hamlet, overlooking it. They had already been down among the squat, thatched buildings, and had found it as described – eerily abandoned. Doors lay unlocked, and there was even rancid food lying half-eaten on the tables.

The entire place made Zachareth's skin crawl, but he also felt a sense of unbridled excitement. He rarely had an opportunity to escape Castle Talon and even less so to journey north. This was the farthest he'd been. He knew that the Mistlands lay just to his right, aptly shrouded in the low-lying fog that had reached out with its tendrils to coil through Mirefield. It was almost midday, but there was no hint of the sun amidst the gloom.

"We should turn back, lord," Skerrif said. He had volunteered to accompany Zachareth, though he made no secret of the fear the north held for him. He still bore the scar across his scalp from Travas's disastrous expedition, made, he had told Zachareth, by a reanimate's axe. If Zachareth hadn't run ahead to get help the day the survivors had made it back to Castle Talon, Skerrif claimed he would have perished. Still, nightmares of the undead haunted him. In the days since turning north, his night terrors had regularly disturbed the camp's rest.

"I am going a little farther," Zachareth told him. "None of you need to come."

He twisted in the saddle to look at the other five members of the expedition, all solid Carthridge soldiery, bedecked in mail and leathers and bearing the black talon upon their burning red tabards and shields.

"Where you go, we go, lord," Skerrif said. "Just lead on."

Secretly, Zachareth was thrilled. They were following him, displaying their loyalty. He had feared they would still view him as the arrogant youth who had bribed them and confounded them around Castle Talon, rather than the sole heir of Carthridge, on the cusp of manhood. But since announcing his intention to go north, none of them had faltered. He was leading, and they were following. It was his first real experience with such, and he was finding it intoxicating.

He rode down and skirted the hamlet, following the track until it became lost in the boggy ground. Skerrif was right about the fog lifting, he realized. He could see a shape looming up ahead now, right where he had hoped he'd find it. As they drew nearer, it resolved into a hillock, north of the village.

"This is the Bogmound," Zachareth said to his companions as they went.

"You know this place, lord?" Skerrif asked incredulously.

"I have not been here, but I know it was the site of a great battle," he said. "Between Baron Rufus of Carthridge and the cursed undead of Waiqar."

He saw Skerrif flinch at the name of the dreaded necromancer. Even centuries later, there loomed no darker figure in all northern Terrinoth than Waiqar.

"Was this one of the battles from your book, lord?" Skerrif asked, as though hoping casual conversation could banish the necromancer's malaise.

"It was," Zachareth admitted. "But it is no fable. It helped preserve Carthridge during the Second Darkness."

He led the small band on up the springy turf of the slope to the crest of the mound. It was larger than the hump they had occupied moments before and would likely have offered a tolerable view into the Mistlands were it not for the fog that still clung to the ground beyond. Zachareth twisted in his saddle to look back past his guards and noticed they'd almost lost Mirefield behind them. The village was now only a vague outline of squat, thatched roofs. It was as though the mist had lifted before them in order to draw them in before descending once again.

"This is it," Zachareth told Skerrif, who advanced his horse to once more be alongside Zachareth's. "This is where Baron Rufus made his stand against the deathless horde of Waiqar, led by his lieutenant, Ardus Ix'Erebus."

"I fear we're too few to recreate that particular battle, lord," Skerrif said dryly. Zachareth smiled in an effort to hide his emotions. Every instinct in his body was screaming at him to turn back now. There was a malice about the hidden land ahead, something that crawled and crept, unseen, right up to Zachareth's body, seeking to slither up his spine and graze its fangs along the nape of his neck. The utter stillness that surrounded them only made it worse. Briefly, it seemed as though the Bogmound was a small island in an ocean, an outcrop of safety and sanity in bleak, icy waters that held unknown and unknowable horrors.

And yet, a small part of Zachareth still wanted to go farther.

"Look," said one of the other guards, Yarrow.

Skerrif's earlier comment about the mist lifting had been correct. As Zachareth peered ahead, he realized he could see the bottom of the mound's north-facing side where the relatively firm slope became a flat expanse of marsh grass and black, tepid muck. The fog continued to recede as though commanded to withdraw. As it went, it exposed more and more of the bog, stretching away from their small mount.

"Oh gods," Skerrif murmured. Zachareth was about to ask what it was he saw before spotting it himself. The marshland was an expanse of greys, browns, and blacks, rotting and cancerous, but things were breaking that uniformity. Zachareth leaned forward in his saddle, peering at what appeared to be hundreds if not thousands of small white objects jutting up from amongst the mud and tall grass.

He knew what he was looking at. Bones. Human bones from, at the very least, hundreds of bodies. They were scattered throughout the marshland before him, a harvest of remains, left to decay amidst the festering mire.

"The remnants of the battle of Bogmound," Zachareth said with equal parts horror and wonder.

"I'm not sure all of them are quite that old, lord," Skerrif said, pointing down. Zachareth followed the gesture back to the base of the hillock where the marsh began.

There were other shapes down there. These were not the pale and jagged forms of the bones of long-deceased warriors but were lumpen and more whole. Zachareth had first dismissed them as rocks and stones, but now recognized, with a pulse of fresh horror, that they were dead bodies, caked black and filthy by the bog.

"The villagers," he said, understanding that the mystery of Mirefield's disappearance had been solved.

"They must have been drawn to the marsh by fell sorcery," Skerrif said. "Drowned and added to this mass grave. My mother had the sight, lord. She had magic about her, and I can tell you now that this place is rank with the worst of its kind."

"I don't doubt it," Zachareth murmured, secretly jealous that Skerrif possessed even the vaguest hint of aptitude in the magic arts.

He sat astride his mount for a while longer, trying to come to terms with what they had discovered. He was as angry as he was afraid. These people were of Carthridge, and they fell under the protection of his family. House Carth had failed them. He had failed them. It stung him to acknowledge as much.

Movement caught his eye. At first, it was so slight it failed to penetrate through his grim thoughts, but as it spread – albeit still subtle – he noticed what was happening before him.

The bones out among the marsh had started to twitch. The motions were small, jerky, and disjointed, but there was no denying what Zachareth was seeing. It made his blood run cold.

"Oh gods," one of the other guards murmured.

"I would not have you take me for a coward, lord," Skerrif said quietly. "But I really think we should be going now."

"Yes," Zachareth said, his anger evaporating. "You have my thanks, all of you, for coming this far. Now, however, we return to Castle Talon. Skerrif, lead us off."

Zachareth forced himself to be the last to ride down from the Bogmound, though every second he spent flooded him with chilling terror. He tore his eyes from the twitching bones just as the mist came rolling back in, shrouding the scene from his sight.

The band rode south.

They were waiting for him. The hall was silent.

Zachareth paused in the antechamber, pulling his doublet straight. It was black with a silver belt about his waist. There was a sword at his hip, newly forged and presented to him during a ceremony by Golfang the day before. He wasn't wearing the hat that had been laid out for him.

Three days had passed since his return from the northern border. The journey back had passed uneventfully, but still he had felt the lingering horror of what they had found at Mirefield and had been haunted by the night terrors that continued to plague Skerrif.

He glanced briefly at the statues of the Carths that lined the way into the hall. As ever, they offered no practical advice, just stony indifference. He was nervous and uncertain. He knew he had to overcome that. Right now, he could do nothing more about the evil he was certain was growing on their northern border. Zelmar wouldn't listen to him, and he didn't have the authority to raise the Carthridge host and march north of his own volition. Even if he did, he doubted he was ready to face the terrors of Waiqar's legacy. He lacked the sorcerous power to do so, just as he lacked the magic to challenge Leanna's direct hold over the court.

Zachareth hoped to change that, starting that day. He had played out what was about to happen a thousand times in the last few months as he laid his plans. He knew what he was going to say and do. The only thing now was to actually say it and do it.

He stepped through the doors and into the great hall.

It was full but disconcertingly quiet. There was a faint murmur as Zachareth entered, but it quickly stilled. He glanced about at the faces, each one of them turned toward him – relatives near and far, allies and ambassadors, all dressed in the finery of Terrinoth's nobility. It was not just Carths and those of neighboring Rhynn and Cailn either. Eight of the twelve baronies had sent representatives. Several barons or their heirs had also attended in person – Greigory, Wilem, as well as Elain of Dhernas and her daughter Magrit, and Adelynn of Forthyn. All had come to see Zachareth's banner hold.

Today, in the eyes of Terrinoth, he became a man. Eighteen Deepwinters had passed since his birth, and the eighteenth Highsummer was on the brink. Today he was expected to adopt the full responsibility of his role as the sole heir to the house of Carth.

He began to walk down the aisle between the assembly. His heart was racing, and his stomach was in knots, but he tried to keep his expression serene as he went, a hand grasping the pommel of his sword so it didn't scrape along the floor or trip him.

Zelmar awaited him. The dais had been erected, and he sat on his throne upon it. It was strange to see him alone without

Leanna's cloying presence – for once the sorceress had been relegated to the crowd. Zelmar was still seated, his wounded leg propped up, but in his right fist he grasped the Silver Banner. It had been attached to its pole, a stout haft of iron-oak, for the purposes of the ceremony.

Zachareth climbed the short flight of stairs onto the dais and knelt before his father. Normally, he would have stood, but his father was unable to rise, and the ceremony required he hold the banner lower than Zelmar.

His sword bumped on the wooden boards as he took a knee, the sound uncomfortably loud in the stillness. He could feel the huge expectation of the crowd behind him, bearing down on him, attempting to crush him beneath its weight. He instinctively wanted to stand and face them, but he couldn't, not yet.

His father watched him steadily. He seemed unusually solemn. Perhaps even he had become invested in the moment.

Zachareth reached up and grasped the banner pole, just below Zelmar's hand. He held it tight so there was no hint of trembling.

"Zachareth Carth," Zelmar said, his voice scratchy. "Firstborn heir of Carthridge, lord of the Carthmounts, inheritor of the lineage of Carth. Today is the day of your ascension from boy to man. Do you once more affirm your fealty to the Barony of Carthridge, and do you likewise swear by the Flames and Hand of Kellos that you will protect these borders against the scourge of undeath?"

"I do," Zachareth said.

"Louder, boy," Zelmar growled.

"I do," Zachareth repeated, the words reaching the hall's timber rafters.

"Do you swear also that when I, Zelmar Carth, perish, you will take up my role as Baron of Carthridge, and that in doing so you will rule justly, protect the weak, uplift the poor, and defend the laws and lineages of Carthridge?"

"I do," Zachareth said firmly.

"Then, as of now, you are a man," Zelmar said. Zachareth was surprised to note the emotion in his voice. "Raise your standard."

Zelmar let go of the Silver Banner. At the same time, Zachareth shifted his grip higher up and stood. He turned around and hefted the standard, looking for the first time out over the assembly.

A herald, bedecked in black and fiery red, took a post at the bottom of the dais and likewise turned to the crowd, addressing them in high, precise tones.

"I present to you Zachareth Carth!"

The onlookers cheered. Zachareth felt his face flush as the moment washed over him. He tried to keep his gaze level, slightly over the heads of those giving him their acclaim, but he couldn't help but glance at them. He saw Greigory, now sporting a bristling mustache, applauding hard. Near to him was Leanna, her smile never reaching further than her lips. Foremost on the right was Bernard. An invitation had not initially been extended to him, but Zachareth had refused to attend unless he was present. The situation had been aided further when the scribe who was supposed to be recording the ceremony had abruptly fallen ill. Bernard was the ideal replacement, and Zachareth had ordered that his lectern be carried down to the hall from the north tower. He stood behind it now, quill poised, beaming from ear to ear as he beat his free hand against the woodwork in applause. Despite his nervousness, Zachareth couldn't help but smile back.

The banner was heavy, but he was strong. He held it aloft firmly. Finally, the acclaim died down, and an expectant hush settled across the hall.

He took a breath. This was the moment he had anticipated. The moment he finally took control. He spoke.

"I thank you all for attending, and I bid the nobles of our fellow baronies especially welcome. To my great regret, though, I will not have time to greet you all in person. Tomorrow, I am departing for the University of Greyhaven."

Silence greeted his words. He let it stretch, forcing himself not to waver. It was Zelmar who broke it.

"What do you mean, departing for the University of Greyhaven?" he asked incredulously.

"I have enrolled there," Zachareth said, half turning to better address him directly. "Last Stormtide I sent a letter to the College of Runemasters, requesting that I be taken on for a full term of study. I will be learning the secrets of runemagic as well as finishing my more general education."

"I was not consulted about this," Zelmar declared, glaring up at Zachareth. "No son of mine is going to waste his banner-day inheritance on those tricksters and bookworms!"

"I have already sent the deposit, courtesy of my allowance," Zachareth said.

"This is an outrage," Zelmar carried on, rising up as best as he was able in his throne, seemingly forgetting the presence of Terrinoth's great and good before him. "How dare you, boy! I will have you confined to your tower for this!"

"You forget yourself," Zachareth said sharply. "Legally, unless I break the laws of this barony, I may go wherever I wish. You have no power to hold me. And while you will always be my father, I am no longer your boy. I am a man and your sole heir."

Zelmar seemed lost for words, his face turning a shade of puce, mouth opening then closing like a gaffed fish. Zachareth turned back to the assembly, speaking before the baron had a chance to recover.

"I am sure my father's reaction here is not unique," he said levelly. "Many of you, I suspect, see no benefit in a highborn such as myself attending Greyhaven, certainly not at my age. Even your father, Baron Cailn, had long been established as a ruler before he chose to study the runes. I submit to you, however, that if I am to effectively rule this barony someday, such an education is essential."

He could sense the hall's unease, but he undoubtedly had their attention. Zachareth pressed his advantage, knowing he had to make the next few moments count, silently praying to all the gods that he didn't look and sound half as nervous as he felt. He'd gone through this so many times in his head, it was strangely surreal knowing that it was finally happening.

"Many of the benefits of a Greyhaven education speak for themselves," he said. "I have been well taught by Bookkeeper Bernard here – himself a lauded graduate of that same university – but there comes a time when a student outgrows his classroom."

He nodded to Bernard, who was simply staring at him in shock, his quill abandoned.

"At Greyhaven, I will learn the finer points of Terrinoth's history, of the humors, of mathematics and matters of philosophy. Were that all, however, I would not think of abandoning Carthridge for the next three years. Greyhaven is, of course, the greatest seat of magical learning in this part of Mennara. I will be the first to admit that I have never sensed an inkling of what some might call 'natural' magic about my person. But that is not a prerequisite of the runemagic Greyhaven teaches. Any may become adept in it, and I am of the firm belief that if Carthridge is to weather the struggles already afflicting her, it must have a ruler who is versed in the arcane arts."

None in the hall reacted. Zachareth couldn't tell if his words were striking home yet. He almost panicked but forced himself to press on. He had committed now. He had no choice other than to continue.

"Apart from runemagic, there is more I must learn about the world at large. I can count on two hands the number of times I have journeyed beyond the Talon Valley. I have only left Carthridge itself on four occasions. I have visited Greyhaven once, for only a few days, yet it is easily the greatest city in the region. If I am to start my reign well, I must know more about existence beyond these walls, proud and firm though they are."

"I will disinherit you," Zelmar snarled from his throne, finally finding his voice. "I will cast you from Carthridge!"

"I doubt that," Zachareth said, this time barely glancing at his father. "Disinherit me and the Council of Barons will reinstate me, and you know it. What claim will you make? That I sought to complete my education? That I took the threats besetting Carthridge seriously enough that I received tutelage in runemagics?"

He kept speaking, giving no time for Zelmar's dissent to spread. He gestured toward Baroness Kalrif and her daughter, Magrit.

"Noble lady," he said. "Your court is not ignorant of the ways of magic, be it the Turning, or the runes, or matters even stranger. Have you not employed battle mages in defense of Dhernas before?"

"We have," Kalrif acknowledged tersely, sounding as though she wanted to avoid being drawn into the argument.

"How much better, then, if a baron could rely on his own skill in such matters?" Zachareth pointed out, turning his attention to Wilem of Cailn. He stood alone apart from two retainers – Mikael had not journeyed with him.

"Lord Cailn," Zachareth said. "Did the subjects your father learned at Greyhaven not stand him in good stead in the latter years of his rule, and help inform your own upbringing?"

Wilem looked uncomfortably past Zachareth at the furious Zelmar and hesitated. Zachareth pressed on while he still had the edge.

"Lord Rhynn," he began to say, but Greigory held up a hand sharply, smiling.

"Save your pretty words, Lord Carth," he said. "It is clear you have already cast a beguiling spell upon the rest of this hall, and I fear if you turn your abilities on me, I shall end up enrolled with you!"

A smattering of laughter ran through the hall, helping to dispel the pained mood that had struck the assembly.

"I am altogether too dull to be able to engage with runemasters and scholars," Greigory went on. "But I suppose someone must pay them and occupy their time. Rhynn fully supports your attendance. Rather you than I!"

"Only the very wise admit to their own foolishness," Zachareth said with a smile of his own, quoting Atrikus the Hermit. He had hoped that, at the very least, he could count on Greigory. Over the past few years they'd remained close, exchanging mail and sparring whenever Greigory's duties took him to Castle Talon. The Baron of Rhynn hadn't let him down.

"I hope some of you will see the sense in my decision," he

said. "Even if my father does not. I hope also you will enjoy tonight's feast. Regrettably, I will be too busy packing to attend, but the presence of so many of Terrinoth's noble houses honors me greatly. Gods willing, I shall see you all again soon."

With that, he handed the banner to the herald, stepped from the dais, and headed for the doors, pointedly avoiding making eye contact with anyone. The hall remained deathly silent until Zelmar's voice rang out behind him, demanding he return and cursing him to the Ynfernael and back.

Zachareth ignored the furious words and, as he did so, felt a surge of power and resolve. Zelmar had no more hold over him anymore. None of them did. He was Lord Zachareth of Carth, and soon he would be more powerful than any of them could imagine.

CHAPTER EIGHT

The pale king was communing with the dead.

His servants had been banished from the throne room or had fled – he couldn't recall which. His mind was elsewhere, his body cold, heartbeat almost still.

The darkness within the lofty, damp hall had grown near absolute. Strange shapes flitted at the corner of the eye, and stranger noises emanated around the barren fastness – scratches, and susurrations, and the barest hint of what could have been words or worse.

The pale king paid them no heed. He was communing, surrounded by the dead. Dozens of spirits filled the hall, their essence visible only to him. They had been called from across Terrinoth and beyond, sent to him via unimaginable curses. Their fear and confusion filled his thoughts with a rank, unwelcome discord. He focused through it, his own spirit form working to lance and bind them with ethereal fetters so he could interrogate each in turn.

They brought him news. It was an indirect process, but it was the best means of gathering knowledge from those loyal to him. Around Terrinoth, from pathetic farming hamlets to Free Cities bustling and lousy with life, those who did his bidding gave their reports. Each made a sacrifice on the last Moonsday of every Highsummer and every Deepwinter. That soul, stabbed or bludgeoned or strangled or drowned or otherwise dragged from its frail, mortal body, was trapped by enchantments as old as barrow hills and broken cairns and sent to him across vast distances. Each arrived full of terror and dismay, many still screaming, their disembodied howls filling the ancient stronghold's cold halls and corridors.

The pale king silenced each in turn, sewing their maws shut with curses so they could only whimper and moan. He had no intention of having to deal with the gibbering horror that so often beset the newly deceased. He did not need them to speak. He just needed them to remember.

The souls themselves did not understand why they had died or why they did not know rest. But they had all been imprinted with the information the pale king needed. It was merely a case of drawing it forth.

He entered the minds of each of the summoned spirits one after another, seeking out the knowledge he had been sent. Doing so required that he strip away the other thoughts and emotions still clinging to them. Silently, he interrogated a murdered maidservant, finding her initial emotions – horror and dismay – almost overwhelming. He worked past her memories of bidding farewell to her parents just earlier that morning, of the drudgery of cleaning out fireplaces and laundering bedsheets, until he arrived at the moment she had been seized.

Once upon a time, he might have enjoyed sampling her terror secondhand, but such petty evils no longer amused him. He forged through it until he found the words the leader of the death cult in Fairhaven had spoken to her before ending her, a message she had no comprehension of whatsoever but which she unwittingly carried to the pale king.

Matters in the city were, it seemed, progressing well. Fairhaven's investigations into the cult's presence there had stalled. Several aldermen had already pledged their allegiance in secret. The cult's influence continued to spread.

He moved on, releasing the maidservant and allowing her to dissipate. Next was a seamstress, then a porter, a ferryman, a farmhand, a collier. People who would barely be missed, chosen by the pale king's servants to carry their news to him in the distant north.

He arrived at a stable hand, his form phasing in and out of permanence as he writhed and twisted in the fetters the king had so patiently and firmly bound him.

"What do you bring me, boy?" he mused aloud, idly twisting his fingers through the phantom's plasmic essence.

He pierced the spirit's consciousness and slowly pieced together what he recalled. What he found was disturbing. All was not well in the Barony of Carthridge. The plans that he had started to lay years before were under threat, albeit only tangentially. The youngest Carth had gained some foolish notions about magic and its importance. That in itself might not have been so great a problem had he not been filling his head with other nonsense. Tales of battles and heroes, shining knights and terrible, skeletal monsters.

The pale king scoffed as he reviewed what the servant had been told. The ignorance of the people of Terrinoth never ceased to astound him. Eventually he withdrew from the soul, releasing it almost subconsciously as he sat and brooded on his tarnished throne.

There was no need for a direct intervention, not yet. Such dangers often proved to be inconsequential given time. And time was something he had plenty of. He would monitor Zachareth of Carth and make a decision on his fate at a later date.

He dragged forth the next spirit.

PART TWO

GREYHAVEN

CHAPTER NINE
Icetide, 1829

The cold woke Zachareth.

That was not unusual. When winter descended in the north of Carthridge, the great hearths throughout Castle Talon would remain burning all day and smoldering all night while bolts of wool would be used to stopper up window slits and extra rugs would be laid in bedroom chambers.

Greyhaven possessed none of those comforts. Zachareth had genuinely feared he would freeze to death during his first Deepwinter in the Free City. The lecture halls were without fireplaces, and the one that occupied the main dormitory could hardly be called as such – it was a small hole in the wall, and the students were expected to pay for firewood out of their own pockets, which of course meant that hardly a log was burned.

It was still dark for the most part, but dawn was adding the faintest luminescence to the beds nearest the dorm's high windows. The rest of the cohort was still asleep, Krellen's bass snoring ringing out. Zachareth sat up slowly, shivering. During the night, the chill had crept into his limbs, his hands, and his feet, heedless of the fact that, like most of the students during the winter months, he'd worn his class robes to bed under his blanket.

He knew from experience that this was the hardest part of the day. He was miserable and cold in bed, but that still seemed preferable to leaving it and facing the washing basin. He closed his eyes, feeling his tiredness trying to haul him back down in defiance of the oncoming day.

Fight it, he told himself. You haven't got a choice. Better now while everyone else is still asleep.

He pulled himself up and out of bed. The flagstones underfoot were painfully cold, but he made himself ignore the discomfort as he padded to the basin at the far end of the dorm, next to the miserable, dead fireplace.

Stretching out, he tied back his hair then probed the basin in the darkness. As he'd feared, the water within was filmed with a sheet of ice. He cracked it with his fingers. One of the nearest students, Hamar, he thought, whimpered in his sleep.

Zachareth skimmed the broken ice to one side and cupped the frigid water, splashing it across his face. It was a shock, but he embraced it, gritting his teeth to stop them from chattering. He stooped low over the basin to avoid getting water on his robes, scrubbing with his fingers around his eyes, nose, mouth, and ears. He wiped the excess off on the hem of his long sleeve, turned inside out.

The water had brought freshness and clarity if not warmth. He paced back down the dorm's central aisle, holding his freezing fingers up under his armpits until he reached his bed. Kneeling down, he pulled on his soft leather shoes and retrieved the books he'd need for the day, slipping them into the small leather satchel every student at Greyhaven was issued on their first day along with their robes.

He heard movement in the surrounding semidarkness, coughing and scratching, a few muttered words. The rest of the cohort beginning to awaken. He stood up, stretching his cold, stiff limbs again before shucking the satchel onto his back and making for the door.

The early hours, before the university had really come alive for the day, were when he enjoyed Greyhaven the most. He had never seen anything like the austere grandeur of the Hall of a Thousand Scribes, or the imposing dome of the Celestial Observance, or the towering pillars of Hallow Library. Filled with bustling students and lecturers, they were impressive, but in the cold, gray dawn they still possessed a quality beyond anything Zachareth had known before, a majesty that remained striking even two years after his arrival.

In another month and a half, Zachareth would be entering his third year at Greyhaven. The first winter had been the hardest. He'd hated the cold, and the terrible food, and not having any money. He had been lonely and perpetually tired, and Zelmar would not send any funds, would not even respond to his letters. Golfang wrote occasionally, but his duties kept him busy, and he clearly had little love of letters. Zachareth had taken on a side job scribing for one of the runemasters, Baelwich, writing her letters and organizing her mail. The venerable scholar paid a pittance, however, and Zachareth was deep in debt to everyone from the university itself to the bakery on Dock Street. It was something he had decided not to worry about yet – he had enough troubles right now, and he was certain the finances would resolve once he received his inheritance.

He passed through the dorm's deserted corridors and out

into the quadrangle that joined the accommodation block to the Hall of a Thousand Scribes. It was the foremost of the university's buildings, a sprawl of dark, weathered stone, fashioned like the palace of some austere king. The windows were high and arched while the roofs of the various adjoining lecture theaters, demonstration halls, and sublibraries were each dominated by a series of domes, lined with black slate that glistened whenever it rained. The quadrangle itself, a small space of open grass the students were forbidden to step on, was overlooked by statues set into niches along each of the four surrounding walls. They might have reminded Zachareth of the statues of his ancestors in Castle Talon's antechamber, but these were representations not of nobles and rulers but of scholars in their long robes or runemasters holding carved renderings of the shards of Timmoran. University legend claimed the souls of the Greyhaven worthies they represented were yet bound to them, and should the Free City be threatened, they could be awoken in its defense. Standing beneath their fearful bulk, Zachareth found himself believing the stories.

He passed beneath their stony eyes, resisting the urge to cross over the grass directly. He had survived his first year partly because he had worked out quickly when to follow the rules and when not to and partly because all the other students seemed just as miserable, and that gave him the determination to press on.

His fellow pupils were an eclectic mix, hailing from Terrinoth and beyond. Their ages varied, but most were younger than Zachareth. Their social standing defied categorization. Greyhaven prided itself on setting its fees to match the levels of individual entrants, nominally ensuring the university was open to all. In Zachareth's dorm, there was a butcher's son from Dawnsmoor, a merchant from Tamalir and a former Kellos initiate who'd given up the fiery cloth in an effort to learn the secrets of what he now considered true power – runemagic.

The presence of many of them had initially stung Zachareth. As the heir to a barony, he was expected to pay many times more than them in fees, despite the fact that in reality he was as destitute as any if not more so. He had come to realize, however, that matters of inheritance meant little in Greyhaven, to either the university staff or those enrolled under them. This was a Free City that knew no single direct overlord or master. It possessed a burgh council, but in truth, it was run by and for the university, specifically the Lords Regent.

Almost every family within the city had someone enrolled at it or employed by it, from the runemasters themselves down to the cleaners and serving staff. Those who didn't work for the institute directly usually earned their livelihoods catering to those who did, be they food sellers, parchment makers, or the tailors and the merchants and traders who sold the goods to all of them. The university ruled, and all others were there by invite only.

The lack of deference shown to him, even from many of the runemasters, had been a shock to Zachareth. He had survived, though, and steadily learned to adapt. Merit was key, he'd come to understand. Those who applied themselves – noticeably – to their studies won the approval of the runemasters and scholars. That meant leniency in other matters, whether it was late fee payments or marginal examination results. Zachareth had made sure he was known to his tutors and had pushed the limited influence he held as far as possible.

That included letters from Bernard. He had found several lecturers who remembered the tutor from his own days studying in the Free City. Zachareth was relieved to find that he had left a good impression. He had written to Bernard and received letters of recommendation that had helped secure his place on several of the more popular courses, all of them dealing with runemagic in one form or another. That form of influence, seemingly so easily acquired, had secretly pleased him. He had feared that in some way his power extended only as far as Castle Talon's gatehouse, but it was clear there were many ways to wield power in the wider world.

His old tutor had initially been shocked by his decision to attend Greyhaven, but that had given way to delight. He'd even claimed he was going to visit, though that had yet to materialize. Zachareth didn't begrudge him that. He knew that, even when he'd been younger, Bernard had not been in the best of health.

Zachareth entered the western wing of the Hall of a Thousand Scribes, taking one of the vaulted corridors to a wide set of stone stairs, which he climbed to the lecture room hosting his first class. Normally the route was churning with students going to and from their sittings, but right now there was nothing but the soft scuff of his shoes on the worn flags and the creak of the door as he stepped out into the upper tiers.

There were four identical lecture rooms in the Hall of Scribes, one at each point of the map. They were arrayed like amphitheaters with tiered wooden benches upon concentric stone steps that culminated at the bottom in a display pit. The ceiling overhead mirrored the sloping architecture in reverse, rising in a dome that culminated in a glass circle. The strengthening dawn light was currently spilling through, illuminating the pit directly below and leaving the higher viewing tiers where Zachareth had entered still wrapped in darkness.

He was no longer alone. The lecture theater had a single other occupant down below him in the pit. It was the morning's lecturer, Runemaster Gemil. He was a dwarf, formerly of the great Dunwarr city of Thelgrim, an irascible, white-bearded scholar with a wooden leg and a patch over one eye. Stories abounded as to just how he had sustained his grisly injuries, most of them involving a past calling as either a prospector, or a dangerously experimental runescribe, or both.

Gemil peered up at the shadows where Zachareth had entered, then grunted, looking back down at the texts he was busily laying on the table before him.

"Knew you'd be early," he grumbled. "Well, you might as well make yourself useful. Get down here."

Zachareth paced down the steps that divided the tiered rows, joining Gemil at the amphitheater's bottom. The dwarf carefully set a runestone down on the table. It was small, barely larger than Zachareth's thumbnail, a pebble that would have appeared wholly unremarkable if it wasn't for the tiny marking etched into its smooth surface. It was a series of whorled lines that encompassed it in a ring.

"Lay these out on every second bench space," Gemil said, tapping the top of a sheaf of scrolls set beside the stone. Zachareth picked them up, looking surreptitiously at the subject matter as he started to distribute them around the empty chamber. They detailed the nature of runes of strengthening and weakening, explaining the usefulness of both, as well as how to manipulate runestones stamped with such powers. He felt a flicker of excitement. Since arriving at

Greyhaven, those particular subjects had interested him the most. They seemed to be the most direct route to acquiring arcane power.

Zachareth's classmates began to arrive as he set out the last of the scrolls. He returned to the bench he usually occupied, at the lowest tier of the amphitheater closest to Gemil, as the domed chamber slowly began to fill with conversation. He ignored the chatter, reading through one of the books he'd brought with him, until a voice from the end of his row disturbed him.

"I thought we had Runemaster Yeng today?"

"That's tomorrow," Zachareth said without looking up from the book. "Runemaster Gemil always takes the strength rune classes."

"Makes sense, I suppose," Mikael said. "I don't think a willow like Yeng could tell us much about strength."

Zachareth was tempted to point out that there was more to strength than appearances, but he didn't want to get into a debate with Mikael just as the lesson was about to begin. The heir to Cailn slid along the bench so he was sitting next to Zachareth, who finally glanced up and acknowledged him.

"Did you do the reading for the transmutation class?" he asked. Mikael grinned sheepishly.

"I tried, honest. I fell asleep halfway through and seem to have forgotten the half I read."

Zachareth scoffed. "You won't pass the review if you haven't memorized the right formulas. The first year is the hardest."

"Good," Mikael said, clearly trying to sound nonchalant. "Then I can get kicked out of this miserable, cold dung heap and go home."

"I suspect Cailn is just as miserable and cold at this time of year," Zachareth pointed out. Mikael shot him a look but said nothing.

Zachareth's childhood rival had arrived at Greyhaven the summer past. They had found themselves sitting beside one another in Runemaster Sevril's runeshaping class. Zachareth hadn't seen Mikael for almost six years, and the changes were as stark to him as he assumed his own were to Mikael. The tall and somewhat ungainly youth had become strong and handsome, though he admitted he had not taken on the broadness of shoulders and limbs that Zachareth now possessed. Initially, they had greeted one another cautiously and avoided each other as much as possible, more out of awkwardness than anything else. Memories of various incidents at the last Silver Tourney, and the one before, were still fresh.

It hadn't taken long, however, for both of them to realize their days of scrapping were behind them. Childhood enmities now seemed small and insignificant compared to where they found themselves. Zachareth remembered well the loneliness and misery of his first year in Greyhaven, and even now a familiar – if much-changed – face was a welcome one. Bound together by circumstance, they had unearthed a friendship that perhaps had lain there, dormant, all along.

"Do you think there's a runestone that cures hangovers?" Mikael asked, leaning over to peer at the text Zachareth was reading. Zachareth moved it to one side so he could get a better look at it.

"Better one that stops you getting drunk in the first place," he pointed out, noting Mikael wincing as Gemil banged his runemaster's gavel on the table below them. In their time together, he'd found Mikael altogether more amusing than he had as a child. His lack of care regarding his studies almost made Zachareth envious. He wished he had such a luxury. He wished he didn't feel like the fate of his barony rested on his success here.

"That's enough idle nattering," Gemil barked at the assembling cohort. "You can address the scrolls laid out on your benches in silence while we wait for the last of your sorry lot to arrive."

There was a heavy, low tolling sound coming from outside. Zachareth recognized it as the university's bells, summoning tardy students to their first class of the morning. All across Greyhaven they would be ringing, as late youths struggled to pull on robes and locate books or, if they were unlucky, only just start awake from their slumber. The cookhouses would be sliding bread into their ovens and the taverns would unlock to admit fresh casks of ale into their cellars while the first of the day's river commerce would be pulling up to the docks. As in all other matters, the city set its time by the university's bells.

Gemil ordered the doors to the upper tiers be shut. Once closed, he began to deliver the lesson in his usual brusque style, remaining rooted firmly to his spot in the amphitheater's pit rather than pacing around as most other runemasters did. He explained the concepts behind runes of strengthening and weakening, two categories that had long intrigued Zachareth. Compared to elemental fragments, or mind-breaker pieces, or twinned teleportation stones, such shards were almost commonplace, but that did not necessarily make them easy to master. At a basic level, the former could increase the physical power of the wielder while the latter could weaken selected targets. Depending on how they were manipulated, they could also affect physical objects, be it swords, shields, gates, or windows, alternatively strengthening them or making them more brittle.

Zachareth recalled that one of Greigory's longswords had included a rune of strength set into the pommel, and Mikael had confirmed that his own grandfather had once used one during the Silver Tourney before runemagic was banned from the competition. Zachareth found himself wondering just how powerful a whole host could become if its warriors were imbued with such runes. How many would he need for the entirety of the baronial guard? A hundred or more? It would take decades to amass such a collection, but by the end of it, surely no force in Terrinoth or beyond would be able to stand before them. Not even the undead of the Mistlands.

"Novice Carth," snapped Gemil, startling Zachareth back into the present. "Would you care to demonstrate?"

"Of course, runemaster," he replied without hesitation, silently cursing himself. He didn't even know exactly what he was meant to be demonstrating. Nevertheless, he stood, and Mikael and his two neighbors shuffled along the bench to allow him out and down into the pit.

"I take it you have read the literature I told you to dispense earlier?" Gemil demanded.

"Yes, runemaster," Zachareth said. That at least was true. The scrolls had laid out the basics of manipulating strength runes, the act of grasping the runestone itself, and the simple mantras that helped the wielder find focus and safely unlock the shard's magic.

"Pick up the Bonesplitter," Gemil said. Zachareth looked down at the small runeshard on the table, the one he had seen laid out before the other students had arrived.

He had handled similar ones before. During their very

first day, students wishing to study runemagic at Greyhaven were expected to take up and attempt to unlock the power of a simple stone. Those that failed were immediately expelled while those who succeeded were allowed to complete their enrollment. Zachareth had passed using a pebble inscribed with a water rune, successfully managing to twist and coil the liquid inside a goblet before the eyes of a trio of runemasters, albeit only for a few seconds before losing control and watching the cup tumble. It had, apparently, been enough.

Zachareth knew the basic mantras and had experienced the power of the runes before. At first, it had filled him with fear and concern – the energies he felt when he grasped one of the stones were not his own. Their power was not his power, and without a shard in his grasp, he knew he would not be able to retain it. That truth still troubled him, but he had come to embrace the arcane energies as he'd grown more familiar with the strange, unique sensations they caused. Each runeshard had its own effect, but all made him feel more aware, more alive. They caused his skin to tingle and his hairs to bristle, and while he was using them, he often felt as though he was capable of anything. He was reluctant to relinquish them at the end of a lecture or demonstration.

Zachareth picked up the stone. Immediately, he felt its power. It was heavy, far heavier than it looked. It felt dense and compact as though the little pebble could have survived the strike of a battering ram or an ogre's hammer without so much as a chip.

"Now, channel it," Gemil said as the rest of the class watched on. "And lift this table."

Zachareth looked down. The table itself was more of a stone slab, its flanks carved with the same runic etchings that inscribed so many of the walls, floors, ceilings, and pillars in Greyhaven. Even knowing the purpose of a shard of strength before grasping the stone, Zachareth would have balked at the prospect of trying to lift it.

He could feel the rune's power, though, the untrammeled energies of the arcane that suffused him at its touch. Its potency helped drive away his doubts.

As the class looked on, he closed his eyes. He had noticed it helped some initiates focus themselves and was not expressly forbidden by the runemasters. It shut out the pressure of the watching cohort and Gemil's stony presence beside him.

He felt the stone in his palm, heavy and unbreakable. He ran his thumb over it, touching the runemarks that bonded it. He felt the weight respond to his touch, clasping like a strong hand around his wrist. It seemed to sink in, that heaviness running up his arm, around his shoulders, bleeding into the rest of his body. He invited it to spread further and sink deeper, repeating in his mind the short canticles of focus and preparation.

Suddenly, the runeshard was lighter. That wasn't really the case, he knew. He was stronger. His body felt like a coiled spring, full of potency, as it often did after he had completed his exercises prior to sparring with Golfang.

He opened his eyes and crouched down, squatting so he could plant his hands beneath the table. With the runestone still in his palm, he tensed for a second, then heaved.

There was resistance, but it was only momentary. The table shifted, then as Zachareth adjusted his grip and stance he felt it begin to lift. He rose from his haunches, his teeth gritted, muscles straining as he raised the slab up with him, still heaped with books and scrolls. It was heavy enough to make his arms and legs tremble, and his muscles ache, and his shoulders twinge, but it was all bearable. Soon he was standing up fully, the table raised to head height. He felt the rune's strength multiplying and enhancing his own, extending the horizon of his capabilities, making him feel as though he could stand solid with the table for hours.

Then Gemil stamped on his foot.

Zachareth yelped. The unexpected pain shattered his concentration. Quick as thought, the power of the runestone left him, reduced only to a vestige in the arm still grasping the shard.

He let out a cry as the table fell, the books on top of it scattering. It might well have broken his back, or at least his arms, had Gemil not reacted. The runemaster had a shard of his own clenched in one fist and raised it up as Zachareth stumbled. A blue glow suffused the table's edges, emanating from the stone in Gemil's hand. It stopped the slab from falling, leaving it levitating in the air where Zachareth had let go of it.

Gemil lowered his hand slowly, and the table likewise eased back down to the ground, reaching it and settling with only a slight thump. The runemaster returned his shard to an embroidered pouch at his waist, the blue glow vanishing.

"Novice Carth shows commendable ability when it comes to manipulating the shards," he announced to the class as Zachareth stood back, feeling suddenly self-conscious. "But his concentration is not flawless. Far from it. The minor inconvenience of a sore toe is enough to spell disaster. The runes, especially ones such as the Bonesplitter, demand our full respect and attention. Lack of either can lead to disaster. Take note of that."

The chamber filled with the scratching of quills on

parchment. Zachareth looked down at the runeshard in his hand. Its strength was still there, just waiting to be called on, to be unleashed. For a moment, he was almost tempted. He realized Gemil was watching him closely.

He placed the stone back down on the table and returned to his seat.

CHAPTER TEN

"You always get picked for the demonstrations," Mikael said as they packed up at the end of the lecture.

"It's because I sit at the front," Zachareth replied.

"I'm sitting right next to you!" Mikael exclaimed.

"I'm also more talented and stronger. I'm sure he'll pick you for the weakening stone tomorrow."

Mikael punched him in the arm while Zachareth laughed. The pair joined the flow of students making their way back up the amphitheater stairs to the upper doors.

"Makari's, tonight," Mikael said over the hubbub, keeping next to Zachareth, who shook his head.

"I've got plans."

"What plans could possibly be superior to an evening spent in Greyhaven's finest, cheapest alehouse?" Mikael demanded. There rarely seemed to be a night when he wasn't out and about in Greyhaven. Zachareth had realized early on that there was no point in trying to keep up.

"I'd rather keep it a secret unless it goes well," Zachareth said. "Actually, no, even then I'll probably still not tell you."

"You're probably seeing Maria again then," Mikael said teasingly. "You know she has her eye on you."

"She pays me to help her study," Zachareth said, his tone prickly. "Nothing more. Given the number of times I've assisted you, perhaps I should start charging you as well."

They processed out into the upper corridors where the press of robed, chattering students began to ease off. Zachareth waited while Mikael checked his schedule, the university's bells tolling again.

"Zachareth," said a voice from amidst the flow of bodies. He looked around, surprised that someone was calling his name.

"Zachareth," it repeated, the speaker becoming clear. It was Runemaster Morrow, a tall, gaunt man with receding black hair streaked with silver and a black goatee. He was dressed in the dark red robes of the Ignis Order, a subbranch of the Greyhaven faculty that specialized in fire-attuned runestones.

"Good morning, runemaster," Zachareth said, privately cursing his luck. Of course he'd run into Morrow while he was still with Mikael. He'd hoped his friend wouldn't discover the plans he had laid with Morrow. He'd been singled out by him, and he had no doubt Mikael would mock him for his studiousness.

"I have the next class," Morrow said with a slight smile, nodding at the chamber Zachareth and Mikael had just left. "Novice pyre rune manipulation. Something you've long become adept at, I'm sure."

"Still learning, runemaster," Zachareth said humbly, hoping the lecturer would move on. "Always room for improvement."

"Well, I won't keep you," Morrow said, perhaps sensing Zachareth's discomfort. "But I'll see you this evening, yes? I've several colleagues who're eager to meet you. The Four Hawks at the seventh bell. Don't be late!"

Morrow strode off into the lecture chamber before

Zachareth could respond. He sighed, deliberately not looking at Mikael as his fellow student whistled.

"So that's what you're doing," he said, his voice full of gloating. "Being summoned to private dinners by high-ranking runemasters! You might be the heir to Carth, but you're already the baron of popularity!"

"When a senior member of the university invites you to a private dinner, you go," Zachareth said. "Besides, it's free food. Take my advice in future, Mikael. Not that I imagine there'll be many staff members jostling to include *you* in their meetings."

"Nobody wants to make friends with the future Baron of Cailn," Mikael said with pretend despair. "Will you keep a few scraps to bring back to me in the dorm, good sire?"

It was Zachareth's turn to punch Mikael in the arm. Mikael located his planner and with it, the location of his next class, setting off with Zachareth.

"How did you meet Morrow anyway?" Mikael asked, unable to properly mask his curiosity. "I didn't think you took any fire rune classes."

"I was given extra lettering to copy, and he was the one overseeing it," Zachareth said. Mikael looked amazed.

"You, given extra lettering? You mean you were being... punished? That you actually... committed some sort of infraction?"

"I was a less model student in my first year," Zachareth said evasively, recalling how he had gotten into a brawl during elementalism with a cousin of the heir of Dhernas, who'd insulted the honor of the line of Carth. It seemed childish now, but it had born out positive results. Morrow had struck up a conversation and, realizing who Zachareth was, had made a point of greeting him whenever they encountered one another over the years. Then had come the invitation to dinner, a little over a month earlier. It seemed Greyhaven's runemasters weren't all quite as egalitarian as they liked to pretend.

"You be careful tonight, then," Mikael said as he arrived outside his next class, ready to part ways as Zachareth carried on to elementalism. "You know the university's overlords like to kidnap notable students and drain their essence on moonless nights."

"Even if that were so, I'd still be safer than you will be at Makari's," Zachareth pointed out. "I'll see you tomorrow!"

Mikael was in the doorway of the lecture hall when he turned back, calling after Zachareth.

"I almost forgot, a letter arrived for you this morning after you left. I've put it under your bed."

Zachareth discovered the sealed piece of parchment at the end of the day. He sat on the edge of his bed and tore it open hastily. Time was pressing, and if he didn't get changed and leave soon, he would be late to the dinner. Still, he couldn't leave without scanning the letter's contents. He knew the handwriting of the sender all too well.

It was from Bernard. His old tutor was the only one to write to him. Sometimes he sent news about home, but often he preferred to exchange stories about Greyhaven. When Zachareth had first arrived, he had found Bernard's inside knowledge about the cheapest taverns and the most reliable merchants gave him a degree of trust and status among his fellow students. The letters contained all sorts of warnings and advice about everything from the best classes to take to the runemasters he remembered from his own studies. Zachareth had put it all to good use, valuing the knowledge as a tool to advance his work. He knew his time here was vital if he was going to avert future disaster in Carthridge.

Today, though, there was little by way of advice from his former tutor. Bernard's tone seemed labored as he recounted the latest rash of difficulties to have beset the barony. The bandits in the silver mines had ceased paying their tithe, and Zelmar was refusing to even meet with Ragasta and Amalie, preferring Leanna's company alone. Worst of all, attacks from the Mistlands were increasing. More and more hamlets were being found deserted, and it was said the dead walked abroad far beyond the barony's borders.

The news filled Zachareth with a simmering anger, one which he turned with some difficulty into resolve. Matters were progressing at the university. He was growing stronger, sharper. He was learning. He only hoped that he attained the abilities he needed to confront Leanna and the wider threat of the undead before either became too powerful to stop.

He wrote a quick reply to Bernard, thanking him for sending word and passing on the compliments of several runemasters, then changed out of his university robes. Wearing a shirt, hose, and an open jerkin underneath a fur-lined cape, he left without telling anyone else in the dorm where he was going.

Evening was settling over Greyhaven. A cold winter fog had crept slowly across the city, pierced in places as candles and fires were lit within homes and taprooms, and lamplighters touched flames to the shielded slow torches that lined the wider thoroughfares, paid for by the university. The streets were quiet, the last few students hurrying back to their dorms or lodge houses, breaths steaming and cloaks drawn tight. Stores and shops were beginning to lock their doors and shutter their windows for the night.

Zachareth climbed Winding Hill, then took a right past the apothecary. He knew the alleyways, the small squares, and the steep, narrow lanes well now, comfortable in what had once been a strange environment full of unknown sights, smells, sounds, and characters, all far removed from the insular existence of Castle Talon. He had missed the seat of Carthridge's power during his first year, had missed the familiarity of Golfang, Bernard, even Zelmar, but his confidence had steadily grown. Greyhaven now felt like a second home, even more so since he hadn't returned to Castle Talon since departing for the university.

At the top of Winding Hill stood the Celestial Observance. It was the tallest building in Greyhaven, a great slate dome that stood proud of the jostling towers and spires of the other university buildings. Protruding from it was the great lens of the oscilloscope, a huge device that the masters of the celestial and divination schools used to scan the heavens. Zachareth had been told that it magnified everything, even the stars themselves, something he still struggled to imagine.

He skirted around the base of the Celestial Observance, which was steadily filling up with an evening class, and made his way down the other side of the hill toward Eastdock. He was nervous. Assisting an academic like Runemaster Baelwich with her letters was one thing, but being invited to a private function with a whole group of them was another entirely. He didn't even know Morrow particularly well. He had already resolved to be careful about what he said, to make no promises he might be expected to keep when he became Baron of Carthridge.

The Four Hawks was an eating house halfway down the northeastern flank of Winding Hill. It was a salubrious establishment well known to be frequented by Greyhaven academics, a factor that combined with its expensiveness to ensure it was typically shunned by the student body. It was certainly far removed from the cheap taverns and semi-illicit gambling dens that Zachareth had grown familiar with down by the Westdocks or the Triangle.

He arrived outside the eatery, glancing up at the sign of the four raptors emblazoned above the door as he paused to collect himself. A warm glow was spilling out onto the street from the windows flanking the entrance, but the glass was too opaque to be able to make out more than the blurred figures of those sitting within.

He opened the door and stepped inside. Welcome warmth washed over him, accompanied by a babble of voices and the scents of roasted meats and ale. It made him realize how hungry he was.

The front room was occupied by half a dozen tables crammed with clientele with more sitting at the bar that ran along the far wall. Zachareth stood awkwardly, searching for any sign of Morrow among the room's convivial occupants, until one of the waiting staff noticed him by the door. He hurried over with a slight scowl, clearly thinking he was some gormless youth who had wandered into the wrong part of town.

"My name's Zachareth Carth," he told him before the waiter could speak. "I was invited by Runemaster Morrow."

The staff member took a second to recompose his expression.

"The runemaster's party is in the back room, sir," he said, doubtless thankful he hadn't ordered Zachareth out on sight. "Might I take your cloak?"

"You may," Zachareth said, removing the garment while trying to disguise his relief. Morrow must have told the

Four Hawks to expect him. For some reason, he found that reassuring. He was in the right place. Besides, impoverished student or not, his standing was greater than any currently eating at the tables around him. He couldn't allow himself to forget that.

"Right this way, sir," the waiter said after he had hung up Zachareth's cape by the door. He led him briskly between the tables to a door by the bar, opening it and ushering him inside.

The rear room of the Four Hawks was considerably smaller than the front. It was lit only by the flames of a small fireplace, leaving dancing, flickering shadows on the dark wooden paneling that covered the walls. A single table at its center was occupied by three women and four men. Four of the guests had on the russet-red, gold-edged gowns of the Ignis Order while the others were dressed in a style that betrayed their wealth.

Zachareth's entry went unnoticed by the room's chattering company until Morrow, sitting at the head of the table, let out an exclamation and half rose from his seat.

"Zachareth," he said, clapping his hands together like a conjurer who had just performed a trick. "You made it! The first course is just on its way!"

Zachareth felt himself wilt as the attention of the room's occupants turned suddenly toward him. He was reminded abruptly of the sensation of being singled out during one of his father's feasts at Castle Talon. He smiled, putting up the confident front he had learned in Carthridge's court as Morrow saved him the awkwardness of responding.

"Come, sit!" the runemaster said, patting the sole empty chair set at his left hand. Zachareth obeyed, edging around the table until he was at Morrow's side.

"This is Zachareth Carth," Morrow declared, placing his

hand on Zachareth's shoulder as he took his seat. "Son of Zelmar and heir to the Barony of Carthridge."

"We should make you a herald, Morrow," one of the red-robed women said with a smirk. There was laughter and some table thumping.

"Welcome, Zachareth," a large, jowly man in a yellow cassock sitting opposite Morrow said. He had a golden amulet on a heavy chain around his neck, fashioned like the burning Hand of Kellos. "It's always good to add some young blood to our rather stale mix! I'm Martyn."

"Deacon of the Flame Simon Martyn, foremost clergyman of the Church of Kellos in Greyhaven," Morrow elaborated cheerfully, beginning to introduce the rest of the table. "You'll be familiar with some of the other faces I'm sure."

Zachareth was, at least with the other three Ignis runemasters, Lyrella, Drussus, and Zema, though he had never been to any of their classes. The other non-academics, besides Martyn, were a merchant named Potts and Olivia, who Morrow introduced as a writer.

"You're about to enter your third year, Zachareth?" Potts, a heavyset, salubrious-looking gentleman, asked.

"I am, sir," Zachareth responded. "I recently passed my mid-examination under Runemaster Holt."

"Zachareth's ability to manipulate fire runes seems to be quite exceptional," Morrow said. Zachareth felt abruptly embarrassed – he hadn't expected such high praise, and to have it come from a runemaster meant more to him than he had initially expected.

"I've not been fortunate enough to have many classes with Ignis tutors," he admitted. "I'm sure I have much still to learn."

"Humble too, unlike most baronial heirs," Martyn said,

watching Zachareth carefully. He caught the teasing tone in the priest's voice and smiled at him.

"That may change when I begin to achieve things of note," he said.

"Ambitious then," the writer, Olivia, noted.

"As all barons should be," Zachareth said, looking at her in turn.

There was a moment of silence before one of the academics, the one called Zema, spoke up.

"Which runes in particular do you hope to specialize in next year, Zachareth?"

"Strengthening runes have always interested me," he replied. This was their world, he tried to remind himself. His noble title meant little to them. Their concerns were not with lineages or family stock but with the power of the arcane, power that was still far beyond him. He hadn't been lying when he had said he still had much to learn.

"You are clearly direct enough to appreciate strength," Lyrella, another of the runemasters, said. "But have you not considered the natural runes, the elementals? Fire, ice, lightning, and more besides. Most students find an affinity with one. After all, their power is all around us."

"Already trying to recruit him to the ways of the flame, Lyrella?" Olivia asked with a little laugh.

"And well she may," Martyn said.

"I can see the benefits they bring," Zachareth said, trying to tread a fine line between matching the runemaster's questions and not appearing combative. "But all power originates from strength, and thus, to my mind, the runes of strength are the basis of all efforts at arcane enhancement."

"Paraphrasing Selgar the Twice-Blind," another of the

runemasters, Drussus, mused aloud. "I doubt even you were familiar with him at the end of your second year, Morrow!"

"My awakening to the Strictures of Power followed soon after," Morrow said, brushing away the claim with a charming smile. "But come, my friends, enough of this. I did not bring Zachareth here to interrogate him! Y'gath knows, if I were him, I'd never wish to make our acquaintance again!"

A few of those around the table frowned, and Zachareth sensed an abrupt chill in the silence that followed, one which Morrow seemed either oblivious to or unwilling to indulge.

He was saved any further embarrassment by the arrival of the first course, consisting of fresh bread and steaming bowls of leek soup. The conversation resumed and meandered warmly enough throughout the evening. Zachareth made a point of listening and speaking only when spoken to. For the first time, he saw beyond the stern exterior projected by most Greyhaven scholars toward their students. Those present spoke in a way he imagined parents might when discussing an extended family. There were expressions of annoyance and frustration when mentioning flagging or disruptive students, regret regarding those failing, and a materialistic delight for those expected to progress. Even the university's administration and the attitudes of certain other runemasters and faculties were questioned, something Zachareth had never expected to hear. He began to realize that there was a lot more to the university than the united front its staff liked to present to the student body. Rumors and squabbling abounded, with certain high-ranking runemasters clearly acquiring what Zachareth found himself likening to retinues of followers and adherents, some of whom were directly opposed to the adherents of others.

The first course was replaced by the second, oysters and

pickled cod from the Kingless Coast. Wine was poured liberally. Zachareth did his best to pace himself, but it was a struggle. It felt like a lifetime since he had last enjoyed a similar feast, and the warmth in the small room was making him light-headed.

Eventually, the conversation meandered back to him. He did his best to focus through his dull, tired thoughts. Olivia, the writer, was asking him something.

"Is it true your father counts a Latari elf among his advisors?"

Zachareth felt a spike of anger at Leanna's mention.

"Advisor would be too charitable," he growled. Olivia arched an eyebrow in a way that reminded him rather too much of the elf.

"She is not currently in favor at your father's court?"

"No," Zachareth said. "She is not in my favor, and soon that will be all that matters in Carthridge."

Potts, Drussus, and Morrow had been having a concurrent conversation about the merits of Greyhaven's geomancy guild while Potts dished out the last of the oysters, but they stopped and glanced at Zachareth as he spoke.

"She is a trickster and a fraud," he went on, the words rushing from him suddenly as though eager to be free. "I curse the day she arrived at Castle Talon and began to turn her dark magics upon us."

He had told no one at Greyhaven of Leanna or her hold over his father. His earlier determination to keep his own matters private seemed to have fled. He felt his anger twisting into embarrassment and concern as he realized everyone was looking at him, but it was too late now.

"Some, most of them elves, claim that the magic we study here is only a lesser version of what they practice," Morrow said carefully, filling the silence left by Zachareth's outburst. "They think the power of the Empyrean is superior, and that their ability to access magics at will, without recourse to runeshards, means that we are only dabblers and amateurs."

"A fact we enjoy disproving whenever an elf thinks to challenge Greyhaven," Lyrella said with obvious relish.

"I have no innate magic," Zachareth said, seeing no point in keeping his distance from the conversation any longer. "Nothing to challenge her with. The runes are my only hope."

"Why would you need to challenge her?" Olivia asked, clearly hoping he would elaborate on his dislike for the elf. Zachareth tried to pick his words more wisely. The heat in the back room was making him sweat, and he felt drowsy and dangerously slow.

"She has a ... negative influence on my father," he said. "At a time when Carthridge can ill afford it. We are beset by threats and difficulties, and Zelmar does nothing. He is confined to Castle Talon."

"I had heard the silver mines of the Carthmounts aren't producing what they once did," Potts said, chair creaking under his weight as he shifted.

"It is not the mines themselves but the bandits that beset them," Zachareth said. "And they are inconsequential next to the danger that comes creeping from the Mistlands. Just today I received a letter that tells of fresh attacks. The dead walk abroad. There is a malice that covets my barony, and none seem to know or care."

Again, Zachareth wondered if he had gone too far. It had felt good to unburden himself, though. He had kept his troubles close ever since leaving Castle Talon, rarely confiding even in Mikael. Hardly a day passed when he didn't worry about what was happening beyond Greyhaven and its twin rivers. Bernard's letters so rarely carried good news.

"You were right to come to Greyhaven, Zachareth," Morrow said. "Too many of the great and the good think little of learning and of the potential of runemagic. If it is power, and the strength to wield it in defense of your people, you seek, then we here can help you."

There were murmurs of support from around the table. Zachareth felt a surge of affinity for them. They were from amongst the great and the good of Greyhaven, each with years of success in their own trades, yet they were willing to sit and give consideration to him, a student who, while he was in the Free City, bore next to none of the influence his lineage would usually guarantee him.

"Have you thought about taking your Trial yet?" Morrow continued. Zachareth frowned.

"That would normally be at the end of my third year, would it not?" he asked uncertainly.

"Normally students sit it then, yes," Drussus said. "They hope to have acquired the necessary skills to pass it by then. There is not a fixed length of time that must elapse before it can be taken, though. It is not unheard of for students to participate at the beginning of their third term of study or even at the end of their second."

"So, you're saying I could?" Zachareth said slowly, trying to work out just how wise of an idea that was. He felt instinctively cautious about the proposal.

"We're saying you should," Morrow clarified, to his surprise.

"You are clearly talented, and matters are becoming pressing," the runemaster continued. "I do not believe I am being overly optimistic in encouraging you. If, say, you wished to undertake the Trial of Fire, I'm sure my colleagues and I could facilitate that. It could be organized before the month is over."

"That would mean I would be able to graduate almost a year early," Zachareth said, pondering the suggestion's potential, trying to weigh it against the risk of failure. He knew he still had more to learn. He couldn't leave Greyhaven unprepared, still ignorant of the true potential of the arcane. But time was pressing. He had no doubt Leanna's influence at Castle Talon was growing greater by the day. It already felt as though he had been absent for too long.

"And then you can return to Castle Talon," Morrow said. "And show your father and his Latari just what it is you have learned."

CHAPTER ELEVEN

There was a boat moving through the evening fog, sliding silently along the East River. Zachareth watched it for a while from where he was sitting on his rooftop perch, legs dangling over the wall's edge. The mist and the early evening made it difficult to discern the ship, but it looked big. Probably a merchant from Archaut or Jendra's Harbor, he decided, a large, indistinct bulk cautiously feeling its way through the fog, seeking passage via the Fork into Greyhaven's docks.

They had clearly paid the toll to hire out a local pilot to guide them because they had successfully avoided the Island of Trials on their way into the Fork. It was a small outcrop of rock that lay directly to the south-west of Greyhaven in the channel where the East and the West Rivers joined, coming down from Korrina's Tears. It was occupied by a building known to the students of the university only as the Manse, a crumbling edifice of stone that had, seemingly, lain abandoned for centuries.

Zachareth had been its only occupant for the past three days. He had been ferried over and left to his own devices, sent forth and told to wait by the university's runemasters. Since then he had grown increasingly familiar with the boats – merchant haulers, produce loggers, some private luxury craft – that plied Greyhaven's waterways.

They gave the island a wide berth, and Zachareth didn't try to hail them. Everyone knew the place's reputation and knew that seeking to interact with the lone figure sometimes seen on the Manse's roof or through its gaping windows would be a bad idea indeed.

Zachareth had spent the afternoons since his arrival exploring the place. Its age was difficult to determine, but from what Zachareth had learned in his studies, he suspected it had first been raised up sometime after the Second Darkness. That made it old, though not as ancient as some of the stories told about it in the student dorms.

The structure was mostly still intact, barely. The rooms were clad in stone, the affectations of furniture or timber paneling long since rotted away. Debris littered the building – old birds' nests and droppings, small bones, and the skull of what Zachareth thought was a dog down in the main hall. The stairs leading up from it had partially collapsed, but a sturdier-looking set of spiral steps in a small tower facing the eastern bank of the Fork gave access to the next floor as well as the roof.

The upper section of the Manse's east-facing wall had given in, leaving the rooms and the separating internal walls of the upper floor exposed like the ribs of a decaying torso. Parts of the roof had collapsed onto the second floor, though not yet to such a degree that they had caused a general cave-in. The roof itself, part curving and slated, part flat and traversable, offered a good view of Greyhaven's sprawl, from the warehouses and wharves cramming in at jutting angles on the East and West

Rivers to the dome of the Celestial Observance and its scope on Winding Hill, crowning the city.

It only lay a few hundred yards away across the water, but it felt like a whole other world. It felt like far more than three days since Zachareth had been dropped off at the tiny jetty and the short, narrow set of steps that led up the sheer rock face to where the Manse sat. Zachareth had never known isolation like it. Even when Zelmar had ordered him confined to his room in Castle Talon, he had simply bribed the guards or sat talking to them.

There was none of that here. No guards, no means of escape, arcane or otherwise. The figures bustling on Greyhaven's docks were too distant, and the passing boats knew better than to pick up anyone left on the island. Zachareth's only company, the only acknowledgment of his continued existence, were the gulls who had taken over much of the roof and upper rooms and squawked and gibbered at him if he approached too close. He felt abandoned, though he knew that was not really the case. He'd been sent there to be tested, and in a sense that test had already begun.

He had heard enough stories about the island to know the remoteness would affect him. He did his best to regulate his days by the bells of the university that still reached him from the city, tolling the hours across the waters. In the morning, he read from the two books he'd been allowed to bring with him, Caro's *Metamorphic* and a translated and abridged copy of *The Seven Platitudes* by Kazim of Thaj. The former he'd already read, though he enjoyed the stories of the Hyrrinx fable and the story about the farm boy and the runic animus he succeeded in summoning. In the afternoon, he searched the Manse, familiarizing himself with its dank, echoing chambers. In the evening, he wrote on the length of parchment he'd brought, trying to memorize the most useful focus mantras until the light grew too poor to make out his lettering.

In between it all, he ate. The food he'd been supplied with by the university for his sojourn was poor – heavily salted pork, hard biscuits, a few apples, and a hard block of cheese. He'd tried to make the most of it by looking for fish swimming in the shallows around the jetty, but he had no fishing equipment and no experience with it anyway and was not yet so hungry that he was willing to stoop to trying to snatch the darting little silver scales directly from the water.

He watched as the boat he had spied in the mist dissipated into it once more. The fog had descended that afternoon, prowling in off the East River. It made everything cold and damp and reminded him too much of the Bogmound and its horrors. He remained sitting on the roof's edge a little longer, watching the waters lapping at the rocks directly below and trying to feel kinship with the gulls glaring at him nearby, then abruptly rose and shook out his robes before heading back downstairs.

It would happen soon, he tried to tell himself. The Trial was the most important, as well as the most dangerous, examination taken by a student at Greyhaven. There were four that could be chosen from, each based on rune-elemental principles first theorized by Wellen of Riverwatch. On Morrow's advice, and with the implied backing of the Ignis Order, he had chosen to attempt the Trial of Fire.

He had been assigned to the Manse. It was one of the locations where the Trials occurred – the others were the Wending House, down amidst an abandoned stretch of the Westdock, Gallow Hill just outside the city to the south, and the Attaining Rooms, which were said to be buried somewhere deep beneath the Hall of a Thousand Scribes itself.

Once they were given a location, students were sent to it and left. Their chosen Trial would begin without warning. It could take days, even up to a week, but at some point, the student would find themselves assailed.

The wait in itself was half the test. Despite his best efforts, despite the meditation techniques he had sought to employ, Zachareth found it maddening. His fate at the university was about to be decided, and it could all happen in a flash.

Doubts haunted him as he descended to the Manse's main hall. It was so early to be taking his Trial. He was risking everything on Morrow's belief that he was ready. He almost resented being pressured into the examination, but he knew that in truth it was what he wanted. The letters from Bernard had spurred him on. Darkness was descending on Carthridge, and there were none to act as its light. Nobody else had his potential. He was the barony's heir, and he was on the cusp of being able to wield the power necessary to save it. Pass the Trial of Fire and he would have access to Greyhaven's final courses. Once he had graduated, he would be able to wield the runes and strike down all the ills that threatened his home.

Those were the thoughts he held onto tightly as the hours and days passed by, drifting like a boat out on the river. He had taken up residence in its main hall. It had once been a grand place, he was sure – its high ceiling and single, arching window spoke to the wealth of the house's original owner. Zachareth fancied that said owner was immortalized in stone at the hall's far end, beneath the long-shattered window. A statue stood there, larger than life, a woman, he believed, in a flowing gown.

He liked to think they were the same university robes he wore, though it was impossible to be sure, just as it was impossible to be sure about her features. Wind and rain and the gnawing effect of time had eroded her so that much, including her face, was just rugged, indistinct stone, blotched with moss.

He had his suspicions about the statue. He had read enough to know that many things during the Trial were not as they seemed. He had inspected it closely, wondering if it contained some sort of trap or acted as a sort of magical locus that would activate when the Trial began. Perhaps it was an animus, just waiting for the right incantation to awake it?

Her blind stare had made him feel uncomfortable, so he had chosen to roll out his sleeping blankets in the one place where she couldn't see him – beside her. He had soon discovered he wasn't the first to do so. The cracked, ancient-looking flagstones were darkened and smudged with soot, the marks of a past fire. He found the sight to be a strange comfort.

Zachareth knelt beside the fresh bundle of sticks he'd been allowed to bring and lit a knot of kindling with a flint and striker. He was wary about fire – it would be part of the Trial after all – but he didn't fancy spending the nights without it. He had slept little since he had arrived. It wasn't just the cold, though that was so much worse than even his dorm. Grim stories about the Manse abounded, from the ghosts of its near-mythic founders to foundations supposedly composed of the bones of students who had failed their Trials.

The dead should hold no fear, he told himself over and over. His ancestors had faced the restless corpses of the Mistlands countless times, and in every clash had sent them howling back to their graves. An heir of Carthridge should never quail before those who had escaped from the clutches of Nordros.

He prayed to the god of the dead, asking him to keep any spirits that lingered in the Manse silent as he opened the pouch at his waist and checked its contents. Nestled within were three small stones, shards of rock that might have seemed incongruous were it not for the inscriptions upon them.

They were the Tide-Turner, the Deepwinter Heart and the Stonecrusher, runestones all, each of them inscribed and imprinted with a specific brand of magical potency. Before being sent to undergo their Trial, a student was permitted to choose three runestones to take with them. Their ability to use them to survive the Trial was of vital importance.

Zachareth had mapped out his expectations and had chosen the ones he hoped would be most useful. He kept the pouch tied about his waist at all times and checked it every few hours. The Trial would begin without warning and to be caught unprepared could prove fatal.

The nature of any Trial was simple enough, though that belied the difficulty of passing it. After settling into their chosen location, an aspirant could expect to be beset by an elementalist form of magic. To pass, the student had to overcome the particular element – be it lightning strikes, a flood, a hurricane, or an earth-rupture – or escape from the location without major injury. The fact that there was no defined start point, and that the Trial could begin at any moment, only added to the difficulty. A student had to remain constantly alert without succumbing to the strain of doing so.

The runestones were all still where they should be. Zachareth looked up as he heard a faint ringing sound before recognizing it as the bells of Greyhaven, tolling the hour once more across the water.

Setting down the rune pouch next to him, he drew his

blanket up around his shoulders and found where he had left off in *Metamorphic*.

The Trial started later that night.

Zachareth awoke to the horror of fire. As he had feared, it had begun while he was asleep, shivering in the meager blanket he had wrapped himself in. Just where it had first leapt from he didn't know, but as he sat up, he saw that part of the hall was ablaze.

No natural flame would have taken in the Manse, for those pieces of the building that might have burned had long since rotted away. The Trial was in no way natural, though. Fire ran like liquid across the flagstones and up one wall, eating away at the stonework, tinged with the purple glow of sorcery. It crackled and snapped hungrily, its fingers questing further into the chamber. Zachareth realized that it gave off no smoke.

He surged to his feet, heart pounding, desperately freeing himself from his blanket before it could catch light.

Stay calm, he tried to tell himself. This was what he had prepared for. It was what he had wanted as well. To prove himself, to acquire the strength and knowledge he needed. Mere sorcerous flames were nothing before the might of the runes he had brought with him.

He snatched up his pouch and fumbled in it, clutching at the stones within. Immediately, power surged through him, altogether too much at once, making him gasp and almost drop the shards.

Picking up three runes at once was a basic mistake. He let go before his mind was overwhelmed by their joint energies, feeling each in turn until he found the Tide-Turner.

Instantly, he felt the more focused, specific energy of the

single shard. It made him sense the coldness and the pressure of the two great bodies of water that surrounded the island on either side. The runestone attuned him to the coursing rivers, made him briefly as one with the flowing waterways. He could feel their life-giving potency, how they met and churned at the Fork around the island, a rushing force of nature whose memories stretched away for leagues and across millennia.

He called out to the rivers to aid him. A mantra kept his mind focused as the Tide-Turner acted as a conduit, grasped firmly in his left hand, his thumb running across the small stone's intricate inscriptions. It was, to use one of Runemaster Holt's metaphors, the translator that enabled him to speak to the energies around him.

Those energies answered. He felt the waters where the rivers met twist and coil, just beyond the Manse's wall. They churned up into a great surge that Zachareth could see in his mind's eye. He raised the fist holding the stone, remembering the lessons about directional motioning. Energy responded to action.

He drove his fist toward the flames, which seemed to be rising and spreading at an ever-greater speed. There was a roaring sound, faint at first but building rapidly.

With a crash, a torrent of water stirred up by the Tide-Turner slammed through the broken arch of the window behind Zachareth and the faceless statue. It washed over him, its drenching, icy touch making him gasp, but he held into his concentration, determination giving him the focus he needed to keep the water under his control.

It surged like an undammed flood past him, slamming into the flames as they reached for him. There was a piercing hiss, and a great cloud of steam exploded through the derelict hall.

Zachareth snarled, his grip on the runestone shaking. Its

power was close to overwhelming him. He could feel an invisible pressure around him, the magical essence of the Tide-Turner made manifest. It was the intensity of the depths, and he knew that in a few moments more it would be too much. It would crush him, and the Runemasters would arrive the next day to find him broken and drowned by the might of the waters.

At the last moment, he let go. It was the crudest form of breaking the conduit between a runestone and its wielder, and doubtless the masters of Greyhaven would have chastised him, but survival was all that mattered. He released the Tide-Turner and it clattered to the flagstones. As it fell, so did the water, all direction and motion lost. Zachareth was struck by a final spray as the jet he had been master of collapsed across the chamber.

Zachareth gasped, dragging in a breath. The pressure, which had been building so relentlessly, was gone.

The Trial was over. He found himself laughing, relief flushing through him. All that time, all that preparation, and it was done. It had been close in the end, but not that close. He hadn't even needed the other runestones he'd brought.

He was about to try to wring the worst of the water from his robes when he caught a purple flicker reflected in the surface of the shallow pool that had flooded the hall. He looked up and felt an upwelling of horror.

The magical flames had reignited. Across the chamber floor, dozens of fresh tongues leapt into existence.

"Kellos preserve me," Zachareth exclaimed, trying not to panic. The flames, unnatural to begin with, were now almost wholly purple in color and danced across the top of the water even faster than they had spread over the stone. They rose up to clutch at him with flickering, hungry fingers. He could feel the heat of them on his drenched skin, making his hairs prickle, driving him back toward the dripping statue.

He drove his hand into his pouch, clutching at the second of the three runestones. It was the Deepwinter's Heart, and in his palm, it felt like a small, bitter shard of ice.

There was no time for finesse. He closed his eyes, screwing them tight shut, and sought out the winter chill the Heart carried.

The hissing returned, and he felt the heat on his face recede. He dared open his eyes and found the flames once more in retreat. Ice was emanating from him, turning his soaked robes brittle and stiff and spreading to the water swilling about his ankles. It hardened and frosted over as he watched, extending in a sphere until it met the fire and drove it back.

The Deepwinter Heart responded quicker than the Tide-Turner had, aided by the bitter seasonal cold that still lay over Greyhaven, but its effects also struck Zachareth faster and harder. After only a few moments of holding the runeshard, he felt its chill not only creeping over his body but penetrating it as well. Warmth fled from him, stealing his breath away and turning him numb. Limbs shaking, he desperately tore at the hand which holding the stone as he tried to regain control.

The flames had been held at bay, their heat overcome by the glacial cold as the temperature in the hall plummeted. As Zachareth struggled however, they seemed to redouble their efforts. They rose around him from all sides now, roaring and crackling, odorless and smokeless but full of the fury of utter destruction.

Zachareth didn't know what to do. He was being burned from without and frozen from within. Steam wreathed him, his soaked robes melting and refreezing. He couldn't breathe. He'd made a terrible mistake, and it was too late now to change it, too late to do anything. He had trapped himself between two elemental forces, and he was about to be destroyed utterly.

There was a splitting sound, louder than the hiss and roar of the war being waged between ice and fire. He felt his balance abruptly go as something shifted beneath him. He didn't even have enough breath to scream as he felt the floor giving way.

He fell.

CHAPTER TWELVE

Zachareth felt the crushing power of tumbling masonry around him and heard the splitting thunder of falling stone. A moment of hideous dislocation – free fall – and a brutal impact that drove the wind from his lungs and made him think his legs and spine had shattered. He brought his hands and arms up instinctively, the ice that had been forming over his clenched fist shattering as his grip on the Deepwinter's Heart was lost.

For a few frantic moments, he expected to feel the final, crushing impact of the stones of the Manse as they followed him down, pulverizing flesh and splintering bone. There was the rattle and clatter of settling rocks, and he felt the splash and patter of water raining down on him, but that was all.

Gingerly, he opened one eye and then the other and discovered what had happened. There was a space beneath the hall. The combination of extreme heat and cold must have caused the floor, already cracked, to split and come apart beneath him. He'd fallen down into what was probably a crypt or a sealed-up family tomb. A hole remained above him, water cascading down from the jagged edges.

He managed to sit up, cautiously checking for broken bones

and torn muscles. He was shivering with the residual cold of the Heart, but the worst of the chill had left him. He couldn't see the runestone though. Like the Tide-Turner, he'd lost his grip and lost control.

The featureless statue had fallen in with him and was now lying crooked at his back. He found his books as well and his blanket and satchel, all drenched through. He didn't have time to consider how he might make his way out of a sealed tomb, however. The fire was still coming.

It raced down with the cascading water, coiling and darting like a ferret unleashed into a burrow, hunting him with relentless, wicked ferocity.

Despair threatened to overwhelm Zachareth. No matter what he did, he couldn't extinguish the flames or stop their spread. His only hope now was to get out, but even that desire lay in ruins. In the hall above, he could have thrown himself through the window and hoped he survived the impact with the rocks and the waves. Now, however, he was surrounded by cloying darkness, and unable to get back up into the hall. He'd heard nothing about a crypt, let alone a way in or out of it that wasn't blocked.

The flames began to flicker over the mound of broken masonry that Zachareth had come down atop. The heat had returned, searing at him.

He cast about for something, anything that might offer him a way out. He'd been a fool to think he could fight the fires head-on. He should have sought escape immediately before he'd been cornered.

He noticed the pouch was still tied around his waist. His third and final runestone was within – the Stonecrusher. He grasped it, trying to draw courage from its familiar weight. He hadn't expected to need it. He'd brought it to study, thinking it would be useful to cram in extra research while waiting for the Trial to begin.

That had been another mistake he was now sharply regretting. The Stonecrusher couldn't help him against the arcane fires of the Trial. He couldn't fight them. His only hope was that he could use the stone to break his way out. The wall that was to his back was, presumably, an external one. Whether it was buried into the bedrock of the island or not, he didn't know. If it was, even the strength afforded to him by the shard probably wouldn't be enough. But he had to try. He had no doubt he was being observed by arcane means. If the runemasters intervened at the last moment to save him, he would be faced with the reality that he had failed. Such an outcome was inconceivable.

He pressed his thumb to the shard's binding markings and summoned the strength within. It revitalized his body, and with it gave him a fresh sense of determination. He scrambled down from the mound and over an ancient-looking tomb slab that lay between him and the wall. The ceiling's collapse had half shattered it and left dusty, skeletal remains jutting from its broken portion.

Zachareth apologized to them as he vaulted over, heading for the crypt wall. He landed and lunged, hoping the momentum would provide further force as he clenched his fist around the Stonecrusher and slammed it forward. Pain exploded through his knuckles, but the punch had the desired effect. It shuddered through the undercroft, causing great splits to appear in the brickwork in front of him.

He gritted his teeth and punched again and again. Pain followed every blow, but he could feel masonry shifting and giving way. The Stonecrusher gave him strength beyond mere force, a resilience to the shuddering impact of knuckles meeting stone. Lumps of broken brickwork fell around him, the heat of the flames and the straining of his muscles slicking him with sweat.

But still, it would not be enough. Masonry tumbled away from Zachareth as the last of the wall crumbled, but it only revealed more stone beyond it, dark and uncut.

His fears had been correct. There was bedrock between him and the outside, and he didn't have the time to break his way through it.

Zachareth expected to feel fear then, horror at the fiery, certain death that was about to engulf him, but instead, he found his thoughts turning cold and calm. There had to be another option. There always was. That was the purpose of the Trial.

The fire hadn't yet reached him around the mound of rubble. On an impulse he scrambled back up onto it, intending to gain higher ground and hopefully find a way back up into the hall above. Perhaps he could use the statue?

As he climbed, hand over hand, he noticed one of his books that had fallen in amongst the rubble. It was Caro's *Metamorphic*, though between the water, the dust, and the debris it was now undoubtedly ruined. One of the stories it told, though, of a young farmhand who summoned an animus to defend his family from borderland bandits, flashed abruptly through Zachareth's thoughts.

It was a tale he had first read in Bernard's loft, and he had long memorized the incantation used to bring the animus to life. As a child he'd tried to use it on the effigies in Castle Talon's antechamber to no avail – they had not been imprinted with the proper magics, Bernard had told him. In the story, the elemental creature had been a conglomeration of a watering trough and a drystone wall, but Zachareth realized that now he already had something better. He had a statue, one that he had felt was conveniently placed since arriving at the Manse.

Animus magic was one of the most famous disciplines practiced in Greyhaven. It was said that, should the university ever be threatened, the runemasters had it within their power to raise up the statues that lined the halls and cloisters and turn them to the Free City's defense. Animus creation was considered beyond all but the most senior and accomplished of students – Zachareth had only sat through a single, basic, preparatory lesson. Still, he believed he understood the core concepts. With the correct focus of energies a runeshard, sometimes multiple ones, could be used to imbue otherwise base and unfeeling materials with a semblance of life. Brought under control, they could be employed to serve the summoner in whatever way they wished.

Zachareth had no idea how accurate the account of the summoning in the *Metamorphic* was. It might just have been an approximation or an author's flight of fancy, but he didn't have any other techniques for raising up an animus memorized. It was his only chance. He just had to hope that the statue had been left deliberately, pre-prepared with the runic lines and already imbued with a trace of the arcane.

He did his best to ignore the flames that were just feet away now, standing before the statue that lay partially wedged and buried amidst the rubble. He closed his eyes, seeking focus and control.

"Concisus expergiscim," he said, enunciating the words carefully. "Lapis ori."

Nothing happened, but he could still feel the power of the Stonecrusher, clutched in his raw, bloodied fist.

Gritting his teeth, he opened his palm and slammed it against the featureless head of the statue. There was a cracking noise, and he felt a shockwave of energy slam through the crypt, dislodging rubble underfoot and causing the flames to shiver for a moment as though suddenly uncertain about their supremacy.

"Ligari, ligari," he said, wondering if he was even remembering the phrases correctly, let alone pronouncing them right. Even if the manipulating incantation was effective, the statue would have to have been imbued with reactive markings when it had first been sculpted to act as a vessel for an arcane, elemental consciousness. Zachareth was just hoping its presence in the Manse was intended as something he could use during the Trial rather than mere decoration.

He withdrew his hand, trembling and blinking through the sweat, expecting the Stonecrusher to simply slip from where it had been pressed against the stone. Instead, he found that his blow had buried the shard into the statue's brow, leaving cracks emanating like a web across its face. The stone's runic patterns were glowing a fiery yellow now. As Zachareth watched, they spread along the cracks, starting to pulse and flicker.

Without warning, the statue began to shift. At first, he thought it was simply settling in the dislodged rubble, but then he realized it was actually moving on its own. Its arms grated and scraped, then its lower limbs, cracking and shattering the lower portion of the graven gown. Then the head moved too, first fractionally left and then right, stone grinding. It reminded Zachareth of someone cracking their neck and working out their shoulders after a long, uncomfortable slumber.

He stumbled back, almost tripping, suddenly as afraid of the statue as of the purple flames reaching for him. He could feel its consciousness like a dull, heavy weight on his mind, linked to him by the rune's presence.

The statue got up onto its feet. The runeshard remained wedged in its brow, flowing with magical power, giving the construct a fierce and terrible appearance.

Zachareth had just raised an animus.

Part of him expected it to lash out and crush his skull in its cracked, stony fingers. But it did nothing, merely standing as still as it once had, smoldering. He felt its thoughts, or rather its emotions, in his head, impressions of consciousness overlapping his own. It was waiting.

The fire was reaching up the rubble, licking at his feet and making him yelp with pain. He pointed at the dank stone of the crypt wall, staring into the animus's burning eye.

"Break through," he shouted, voice lent strength by his desperation.

The construct responded. With a speed and alacrity Zachareth hadn't anticipated, it lunged down toward the wall, ignoring the flames that rose up as though to block it. It struck at the same point Zachareth had already hit but with far greater force.

It seemed as though the impact would bring the whole crypt down. Dust and debris rained from overhead, and the crack in the ceiling split wider. Splintered shards of bedrock burst from around the animus's fist as, augmented by the Stonecrusher, it plowed into the wall. A second strike followed the first, and then another, and then another, making Zachareth's ears ring.

The wall was starting to properly collapse now, not just the brickwork but the stone of the island itself, giving way before the relentless hammer blows. The animus struck alternately with one fist and then the other, implacable. It didn't know the meaning of pain, exhaustion, or fear. Zachareth felt none of those emotions in his mind.

The fires were snapping at his robes as he was forced back to the animus's side. The entire crypt was engulfed now, the unnatural purple flames choking and blinding. Through stinging eyes, Zachareth saw a more welcome illumination, one that didn't belong to the arcane inferno. It was pale and weak, but it was unmistakable. Daylight.

The animus had broken through. A gap had been pounded in the wall, a gap that rapidly widened as it thrust its fists through and tore at the jagged edges. After ripping the opening apart, it stood upright and still just as the fire caught about its ankles and surged up over its stony, moss-covered frame.

Zachareth threw himself for the gap, desperation driving him to a near frenzy. The fire had caught at the edge of his robes, and he cried out in pain at the scorching heat around his ankles. He tumbled through, clawing his way, before falling headfirst out the other side.

He half expected a short, plunging drop into the choppy waters around the isle or, worse still, to be met by the jagged rocks that surrounded it. Instead he realized, to his relief, that he had come out just above the stone stairs leading from the jetty to the front of the Manse. He tumbled halfway down them, grunting as he cracked a knee and an elbow on the rough, dark stone. Finally, he was able to snatch onto one protruding piece of rock and arrest his fall.

He sat up, dazed, and looked back. The Manse towered over him in the dim light of dawn, purple flames licking from the hole smashed in the bedrock it sat on. They didn't pass into the outside and continue their pursuit of him, though. He realized he could no longer feel the animus's presence in his mind either. The absence came with an unexpected pang of loss, but it was insignificant next to the relief he felt. The cold, wet air, the biting wind, all of it served as proof that he had made it out.

He turned back around and discovered he was not alone. A small assembly had gathered on the jetty, framed by the sprawl of Greyhaven behind them, rising up out of the dawn. They were gazing up at him, their faces lit by the pallid sunlight that was starting to leach life back into the world. Zachareth recognized the senior runemasters who judged the Trials, Corwin and Palais, as well as Morrow, Drussus, and Zema in their dark red robes. Most looked shocked, but Morrow was smiling.

Zachareth stared at them for a moment, then began to laugh. This time he didn't stop.

He had survived. More importantly, he had passed. The Trial was over.

CHAPTER THIRTEEN

The noonday bells were tolling, calling the students to class as assuredly as they might have summoned the faithful to worship. Zachareth arrived outside the door to Morrow's private chambers and hesitated. He heard voices within, the words more or less indecipherable. It sounded like Morrow and a woman. There was a question, a name – Olliven, he thought – and a low laugh. He realized someone was walking down the corridor to his left and would see him eavesdropping. Quickly, he knocked.

"Enter," came Morrow's voice. Zachareth opened the door and stepped inside.

It was the first time he had visited Morrow directly and the first time he had seen the inside of where the runemaster spent his time at Greyhaven when he wasn't lecturing. A large oaken desk, its timber blackened with age, dominated the room's center with a fireplace behind it and a small, arched window to the left. On the right was a single small door that led through to what Zachareth took to be a bedroom. The floor was covered by a black rug with intricate, intertwining golden-yellow patterning, and high bookshelves lined the wall on either side of the door Zachareth had entered through. A glance showed several strange objects among the tomes, small statuettes that didn't seem to obey any anatomies Zachareth knew or understood.

Morrow was seated behind the desk, while Drussus was lounging on the other side, seemingly interrupted mid-conversation. Zachareth hovered uncertainly just inside the door, glancing about.

"Come in, come in," Morrow said, his quick, easy smile replacing the frown that had been on his face when Zachareth had first opened the door. Drussus smiled as well, relaxing after the unexplained moment of tension.

"I'm not interrupting?" Zachareth asked.

"Not at all," Morrow said, waving at him. "We were just discussing your progress, actually."

"Is that... a good thing?" Zachareth wondered, carefully closing the door behind him and moving across the room to take the seat Morrow nodded to next to Drussus. Both of the runemasters laughed.

"That depends on your point of view," Drussus said. "In fact, Morrow has a proposal for you."

Zachareth tried not to frown. He wasn't sure what to expect. Three weeks had passed since the end of the Trial. The weather was turning, Snowmelt surrendering itself to Planting, the first month of the new year. The bitterest cold had withdrawn from the cloisters and dorm rooms, and the sun rose a little earlier and set a little later every day. Between the scents of woodsmoke and old vellum, the air smelled of spring. And as Greyhaven looked forward to nature's renewal, Zachareth had received the unexpected summons. It was the first he had heard from Morrow since the runemaster had congratulated him on the steps below the Manse.

"Myself, Drussus, and a few other interested parties have been in discussion for some time now," Morrow said, as Zachareth tried to work out just what was going on. "We were more than impressed by your success during the Trial. To awaken an animus at your age, and under such extreme stress… certainly neither of us have heard of that happening during our time at the university, and between us, that's quite a while!"

"Thank you, runemaster," Zachareth said, keeping his expression neutral. He'd learned to absorb praise and knew to temper his elation. He was sure he hadn't been summoned to Morrow's own quarters just to receive another round of plaudits. Something more was at play.

"We've already introduced you to many of our fellows in the Ignis Order," Drussus said, taking over from Morrow. "Your work is known and approved. There are further contacts we might make for you, however. Ones that will take your studies to the next level."

"I see," Zachareth said guardedly, still trying to work out just where the conversation was going.

"There are, as you are probably aware, a number of societies and collegiate groups associated with the University of Greyhaven," Morrow said. "The Ignis Order is a collection of like-minded faculty members, but many of us are part of a wider group, one that concerns itself with more than just runes of fire."

"Have you ever heard of Silver Horizon?" Drussus asked.

"No," Zachareth admitted after a moment's thought. "But given my heritage, such a name sounds auspicious."

Both runemasters laughed, though there was little mirth in it. Zachareth once again sensed the tension in the room, the same he'd felt when he had first stepped in.

"You are right to make the connection with the Silver Barony," Morrow said. "One of your ancestors was a founding member, though few today know it. Have you read of Marellus Carth?"

"Baron between the end of the sixteenth century and the start of the seventeenth," Zachareth said, his mind automatically going back to fragile lineage parchments learned by rote in a dusty garret. "He only ruled for eleven years before his unexplained death."

"Marellus didn't leave a lasting impression on the formal histories of Carthridge," Drussus said. "But he held influence in other things, ones less well documented."

"Like you, he had an interest in runemagics," Morrow said. "And the arcane in general. He founded Silver Horizon along with several others. We still continue his legacy today."

"What sort of legacy?" Zachareth asked, unable to avoid sounding suspicious. He could sense that, at some point, there had been a fierce debate about whether or not he should hear what he was currently being told. It was clearly a matter of controversy, but why he still couldn't fathom.

"Like you, Marellus appreciated the threat posed by the restless dead," Drussus said.

"By Waiqar?" Zachareth asked. Drussus glanced at Morrow, though what the look meant he could not tell.

"Yes, like Waiqar," Morrow said, seemingly determined to forge on. "The dead rose up from the Mistlands during his rule, much as they do now. He banished them with a combination of military strength and sorcerous might."

"At the battle of the Barrows," Zachareth said. "But I remember reading of no sorcery?"

"The record keepers tend not to look favorably upon the magic arts, at least not all of them equally," Drussus said.

"It wasn't runemagic Marellus used?" Zachareth asked.

"Not solely," Morrow replied. "He had aid from other, even greater forces."

"I see this is a tale you are cautious to tell, runemaster," Zachareth said, deciding to go on the offensive. Impatience was starting to wear down the intrigue. "Perhaps it is best to simply tell me what you expect from me for the time being."

"See? He does have sense," Morrow said to Drussus before looking back at him.

"Silver Horizon is a private club for scholars and arcaneists interested in the full potential of Mennera's magics. We would like you to join us."

"What would that achieve?" Zachareth asked pointedly. He wanted to know exactly what was being suggested. Until then, until he knew for sure, he didn't want to be drawn in.

"We believe there is more you need to know, more than some of our colleagues here in Greyhaven may wish to teach you," Drussus said, rallying once more to Morrow's narrative. "We fear there is another great battle against the living dead coming. None are better placed to defeat them than you. But you need to be prepared."

"You need the magics we can teach you," Morrow said. "With them at your disposal, the coming night might be kept at bay."

"You would teach me in addition to my final classes here?" Zachareth asked.

"Not entirely," Morrow said. "There is little more for you to learn at Greyhaven. I hoped you would apply for a sabbatical before your graduation, one that I would make sure was approved. I wish to take you to Nerekhall to study under me directly. That is where Silver Horizon has its headquarters."

Zachareth had heard plenty of stories surrounding Nerekhall, a few when he'd been growing up and many more since arriving at Greyhaven. It too was a Free City, and, like Greyhaven, it had a reputation for the arcane, albeit of an altogether darker nature. Centuries before, its sorcerers had gone too far in their quest for knowledge and power. Now it was a shadow of its former self, ruled over by uncompromising magisters ever on the lookout for the first hint of dark magics.

"You really think it would be for the best to conclude my studies here and travel to Nerekhall?" Zachareth asked. There was an allure to what Morrow was suggesting. Even after the Trial of Fire, he had come to realize that he didn't feel ready to return home. If there was so little left for him to learn in Greyhaven, could he really oust Leanna with what he had learned so far? And if he did, what about after? He didn't possess any runes of his own. Just how he could acquire and keep any was a subject that had vexed him almost since his arrival at Greyhaven. He needed to attain the power of at least one, but he didn't know where to start. If the situation was as dire as Bernard's letters made out, what good could he do? He had barely survived his Trial, had barely even been able to keep a grip on the runestones he had been wielding. He needed more permanent power.

"These new magics, they will give me … strength?" he asked. "The power to save my home? To save Carthridge?"

"To save all of Terrinoth, I pray," Morrow said.

"I am honored that you would tell me of this," Zachareth said. "And happy that you believe that I have such potential, runemasters. It is a lot to take in, though. I hope you will understand if I take a little while to consider your offer?"

"Of course, Zachareth," Morrow said, leaning back in his chair with that easy smile. "Take your time! You know where to find me."

"Were there any new letters for us today?" Zachareth asked Mikael as they headed to the dining hall adjoining the dormitories.

"None," Mikael said casually. "I don't think so, anyway."

Zachareth felt his mood, already dark, plummet further. He hadn't heard from Bernard for over a month. Even the excited letter he'd scribbled in the aftermath of the Trial of Fire, describing his success, had been met with only silence.

In the past few days, he'd sought out traders in Greyhaven he knew visited northwest Carthridge, but none had any news from Castle Talon. It seemed life went on there, but then it would have to anyone not aware of the barony's inner workings. What if Leanna had now assumed full control? What if Zelmar was completely enthralled and Bernard had been imprisoned or worse?

"It's Maxev's birthday tonight," Mikael said, speaking about one of the other students. "He's headed to the *Mage's Staff* to celebrate. You should come."

"I wasn't invited," Zachareth said, still brooding about the lack of news.

"The whole dorm's going, invitation or not," Mikael pointed out.

"I need to study," Zachareth said evasively.

"For what exactly?" Mikael asked. "You've already passed the Trial. It's little more than a procession now until you graduate. Have you got another of those fancy dinners with Morrow?"

"I wouldn't be going with you right now to get food if I did," Zachareth said, instantly defensive. Mikael grunted.

"You must have known that coming here to study would mean leaving behind all your troubles at home for the time being," the heir of Cailn said. "You used to enjoy yourself, Zachareth, or at least it seemed you did. By Fortuna's lucky dice, you completed your Trial this month, and you're barely in your third year! Let's celebrate!"

"No," Zachareth said, coming up short as they reached the entrance to the dining hall. He had grown to enjoy Mikael's carefree attitude, so often a tonic to his own stresses. Right now, however, he wasn't in the mood. "I'm nowhere near where I need to be. Nowhere near ready. I'm still a novice. An amateur. I'm in no fit state to protect Carthridge."

"What makes you think you need to right now?" Mikael asked.

Zachareth tried to articulate his fears and Bernard's silence, but he realized that their raised voices had drawn the attention of other students headed into the dining hall. He glared at Mikael wordlessly, then turned and stalked back to the dorm.

Zachareth pulled the letter from the sheaf he kept bound under his bed and, sitting down on the edge, eased its creases over his knee.

Again, he read the dire news Bernard had sent, the last communication before his silence. The dead rising. Zelmar growing ever weaker. Carthridge, its core steadily rotting away, unnoticed by the rest of Terrinoth.

He had two choices, he knew. He could ride tonight for Castle Talon, sweep through the gates and challenge Leanna. Or he could take up Morrow's offer.

His first instinct was to go home, to end the terrible uncertainty he felt and confront his fears. But it was too early. If he fought Leanna and lost, everything he had done so far would be in vain. Carthridge would have fallen without an army from the Mistlands having even crossed the border.

On the other hand, he could stay in Greyhaven, but he knew what Mikael had said was true. There was little more he could be taught about runes. They weren't going to equip him for the battles ahead. Staying wasn't an option. He needed the power of the runes and the knowledge to wield them. He had to become one with the strength they offered.

And that left only Silver Horizon. After a few moments more, he returned the letter to its sheaf and rose, heading for Morrow's chambers.

CHAPTER FOURTEEN

"What do you know of this place?" Morrow asked.

"Just the stories," Zachareth responded.

"What stories?" Morrow pressed.

Zachareth shrugged, suspecting the runemaster was merely forcing conversation in an effort to distract from the violent bouncing of the carriage as it clattered along the street's old, uneven cobbles.

"Nerekhall is cursed," he told Morrow simply.

"I think the city's magisters would prefer it if you used the past tense," Morrow said with a small smile. "Nerekhall *was* cursed. But it has been cured of that particular ailment. Or so I believe."

Zachareth didn't ask him to elaborate. As he said, he knew the stories. Centuries before, misguided sorcerers within the Free City had unleashed a legion of Ynfernael demons upon Terrinoth. A series of terrible battles had been fought to drive off the invaders, sealing them back on the far side of reality. Afterward, demands had been made to raze what little remained of Nerekhall to the ground and leave it scoured and barren, but Terrinoth's Council of Thirteen had voted, by a single ballot, to permit the city to be rebuilt. Zachareth found himself wondering just how much it ever could truly be cured. He also suspected Morrow was not naive enough to think that no trace of the taint remained. The runemaster knew more than he was letting on. Zachareth suspected that was often the case.

"Safeguards were put in place," Morrow said as though sensing his doubts. "Legal and arcane."

"The Ironbound," Zachareth said, wincing as the carriage hit a particularly deep rut. "They're like the animus of Greyhaven?"

"They may seem as such to those unaware of the magics involved," Morrow said. "But their natures are very different. They were forged by the priests of Pollux to guard against even the slightest hint of the Ynfernael. They are only the most famous of Nerekhall's defenses, though. The Church of Kellos has its agents here, and the laws of this Free City ban all but the most basic magics."

"Seems a strange place to bring me if you wish to teach me more than basic magic then," Zachareth pointed out. Morrow laughed.

"For every rule, an exception, Zachareth," he said. "Silver Horizon is part of the Academy, which has special dispensation to practice magic. It is Nerekhall's answer to Greyhaven's university. It might not be as large or as prestigious, but I fancy it superior in other, more important ways. Its library is more extensive, for starters."

Zachareth pondered the runemaster's words as he drew back the carriage curtain and gazed out at the city beyond. It was late and raining, which made it difficult to discern much. Buildings loomed along the way, dark timber edifices only occasionally lit from their windows and doorways. The firelight made the raindrops streaking across the window shine briefly before throwing them back into darkness, oscillating from one to the other. The light never quite reached Morrow's face across from Zachareth in the carriage.

"There are other students here?" he asked, wondering just how the place would compare with Greyhaven.

"Only by appointment," Morrow said. "And far fewer than you'll be used to. The Academy does not flatter itself as a teaching institution nor seek the exorbitant fees of one. It is a place dedicated to mastering the true arcane. Few are called to that."

"You speak as though you were not a runemaster at Greyhaven," Zachareth pointed out. Morrow laughed again.

"I have taught there for many years, of course," he said. "But the Academy was where I first learned the art. By Y'gath, it is special to me."

Zachareth had suspected as much. He had first mentioned Morrow to Bernard after the last letter, wondering just what his childhood tutor knew about the fire rune manipulator. He regretted not bringing him up sooner because without contact with Bernard he suddenly felt blind to the world beyond Castle Talon. The prospect of visiting another Free City, especially one with an infamous history like Nerekhall's, had filled him with a sort of nervous excitement, but he was cautious too. All this was necessary, he told himself, if he was going to attain the abilities he needed in the shortest amount of time possible.

The carriage lurched suddenly to a halt, forcing Zachareth to put a hand out to steady himself. There were voices outside, muffled by the steady drumming of the rain on the roof. Morrow's expression was invisible in the dark.

The carriage door was hauled open. Light spilled inside, illuminating Morrow and making Zachareth flinch. A man peered in at them, lamp raised. He was heavyset and pox-scarred, clad in a drenched oilskin cape and a feathered cap that was drooping miserably in the rain.

"Runemaster Morrow," the man said gruffly. "Welcome back to Nerekhall. Who's this with you?"

"This is Zachareth Carth, one of my students from Greyhaven. He's also the heir to the Barony of Carthridge. Zachareth, this is Gilmar Ruben, servant of Kellos and a captain in the night's watch."

Ruben inclined his head, though he didn't seem particularly awestruck by Zachareth's title.

"I'm afraid I'll need to scent you both," he said. "Standard protocol. I'm sure you'll understand."

"Of course," Morrow said diplomatically. "I was just describing the Ironbound to Zachareth. It will be good for him to encounter them in person."

Ruben stepped back, and Morrow ushered Zachareth out. He stepped into the rain, pulling up the cowl on his cape as he did so, but Ruben immediately snatched it and pushed it back again.

"No hood," he said. "They don't like hoods."

Zachareth's attention was too focused on the figure he'd just noticed standing by the carriage to be bothered either by Ruben's impertinence or the rain.

It was a giant, even taller than Golfang, and clad head to toe in gilt-edged plate mail. The rain seethed from its helm and its broad shoulders and ran down the great shield resting in its left hand and the massive glaive clenched in its right. The only part of it that wasn't glistening metal was its tabard, bearing the black and purple heraldry of Nerekhall.

"An Ironbound, guardian of Nerekhall," Morrow said as he stepped out beside Zachareth. "Fearsome, isn't it?"

Zachareth was lost for words. The thing took one clanking step toward them. The sound of the rain hitting its armor was loud. He realized there were runes inscribed into the metal, sigils of warding and anti-magic.

"It will only detain you for a moment," Ruben said, moving away from them.

Zachareth felt an overwhelming urge to cower before the giant. He found himself looking up into its faceless helm. There was nothing to see past the cold steel, but he could feel a tireless, cold intelligence, one that seemed to be interrogating more than just his physical appearance. It felt as though it was sniffing through his thoughts like a hound on a trail, searching for any hint of the darkness it had been built to destroy.

"Be at ease, Zachareth," Morrow said, sensing his tension. "It is a guardian, not a threat. It protects us all."

Zachareth tried to take comfort from the words. As Morrow spoke, the thing's helm turned to regard him. Morrow met its wordless appraisal, rain dripping from his goatee.

The Ironbound remained chillingly still, then abruptly looked to Ruben and nodded once.

"All is well, sirs," the watchman said brusquely. "You may be on your way. And welcome to Nerekhall."

The Academy was grander than Zachareth had anticipated. Whereas Greyhaven left the impression of some austere king's palace with echoing, high chambers and cold cloisters, the chief center of magical learning in Nerekhall felt more like the mansion of some learned gentleman scholar. Much of it was comprised of timber or clad in wooden paneling, darkened with age. Walls were occupied by tapestries or paintings of what Zachareth took to be venerable faculty members. In the first hallway Morrow led him down, there were alcoves with stands and glass pedestals that bore upon them an eclectic array of objects. There was broken pottery, old, rusting daggers, fragments of cloth, and a few strange, twisted little statuettes that reminded Zachareth of the ones he had seen in Morrow's chambers back in Greyhaven.

"Those are representations of the Djinn of Al-Kalim," Morrow said, noticing his attention in one of the hallways. "Mystical beings of immense arcane power. The Academy has close ties with a number of eminent Al-Kalim scholars and sorcerers.

They carried on with Morrow showing him the lecture chambers – tiered downward around a raised central podium, in reverse of the style at Greyhaven – and several study rooms, complete with crackling, lit hearths and well-worn leather couches and reclining benches. There seemed to be few people around, which Zachareth attributed to the lateness of the hour. Those he did see appeared to be robed members of staff, and most were too absorbed in their own thoughts or in the books they were reading to acknowledge either him or Morrow.

Eventually, their route led to what Morrow described as Zachareth's chambers. It was not, as he had anticipated, a drafty dorm room already filled with other students. Instead, he was shown into a small but well-appointed bedchamber in the main building's eastern annex. It even included a writing desk, a fire nook, and a bookshelf.

"The Academy has far fewer students than Greyhaven," Morrow explained. "It can afford better living conditions. Personally, I've always felt that good quarters lead to better study."

"Perhaps I should have come here in the beginning, rather than Greyhaven," Zachareth said as he set his satchel down on the bed, only half joking.

"Greyhaven is a fine place to learn the simplest tenants of runecraft," Morrow said, taking the statement seriously. "But the Academy is where those with a wider interest in the arcane arts come to hone their skills."

He paused at the door, his expression unusually grave.

"Your studying is over, Zachareth," he said. "Tomorrow, your training begins."

Zachareth picked up the rune. Unusually, he felt nothing, not even a hint of the magical energies that should have infused it.

"Is it a dud?" he asked Morrow. "A fake?"

The pair were standing outside in a small, walled-off courtyard, one of a number that lay within the grounds of the Academy. It was a pleasant space with rows of flowerbeds and yellowbranch and copper beech trees set before walls lined with ivy. Zachareth imagined that during Greentide it was full of the scents and colors of ryeflowers and brightblooms and busy with industrious insects. For now, though, with spring still a month off, it hosted only the gentle flow of a small fountain, leading into a brook that babbled its way out under one of the walls.

Morrow had told him that such secluded gardens were used by academics and students alike for both contemplation and demonstration. Zachareth couldn't imagine such a place in Greyhaven, with its austere colonnades leading out to the crowded, busy streets.

"It isn't a fake," Morrow said, as Zachareth looked down at the mysterious runeshard in his palm. "Can you hear anything?"

Zachareth paused, straining to make out something over the trickle of the fountain and the creak and sight of the trees overhanging the garden.

"There's nothing," he began to say. Morrow scoffed.

"You're not trying, Zachareth. Come now, treat this like a class demonstration back at Greyhaven. Focus!"

Zachareth looked back down at the runeshard. It was a strange one, unlike any he had seen before. Whereas most were smooth fragments of stone, or pebble-like rocks, this piece seemed rough and twisted, as though it had been melted and fused in some unimaginably hot furnace. The rune markings, three concentric rings sunk into its warped surface, were equally unknown to Zachareth.

"It's called the Whisperer with good reason," Morrow said. "There are few others like it. Focus on it. Close your eyes if you need to."

Zachareth felt a pang of embarrassment at the idea of using so basic a technique in front of the runemaster, but he did it anyway. Almost immediately, he heard a susurration that didn't belong to the wind in the eaves.

The sound made the hairs on the back of his neck prickle. He realized it was a voice he could hear, whispering to him. It was too quiet to discern what was being said, though. It lingered, right on the edge of hearing, the faintest murmur.

"It's speaking to me," he said uncertainly, wondering if he was imagining things.

"Not it, though it has its own voice," Morrow said. "The words are mine, though. My thoughts."

Zachareth opened his eyes in surprise and lost the faint mutterings.

"The shard reads minds?" he asked incredulously. He could see now why it was so rare and unusual. Morrow nodded.

"It takes a great deal of practice to be able to hear them properly," he said. "And an adept sorcerer is capable of hiding his true thoughts from it. Still, it is a powerful tool, no?"

"It is," Zachareth said, then flinched as he felt a sudden pain behind his eyes.

"Those are its aftereffects," Morrow said, holding his hand out and taking the shard back. "Without proper technique, it can be punishing to use."

"I see," Zachareth said guardedly. Morrow smiled.

"You still doubt it. I can hear you. Your thoughts."

"What am I thinking, then?" Zachareth asked, hastily attempting to clear his mind.

"Before you started to mentally recite the Five and a Half Verses of Tranquility, you were wondering at the power of such a shard, where I found it, and just what ends it could be put to. You were thinking, more generally, about how you can more quickly accelerate your learning here. You also... want one of the Ironbound to spar with?"

Zachareth took a step back, shaken at just how much Morrow had been able to discern in an instant.

"Put it away," he said with a flash of anger. "My thoughts are my own."

"Of course," Morrow said, slipping the twisted shard into his rune pouch. "Rest assured, Zachareth, I would never use the Whisperer without permission. With power comes responsibility."

"Well, if that's the truth, then I think it's foolish of you," Zachareth replied, mustering up a smile. "Such a shard would bring you great power indeed."

"The power will be yours once you master it," Morrow said. "How you use it is then up to you. Likewise with the other runes I will show you. And do not concern yourself with the pace of your training. You are already progressing far faster than anyone I have known. A little longer and you will have all that you seek."

Morrow once more held his hand out, palm flat. As Zachareth watched, a small tongue of flame sprang into existence just above his fingers, flickering from nowhere. Zachareth stared, looking at his other hand, searching for a runestone but finding none.

"You are a sorcerer," he said, awe and surprise making him forget himself. "More than just a runemaster. You can tap into the energies of the Turning?"

"I am no more capable of accessing the Turning than you are, Zachareth," Morrow said, clenching his fist and making the flame disappear. "But there are a great many forms of magic in this reality we inhabit – and even more beyond it. Give me a little time, and if you are willing, I will show you."

Zachareth felt suddenly cautious. Discovering Morrow possessed powers beyond the runes he taught was strangely embarrassing. He had never even considered the possibility. Briefly, he wondered if he had been naive to never question more of what was happening, why Silver Horizon would want to teach him their magics, or what they intended for him when they were done. He couldn't allow himself to be used. He had to turn it around, ensure that he was the one who benefited from the new relationship. And through him, Carthridge.

He remembered the Whisperer and tried to wipe his thoughts clear. Morrow was smiling again.

"Come," he said. "Let us see what we can do about finding you an Ironbound to put you through your paces."

CHAPTER FIFTEEN

Planting gave way to Newbloom and then Greentide. As the gardens of the Academy blossomed and summer set in, Zachareth learned. He rarely left the grounds for the city beyond but sat in private studies or in the walled-off spaces outdoors, doing his best to absorb everything Morrow told him.

His favorite place was the library. It was even larger than Greyhaven's – according to Morrow it was the most extensive in all of Terrinoth. Zachareth had been filled with awe when he had first been led around it. The building, at the heart of the Academy, was circular and domed with multiple tiers – six in all – rising to the curved ceiling, packing row after row of books, parchments, and maps. He had quickly established a reading desk on the second level as his own and spent most of his spare time there, devouring everything from philosophical ponderings on the Aenlong to detailed charts of the Sea of Kingless Coast. Sometimes he simply sat and gazed about at the vast collection of texts and scrolls and remembered how he had started with a few stacks in Bernard's musty old tower loft.

He had sent a letter to his old tutor before leaving Greyhaven, asking for news and advising him to send any correspondence to Nerekhall. It didn't seem to make a difference. There had been nothing. In the first month at the Academy, feeling isolated and friendless, he had ended up confiding his fears to Morrow. He had told him that he worried Castle Talon was already in the thrall of dark forces and that he was certain the dead stood poised to march upon Carthridge any day now.

"I have heard nothing of immediate concern from my friends in the north," Morrow had told him, the words offering Zachareth a momentary reprieve from his worrying. "You are making such progress. Another few months here, and a few more in Greyhaven, and you will have everything you need to protect the barony. I will have taught you everything I know. Well, almost everything."

The training continued. Zachareth learned the nature of runes considered too powerful for use by students at Greyhaven. There was the First Sight, which, with immense, headache-inducing concentration, could provide accurate – but malleable – premonitions a few minutes into the future. Even more impressive were the Twins, two identical runestones that allowed instantaneous transportation from one to the other. Zachareth started with one in Morrow's study and, in a blink, found himself where the other had been placed, beneath an oak in the garden they often practiced in.

Morrow even permitted him to carry some of the runes around on a day-to-day basis, something strictly forbidden in Greyhaven. He employed a rune of speed sometimes when reading, devouring weighty old tomes in a matter of minutes, and became particularly attached to a simple rune of strength called the Sunderer.

In a few weeks, he felt more familiar and comfortable with runemagic than he had after years at Greyhaven. He pressed

Morrow for more, however. The realization that he was a fully-fledged sorcerer, while initially shocking, now filled Zachareth with hope. There were magics in the world that he might yet learn that would give him power beyond the shards. He begged Morrow to teach him more.

"It is not for novices, even talented ones like you," Morrow had said. "The magic I use is not of the Turning. It is from the realm of spirits, the sorcery of entities and powers beyond our comprehension."

"Not the souls of the dead, though," Zachareth said cautiously.

"No, not necromancy," Morrow said. "No good comes from that foul practice."

"Like the djinn you spoke of?"

"Sometimes, yes, but there are many spirits and powers in that other place. And many of them are dangerous."

Zachareth didn't care about danger. If there was more he could learn, something that would give him the edge in the clash that was coming, he needed it. He asked Morrow until the runemaster finally acquiesced enough to teach him a short incantation.

It was fire magic. After spending hours attempting to pronounce each syllable correctly, he was able to briefly conjure a small tongue of flame above his palm. The effort singed his hand and made his head hurt so badly he could only recite it once or twice in a session. It excited him, however. There was potential there, power to be used and controlled. Perhaps he wouldn't have to rely on runes after all. Morrow advised him that he would need to be patient.

When he wasn't reading or attending Morrow's private lessons, he was sparring. He had missed out on it at Greyhaven where there had never been the time or a fitting opponent. It felt good to have a blade in his hand once more. The runemaster had been as good as his word, convincing the city's militia to furnish him with an Ironbound to train with, the only stipulation being that the sessions take place outside the Academy. The Ironbound were forbidden from entering the school without express authority. It was the only place in Nerekhall where their presence was restricted.

A deal had been struck with the city's merchant guilds, who seemed to have a close relationship with the Academy. Zachareth journeyed there regularly, trying to hone the edge he felt he had lost during his time at Greyhaven. Amidst all the books, he couldn't forget the sword.

He went again on the second Moonsday of Greentide. The streets of Nerekhall were close and sultry in the midday heat. The guild hall seemed quiet, the auctions and trade councils suspended for luncheon. He found the Ironbound waiting for him in the lower hall, a timber-clad space that looked out over the Iron Tower, in the city's southern quarter.

"Good afternoon, silent one," he said to the Ironbound as he always did. It didn't respond. He had yet to hear any of the constructs utter a sound beyond the grating of their armor and the occasional clicking noise made by what he assumed to be their internal workings.

Zachareth removed his cloak, scratched briefly at the goatee he'd been attempting to grow, and stretched, waking his muscles. Ironbound were devilishly swift and seemed impervious to the hardest sword stroke. He suspected even Golfang would have struggled to best one. He was just thankful the one he had been loaned bore instructions not to harm him.

He rebuckled his sword around his waist, checking it, then

slipped his hand into the pouch he wore and gripped the Whisperer. The strange, warped runestone was with him most days. He was desperate to learn how to manipulate it properly. When he focused hard enough, he could just about discern the shard's muttering, sometimes even specific words. He had discovered that if he trained his attention on someone in close proximity, usually in the same chamber, he could almost catch snatches of what sounded like conversation. He had brought the shard with him today to see if he could manipulate it more easily in a private, quiet environment.

The Ironbound's helm scraped slightly as it turned to regard him. That was strange – normally when he entered it remained unresponsive until he drew his sword and raised it in salute. He felt the cold, soulless nature of its attention, only accentuated by the flat, featureless helm.

"What are you thinking, Ironbound?" Zachareth asked it. He wasn't expecting an answer as such, but he was curious. He wanted to know if there were thoughts amidst the apparatus within its armored shell. Would he be able to hear the whirr and click of its mind cogs? Or, if its directives were set by the artificers of Pollux, would it be their words, their thoughts, that had been inscribed upon the runestone?

He began to raise it in his palm but had barely done so when the Ironbound moved. It lowered its glaive and, without any warning, lunged.

Zachareth yelled and threw himself aside. If he hadn't, the glaive would have run him through. Despite missing him, the Ironbound recovered instantly, sweeping the haft of its weapon sideways and connecting with Zachareth's midriff. He grunted and windmilled with his arms but was unable to stop himself from being thrown painfully to the ground.

He tried to tell the Ironbound to stop, but the glaive haft to the ribs and the fall had winded him. Gasping, he attempted to stand, seeing only the Ironbound's armored feet as they pivoted with a scrape, leaving gouges in the timber floorboards. He twisted to look up and found the glaive reversed overhead, about to slam down with unyielding, mechanical force.

He rolled as the glaive descended, its long blade burying itself almost to the hilt in the boards beside him. He hadn't even had a chance to draw his sword yet, but he did so wildly as he made it up onto his knees, attempting to chop through the glaive's haft two-handed. The weapon Golfang had presented to him for his banner hold, the one he had yet to even give a name to, cut deep but failed to cleave all the way through.

He attempted to wrench the sword free, but it was stuck fast. He had a sickening recollection of Captain Travas, his armor shining in the burning sun, his sword wedged and useless in the lists.

The Ironbound responded. It released its glaive and snatched Zachareth by the throat. He felt cold, hard, rune-etched steel clamp like a vise, instantly cutting off the air and putting a terrible strain on his neck, head, and shoulders. The massive automaton began to lift.

It hoisted him up like he weighed nothing, his legs kicking and his hands clutching against the Ironbound's vambrace. He desperately needed to relieve the pressure and drag down air – just then nothing else mattered. Panicking, he was sure his neck was a single, small cog turn away from snapping.

Choking to death, he didn't realize he'd dropped the Whisperer until the Ironbound itself reacted.

The construct released him. He fell abruptly on his rump, clutching at his aching throat, gasping and panting. His lungs burned, and it took a moment for him to realize why the out-of-control machine had dropped him.

The Whisperer had hit the floorboards and skittered across them. The Ironbound turned sharply and strode toward it, its clanking footsteps heavy and full of menace. As Zachareth continued to try to drag down air, he saw it raise its shield and slam the pointed end down onto the twisted runestone. The furious motion was both shocking and horrifying, and only added to Zachareth's confusion.

There was a crash and a blast of energy that threatened to throw Zachareth onto his back. A red glow suffused the room, emanating from the stone. It was accompanied by a disembodied roar of fury and pain as though the voices the Whisperer stole had cried out as one.

The Ironbound struck with its shield again, the blow ringing like a hammer upon an anvil. Again, magical energy blasted through the chamber. Zachareth felt a sudden, splitting pain in his skull. He clutched it, moaning in fear and agony.

The Ironbound was trying to break the runestone, he realized, and the runestone was fighting back. The sigils engraved across the machine's armored shell had started to glow white-hot, and Zachareth could feel tremors running through the whole guild hall as though Nerekhall were in the midst of an earthquake. The hellish red light emanating from the Whisperer was suffusing everything.

The Ironbound's great rune-etched shield fell one last time. The Whisperer howled, a chilling, inhuman noise, before shattering into pieces. Fragments scattered across the room. The bestial voice's agony was ended, and the red glow vanished like a torch being abruptly snuffed out.

Zachareth stayed where he had fallen, eyes wide, thoughts

racing. The tremors were subsiding, though pain still throbbed in his temples. He was still trying to process what he had just witnessed as the Ironbound slowly lowered its head, shoulders slumping. The runes on its armor began to lose their glow, steam rising gently from them. There was a soft ticking sound, gradually slowing, as though the mechanism within the armor was beginning to shut down.

Zachareth roused himself. Whatever had just happened, the Ironbound had gone dormant. He wasn't going to wait for it to wake up again. Getting up unsteadily, he paused only to grasp the hilt of his sword and deliver a few savage kicks against the glaive haft it was still wedged into until it gave way and the blade came free.

He glanced one more time at the Ironbound, still towering, head bowed, over the fragments of the broken runeshard, then ran for the Academy.

As Zachareth raced through Nerekhall's darkening streets, his mind was in turmoil. He didn't know runeshards could be physically destroyed, and he certainly hadn't heard of sentient ones that cried out in pain and sought to defend themselves. Such magic felt wholly unnatural. In fact, he realized that there had been something unsettling about the Whisperer ever since he had first held it in his palm. The headaches, the disembodied voices – at first, he had just put it down to the stone being of a power he had never before encountered. Now though, he wasn't so sure.

One thing was certain. The Ironbound hadn't been attacking him. It had been trying to attack the runeshard. Suddenly, he began to understand why the constructs weren't allowed in the Academy.

He swept into the Academy, making directly for the library. A horrible realization was starting to dawn on him, one that at first seemed outrageous. The more he considered it though, the more likely it seemed.

He strode into the library, his footsteps loud on the flagstones of the lower floor. The curator, Dolman, looked up from his desk with a scowl. Zachareth watched the expression turned to bewilderment as he saw him approaching, sword at his hip, hair unkempt, damp with sweat.

"Is something awry, Master Carth?" the wizened librarian asked, clearly alarmed at Zachareth's fierce expression.

"It would seem so, sir," he responded. "But I have need of your assistance if I am to be sure of it. Tell me, do you know of any texts here that document the ancient spirit known as Y'gath."

Zachareth watched Dolman's face turn from concerned to afraid in an instant.

"I can't say I've ever heard of such a being, sir," he said far too hastily. Zachareth's expression hardened.

"Then you are not well acquainted with Runemaster Morrow, for I have heard him utter the name a number of times in passing."

"That's really no business of mine," Dolman began to say, but Zachareth cut him off.

"I will have a look for myself," he said, striding past the desk. Dolman called out after him, but he ignored him.

The library of the Academy was arrayed according to the scholarly view of the plains of existence. Works detailing what Hironemous Zech called the "lower planes of the many realities" lay in the subsurface level, accessed by a spiral staircase set into the center of the great, circular library. Zachareth hurried down it, ignoring the echoing voice of Dolman.

The undercroft was quiet and appeared empty. Zachareth swept through to the section on the spirits of the lower plains and began rifling through different glossaries and compendiums, letting books drop when he found nothing. He heard Dolman's voice, in urgent conversation with someone, up in the main section of the library.

He found what he was looking for – an entry detailing Y'gath in a section of a crackled tome entitled *An Account of the Fouler Entities.* As his eyes darted across the words, a dark rage gripped him. How could he have been so blind, so foolish? Was it already too late? Was he already damned?

"Master Zachareth."

He turned and found himself being confronted by Drussus and another of the Academy's dark-robed tutors, Ollen. Dolman was lingering nervously behind them at the foot of the stairs.

"You are disturbing the peace and order of the library," Drussus said sharply. "Pray tell, what in the name of the gods are you doing?"

"Seeking enlightenment," Zachareth said angrily, slamming the book shut. "And I fear I've found plenty of it."

A bell began tolling somewhere in the Academy. Zachareth thought it was for him until he saw the looks of confusion and alarm on the faces of those who had accosted him.

"The main doors?" Ollen asked.

"I'll go and see," Drussus said. "Stay here with Zachareth."

"No," Zachareth said sharply. "If this is what I think it is, they'll want me. I'm coming as well."

Drussus looked conflicted, but after a glance at Ollen, she nodded.

"You don't say a word unless you're spoken to, understood?" she demanded.

"Understood," Zachareth replied.

CHAPTER SIXTEEN

Unusually, the front doors of the Academy were lying open. Zachareth, Ollen, and Drussus found Morrow standing on the steps beyond, facing out onto the street.

Before him was Ruben, and at his back, six Ironbound, arrayed precisely in two files of three. The Nerekhall watchman was speaking loudly but paused midsentence and pointed at Zachareth as he came through the door.

"Him," he said.

"I told you, there has been some misunderstanding," Morrow said in an altogether calmer tone. "Zachareth Carth merely studies here until his return to Greyhaven next month."

"That means nothing regarding his innocence. He has been sparring in the guild hall with an Ironbound we provided as a token of goodwill. He was there today, was he not?"

"He was not," Morrow said, his voice tight with controlled anger. "He hasn't left the Academy today."

"He was seen fleeing through the streets with a sword this morning. And he doesn't exactly look as though he has just come from a quiet studying session."

Zachareth was tempted to speak up. He wanted to tell Ruben

about the Whisperer, about everything he had discovered in the library. A part of him even wanted to see the Ironbound lower their spears, march up the steps with their terrible, silent implacableness, and set about slaughtering everyone in the Academy. He had been deceived, and he was furious.

But he had also learned much about the values of silence and patience. He forced himself to think rationally about the consequences of speaking up. Morrow would regret what he had done, no doubt. The Academy would suffer, and Nerekhall itself would likely know a level of turmoil it had not seen since demons stalked its streets. But it would not help him, and it would not help Carthridge. And that, he told himself repeatedly, was the only thing that mattered.

As Morrow lied, he stayed silent.

"Zachareth was just with one of the Academy's members, Lady Drussus," the runemaster said, gesturing. "I have multiple witnesses that can vouch for him."

"As have I," Ruben said, his tone rising again. "The Ironbound he was assigned was found with the broken shards of a tainted runestone. Dark magic, forbidden even here in this den of sorcerers."

"That is an outrageous accusation," Morrow snapped. "Don't think I don't know what this is about, Ruben. Your little inquisitorial searches here never turn up anything. The magisters want to remind us of our place, so they send you to make their threats with Ironbound at your back."

"Now you are the one making outrageous accusations," Ruben barked. "Despite your vaunted status, you will still obey the laws of Nerekhall!"

Zachareth stepped forward. He did so impulsively, knowing that if he didn't act, matters would spiral completely out of control. His experiences with a single Ironbound meant he had no wish to test himself against six.

"I know nothing of the accusations you make, sir," he told Ruben, trying to focus on him and not the looming threat behind him. "But if need be, I am happy to submit myself. At the very least, though, I would expect a formal warrant. I am, after all, a baronial heir. I cannot simply be seized if the evidence is circumstantial."

"He is correct," Morrow said before Ruben responded. "If the magisters want one of my students, they'll have to come themselves, not send some watchman lackey."

"I am no lackey," Ruben snarled.

"Regardless, I wish to see one of the magisters," Zachareth said. "And until one comes here, I will not go with you."

Zachareth could sense Ruben weighing his options. Regardless of the antipathy between the Academy and the inquisition, Zachareth doubted the watchman wanted to be the one responsible for starting a war between Nerekhall and its wizarding institution. Zachareth knew the best way to defuse a threat in circumstances like these was to offer the easy way out.

"Bring a magister, and all this will be resolved," he urged, spreading his hands in a placatory gesture.

"You will see me again, and soon," Ruben said, looking pointedly at Morrow. Then, without another word, he turned and stalked away through the files of his Ironbound. The automatons raised their glaives with a scrape and, feet thumping against the cobbles in unison, reformed to follow the watchman back into the town.

"Well done," Morrow said quietly to Zachareth as they viewed the withdrawal. "I am too prone to bouts of anger when it comes to the inquisition. We have… clashed too many times."

"Send the others inside," Zachareth said harshly, in no mood to indulge Morrow's conversations. The runemaster frowned at him but nodded at Drussus and Ollen. They entered the Academy, leaving Zachareth alone with Morrow on the steps.

"I know," Zachareth snarled, looking Morrow in the eye. "About everything."

"As fine an education as you've had over the last few years, I rather doubt that," Morrow said, daring to smile at him.

"I know about the magics you use," Zachareth went on, his anger given voice. "The spirits you call upon. It is dark sorcery. The Ynfernael. You consort with demons."

"I told you it was dangerous magic, Zachareth," Morrow said, losing the veneer of humor he so often affected. "I told you it would be unwise to try to learn it."

"Dangerous is one thing. The Ynfernael is another," Zachareth hissed. "You make truck with the very powers that almost destroyed this city. Ruben and the others are right to be suspicious. How much more darkness is the Academy hiding within its quiet studies and the alcoves of its library?"

"You see conspiracies where none exist," Morrow said. "That is understandable. Your revelation is doubtless quite a shock. That is my fault. I should have told you from the beginning. I should have explained that part of the power you crave is rooted in the lower realms of sorcery."

"The Ynfernael," Zachareth said. "Call it for what it is. That runeshard, the Whisperer, it was tainted. It would have corrupted me, given time. Enslaved me to the will of some demonic horror."

"You misunderstand," Morrow said, his tone growing brusque, clearly unused to being on the receiving end of a lecture. "How much do you know of this thing you call the

Ynfernael? Your knowledge comes from stories and fables no doubt, silly old tales about horned monsters and fires and snarling hellhounds. The reality is very different."

"In what way?" Zachareth demanded. "Do not try and tell me the laws of this place and the likes of the Ironbound would still exist if the threat was not grave."

"The spirits of that place – demons, yes – are neither mindless terrors nor inscrutable gods. They have goals and ambitions and, most importantly, they have weaknesses. They can be bargained with. The power they can bestow is immense."

"But at what price?"

"That just depends on how good a negotiator you are. As we've just seen, you appear to have developed something of a talent for it."

Zachareth tried to collect his thoughts. The fact that Morrow hadn't even tried to deny his involvement with the Ynfernael now that he was confronting him felt strangely reassuring – perhaps it didn't hold as great and terrible a sway over him as Zachareth had first imagined? He knew the stories about how the energies of that terrible realm could bleed into both body and soul, warping and turning noble men into murderous beasts. Yet Morrow seemed neither of those things. He was a refined, knowledgeable scholar who had always shown Zachareth care and consideration and had yet to display dishonorable, ulterior motives.

"You should not be quick to dismiss the lower realms," Morrow said. "With all due respect, Zachareth, you are a northerner, a son of Carthridge. Necromancy and the foul, festering arts of the Mistlands are what you know and fear. Do not pretend to understand the nature of the Ynfernael. The power you seek, that is where it can most readily be found."

"Would you have taught me dark magics if I hadn't asked?" Zachareth said, looking to gauge Morrow's response.

"Perhaps," the runemaster admitted. "But not before you were ready to control them. If you display half the aptitude you've already shown for runemagic, you should have nothing to fear."

"You would have me consort with nightmares," Zachareth accused.

"I would have you attain the power necessary to protect your people, to protect us all! Or do you think you are the only one who takes the threat of undeath seriously? Silver Horizon was created to guard against the curse of necromancy. Against the return of Waiqar! Or did you really believe only you took the stories seriously?"

"You expect me to think Silver Horizon isn't a front for the worship of the Ynfernael?" Zachareth asked. "That they aren't a cult?"

"We are a group of individuals willing to do what must be done to protect Terrinoth," Morrow said, and for a moment, Zachareth thought he saw his eyes flare yellow. "The Ynfernael is necessary for the power it offers. There is no bargaining with the servants of death. Their victory, if it ever comes, will be final, total. It must be stopped."

"What if I can stop it without dark magic?" Zachareth said. "My ancestors did."

"And one of them also founded Silver Horizon," Morrow pointed out.

"How dare you suggest a baron of Carthridge–"

"I suggested nothing," Morrow interrupted. "You are showing an unusual level of naivety, Zachareth. If you are done, then perhaps we can go inside and formulate a response to the magisters once they turn up, preferably one that doesn't involve leveling the Academy and half of Nerekhall."

"You won't need a response," Zachareth said. "I'm leaving. Now. I'm going back to Greyhaven."

"You can't be serious," Morrow said, his voice low.

"I'm entirely serious," Zachareth said, brimming with angry defiance. "I only hope Greyhaven is less riven with... questionable practices."

"You can't reveal what has happened here," Morrow said. "Since we first spoke, I have only tried to help you!"

"I will say nothing," Zachareth said. "But I will remember. If you return to Greyhaven as well, you would be wise to stay out of my way."

"And what of the Ironbound?" Morrow asked, showing a flash of anger. "It was foolish to try to use the Whisperer on one. I should have been clearer and stricter in my instructions. You have caused the destruction of a valuable artifact."

"The Ironbound have no jurisdiction beyond Nerekhall," Zachareth said. "They will not pursue me, and I have no intention of returning here. If I do, I will tell them all that happens within the walls of this cursed place."

He turned and began to walk into the Academy, intending to collect his belongings.

"You're making a mistake, Master Carth," Morrow called after him. "I only hope it is not the first of many!"

"We will find out soon enough, Runemaster Morrow," Zachareth replied without looking back.

CHAPTER SEVENTEEN
Stormtide, 1830

The pounding of a fist at his chamber door woke Zachareth. He sat up sharply, and for a moment, he had no idea where he was or what the hammering sound meant.

"They're waiting for you," called an urgent voice. "You're going to be late!"

He knew the voice. It was Mikael's. He knew where he was too – the miserable space, scarcely larger than a broom closet, that passed for his private chambers in Greyhaven. The fact that he'd been granted any such room at all was due only to the fact that he was undertaking his final treatise defense. And that defense was about to begin.

Zachareth cursed and threw himself from his bed. Mikael was right, he was going to be late. He fumbled his formal robes over his head and snatched up the mirror shard by his bed. His hair was unkempt, but he was able to tie it back presentably enough. He splashed water from the basin over his face, cuffed it off with the inside of his robe sleeve, and raced for the door.

Mikael was still knocking incessantly and almost fell into the room as Zachareth swept out past him.

"Thank you," Zachareth called as he went.

"The examination hall is to the left, not the right," Mikael shouted back.

Zachareth swerved, cursing again. His mind was addled. He'd been averaging four, maybe five hours of sleep for the past days. He could do it, he kept telling himself. He could handle the load. He had to.

The defense was the final part of his Greyhaven education. In the four months since leaving Nerekhall, he had thrown himself into his studies like never before. As other students had enjoyed the summer markets and the sunshine on Gallow Hill, he had locked himself in his tiny room with stacks upon stacks of books from the library.

On the rare occasions he'd seen him, Mikael had professed worry. He wasn't eating. He wasn't sleeping. He'd become more distant since Nerekhall. All of that was true, but it didn't change anything.

Zachareth had told no one of what had happened at the Academy. The revelations about Morrow and the source of his magic – the source of much of the magic in the Academy, it seemed – had shocked and disgusted him, but it was something he'd resolved to store up for the future. He was in no position to do anything practical about what he'd found out. He didn't even know if the taint stretched as far as Greyhaven. He'd been on his guard, alert to any hint of the signs he'd unwittingly come across in Nerekhall – strange statues and stranger incantations, sorceries that made his head ache, runestones that looked twisted and misshapen. He'd not spoken to Morrow and had seen him only in passing. He had been afraid the runemaster would seek some form of vengeance, but so far there'd been nothing.

A part of him was afraid that he'd walk into the examination hall and find the goateed sorcerer sitting on the judgment panel.

He hurried up a set of stairs, the skirts of his robes hiked up, and came to a panting halt outside a heavy set of doors. A few other students were passing by, and they gave him a wide berth as he took a moment to catch his breath and wipe the sweat from his brow. There were rumors about him, he knew, rumors about the novice who'd vanished to Nerekhall one day and returned, months later, alone and in the dead of night. They said that he had been involved in dark sorcery, in forbidden practices. The gossip made him angry, but he knew denial would likely quicken the accusations.

He opened the doors and passed through, leaving behind the shuffle of feet and murmured conversations out in the corridor.

The examination chamber was a large, grand space at the heart of the Hall of a Thousand Scribes. Its stone ceiling soared far above while great pillars, carved to resemble Greyhaven's worthies, seemed to glare down upon Zachareth as he haltingly began to approach the table raised upon the dais at the far end.

He tried to think about his thesis, about his arguments, about the passages of texts he'd memorized and the examples he could give, but all he was able to recall was the hall in Castle Talon. The examination room was twice the size, but the feelings of loneliness and threat were identical. Briefly, he was twelve years old again and trying to find the courage to face Zelmar and Leanna at the end of that long, solitary walk.

There were three runemasters waiting for him, and the only relief was that Morrow wasn't among them. He recognized two, the white-bearded Chia and Akali, the left side of her face twisted by terrible burn scars. The third he didn't know –

she was shaven-headed, with runic markings tattooed into her scalp. Her eyes were green and seemed to glitter in the pallid light shafting through the windows high in the hall's walls.

"Novice Carth," Chia said as Zachareth came to a standstill before the high table, still feeling horribly exposed. "I believe you already know myself and Runemaster Akali. Allow me to introduce Runemaster Falla."

Zachareth bowed, meeting Falla's eyes as she nodded to him. She was at least part elf, he realized. He tried not to think about Leanna, about anything besides what he had spent the last four months writing.

"We have read through your offering, Novice Carth," Akali said, raising the bundle of scrolls he had submitted to them the week before. She unfurled the sheaf to read the title aloud.

"'Of the Natural Runes and the Principles of Binding to the Mortal Form'. An interesting concept. Where did the inspiration for all this come from?"

"My own experiences, in part," Zachareth said, having to clear his throat. He suddenly wished he'd taken a drink before leaving his chambers. His mouth was dry, and his heart was racing. He was amazed his words came out clearly as though someone else was speaking them.

"Since starting my studies here, particularly after my Trial of Fire, I have come to respect the importance of permanence. Runestones lack that unless it is possible to guarantee absolute control over them, and there is no better guarantee of control than physical inscription."

"It's interesting that you say this is based on personal experience," Chia said. "Because I doubt that experience has a great deal to do with this university. Physical inscription is not something we teach here."

"Perhaps it was a lesson learned at another institution," Akali added. The inference was obvious. They believed he was proposing something picked up at Nerekhall.

"That is not the case, runemasters," Zachareth said, deciding to meet the claim head-on. "If anything, my brief spell away from Greyhaven left me with a... tarnished view of other forms of magic. I wish to dedicate myself to the mastery of the runes."

"And you believe binding is the final goal when it comes to said mastery?" Chia asked. "You do realize that the melding of runes with the physical form is considered to be a radical form of magic?"

"I do," Zachareth said. "Radical not because of any particular form of taint or corruption but because it is exceptionally dangerous."

He had anticipated this. Rune binding was an extremely rare undertaking, so uncommon that some even considered it to be near-mythical. It involved tearing a rune from its shard and searing it physically into the caster's flesh, imbuing them with the ability to call upon whatever power the runestone had once possessed whenever they desired. Zachareth had been thinking about it since the Trial when he had been forced to scramble and fumble for his stones. Grasping a shard and manipulating it with a combination of motions and mental focus required a great degree of balance. According to everything he had read, someone bound permanently to a rune possessed a far more intimate and easily accessed connection. If he could prove it could be done with a degree of safety, he would be permitted to enact the necessary rites as part of the final, practical test. He would be granted a runestone, and the power he needed would be his forever.

"It is difficult for me to tell just how much this submission is fueled by arrogance and how much of it is born out of stupidity," Runemaster Falla said. It was the first time she had spoken since Zachareth had entered the hall. He instantly hated her.

"I believe that is for you to judge, runemaster," he said with a slight bow.

"Arrogance it is then," Falla said, placing her hand on the parchment spread across the table before her. She held Zachareth's gaze in silence before speaking again.

"It is madness to attempt a runic binding. The chances of success are less than one in ten thousand. Failure invariably means death."

"It is a matter of experience and force of will," Zachareth said. "According to the writings of Dalamar the Great–"

"Contrary to some accounts, Dalamar never completed a binding on himself, nor did he claim to have," Falla said. "His son succeeded in binding a rune of keenness upon his mind, but his body was left broken. You would be fortunate to suffer such a fate."

"The only case to be made in your defense is that at least you are not proposing to attempt a binding with a rune of great power or complexity," Akali said, briefly scanning the parchment. "You correctly identify that runes of basic strength or resilience hold the greatest chance of success."

"The only chance of success," Chia clarified. Akali nodded.

"A binding is more likely to occur if a body is physically as well as mentally strong," Zachareth said. "I have been preparing for this for almost a year. I am capable of at least attempting the rite, under supervision if need be."

"Greyhaven cannot be seen to encourage such an

undertaking," Falla said in a firm voice. "If we did, we would be endangering the lives of our students and spreading unsound practices."

"I am not asking for Greyhaven to teach the binding rites," Zachareth said, feeling exasperated now. "I am simply asking to be allowed to try them myself in order to complete my studies here."

The trio exchanged glances. Zachareth tried to be patient. He had understood there would be reluctance, but he had hoped the arguments in his thesis would prove persuasive and that he could ease any remaining doubts in person. But it seemed the runemasters didn't even intend to debate him.

"We discussed this before your arrival," Chia said, the aged academic looking almost sheepish. "And we were unanimous in our agreement. This thesis, and your further proposal concerning it, is not appropriate. We will be failing it and requesting you come up with a different proposal to bring before us."

"A different proposal?" Zachareth repeated disbelievingly.

"Entirely different," Falla said, leaning into her high-backed chair.

Zachareth felt an almost unbearable sense of anger and disappointment. He had spent months researching and crafting his arguments. Now it was all for nothing. The runemasters didn't trust him, and he would have no chance to secure the permanent, unequivocal power he needed. He would always be at the mercy of whatever runestones he could collect and maintain.

"You have shown a great deal of potential, Zachareth," Chia said, clearly attempting to soften the blow. "For that reason, we are not failing you outright. Put aside these foolish notions you have. We shall give you until Deepwinter to come up with a new proposal."

"Carthridge doesn't have until Deepwinter," Zachareth said coldly before turning and leaving.

Two weeks later, Zachareth received a visitor.

The first he knew of it was Mikael's fist against his door once more. He hadn't spoken to him since his rejection during the examination. In fact, he hadn't spoken to anyone. He'd locked himself in his room, leaving only to get food. He had barely slept, spending hours agonizing over his failure to convince the runemasters and poring over his submission. He couldn't face embarking on new research. He had come to Greyhaven to attain the power he needed to defend Carthridge, and there was no surer power available to him than the binding. He couldn't give up on it.

"I know you're in there, Zachareth," Mikael called from beyond the door, clearly annoyed. "It's about time you left that damned pit and spoke to someone. Not just me. Anyone."

Zachareth said nothing, sitting on the edge of his bed, his head in his hands.

"I thought you'd say something like that," Mikael said, the humor forced. "But if you won't talk to me, maybe you'll talk to that old tutor of yours, Bernard. He's in the infirmary right now, and he's asking for you."

CHAPTER EIGHTEEN

Questions had plagued Zachareth as he'd made his way down to the infirmary. His worry was so overwhelming that he'd run the last few corridors, heedlessly shoving both students and startled, indignant runemasters out of his way.

All thoughts vanished, however, the moment he set eyes on Bernard. The aged tutor was lying in a bed in the otherwise empty infirmary wing of the university. A surgeon's assistant, passing along the row, noticed Zachareth enter and simply nodded.

Bernard was asleep. Silently, Zachareth sat on the bed next to him, watching him. The shock of seeing his old teacher dispelled all other considerations.

It looked as though he was dying. Gone was the rotund, ruddy figure who had hunted him through Castle Talon's stairways, halls, and cellars. The man in the bed was gaunt and pale, what remained of his white hair tousled. His breathing rattled softly as he slumbered.

Zachareth rose and caught up with the assistant, speaking quietly.

"When did he arrive?"

"This morning," she replied, looking past him at Bernard. "He said he was looking for you, then he collapsed. He's been slumbering since."

Zachareth returned to the side of the bed. He felt an aching sorrow coupled with a simmering sense of dread. Even years ago, Bernard had known a trip to Greyhaven would likely be too much for his aged body. What had possessed him to make that journey now? What had he risked his life to tell him?

He waited until Bernard awoke. The tutor's eyes fluttered, and he moaned feebly before looking up at Zachareth.

"Hello, Bernard," Zachareth said softly and smiled.

Bernard made a small grunting sound that turned into a series of coughs, the ugly noise echoing through the drafty hall. Zachareth hastily poured water from a pitcher on the floor beside the bed and helped Bernard to sit up and drink. The old man panted for a few seconds after the cup left his lips, then managed a few wheezing words.

"I didn't recognize you, boy."

Zachareth smiled.

"Nor I you, tutor."

Bernard smiled thinly, giving the cup back to Zachareth. His hands were trembling.

"Why have you come all this way?" Zachareth asked, squatting next to the bed, a hand on his shoulder. "This is no time to be traveling."

"I wanted to see Greyhaven again, one last time," Bernard said. "And I wanted to speak to you. I received your letter."

"The last one I sent was almost a year ago," Zachareth said.

"I know, and I'm sorry. I was forbidden to write to you. I tried and spent a month in the dungeons for my trouble."

"On whose order?" Zachareth asked, feeling a surge of anger.

"Who else?" Bernard replied. "Your father's beloved advisor. She is all-powerful now."

Zachareth digested the news in silence. It was just as he had feared, yet still, it caused a rage to well up inside him. His grip on Bernard's shoulder tightened fractionally.

"Tell me what she has done," he said.

Instead, Bernard coughed again, his whole body shaking until he was able to swallow a few more mouthfuls of water.

"Your father is ill," he wheezed. "As gravely as I am. Leanna is preparing to make her play. She controls all matters and has subverted Zelmar's will to ensure she is the only beneficiary."

"But I am still his heir," Zachareth said. "No will can change that. I will inherit."

"She is doing her best to stop that too," Bernard managed. "According to Ragasta, she intends to petition the baronial council with a claim that you are illegitimate."

"That is ridiculous," Zachareth exclaimed, standing up impulsively.

"Regardless, it will likely take months for the council to properly resolve," Bernard said, looking up at him grimly. "During that period of time, Carthridge's succession will be thrown into turmoil."

"Leaving us ripe for invasion," Zachareth said, realization dawning. This had to be what she had been working toward all along. The hour was later than he had feared.

"Raids from the Mistlands now happen daily," Bernard said. "There are rumors the walking dead have been sighted as far south as the head of the valley."

"I must return home," Zachareth said. "And put a stop to this foolishness before it grows any worse."

"Forgive me, Zachareth," Bernard said. "I did not mean to trouble you during your studies. I am burdening you with more concerns than you deserve."

"For a man I considered wise, you speak like a fool," Zachareth said. "Eat and rest. I will have need of your counsel in the coming months and years."

Bernard let out a little chuckle.

"I fear my counsel will be counted in hours and days at best. I came here to warn you and to see if you were still the brave young man who left us three years past. I can see you are already so much more."

"But I need you, Bernard," Zachareth said urgently. "I can't deal with all this alone. If Leanna has grown as powerful as I imagine–"

"You have never needed anyone, Zachareth," Bernard said, sinking back into his bed. "You are the most driven and capable man I have ever known. Besides, the truth is I just came here to see Greyhaven one last time. I've spent a few nights in this ward before, let me tell you!"

Bernard's laughter became another fit of coughs, but he waved the water away.

"You spoke of an academic in your last letter," he said breathlessly. "Morrow."

"Yes," Zachareth responded, wondering just what Bernard might know about the devious runemaster. "He showed me favor this past year. First, he encouraged me to undertake the Trial of Fire, which I passed, and then he journeyed with me to Nerekhall."

"Nerekhall?" Bernard repeated, and Zachareth saw concern momentarily break through his exhausted expression.

"It is as you might imagine," he told the old tutor. "There is a darkness about that place. Morrow is a part of it. He dabbles in… unnatural magics."

"I knew Morrow in passing when I was at Greyhaven," Bernard said. "He was a junior lecturer then. He has always been ambitious, but I did not think he would stoop so low as dark magic. Perhaps I did not know him very well. Or perhaps he has changed."

"I suspect so," Zachareth said. "I fear he might have been trying to corrupt me. To lure me with promises of power from the Ynfernael."

"That would be bold, even for him," Bernard said. "More likely he seeks your influence. It is common enough here. The runemasters jostle and compete with one another to teach either the most promising students or the best connected. There is hardly one lecturer in this city who does not enjoy the patronage of one of the wealthy houses of Terrinoth. Of course, they try to hide it and speak often of the independence of Greyhaven, but such is the way of the world. You must choose who you favor wisely."

Zachareth was about to tell Bernard about Silver Horizon but found himself hesitating. He had come to realize just how naive he had been not to properly question Morrow or his motives. Of course the runemaster had been seeking leverage and influence. Zachareth had been thinking like a student, not like the heir to a barony. It made him feel foolish.

"It does me good to see you grown and strong," Bernard said before he could find the right words. "And did I read that Mikael of Cailn is attending here as well? He must be deathly afraid of you now."

"We are friends," Zachareth said absently, still trying to

process all that he had been told. Bernard grunted and smiled, his eyes closed.

"I brought you something," he began to say, his voice becoming a thin whisper.

"Rest," Zachareth replied, drawing his covers up around his shoulders. "I will have food brought and fresh water. Then I will stay by your side until you eat and drink it all. You are in my classroom now, my old tutor."

There was no response. He was asleep.

Bernard died two days later in the watches of the night. Zachareth stayed at his side until the end, full of a hollow, unspeakable pain. It was something he had never known before, a kind of agony that left him feeling numb and hopeless.

He found the surgeon, rousing the grumbling man from his bed to confirm that Bernard's spirit had departed. A priest of Nordros was sent for, and a short prayer was said over the deathbed.

"You will see him buried in the university yard," Zachareth said. "In the shade of the yew trees."

"That plot is reserved for academics," the man began to say.

"Do you know who I am?" Zachareth asked coldly. The man frowned slightly.

"I believe you are Master Carth, heir to the Barony of Carthridge," he replied slowly.

"I am," Zachareth said. "And I swear here and now, upon Nordros, that your church in Greyhaven will enjoy my patronage to my dying day. Bury him properly with full honors. I will check that it is done."

"What should be done with his effects?" the surgeon asked, holding up a satchel that had been under Bernard's bed.

"I will take them," Zachareth said. "Leave us now for a while. I have prayers of my own to say."

The two men departed. Zachareth stood over Bernard, his head bowed in sorrow. A part of him had expected that he would cry, but he found he could not.

He opened the satchel and found a comb, a small mirror, and a few stale bits of bread inside. There was something at the bottom, wrapped in a sheaf of parchment paper. He pulled it out.

It was a book. He knew it instantly. Its cover was battered and stained, but the first page had lost none of its luster. A silver knight, vanquishing the undead, marred only by a dark, stiff blotch of blood, long dried. It was his copy of *The Canticle of Rufus the Bold*.

The numbness at his core vanished. In its place was anger, an anger that blazed and consumed every last shred of sorrow and self-pity left within him. There was no more hesitation, no more uncertainty. The rage gave him clarity. He knew now what must be done.

He closed the book, slipped it into his robes, and departed.

He was going to wake Morrow.

CHAPTER NINETEEN

Morrow came to his door clad in a nightgown, his hair unkempt, squinting in the light of the torch Zachareth held. His expression turned from anger to shock when he realized who it was that had awoken him.

"Zachareth," he said. "What are you doing? What's happening?"

"You wish to have influence over me," Zachareth said bluntly. "You want Carthridge in your debt, to advance your own standing and probably that of Silver Horizon."

"Zachareth, I–"

"Now is your opportunity to achieve that. I want just one thing in return."

"This doesn't sound wise," Morrow said.

"It is necessary. Wisdom is not relevant right now. I need you to unlock the runevault."

Morrow stared at him.

"You know I cannot," he said. "Not if you intend to steal the stones."

"Just one," Zachareth replied. He knew he sounded desperate, but he was beyond caring. He was doing what had to be done. "You have my oath on that. You also have my oath that when I am Baron of Carthridge – and that will be soon – you will have my full patronage. Financial backing for you and Silver Horizon, a safe haven at Castle Talon, even a place on my council if you wish. You can have everything you planned on luring from me, and more, if you help me take the Bonesplitter."

"You intend a binding ritual," Morrow said. "I heard about what happened in your examination."

"That doesn't concern you," Zachareth said. "If you will not help me, you will neither see nor hear from me again. Rumors might even start to spread about your connection to Nerekhall and just what happens there."

Zachareth could see anger in Morrow's gaze now, but it was still nothing compared to his own. He was risking everything, he knew. Challenging a senior runemaster alone was tantamount to throwing his degree onto the fire. That didn't matter right now, though. What mattered was acquiring the Bonesplitter.

"You will not speak of this, ever," Morrow said softly, slipping back into the shadows of his room to pull on his day robes before stepping out past Zachareth.

In silence, he led him down to the runevault. While many of the runestones used to teach and demonstrate at Greyhaven were the personal property of the runemasters themselves, some belonged solely to the university. They were kept in a number of vaults in different parts of the city, but the largest was beneath the Hall of a Thousand Scribes. Like almost all students, Zachareth had never seen beyond its metal doors, but all knew the stories of the arcane wealth held within. It was said to be the most well-protected place in Terrinoth, even more so than the Hall of the Ancestors in the Dunwarr city of Thelgrim.

"You know that theft means we will both be expelled at best," Morrow said as he took Zachareth through the echoing, deserted corridors and halls of the university, Zachareth's torch chasing off shadows that seemed to loom hungrily in their wake. "At worst, we'll be strung up on Gallow Hill."

Zachareth didn't reply. His anger was fueling him, and he didn't dare stop to consider what he was doing. He had to act. If he didn't, he would lose everything.

"Even if this little escapade goes undetected, what you're planning to do with the Bonesplitter is insane," Morrow went on.

"No more insane than the magics you practice," Zachareth said bitterly.

"Oh no, it is," Morrow responded. "I always assess risks. The odds are always on my side. They are against you in this many thousands of times over."

Zachareth knew as much, but he didn't care. He could see no other choice. They began to descend the stair shaft that led to the vault. At the end of it, Zachareth's torch picked out its metal doors, covered in runic inscriptions, wards of resilience, strength, and antimagic. Two vast shapes were crouched on either side of it, brute blocks of stone banded with iron, only vaguely humanoid in shape. They were animus, Zachareth knew, altogether larger and more fearsome looking than the statue he'd managed to manipulate inside the Manse.

As the pair reached the bottom of the stairs, a blue balefire lit within the eye sockets of the animus' helms. Zachareth felt their consciousness awaken. For a moment, he experienced a spike of panic before Morrow stepped forward with a raised hand. He said something in a language Zachareth didn't know – he suspected it was a Latari dialect. The balefires flickered and went out.

"They will not slumber for long," Morrow murmured. "Stay close."

They approached the doors together. Morrow reached up and lightly ran his fingers along their surfaces, muttering under his breath. The runes he passed over glowed briefly, then returned to darkness. At one point, the sorcerer's expression became pained, and Zachareth was aware of a trembling in his breath.

It seemed to take a long time but, eventually, there was a barely perceptible click. The doors swung inward silently.

"Leave your torch in the bracket," Morrow ordered Zachareth, pointing to the wall beside one of the animus. "You'll have no need of it inside."

Zachareth did so and understood why as soon as he stepped into the vault. It was a surprisingly small chamber built into the bedrock beneath the university. The floor was smooth and well worn, but the walls and ceiling were comprised of jagged, uncut stone. There were alcoves set into the former, dozens of small niches that had been dug into the rock like the honeycomb of a beehive. Each only contained a single shard, a runestone.

The chamber was illuminated by a pallid blue light, shimmering with an aquatic glow. It emanated from a film of energy that seemed to lie over the niches, a protective aura that left the air static charged. Even untuned to wider forms of sorcery, Zachareth could feel its power.

"Which one?" Morrow asked tersely. Zachareth paced around the vault, gazing at the stones beyond the sorcerous barrier, trying not to get distracted. The power before him was surely unmatched in all of Terrinoth. Even just half a dozen of the precious shards could make him the most powerful man in the Twelve Baronies.

But all power had limits. What he was doing was already excessively dangerous. Nothing could be allowed to harm his chances of preserving Carthridge.

"The Bonesplitter," he said eventually, pausing at the stone he recognized.

"Stand back," Morrow advised, before moving to the niche and carefully planting his palm against the glowing shield of energy between them and the stone.

At first, nothing happened, but Morrow murmured something and pressed harder. Slowly, to Zachareth's amazement, the shimmering cover began to give way. It did not split or crack like glass but molded around Morrow's outstretched digits as he pushed through. Eventually, the barrier parted completely, like water, and Morrow was able to grasp the Bonesplitter and remove it. The barrier reformed as his hand withdrew, leaving it unblemished.

"Do not make me regret this, Zachareth Carth," he said sternly, handing over the runestone. Immediately, Zachareth felt its power, the strength of its binding markings running through his limbs. He shivered and nodded his thanks at Morrow.

"You will not, runemaster," he said. "Consider me in your debt."

"That can wait," Morrow said. "We must go before this theft is discovered."

Together they passed back through the vault doors. As Zachareth retrieved his torch he realized that the blue balefires were smoldering once more in the helms of the animus.

"They're awakening," Morrow hissed. "Hurry, back up the stairs!"

They fled.

Dawn was fast approaching, and Zachareth intended to be far from Greyhaven when it broke.

He bade Morrow goodbye outside his dorm, ignoring the final, desperate protestations of the runemaster before locking himself inside the chamber.

He felt one final pang of uncertainty and hesitated. The sharp words of the half elf, Falla, came back to him. He was arrogant, perhaps, but he did not consider himself a fool. He knew the odds. He was strong and knowledgeable, but the most likely outcome of any binding rite was still death.

Once again, he tried to consider other options. He could leave and confront Leanna immediately with only the Bonesplitter and what he had learned to aid him. He knew that a contest between him as he was and the sorceress could only end one way, though. Could he bargain with her? He had considered it, painful though it was. What could he offer her that would convince her to give up her hold over Carthridge? He had yet to think of anything.

That left only the binding. With it, he would become a more formidable opponent. She might back down. Perhaps, if he struck hard and fast and was able to rally Golfang and others to his side, he would even be able to overwhelm her. That was assuming Golfang still remained in a position of authority.

The binding was his only hope. Without it, he was convinced Carthridge was lost, and he saw no reason to continue his life without it.

Zachareth set to work. First, he used his torch to ignite the closet chamber's meager fireplace. As it caught, he drew out a series of concentric circles on the flagstones underfoot, carefully consulting Shenwai's *Runic Geometries* in the dim, flickering light as he did so. After he'd checked and rechecked them, he removed his robes so his upper body was bare. He pulled a stick from the fireplace, blew it out, and let it cool for a moment before he slowly started to draw it over and around his upper left arm.

The stick left behind a streak of dark gray ash. He leaned over the small table next to his bed, peering closely at the Bonesplitter, which he had placed atop the books heaped upon it. Satisfied, he began to make the second marking, a swirling spiral that encompassed his arm just above his elbow.

So he continued, little by little, swapping out the stick for others when fresh ash was needed. He was transcribing the runic markings upon the Bonesplitter onto his own flesh. He forced himself not to do so in haste. One mistake, one misplaced line, and when he called upon the rune's power to enter him, he would be annihilated. As much as he wished to, now was not the time to rush.

He just hoped he could finish before Morrow did anything stupid.

Mikael had been dreaming about the barmaid in the *Magi's Scroll* when a hand shook him roughly.

"Oh gods, is it last orders already?" he slurred, trying to roll over and ending up with a face full of his own drool.

The hand turned him back, this time accompanied by a low, harsh whisper.

"Wake up, boy!"

Mikael groaned, opened his eyes, and realized an indiscernible figure was standing over him in the dark of the university's main dormitory. The figure's eyes were glowing the faintest yellow. He yelped and was silenced by a hand over his mouth.

"Are you Mikael of Cailn?" demanded the man. Mikael had no idea if he should confirm or deny that. He nodded.

"I'm Runemaster Morrow," said the figure, taking away his hand. "I need you to come with me. Now."

Mikael hesitated but didn't want to make those yellow eyes any angrier than they already looked. Fumbling and clumsy in the dark, he managed to find his robes under his bed and pulled them on before getting up.

The rest of the dorm continued to slumber. It was the height of summer, and the air was close and sultry. The faintest hint of light about the windows betrayed the coming dawn.

Mikael didn't know what was happening, but he had a grim feeling it involved Zachareth. He hadn't been the same since he had started to encounter Morrow more regularly. That made Mikael wary, but there was no way, woken urgently in the middle of the night by a runemaster, that he was going to just stay in bed.

"Runemaster, what's happening?" he asked as they passed from the dorm into the private wing of the university's accommodation.

"Your friend is going to get himself killed, that's what's happening," Morrow said, anger in his voice.

"What is he doing?" Mikael asked with an even greater sense of alarm as he hurried to keep up.

"He's attempting a runic binding," Morrow said. "Trying to sear the magic into his own flesh. If you've learned anything in your time here, Master Cailn, you'll know just how uniquely foolish an idea that is."

Despite his august company, Mikael swore. He had known Zachareth was submitting a binding rite – against his own advice – to the council of examination. He'd hoped that with its rejection Zachareth's interest in such a scheme would wane. He should've known better. He felt a surge of guilt for not having talked Zachareth out of his foolishness, for having let him lock himself away. Was it perhaps something to do with the return of his old tutor?

"He's trying the binding now?" he asked incredulously. "Where did he find a shard?"

"I've tried to talk him out of it, but he won't listen," Morrow said, apparently not hearing him. "I thought you might be able to make the difference. He respects you."

Despite the seriousness of the moment, Mikael found himself laughing.

"It's definitely Zachareth we're talking about?" he asked.

"You are a fellow baronial heir," Morrow said. "His peer. I know of no one else here that he confides in so readily."

"Maybe once, but not since you took him to Nerekhall."

Morrow stopped sharply at the entrance to the main corridor of the private dorms. Only a few of the rooms were occupied, and Zachareth had his own corridor to himself. It lay just ahead beyond Morrow. The runemaster was still in shadow, but his eyes no longer had the strange luminescence they had carried before. Mikael couldn't make out his expression.

"What has he said of Nerekhall?" Morrow asked.

"Don't worry, runemaster," Mikael said, not bothering to

keep the coldness from his voice. "I understand how the world works. Why would an academic of Greyhaven seek to curry favor with poor, fallow Cailn when he can win the influence of the mighty Silver Barony."

"Do not let bitterness cloud your judgment," Morrow said. "If we do not hurry, that same Silver Barony may welcome the dawn without an heir."

They pressed on.

"Which is his?" Morrow asked. Mikael walked past him, peering through the gloomy illumination reaching in through the window arches. He found the door belonging to Zachareth and beat his fist against it.

"It's Mikael," he called out, letting his frustration with both Morrow and Zachareth's joint foolishness fuel him. "Stop this madness, Zachareth! You don't need to do this!"

There was silence from within. Mikael wondered if they were already too late. He should have tried harder to speak to Zachareth before rather than leaving him with the worries and concerns he knew so often consumed him.

"When you go back to Carthridge, I'll come with you," he said, smacking his palm against the door for emphasis. "I'll make sure my father sides with you! Cailn will stand with you."

Still there was no clear reply, though he thought he caught a murmured voice from within. That was when Mikael felt it.

In his first year at Greyhaven, he had established that he possessed a minor natural connection to the Turning. He could feel surges in that universal magical energy, could sense when the arcane was called upon.

In that moment, he experienced it like never before. It felt like his very soul had been struck a ringing, reverberating blow, leaving him stunned and speechless.

Morrow clearly felt it as well and, unlike Mikael, knew how to react.

"Get back," he shouted, snatching Mikael by the shoulder and hauling him away from the door. As he did so, he shouted something, something Mikael didn't understand but which made his stomach clench and his skin crawl.

An explosion tore through Zachareth's room. It blasted the door to splinters and pulverized the stonework in a hail of brick and broken timber. Mikael would have been lacerated and crushed had Morrow's spat words not conjured a circle of pure, crackling darkness directly in front of both of them. The force of the blast and the hail of debris that came with it met the circle and seemed to evaporate into it, dragged inside to a different plane of existence by sorcery Mikael had no understanding of.

Even with the nullifying sphere, the shock of the detonation was enough to pitch them both into the far wall of the corridor. Mikael grunted in pain and instinctively shielded his head with his arms.

As he eventually lowered them, the circle of darkness seemed to collapse in on itself with a pop, vanishing just as quickly as it had appeared. Ears ringing, Mikael struggled to rise and was helped up by Morrow. He found himself standing amidst devastation.

The portion of the corridor that had once housed Zachareth's room was in ruins. A thick pall of dust choked the air, stinging Mikael's eyes. He could discern nothing but broken masonry and the shattered remains of the door as well as a few smoldering scraps of paper.

"Oh gods," he said, then wished he hadn't as he began choking on the dust. He doubled over, clutching his chest until he was able to find his breath.

A miserable sense of despair struck him. They'd been too late. He looked at Morrow and realized he was staring in through the jagged remnants of the room's entrance.

Mikael noticed what he was looking at a moment later. There was a light emanating from within, piercing the seething cloud of dust and settling debris. It had a yellow, fiery glow, taking the form of two sets of twisting rings. As Mikael stared, it grew stronger and clearer.

A figure emerged from the wreckage. Mikael's heart leapt as he realized it was Zachareth. The heir of Carthridge was naked above the waist, his powerful, muscular body caked in dust. Mikael realized the light was emanating from his arms. Markings encased them from his broad shoulders down to his wrists. They glowed, lambent with an arcane power that Mikael could feel suffusing the very air.

"Zachareth," he said disbelievingly. The dust-covered figure halted in the remains of the doorway and stared at him as though he didn't know who he was. Then, abruptly, he smiled. It was the first time Mikael had seen the expression for months. For a moment, it made him afraid. He couldn't believe what he was seeing.

"It worked," Zachareth said, then looked past Mikael at Morrow. The smile vanished, replaced by a grave expression.

"I am still in your debt, runemaster, but I am not yet in a position to settle. I am leaving for Castle Talon."

"The university will expel you when they find out what you have done," Morrow said. "You will not be allowed to graduate."

"That doesn't matter," Zachareth said. "I came here to acquire the power of the runes, and I have done so." He raised an arm as he spoke, studying the intricate, swirling traceries of light seared into his skin.

"I can feel it," he said. "The strength of the Bonesplitter. The stone itself is nothing but ash now. Its spirit lies within me, its own strength called to the strength of my arm. Its power is mine to command. Always."

"I'm coming with you," Mikael said. He almost surprised himself with the words, but he realized as he spoke them that he felt no hesitation. He had wanted to get out for months. Now, finally, he had an opportunity and a duty to go with it. He had failed to support his friend recently. Now he could change that. "I'm coming with you to Castle Talon."

Zachareth frowned. "This is not your fight, Mikael. If you leave with me, they will suspect your involvement in this."

"It will be Cailn's fight if Carthridge falls," Mikael pointed out. "Whether by civil war or the undead. Besides, I wasn't lying when I said I would give you my support."

"What of your studies?" Morrow asked. Cailn let out a dry chuckle.

"I rather think I'm not going to progress as far as Novice Carth," he said. "And in all honesty, I hate books, and runeshards probably aren't far behind that. They both give me headaches."

He waved his hand, secretly glad that circumstances had thrown the decision upon him. His father, who himself had been taught at Greyhaven, had insisted after Zachareth had first enrolled that he go as well. Cailn would get left behind, he had worried, if the future Baron of Carthridge became a powerful runecaster. Mikael had never really wanted to study at the university, though.

"Where I go, there is no certainty," Zachareth said. "Death and danger will abound. I do not even know who I can safely count as a friend and who will be my foe. All that is clear is that I must return home."

"If you can't count me as a friend, then gods help you," Mikael said. "I'm going with you, whether you welcome me or not."

Zachareth paused, and Mikael wondered if he was about to rebuff him. Instead, the heir of Carthridge offered him his hand. They grasped forearms, and Mikael felt the power in his grip and the energies of the rune like a tingling sensation that ran through his body.

"I would be honored to have Cailn at my side," Zachareth said.

A shout from one of the adjoining corridors disturbed them. Morrow grimaced.

"If you want to go ahead with this foolishness, then go now," he hissed. "I will attempt to explain all this, Y'gath forgive me."

Mikael shivered, though he wasn't sure why. Zachareth released his grip.

"Come then," he said. "To Castle Talon and whatever fate awaits us."

PART THREE

THE MISTLANDS

CHAPTER TWENTY

Zachareth discovered that he was Baron of Carthridge in a smoky, stinking inn on the road just south of Korrina's Crossing.

Word spread among the patrons that Baron Zelmar was dead. Someone cheered, and someone else ordered a flagon of ale for every table. Mikael put his hand on Zachareth's forearm.

"Could just be a rumor," he said quietly.

"They seem very certain," Zachareth pointed out. "Bernard said it would be soon."

They accepted the ale without question. They were both dressed in their Greyhaven robes, assuming the identity of two poor, traveling students and sitting quietly in the corner of the taproom.

It was difficult to maintain that persona. Zachareth felt a sharp conflict of emotions. He had been steeling himself for news of Zelmar's death but hadn't expected to find out secondhand in a miserable roadside hovel. That many present seemed happy at the baron's passing added a spike of venomous indignation, one he hadn't wholly anticipated. He had always felt he had a connection with his father, but it was one he believed had been trampled and severed by Leanna. A part of him had still held out hope that once he overcame the sorceress, he would be able to return his father to his senses, to enjoy the paternal love he felt had been stolen. Now, however, that hope was gone.

It was a bitter blow, but he had no intention of lashing out at the inebriated revelers around him. No good would come from that, he told himself. He needed to maintain his anonymity for as long as possible if he was going to keep the advantage of surprise. In that sense, Zelmar's death was terribly timed. Leanna would expect him to find out, and return to Castle Talon. Hopefully he would arrive earlier than she anticipated.

The pair quietly drank their ale and retired to their rooms for the night. Another two days' hard riding and they would reach Castle Talon.

Evening was creeping up the valley as they approached the castle rock. The night held the promise of misery. Rain was squalling in from the north, and the clouds overhead were vast and broiling, black and gray shot through with the last of the dying light. Castle Talon loomed on its promontory, a dark bulk of sheer stone lit by the pinprick illumination of arrowslits and slender windows. The black talon flag that flew from the uppermost turret was at half-mast.

"You're sure about this," Mikael called out as their mounts began to climb the steep, winding path up the crag to the gate.

"I am," Zachareth replied. "Just stay alert!"

In truth, he was anything but sure. He felt almost sick with worry, his stomach in knots. He had no idea what awaited him. What if Leanna had turned the whole castle against him?

What if she had prepared a trap for him, knowing he would ride home as soon as he heard word of his father's death?

He focused on his anger and let it drive out the doubts. All his life he had wished for the strength to confront Leanna. Now, the time had come. There would be a reckoning this night.

They reached the end of the path. The gatehouse towered over them, glistening in the rain. A dark figure moved atop the parapet, and a voice called out in the wind.

"Who goes there?"

Zachareth drew back his hood, ignoring the rain that stung his face.

"Do you not recognize your lord?" he called up. "I am Zachareth, Baron of Carthridge!"

There was no reply. He caught more movement, the figures indistinct behind the wall. His nervousness redoubled, and he struggled to avoid showing it by turning to Mikael. He found himself wondering whether the power of the Bonesplitter would allow him to break through the castle's gates.

They seemed to wait a long time. The rain plastered Zachareth's long, black hair to his scalp and dripped from his pointed goatee. He'd grown it in Nerekhall, he now realized, in unconscious imitation of Morrow. He had hoped it would add to the gravity of his appearance. Now he wondered if it made him appear foolish.

Eventually, he picked out a light above them, strong despite the swirling rain. It danced in the air above Leanna's black staff as she arrived at the parapet, draped in a sumptuous crimson cape, its large hood raised. There were others on either side of her, joining her on the ramparts. He spotted Ragasta, then Golfang. Hope surged at the sight of the orc. With Zelmar gone, he'd feared for his place at the castle.

"Master Zachareth," Leanna called, her voice ringing out clear and cold from Castle Talon's battlements. "I did not expect you so soon. This is not the welcome I would have wished for you."

"I am Baron Zachareth," he replied, knowing the elf would seek to antagonize him. "I know of Zelmar's passing. Open the gates immediately."

"I'm afraid I can't do that, Zachareth," Leanna said. "Not tonight, anyway. Unfortunate events have unfolded since you left us."

"Unfortunate events began unfolding the day you arrived at this castle, Leanna," Zachareth responded tersely. "I am your baron, now open the gates."

"I suspect that might not be the case, Zachareth," Leanna said. "There have been... rumors regarding your particular lineage for some time now. Rumors that, sadly, were confirmed by your father before he passed away. You are his son, but you were not born to his wife."

Rage gripped Zachareth. He reached instinctively for his sword and was only stopped by Mikael grasping hard onto his shoulder.

"Don't," he urged and nodded at the towers flanking the gatehouse. Zachareth saw what he'd already spotted – there were figures visible at the arrowslits. Arbalesters, their crossbows loaded and pointed at them both. The sight of them turned his rage cold and icy.

"This is a disgrace," he shouted, voice rife with anger. "To make such accusations, to deny me at my own gates and threaten me. It is treason!"

"The truth is painful," Leanna replied. "I wish it were not so. But you must understand that I have a duty to this place. It will not be usurped. I have already sent word to the Council of Barons and will await their reply. They will decide if your claim is legitimate or not. In the meantime, I think it best if you find lodgings elsewhere."

Zachareth seethed. He tried to consider his options, but it was difficult to think about anything other than breaking his way into the castle barehanded. He had anticipated resistance from Leanna, a fight even, but he hadn't expected to be wholly denied entry. After Bernard's warning, he had expected a false claim about his legitimacy, but Leanna's brazenness was still shocking. Was she really so confident in her own position? What if she had cast spells across the rest of the castle? He looked at the captain of the guard, his expression unreadable in the gloom.

"Is this how it's going to be, Golfang?" he asked. "Have you really surrendered yourself to this sorceress and her lies?"

Golfang hesitated before answering. That at least was hopeful.

"Ride away tonight, pup," he called out. "Let the law take its course. It'll all come good in the end."

"He's right," Mikael murmured behind him. "We should go for now. Regroup and consider our options."

"I won't give up my barony," Zachareth hissed furiously. "I am Zelmar's rightful heir. I'm the Baron of Carthridge!"

"You are," Mikael agreed. "And Cailn will support you in that. Rhynn too. Gods, I doubt a single baron will vote against you when the council next meets."

"That won't be until next year," Zachareth pointed out. It was all he could do to stop himself from dismounting and striking the gate with his fists. "Leanna's power here will be absolute by the time they come to a decision!"

"Then we won't wait for them," Mikael muttered, urging his horse up alongside Zachareth's and putting a hand on the bridle. "Cailn and Rhynn will march to your aid. I'm sure the people of Carthridge will back you as well."

Zachareth was far from sure of that. He remembered the celebrations at the inn when word of Zelmar's death had spread. Carthridge had been steadily decaying for years, and Zachareth had no doubt his family was blamed. The people knew nothing of Leanna's influence or his desperate wish to overthrow her. They saw in the Carths only indolent and ineffectual rulers.

"Let us ride back to the Crossing or Westfurrow," Mikael urged. "Spend the night, then I will go to Castle Tagis and speak with my father, and you can ride to Rhynn and tell Greigory what has happened. They will support us, and we will return with the only authority that matters – two armies."

"I am to claim my inheritance by laying siege to my own home?" Zachareth wondered, unable to hide the bitterness he felt at such a prospect.

"It's a better way to reclaim it than by getting filled full of crossbow quarrels," Mikael pointed out. "That goes for both of us. Regardless of the mystical powers your rune has given you, I'm still a mere mortal. If you try to break those gates, I'll be the first to die. At least I'll be able to tell Nordros you're on your way."

Zachareth knew he was right. Every base instinct wanted to lash out, to vent over a decade of fury on the woman who had tormented his family. But he could not beat her. He had prepared himself to face her and her alone. He had not reckoned he'd be faced with the whole of Castle Talon. If he tried now, there could be only one outcome, then Carthridge truly would be lost.

"I am Zelmar's true heir," he called up to those watching. He looked at Golfang, at Ragasta, and at the arbalesters covering them with their heavy crossbows, ignoring Leanna. "I am the Baron of Carthridge. You all know it. For too long this castle has languished under a curse, the same curse that now stands in your midst, directing you. I do not blame you for being in its thrall. But I will end it. If not tonight, then someday soon. That is my first promise to you as baron. You will be free."

He nodded to Mikael, who released his bridle, then turned to descend the path once more. As he went, he expected to hear the whizz of a quarrel or hear Leanna calling down her magics upon him, but there was nothing, nothing but the seething of the rain and the crunch of hooves in gravel. He forced himself to avoid looking back.

They rode away into the night.

Under an alias, Mikael found them a room in a wayside tavern just north of Korrina's Crossing, not long before midnight. Zachareth sat down on one of the two beds in the cramped, dingy room and let the exhaustion finally catch up with him.

For a while, he contemplated giving up. He had failed. Leanna controlled Castle Talon and through it, the barony. He had underestimated her and made a fatal mistake when he'd chosen to go and study at Greyhaven. He had learned much, it was true, but even now he didn't feel confident in defeating Leanna alone, much less when she had the backing of those he'd once counted as allies, even friends. While he had been away, she had clearly worked hard to dig her roots deep. Ripping them up now seemed impossible.

"Head up, Zachareth," Mikael said as he came into the room.

He'd stayed downstairs to wrangle some bread and cheese from the tired tavern owner.

"Eat," he commanded, proffering the food. "It took a lot of money to acquire this."

"Should you be spending a lot of money if we're supposed to be passing as two Greyhaven failures?" Zachareth asked.

"What's he going to do, ride through the night to Castle Talon and warn them the mighty Zachareth and the distinctly average Mikael are on their way? Bit late for that. Now eat."

Zachareth managed to get halfway through the cut loaf before giving up. He unbuckled his sword and lay back in the unforgiving bed, trying not to think about the lice that doubtless infested it, trying not to think about anything at all in fact.

"I could just go," he said drowsily as much to himself as Mikael. "Travel to Frostgate or head south. I could be a sell-sword, a freelancer. Become the baron who disappeared."

"Very romantic," Mikael said, his voice sounding as though it was coming from far away. "Just abandon the rest of us. Between you and me, Cailn needs Carthridge. So does Rhynn. You're the lynchpin of the north and west of Terrinoth."

Zachareth tried to reply, might have, in fact. He wasn't sure. Everything was so heavy, so slow. He didn't remember closing his eyes, didn't even remember what Mikael was talking about. A few moments more and he was fast asleep.

They came in the night, doubtless with the intent of adding Mikael and Zachareth to their ranks.

The first Zachareth knew of the coming of death was Mikael waking him. It was almost a welcome relief, for a nightmare had been stalking him, a specter that seemed to be seeping into the smoke-stained timber all around. He grunted and opened his eyes, struggling to free himself from the slow, crawling fear.

Mikael was bent over him, barely discernible in the dark. A single candle still guttered by the shuttered window, leaving the shadows to rule the rest of the room.

Zachareth was about to ask why Mikael had woken him when it was still dark, but the heir of Cailn clapped his hand over his mouth and leaned in to whisper in his ear.

"There's someone outside our room."

Zachareth froze, his heart spiking. Slowly, Mikael removed his hand and tapped his ear. He listened, and after a few breathless seconds caught what Mikael had heard. A tiny, soft creaking sound from outside the door.

Zachareth began reaching for his sword. In that exact instant, the world seemed to collapse around him.

The room's window came crashing in. Wood splintered, and the candle tumbled as something slammed inside. Mikael leapt back to avoid a collision and ended up being struck by the door as that too was violently kicked in.

Zachareth threw himself from his bed, sword rasping out, struggling to get it free quickly in the cramped room. As it had fallen, the candle had touched light to the end of his blanket, flames springing up fresh and fierce in the sudden gust. By their light, Zachareth caught a glimpse of the window intruder a second before he struck.

The figure was tall and swathed in a rain-drenched black cape complete with a raised hood. His arms were bare and marked by tattoos, inscriptions of the bones that mirrored those beneath his skin. His face was hidden behind a black mask daubed white to resemble the lower half of a skull. Combined with the ink on his flesh, he had the appearance of a walking corpse. In the brief look he got, Zachareth might have mistaken him for such were it not for the firelight that reflected in his eyes, fierce with an all-too-human hatred.

The man had a dagger in both hands. He launched himself into the attack. Immediately, Zachareth realized that in a cramped tavern room two short blades were better than one long one. He managed to sway aside from the first as it came in low for his gut, and he was forced to snatch the wrist of the man's hand before the other could open his throat.

Parrying the lower strike had left his guard open – the dagger came back in before he could get his sword back across his body. It would have punched into his stomach had he not squeezed with his other fist.

He could feel the power of the Bonesplitter, triggered by his own heightened state. Its strength coursed through him, responding automatically without the need for an incantation or even a moment's focus. The markings on his arms glowed a fiery yellow as he clenched his hand around the wrist he'd caught.

There was a clear, wet snapping sound, and the assassin screamed. He dropped the lower dagger reflexively before it could connect, reaching up to clutch in desperate pain at Zachareth's own wrist.

There was no space for Zachareth to draw back his sword and drive it into the assailant. Instead, he punched it up, slamming the bulky round pommel into the masked face. There was a second brutal crunch, and the white, skeletal jaw that had been grinning at him turned a sudden, bright red. The man's screaming stopped, and he toppled like a felled oak.

Zachareth whipped around as soon as the assailant went down, trying to take in everything that was happening at once. Mikael was struggling to force the door to the room shut again. Multiple black-cloaked figures were attempting to thrust their way inside, and one was making an effort to ram his dagger through the woodwork, seeking to stab Mikael. The heir to the Barony of Cailn was bleeding from a gash across his scalp where the edge of the door had struck him when it had first burst open, half blinding him.

The situation was no better on the other side of the room. The fire had taken to Zachareth's bed and was spreading rapidly, its heat already making his skin prickle and its smoke starting to choke the low ceiling. The only blessing was that it had partially blocked the window where a second assassin was attempting to follow the first in.

Zachareth made a split-second decision.

"Mikael, take the window," he shouted, throwing himself at the door. Mikael saw the power coursing through the markings on his arms and noted his intent quick enough to switch places. He snatched up his own sword and ran the next assailant through as he leaped through the window. At the same time, Zachareth slammed into the door, ignoring the dagger points jabbing through it. The timber swung immediately shut, the efforts of the attackers to force it open barely registering with Zachareth. The frame shook with the pounding of fists and blades.

"We need to go," Mikael shouted, choking on the smoke filling the room. The fire had taken hold of the far wall and was licking across the floor. Zachareth found himself remembering Greyhaven and the Manse. He felt panic gripping him.

"The door won't hold once I leave it," he said, and grimaced as one of the knife tips punching through nicked his finger.

"Too bad. We've got to go out the window," Mikael said, snatching their cloaks up before they caught light.

Zachareth heard a groaning sound that seemed to emanate from all around them. At first, he was afraid it was the building making the noise and that the floor or ceiling was about to give way. His blood ran cold as he understood that it was something far worse.

A shape was materializing in the closest corner of the room. The smoke and ash made it indistinct, but it was humanoid, and it seemed to be hauling itself directly through the wall.

Even before he really understood what it was, Zachareth felt a sense of dread grip him. Despite the fire, the temperature plummeted. The shape reared up above the flames, an ethereal whorl of white smoke that took on the aspect of great, ghostly talons, twisted death shrouds, and a skull that made the ones on the assassin's masks seem childish and pathetic. Deadlights gleamed in its ghastly eye sockets, and Zachareth couldn't help but moan in horror as they seemed to fix on him.

It was a phantom born of foul necromancy, stinking of grave dirt and malice, and he had no doubt that it had come for his soul. Even asleep, he had sensed its presence haunting the tavern.

He had to act, and fast. He grasped the door's edge and, with a roar, wrenched it from its already damaged hinges. Before those beyond it could react, he slammed it into them like a giant shield, crushing the nearest back against those crowding behind. Then, in the precious seconds it gave him, he turned toward the window.

Mikael was already out. The phantom's corposant talons were reaching for him through the flames, the fire cringing back and dying before its terrible chill. Zachareth seized the opening and threw himself at the window, tossing his sword out ahead of him.

His stomach lurched as he jumped out into the dark nothingness of the night. He couldn't remember how many floors up their room had been, but he didn't get long to worry – he hit the mud outside with a squelching thud and got a face full of what he was sure was horse manure.

It was still raining, and the churned-up filth of the tavern yard had absorbed the worst of his brief freefall. He raked through the muck until he found where his sword had fallen. The only illumination was coming from the fire raging from the bedroom window above.

Zachareth found his feet and looked around wildly for Mikael. A loud, urgent tolling made him turn toward the stable block adjoining the tavern. Mikael was there, ringing the bell used for late-night arrivals or emergencies.

"What are you doing?" Zachareth snapped as he ran through the rain and mud to join him.

"I don't fancy letting everyone in there burn," Mikael said, abandoning the bell and throwing open the stable door. "Besides, we could do with a distraction, and everyone leaving their rooms is a good one."

The inside of the stable was dank, musty, and almost pitch black. Mikael and Zachareth fumbled around until they found their saddles and threw them over their mounts. Zachareth was relieved the assassins hadn't slaughtered the animals before moving in for the kill – presumably it would have risked making too much noise.

They mounted up and rode out into the rain. The tavern appeared to have awoken to the horror within it. Flames were now billowing from the window, held in check only by the stinging, hissing downpour, and Zachareth could hear screams and the slamming of doors within. He found himself regretting bringing such a fate down on the place.

"Death cultists," he snarled to Mikael as they rode. "Aided by some sort of summoned phantom. The work of necromancy. Of Waiqar."

Mikael looked at him sharply, his face glistening in the fire-shot rain, but he didn't get a chance to say anything. The light of the fire faded, and Zachareth looked up in time to see the terrible spirit that had materialized in the room surging up directly through the sodden roof. It let out an unearthly, chilling screech, so piercing it made both of them flinch. Then, claws outstretched once again, it surged toward them through the rain.

Bent low in the saddle, the two galloped hard out onto the roadway. They didn't stop until they could see the first light of dawn.

CHAPTER TWENTY-ONE
Snowfall, 1830

The clash of swords rang through the icy hall as cold and as clear as the winter morning outside. Zachareth snarled and went in high, using his strength, the rune marks on his arms blazing. His rival, fully armored, parried over and over, the ringing echoing like the clanging of some ill-struck bell.

The sheer force behind Zachareth's blows was enough to cause his enemy's sword to bend and buckle on the cusp of shattering. He drew back his own blade for one last ruinous strike, knowing that the warped weapon was no longer any danger. With startling speed, however, one of his opponent's hands went down to his waist, drawing the ballock dagger buckled there. Its slender, wicked tip was probing at the weak point beneath Zachareth's raised arm before he could land the final blow. He froze.

The man removed the dagger and stepped back, holding up his brutally bent sword.

"Look what you've done to Keenheart," he complained, voice muffled by his helm. He let the ruined weapon clatter to the floor. Zachareth lowered his own sword.

"Well, you've certainly improved," Baron Greigory said as he removed his helmet and mail coif, shaking out his hair. "I'm still not sure about that goatee, though."

Zachareth smiled. He was tempted to say the same thing about his old friend's mustache, but in truth, he'd grown into it since they had last met.

"You're strong as an ox now, Zacha," Greigory said, clapping him on the arm with one mailed fist and admiring the markings there. "But you let your whole focus be drawn to my sword. Always remember the dagger."

"I didn't think an old man like you could move so quickly," Zachareth said. "Is that silver in your beard, Greigory?"

"You wish," Greigory quipped, snapping his fingers at the group of squires that had been standing, shivering, on the edge of the practice hall. They hurried forward and began to unbuckle and remove the two men's armor.

"Breakfast?" Greigory asked. "There's still chicken and pastries left over from last night."

"Hopefully I can stomach it," Zachareth said. "I'm too used to Greyhaven gruel."

Greigory laughed. Zachareth realized how welcome the sound was. He had arrived at Castle Arhynn the week before on the last day of Chillwind. After fleeing the attack at the tavern, he and Mikael had agreed that their best hope would be to split up. Mikael would ride for Cailn where he would tell his father of the undead threat besetting the north and urge him to raise the barony's host. Zachareth would journey to Rhynn and attempt to do the same with Baron Greigory.

The attack at the tavern had shocked Zachareth. Despite knowing of Leanna's power and duplicity, he had somehow never imagined she would act so brazenly. There could be no doubt now that she was the master of a death cult, in service to some even darker power. The fact that such an organization had been allowed to grow and fester in Carthridge filled him with anger and even greater concern. Things were moving at a dangerously fast pace now, and he felt as though he still did not understand just what had taken place while he had been at Greyhaven.

Doubts had beset him as he had reached Arhynn. What if Greigory had changed since he had last seen him? What if, even worse, the necromantic taint that had burrowed its way into Carthridge had spread to Rhynn?

He needn't have worried. Greigory had welcomed him first with surprise, then merriment. When Zachareth had described what had happened, he had immediately sent out riders summoning the barony's nobles.

"Can't you simply raise the host yourself?" Zachareth had asked. Greigory had shaken his head, his expression grave.

"Regrettably, I do not enjoy the unfettered power of the Baron of Carthridge, current circumstances excepted," he had said. "The laws of Rhynn require that such matters be put toward a vote."

As much as the response disappointed Zachareth, finding Arhynn to be a haven was a vast relief. Greigory at first seemed unchanged, though Zachareth detected a weightiness about him whenever he spoke of his duties as baron. His borders had also been menaced by the growing threat of necromancy.

As the last of the armor was removed, Greigory tossed a doublet to Zachareth for him to put on over his shirt. All the clothes Zachareth had worn since his arrival were borrowed – the doublet had the Grandmother Oak of Rhynn embroidered over its chest. Once, wearing the heraldry of another barony would have given Zachareth pause, but that didn't even occur to him anymore. There were more important things at stake than petty pride.

They walked down toward Arhynn's great hall together, halting in the spiral stairs as Greigory caught sight of something out of one of the arrowslits.

"Sir Telmark has arrived from Castle Daerion," he said. He made way for Zachareth on the stairs, who peered out of the arrowslit and down into Arhynn's courtyard. Three men were just dismounting and throwing their reins to the servants rushing to greet them. One of the trio was a squire, the other a bannerman bearing a pennant embroidered with a variation of the Rhynn heraldry – two smaller trees with a falcon soaring above them. The final man, who Zachareth took to be Sir Telmark, was short and stout with a ruddy, scowling expression. He made for the keep's steps.

"I should go and greet him in person," Greigory said. "The rest of the nobles will arrive over the next day. As soon as they are all assembled, I will call a meeting and ask for their vote."

"Do you wish me to be present?" Zachareth asked. "Perhaps I could impress the urgency of the situation upon them?"

"Best not to, I think," Greigory said as they began to descend once more. "I don't want it to seem as though there is too much external influence over my request. I have to show them that it isn't just Carthridge that is threatened but all of Terrinoth."

Zachareth received news of the vote's outcome as he sat eating alone in the great hall.

He knew immediately from Greigory's expression that the

news was bad. He put his spoon down, saying nothing as the baron came and sat across from him.

"The nobles have voted against raising the Rhynn host and marching on Castle Talon," he said.

Zachareth was silent. Anger and bitter disappointment hit him. He fought to keep his reaction measured.

"Does the plight of Carthridge mean nothing to them?" he asked softly.

"I impressed the desperate nature of things on them," Greigory said. "But the majority decided it would be tantamount to a declaration of war with another barony. It would likely harm your chances when the Council of Thirteen vote on the matter of your legitimacy."

"Then Carthridge is lost," Zachareth said, a sudden, potent sense of despair dousing his anger. Just as in the tavern before they'd been attacked, he could see no way forward.

"It is not lost while you yet live and are willing to fight," Greigory said.

"How can I fight when even my closest allies abandon me?" Zachareth demanded, looking Greigory in the eye. The Baron of Rhynn almost flinched. Zachareth understood the situation wasn't easy for him either. It was difficult to keep his annoyance under control, though. He felt no closer to regaining Castle Talon.

"There are other options still open to us," Greigory said. "I was able to secure the nobles' vote on related matters. An armed expedition is to march to the Carthmounts to help drive the bandits sheltering there from the Rhynn side of the mountains."

"That will only drive more of them into Carthridge," Zachareth exclaimed. Greigory glanced around the hall, ensuring there were no servants present before leaning in and speaking low.

"Once an army is in the field, controlling where it goes and what it does from here in Castle Arhynn is far more difficult. We can help to liberate the silver mines on the Carthridge side. It would cause only minor controversy, enough for me to withstand."

"Less than marching on the neighboring barony's seat of power," Zachareth surmised, realizing what Greigory was hinting at. He felt a fraction of his hope restored. Greigory nodded.

"Exactly. I mean this with the greatest respect, Zacha, but when you've ruled for a while, you'll understand the importance of diplomacy. Being master of a barony is about minimizing risks. At times, you must know when to fight cleverly rather than boldly. A dagger in the armpit, if you will."

"When I rule, it will not involve kowtowing to every petty manor lord in Carthridge," Zachareth said, finding the words coming out sharper than intended. To his credit, Greigory smiled.

"Each barony is different. For my part, I am proud that Rhynn is ruled by committee. It means I don't get blamed as often when things go wrong."

Zachareth sat back in his chair, trying to consider what Greigory had proposed. Recapturing the silver mines would be helpful, but it still didn't solve the root of the problem. He could already imagine Leanna declaring that the mines had simply passed from one set of bandits to another. They gave him no greater legitimacy.

"I just hope Cailn is more able to help than Rhynn," he said, wondering if he could goad Greigory into action. The baron seemed remorseful but otherwise unflappable.

"You have other allies," he said. "Acquaintances from your time in Greyhaven. Will they not help as well?"

Zachareth had told Greigory briefly of Silver Horizon when describing his time at university, but he hadn't mentioned his visit to Nerekhall nor their involvement in dark magics. He shook his head.

"I have little wish to be in their debt any more than I already am. Besides, I doubt I am welcome in Greyhaven's lecture rooms any longer. My departure was… controversial."

"What about that scholarly society you mentioned? You clearly learned much about the arcane during your time with them. Surely they could provide further assistance, unless they were the ones you spited?"

"Magic comes with… great risk," Zachareth said, beginning to feel uncomfortable. He had no wish to delve into the events at Nerekhall or the specifics of his relationship with Morrow. Greigory seemed to sense it, looking at him quizzically.

"For someone with an uncompromising view of how barons should be obeyed, you seem reluctant to enforce the same attitude when it comes to runemasters," he said. "If the forces of darkness have as much of a grip over Carthridge as you say – death cultists, summoned spirits, the borderlands overrun – then we will have need of a battle mage or two of our own."

The words stung Zachareth, but he forced himself to consider their merit. Could he really go back to Morrow, to the cult? It had been dangerous enough placing himself in their debt in order to acquire the power of the Bonesplitter. To call upon them once more would surely risk everything, even his very soul. He remembered what Morrow had insisted, that the Ynfernael was not a simple matter of light and dark as the legends claimed. That the spirits of the lower realms could be bargained with, could be made to obey. That, he was beginning to realize, was one of the most important skills he had yet to acquire. He had to learn to make others obey. Could he do it with Morrow, let alone the demons he was said to command?

"It will be some weeks before an expedition to the Carthmounts can be assembled," Greigory said. "In the meantime, I say we build our strength. I will send a messenger to learn of Cailn's decision and suggest if they don't join you outright, that they assist us in liberating the mines. Success there can be used as a steppingstone to convince everybody to make further moves and support you outright in a campaign to reclaim Castle Talon."

"It's a start," Zachareth said guardedly, still thinking. Events were conspiring to leave him with few options. Greigory stood and leaned across the table to clap him on the shoulder.

"I'm sorry the nobles couldn't be swayed, Zacha," he said gravely. "Those are the realities of politics. In time, we'll get what we need, but while we wait, I suggest you compose a careful letter to the Council of Thirteen explaining your right to rule and think about who else you can call on for aid. I will send messages to the other barons impressing on them the need to hold council and resolve this matter soon. Nobody wants a civil war in Terrinoth."

"Worse than that awaits us if Leanna continues to rule from Castle Talon," Zachareth said. "I am certain she's a puppet of a greater threat. Of Waiqar."

To his credit, Greigory didn't immediately dismiss the claim.

"There's a darkness growing in the Mistlands, that much is

certain," he said. "But there will be a reckoning with it, and on that day, Rhynn will stand with Carthridge no matter what my nobles say. You have my word on that."

"Thank you, Greigory," Zachareth said. Greigory smiled at him again.

"Finish your soup, my fellow baron," he said, turning toward the door. "You'll need your strength. We're going to keep sparring every day. Eventually you'll beat me!"

A figure arrived just over a week later as the first snow began to fall. It came down heavily, a silent curtain of white that blanketed Arhynn and left the day in a perpetual, deep gray twilight.

Zachareth saw the man arrive. He'd been standing at the window of the bedchamber he'd been given, contemplating the onset of the coldest midwinter he could remember for years. It would make everything more difficult. An army did not move in the deep months, especially in the north, not if it wanted to avoid decimation from cold and hunger. The snow might yet save the bandits of the Carthmounts.

The cranking of the gatehouse portcullis echoed up to him through the courtyard. He watched as a lone rider cantered in, unannounced by any herald or bannerman. He was cloaked, snow heaped atop his cowl and shoulders. He shook it off and dismounted as a squire from the keep attended him.

Zachareth had been expecting the man. Deep down he had feared this moment. It was necessary, he told himself. Regardless, he'd been fearing this since he had first written the letter and sent it south.

He descended the keep to meet his visitor. A pair of guards opened the main door, allowing a flurry of snow to sweep in on a bitter wind. Zachareth shivered, pulling his cloak tight and stepping into the entrance.

The figure stood below him on the last snow-heaped step. He lowered his hood and smiled his ready smile.

"Hello again, Zachareth," said Morrow.

Greigory had ordered the fire piled high and lit before abandoning the great hall to Zachareth and his guest. They drew four chairs from the banquet table and set them before the hearth, laying out their cloaks to dry over the backs of two before sitting.

"You are a wanted man in Nerekhall, and your name has been struck from the registry in Greyhaven," Morrow said.

"Fond memories all around," Zachareth replied. "The Academy was able to survive the attention of the magisters and the Ironbound?"

"Concessions had to be made," Morrow said. "But the Academy's influence runs deep. We control the city, not the magisters."

"Covertly, perhaps," Zachareth said. "But I did not call you here for covert assistance."

"Mere months ago you refused to countenance what I could teach you," Morrow pointed out. "Now you would place yourself even further in my debt?"

"Such are the realities of ruling," Zachareth said, recalling Greigory's words about the difficult necessity of diplomacy. He had wrestled with the decision to send word to Morrow night and day before finally deciding that delaying and prevaricating were the worst sins of all. He had already relied on the sorcerer once, and it had strengthened him. Why not do so again?

"Castle Talon languishes in the grasp of Waiqar's allies," he said. "They attempted to murder me. They must be defeated, or Terrinoth itself will be endangered. And that includes both Greyhaven and Nerekhall. You will be on the front line, Morrow."

"What makes you so sure it is Waiqar who is the master of all this?" the runemaster asked. "He had many lieutenants, and there are many other dabblers in the foul arts of necromancy."

"The malignancy in the north is not the work of some petty crypt-robber," Zachareth said. "It has been seeping through for decades if not centuries. It is coordinated. Who else has that foresight, that strategic wit, but the great necromancer?"

"You speak as though you already know him, as though you have already encountered him," Morrow said.

"The tales of my youth prepared me well," Zachareth replied simply. He had been thinking a lot about the stories Bernard had taught him. He still had his copy of *The Canticle of Rufus the Bold* slipped into the pocket of his cloak and salvaged when Mikael had grabbed them while fleeing the tavern. Whenever he felt like giving in to the odds that seemed so heavily set against him, he remembered the struggles of his forebears and resolved not to be the one who failed Carthridge.

"For what it's worth, I think you are right," Morrow said. "Everything points to a darkness growing in the Mistlands unlike anything seen for many centuries. That is partly why I came. You may believe I seek only to bring you into the fold of Silver Horizon, into our debt, but the reasons we were founded by your ancestor still hold true. The plague of undeath must be stopped, and you remain our best hope of doing so."

"Then help me," Zachareth said.

"What do you need?"

"Money. Rhynn will not provide the full weight of their

host, and I have had no news yet from Cailn. I must turn to mercenary bands if I am to build an army, and for that I need coin or, better yet, silver. I am already in... substantial debts."

"Silver Horizon has some financial weight, though that is not what drives us," Morrow said. "Bought influence is the least valuable. We can provide funds, but it will not be enough to raise and maintain your own host."

"What can you do, then?" Zachareth asked, trying not to let exasperation get the better of him. It felt as though difficulties abounded no matter where he turned.

"We can garb you properly for the coming fight. If Waiqar truly is risen, you will face worse than Leanna. The Bonesplitter is impressive, but you will need more if you are to survive, let alone win."

"You speak of more runemagic," Zachareth surmised warily. "Do not try to tempt me with more of your Ynfernael stones, Morrow."

"Your arms and armor must be augmented," Morrow said. He slipped his hand into the rune pouch at his waist and removed two stones, one after the other, leaning over to place them on either arm rest of Zachareth's chair.

"What are they?" he asked without touching them, looking from one to the other as he tried to recall them from his studies.

"The Razorsong," Morrow said, indicating the angular-looking shard on his right. "It offers incredible keenness and durability if forged into a blade's hilt. The other is a variation of a Null Stone, the Turning's Bane. It can earth harmful magics cast upon you."

"You are giving them both to me?" Zachareth asked. He found such a degree of assistance suspicious. He had called for help, but to receive two runestones... His thoughts naturally turned to the Whisperer and how it had almost brought about his ruin.

"We wish to help you," Morrow confirmed. "I will need to oversee the forging that will bind Razorsong to your longsword. Do you have your own armor here as well?"

"Baron Greigory has made a gift of a set of half plate," Zachareth said.

"Then I will see the Bane is sealed to its cuirass too. With all three runes at your command, you have the potential to become one of the mightiest warriors now living in Terrinoth."

"That is well," Zachareth said, carefully picking up the Razorsong and noticing how its edges nearly nicked his palm. "But even the greatest champion cannot face an army alone."

"No, but it will be enough to defeat Leanna," Morrow said. "And once you have reclaimed Carthridge, you can call your people to the Silver Banner."

Zachareth placed the runestone back down.

"How long?" he asked.

"If Arhynn has a good blacksmith, a few days. I want you to have this as well."

He reached into the pouch again and drew forth a third runestone, holding it out in his hand.

"Its name is the Black Key," he said.

Zachareth studied it for only a moment. It looked like a small black twist of roots, a little knot that might emerge from a newly bloomed seed.

"That is a Ynfernael rune," Zachareth said, refusing to try to hide his disgust. As ever, Morrow smiled.

"Do not fear it, Zachareth. It will not make you sprout an extra limb or a maw in your chest. It is as its name suggests, merely a key."

"A key to what?" Zachareth asked dubiously. "The Ynfernael?"

"No," Morrow answered. "To a subsphere of the Aenlong, a place called the Black Realm. It is a nexus of great power and potential."

"It allows the bearer to travel there?"

"Not unless you have attained power beyond even the greatest runemasters," Morrow said. "But it would allow spirits from that realm to enter this one. They can be called upon to aid in all manner of things, but it should not be done lightly. It always bears a price."

"I have no wish of such an ability," Zachareth said sharply, refusing to take the stone. Morrow withdrew his hand.

"I fear there may come a point where it will be necessary to use all the weapons in our arsenal," he said. "The Black Key can be dangerous, but it is still preferable to allowing northern Terrinoth to be overrun by the walking dead and their masters. If all else seems lost, I would urge you to use it. If it comes with a price, then we shall pay it together."

Zachareth said nothing. He was certain, despite Morrow's insistence, that the runemaster was hinting at the use of the Ynfernael. He would not countenance it. It was surely too dangerous.

"That is a bargain I am not willing to strike," he said. "Take it back."

Wordlessly, the runemaster returned the stone to his pouch. Zachareth stood.

"Your help in these matters is appreciated, but do not test my favor," he said. "Set to work forging Razorsong and the Turning's Bane. Those two I accept."

Morrow rose and offered a short bow. Zachareth couldn't tell if he was being mocked or not.

"How you have changed," Morrow said, taking his cloak from the back of the chair and moving past the banquet table. "From a nervous youth, ill-trained in the way of runemagic, to a noble, giving commands."

"It was always going to be so," Zachareth said. "I was born to rule."

"And I pray it is a long and happy one," Morrow said. "I will send word once my work is complete."

He departed. Zachareth lingered, wondering once more if he was doing the right thing. It was only as he stirred himself from his doubts and prepared to call for a squire to request Greigory's return that he noticed the Black Key.

The runestone had been left, glinting, on the banquet table.

CHAPTER TWENTY-TWO

The blacksmith's roof was the only one in Arhynn not to be heaped high with snow. The heat from the furnaces within melted it as quickly as it fell.

Zachareth felt that same heat as he stepped inside. The chief forger, Marta, looked up from her anvil and pulled off her goggles, leaving circular patches of clear skin around her eyes in a face that was otherwise befouled with soot. She smiled excitedly, then, almost as an afterthought, offered a bow.

"Lord Carth," she said. "The runemaster said he had sent for you–"

"Ah, Zachareth," called out another voice from the far end of the workshop. It was Morrow, striding toward them between the sweltering heat of the brick furnace kilns. He had swapped out his red Ignis robes for a sooty leather smock. He seemed quite at home amidst the sparks and ash and unrefined, raw metal. Or perhaps it was just the flames he was used to.

"It's good to have you both here, sirs," Marta said, waving them to her anvil. Zachareth had met her the first time he had surrendered up his sword and armor to the workshop but had deliberately stayed away since then. Morrow had advised that the process of binding a rune to arms or armor was very different than sealing one into flesh. Reactive substances such as burnished bone or certain woods channeled runestones most effectively, but metals tended to be more reluctant. Only now had Zachareth been summoned to deliver the final hammer blows and, in doing so, perform the final rites.

"Can I just say what an honor it is, lord," Marta said, "to be chosen by a runemaster, no less for a forging, and to be the one working on the armory of the Baron of Carthridge. It is this workshop's proudest moment."

Zachareth realized the rest of the smiths and their apprentices – humans, dwarfs, and a gnome – were gathering to watch, seemingly unwilling to miss the last moments of a rune-forging. Zachareth cleared his throat, looking for the appropriate words to utter.

"Carthridge will not forget the assistance you have given me this day," he said. "We stand on the precipice, but with these arms and armor, we shall not fall."

Marta stepped up to one of the kilns and removed the object that had been protruding from it in her heavy leather gloves. It was Zachareth's sword, the hilt's bindings removed and the metal heated until it was red hot. The pommel had been replaced by the Razorsong, the metal partially bent around it.

With a reverent air, Marta placed the hilt atop the anvil's gleaming surface. Morrow held out a short hammer to Zachareth. A binding mark had been inscribed in its head. He took it.

"Strike the final blows," Morrow instructed. "It is tradition. Let the Razorsong know who its new master is."

As Marta held the rest of the blade steady, Zachareth brought the hammer slamming down on the red-hot metal, striking at the point that had yet to be properly set around the runestone. The markings on his arms seemed to glow in sympathy as the hammer blows rang out, shuddering right through him. One, two, three strikes and the metal submitted, clenching to the wicked-edged stone.

Marta lifted the soot-darkened blade once more and sank it into a vat of water next to the kiln. There was a fierce, serpentine hiss, and a gout of steam that momentarily shrouded the workshop. She drew the steel back out, and presented its dripping, gleaming hilt to Zachareth.

He grasped it firmly, knowing the residual heat wouldn't burn him, raising it up before him. Arhynn's smiths had put a new edge on her as they worked, and it gleamed with luster in the firelight of the kilns. The Razorsong winked dangerously on the pommel, beautiful and keen. It seemed to sing in his thoughts, a wordless song that was both elegant and deadly.

"No scabbard will hold her but this," Morrow said, proffering Zachareth a leather sheath stamped with flowing inscriptions. Zachareth tested Razorsong's balance and, satisfied, slipped it in.

Marta moved to the second kiln, where she and an apprentice used large metal tongs to remove the breastplate of the armor Greigory had gifted him. At its center was the Turning's Bane, sealed into the heated metal. It was laid out upon the anvil as Zachareth buckled Razorsong about his waist.

"This one requires greater focus," Morrow warned while Zachareth once more took up the hammer. "Do not lose control."

Zachareth stepped up and took a moment to collect himself.

He found himself closing his eyes as he had once done when seeking the focus necessary to manipulate the runes. Then, opening them, he struck.

The Bane began to glow on the first strike. On the seventh, there was a discharge of magical force that made Zachareth shudder and the surrounding onlookers gasp. The markings on the runestone spread like liquid fire across the breastplate, singeing into the metal. When the flames died, the runestone was left pulsing and glowing faintly at the heart of a latticework of arcane inscriptions, not unlike those that already smoldered along Zachareth's arms.

"Very good," Morrow nodded. "Now you will be proof against Waiqar's foul magics."

He continued to speak as Marta and the apprentice hefted the breastplate and quenched it.

"You are almost ready, but there is one last gift Silver Horizon would give before you travel home. It cannot be granted here, though. It must be done in Carthridge."

Zachareth frowned, wondering what Morrow had in mind. He was constantly alert and worried about Morrow's darker magics. He refused to let himself be tricked as he had been before.

"Why?" he asked. "What is it?"

"You will see soon enough," Morrow said. "We leave tomorrow, if you are ready, bound for the Temple of the Four Storms."

The answer surprised Zachareth even more.

"If this is some dark rite–" he began to say, but Morrow laughed and cut him off before he could say any more before the onlookers.

"It is nothing the learned of Greyhaven don't practice,

Zachareth," he said. "All will be explained on the way there. My associates are already preparing the ground."

"We go tomorrow then?" Zachareth said, still not satisfied by Morrow's evasiveness.

"Yes," Morrow said. "Make your final preparations with Baron Greigory. Carthridge awaits."

The Temple of the Four Storms lay upon Lake Falstar, at the edge of Carthridge, deeply nestled amidst low, rolling hills and dense pine forests. It would have been a picturesque place, a small crag of rocky ground set in the middle of a wide, deep lake that glittered blue beneath a cold, cloudless sky. The natural splendor, however, belied its dark reputation.

Stories about the isle abounded from Carthridge's meanest hovel to the pages of the books in Bernard's garret. Ancient standing stones – elder stones, as they were commonly called – occupied the island in a series of concentric rings. Just who had first erected them was unknown. Theories covered the full panoply from elves to dragon worshippers to servants of Waiqar. Their exact purpose was also a mystery, though all the stories agreed that the Turning flowed especially strong there. Whether the stones acted as a confluence or whether they merely paid tribute to the preexisting energies, no one knew.

It was said that on certain nights, such as the equinoxes or Highsummer's Mideve, cloaked and hooded figures could sometimes be spotted on the isle, conducting unknowable rites. Often a storm accompanied such nights, though, once again, whether the figures summoned it or whether they gathered when they knew it would break remained a mystery.

Zachareth stood looking out across the lake toward the island, his breath frosting in the cold, crisp air. A boat was crossing toward the shore, carrying Morrow. Both he and the oarsman had donned black robes. Zachareth was in his newly reforged armor with Razorsong at his hip. He felt strong, vital, but a wariness hung about him like an unwelcome cloak.

Morrow had tried to reassure him on the journey from Arhynn. The Temple of the Four Storms was not a Ynfernael portal, merely a site where the Turning was at its strongest, and the rites they were going to undertake had nothing to do with spirits or demons. Still, he had refused to divulge the exact reason for their journey, and that left Zachareth with numerous, nagging doubts. He had trusted Morrow too much before. He could practically feel the weight of the Black Key in the pouch at his waist. He had tried to return it twice, but Morrow had refused. He'd considered abandoning it somewhere or leaving it with Greigory, but he didn't want to risk it falling into the wrong hands. He kept recalling Morrow's words about using it as a last resort. Could he afford to throw away any advantage now, even one that might be corrupt?

"All is prepared," Morrow called as the oarsmen sprang out and hauled the small boat onto the pebbles of the lake's shore. "It is time for you to join us."

"You still have not properly explained why," Zachareth pointed out.

"We are summoning an ally for you," Morrow said, then laughed when he saw Zachareth's dark expression. "Do not fear! Once again, I swear to you this has nothing to do with the lower realms."

"With the Ynfernael," Zachareth clarified, disliking Morrow's refusal to use the word.

"Indeed," Morrow said and motioned to the boat. Zachareth grasped the bow and stepped onboard.

"Are the rites you intend dangerous?" he asked as they put out into the lake.

"Not especially, but they are difficult to perform correctly," Morrow said, remaining standing in the prow while Zachareth sat before the oarsman. "A great deal of preparation has led up to today. Let us hope all proceeds as planned."

As the boat drew nearer to the island, Zachareth made out figures amongst the standing stones – over a dozen – garbed like Morrow, their features hidden by their raised hoods.

"Who are these people?" Zachareth demanded, his uncertainty returning.

"Fellows of Silver Horizon," Morrow said. "Several are known to you. Drussus is among them, and Olivia, who you met in Greyhaven."

"They've come here to assist me?"

"All of Silver Horizon now stands ready to assist you, Zachareth. We believe you to be the champion Terrinoth so desperately needs."

Zachareth was wary of Morrow's flattery, but it was a relief to hear that others were taking the threat posed to Carthridge seriously. He gazed out upon the cloaked assembly as they stood awaiting the boat's arrival like a gaggle of black-feathered corvids, silent and watchful. He tried to not feel too intimidated by their sinister presence.

The boat reached the shore, and they disembarked. On Morrow's advice he unbuckled his breastplate and left it in the boat – Turning's Bane was not welcome on the isle. The acolytes parted wordlessly around Morrow and Zachareth and fell in on either side as the runemaster led them to the center of the small island, across the snow freshly fallen upon the craggy turf.

Zachareth inspected the standing elder stones as they passed between them. They stood at teetering angles, their surfaces rough, like disjointed rows of jagged teeth or like a gaggle of drunkards who had been frozen in time. There was no snow on them despite the fact it had been falling just before they had reached the lake. Impulsively, he reached out to touch one as he passed.

Morrow snatched his arm.

"Don't," he said, smiling. "Nothing can disrupt what we have prepared."

Zachareth hesitated, then nodded. Morrow let go.

At the center of the island stood a mound. It looked as though there had once been a single great column at the heart of the elder stones, but it had long since collapsed in on itself, leaving a jagged heap of rubble. Like all the other stones, there was no sign that any snow had fallen upon it.

Morrow led Zachareth to the foot of the mound as the rest of the acolytes spread out into a circle, one before each of the menhirs comprising the innermost ring.

"You brought me here to stand before some old, broken rocks?" Zachareth asked, hoping affected arrogance would mask his mounting fear.

"No," Morrow said. "I brought you here to tame them. Remember what you managed during your Trial of Fire."

The wind began to pick up. With it came susurrations that Zachareth noticed were voices. The acolytes had begun to chant, low at first, but with steadily rising volume and tempo. Morrow leaned forward and placed a hand against one of the broken shards of stone.

Zachareth saw a rune there. It was just one of many, faint from the ruthless erosion of time but unmistakable all the same. They were markers of strength, of resilience, and most of all, of sentient binding. At some point, the central obelisk had been inscribed with dozens, if not hundreds, of arcane marks.

The wind snarled at him, churning up the surface of the surrounding lake with white eddies. He noticed snow had started to fall again, swirling in great white clouds, thickening by the second. A premature twilight had settled across the lake, the clouds a low, impenetrable gray where blue sky had reigned mere moments before. The wind snapped at Zachareth's cloak and at the robes of the surrounding acolytes. Their words seemed to swirl and dance like the snow.

Zachareth's hand dropped to the hilt of his sword. He turned in a tight circle, half expecting to be assailed by the robed figures or by the elemental forces themselves. Thunder rumbled, low and menacing. The snow became a blizzard, stinging Zachareth's face and forcing him to raise a hand. His body was starting to go numb with the cold. What damnable curse were they calling down?

"Place your hand upon the stone," Morrow shouted over the howling of the wind and a louder, rolling thunderclap. When Zachareth hesitated, Morrow snatched his wrist and pressed his palm to the side of the mound before them both.

As he did so, there was a cracking sound and a searing burst of light that imprinted itself on Zachareth's retinas. A fork of lightning lashed down amidst the swirling snowstorm, slamming into one of the menhirs surrounding them. It earthed into the stone, then bounced, striking the ones next to it with a resounding series of cracks. On it went until a chain of coruscating energy linked each standing stone in the inner circle, dancing and fizzing across the craggy surfaces and bolting between them continuously.

"Don't let go!" Morrow urged, keeping Zachareth's hand on the broken mound. "You remember what you did on the Island of Trials? You remember the animus?"

He did remember. The words came back to him, augmented by the lessons he'd sat through since. The air was alive with electricity, the stink of burned stone in Zachareth's nostrils. Blue orbs winked in and out of existence around him. Morrow had started to chant in words he didn't know, running counterpoint to his own. His stomach churned with fear, but he was too in awe of what was happening around him to rip his hand free or to stop the incantation. He knew the words. He would succeed.

Without warning, the lightning jumped again. This time it did so from every menhir, a flurry of separate arcs that leapt in unison into the circle's center. It did so via the acolytes standing before each one, transfixing them where they stood, their bodies contorting.

They screamed. Zachareth stared in horror and realized he could see luminescent outlines of their bones as though each were glowing brilliantly from within. Actinic skulls shrieked, jaws open, as the lightning carried on and struck the stone mound before Zachareth from all sides.

Sparks exploded, and a searing ball of energy momentarily blinded him. His words faltered, as did Morrow's icy grip, but he managed to keep his hand in place. He felt the electrical charge surge up through him, making him cry out, a shock of pure power.

He struggled to breathe, the words almost lost, spots of brilliance still playing across his eyes as his vision returned. He felt the stone shifting and heard a crack that he took to be more lightning.

He was mistaken. It was the broken column itself. Ablaze

with energy, it was beginning to rise up before his very eyes. At first, he thought something was forcing its way up from beneath the stone before realizing that it was the rocks themselves that were picking themselves up.

In fact, they were not rocks at all. It was a beast, a construct of elemental magics. It shook itself free of its stony bed, hunched over on all fours. Zachareth's hand, still upon the stone, was resting on the brow of its angular head as the last words of the spell left his frozen lips.

It was an animus, and it had been awoken.

"Welcome, Back-breaker," Morrow called over the rage of the storm, his voice booming like the elemental wrath all around them. "Bear witness to your new master. Do you feel his presence?"

The last words were directed at Zachareth. He realized he could feel the creature. It was not dissimilar to what he had experienced in the Manse during the Trial of Fire. He could sense the creature in his mind, dense, solid, its thoughts slow but intelligent, measured like the gradual passage of boulders down a scree slope.

"Mount it," Morrow told Zachareth. He realized the runemaster's eyes were pulsing an actinic blue like the lightning. Bolts of power continued to lash and spark across the animus's stone skin. It seemed to growl, a low, grating noise.

Zachareth's fascination overcame his fear. He let go of the creature's brow and moved to its flank, reaching out and grasping onto a spur of stone. The electricity continued to fizz and spark as he stepped up and threw a leg over where its torso narrowed behind its broad shoulders. It had been made for such a role, he realized, crafted and inscribed to act as a hulking, unyielding steed.

The lightning had ceased to flow from the surrounding menhirs. As it had left them, the black-robed acolytes had collapsed, but now they began to rise again, miraculously still alive.

On an impulse, Zachareth drew Razorsong from his side and held the longsword aloft. The storm seemed to whip and eddy around him, casting off and ripping away his cloak. He no longer cared about it, about the stinging, biting, blinding cold. He was rife with power, physically crackling with it. He felt as though he could do anything, defeat anyone.

Overhead, the thunder roared, and lightning flashed once again. It struck the tip of his sword, sending bright, fat sparks flying as it jarred down his arm and through his body. The markings on his limbs blazed, and the runes inscribed into the animus's body lit up in kind, electric blue contrasting with the fiery yellow.

He let loose a roar, venting his rage and uncertainty, his wrath and his determination into the heart of the storm. Amidst it all, a single thought kept the energy surging through him.

He was ready.

CHAPTER TWENTY-THREE

A storm was coming, a blizzard set to batter at Castle Talon's shutters and heap snow upon its parapets. The only thing that surprised Skerrif was that it appeared to be rising up from the south.

He'd drawn the midday shift atop the gatehouse, but it felt more like the evening patrol. Daylight barely seemed to have leached into the world again before it was being driven back. Heavy gray clouds looked as though they were competing to be the first to touch the crest of the valley.

The wind picked up, making the black and red banners atop the castle towers stream and snap. Then the snow started to fall, a few swirling flakes at first, building rapidly to a biting, bitter white deluge.

"Go and get more wood," Skerrif told his watch partner, Mord. The brazier atop the gatehouse was in danger of going out. As the other guard headed for the spiral stairs, Skerrif pulled his cloak tighter and tried to cram himself deeper into the sparse shelter of the small, circular turret abutting the fortification. The wind knifing in through the arrowslits was bitterly cold, and the open walkway of the wall behind him was already covered in a thick, dense layer of snow.

Skerrif cursed his luck, wondering how much longer he had left before he could retreat to the guardhouse. The bailey down below had cleared as the servants and staff had rushed inside. He had no doubt Xaro and Gaillad, the pair responsible for the watch in the north tower, were praising the gods that for once the towering structure of the keep was helping to shield them from a winter storm rather than leaving them exposed as it broiled down the valley from the north.

Skerrif was so preoccupied with his own misery he almost missed the movement out beyond the gate. The blizzard had sharply curtailed visibility, so he didn't catch sight of the approaching figure until it had already started to scale the steep path up the castle rock.

He blinked, raising a hand to try to shield his face from the blinding snow. He didn't understand what he was looking at. It was a rider, but just what was being ridden he couldn't make out. It looked like some sort of massive ape like the one he had seen in the traveling circus that used to stop over in Strangehaven. It seemed to have horns, though, and parts of its snow-encrusted skin were glowing. It scaled the path with a terrible, loping speed, its rider leaning low atop its back.

"Who goes there?" Skerrif called out, but the wind whipped his words away. He was about to try again when he experienced a further terrible realization.

The rider and his mount weren't going to stop.

He lost sight of them as they reached the top of the crag and surged in beneath the parapet. He felt and heard them, though. There was a shattering crack, and the very stonework beneath his feet shuddered. The crashing sound finally snapped him from his shocked stupor.

"Gods," he spat and lunged for the turret's alarm bell.

Zachareth's spirit soared as Back-breaker loped in through the broken gateway, its massive bulk further pulverizing the broken timber before it. Ahead lay Castle Talon's bailey, deserted amidst the snowstorm.

"On," he urged the animus, adjusting his grip on the thick set of leather reins Morrow had given him.

The runemaster had asked to accompany him, but Zachareth had refused. If he was going to retake Castle Talon, he was doing so alone. It was his home and his right to do so. He no longer had any doubt he could do it.

As Back-breaker bore him into the courtyard, he heard the clanging of the alarm from above. Doors slammed and feet scuffed on stone as members of the baronial guard – and a few panicked servants – came clattering from different parts of the surrounding citadel.

Zachareth ignored them. Mentally, he urged Back-breaker on to the foot of the keep's stairs. The heart of the castle towered overhead as the animus halted beneath it.

Guards, some only partially armed and armored, scrambled to intercept and surround him. He caught sight of half a dozen arbalesters taking up posts atop the flanking curtain walls, hurrying to winch back their cords and plant bolts against them.

Back-breaker lowered itself on all fours, allowing him to dismount. As he did so he threw back the hood on his cape, the wind catching his hair. He felt a thrill as he sensed recognition all across the courtyard.

He was about to speak, to demand to know if the guards

knew their own baron, when a voice bellowed from the top of the stairs.

"Hold!"

The garrison froze. Zachareth looked up and saw Golfang striding down the keep's steps. He halted just above Zachareth. His falchion was at his hip but not yet drawn.

Zachareth smiled up at the orc, though in truth a sudden nervousness had gripped him. Perhaps he was wrong after all. Perhaps he really was alone. Golfang's expression remained as stoic as ever.

"You really have grown, pup," he said.

"Still not as tall as you, though," Zachareth replied. "Hopefully I won't have to cut you down to size."

"I'd like to see you try."

"Where is Leanna?"

"In the great hall. I would suggest you reconsider what you're about to do."

"I've reconsidered enough, Golfang," Zachareth said, fresh determination lending his voice strength. "Are you going to let me pass?"

Golfang was silent for a while. Only the wind spoke, howling over the ramparts and through the broken gate. Zachareth forced himself to hold the orc's gaze and not glance up at the crossbowmen. He heard Back-breaker give off a grating growl.

"That's quite the beast you've got there," Golfang said, not looking at the animus.

"Don't worry, it can stay outside," Zachareth responded. "Back-breaker doesn't mind the elements."

Golfang resumed his silence for a few seconds, then turned abruptly toward the keep. He was halfway up the stairs before he looked back down at Zachareth.

"Well, are you coming or not?"

Zachareth followed. His heart was racing. Was Golfang with him? It seemed so. He stepped in out of the snow, shaking off his cloak and walking with Golfang into the keep. It felt utterly surreal to be back home, to be doing what he had imagined doing for almost as long as he could remember. Every step felt like a dream, divorced from the firm anchor of reality, something that might unravel in an instant and dissolve around him. But it didn't. It was truly happening.

The doors to the great hall stood open. A number of servants waited around the edges, their muttered conversations falling deadly silent as Zachareth and Golfang entered.

Leanna was waiting for them at the far end of the hall. She stood atop the dais before a single throne. Zelmar's was gone. Amalie and Ragasta were off to one side, their expressions guarded. Leanna's wasn't. She smiled.

"Zachareth," she exclaimed, opening her arms. Her twisted black staff was held in one hand. "Welcome home."

Zachareth said nothing, feeling his anger spike. He advanced down the hall, the only sound his boots upon the flagstones. He felt the eyes on him, not just the servants and advisors but the hawks and hunters and knights of the tapestries adorning the walls. They were judging him as they always had every time he had undertaken this same long, lonely walk.

Leanna lowered her arms, resting her staff against the floor. Zachareth halted before her.

"You are to leave, immediately," he said, loud and clear. "As baron, I formally banish you from Castle Talon, and from Carthridge, under pain of death."

Leanna kept smiling, but her yellow gaze was unblinking and sharp as a knife.

"You are speaking in haste and anger, so I will forgive you that," she said. "You should have sent a rider ahead, and we might have been able to prepare a more civilized reception for you. This merits conversation."

"There will be no conversation," Zachareth said stonily. "You will leave and never come back."

"Why?" Leanna demanded, her tone turning suddenly as cold as the storm outside. "If you are following the old ways, the laws of King Daqan, you must give a reason for my banishment."

"Foul sorcery, among other things," Zachareth said. "For years you have used dark magics to undermine the safety and stability of this barony."

"Preposterous," Leanna exclaimed. "To think I hoped that a Greyhaven education might rid you of your parochial fear of the arcane. Not all magics come from darkness, Zachareth."

He knew she was trying to lure him into a debate instead of action. He kept glancing at her staff, wary of the first hint that she was starting to use her sorceries. He wanted desperately to just draw Razorsong and strike her down, but he fought the urge. In a sense, she was right. He had to do it properly before the eyes of those she had enthralled. He had to give her a chance.

"If you are not a practitioner of foul magics, then you will have no complaint if I have your chambers searched for forbidden texts and artifacts," Zachareth said, carrying on before she could protest. "Captain Golfang, take three of your guards and go to the sorceress's rooms. Search them thoroughly and bring anything you consider dubious back here."

"You will do no such thing, Golfang," Leanna snapped. "Zachareth Carth is not your ruler, not until his legitimacy has been examined by the Council of Thirteen. You do not obey him."

Zachareth made himself keep facing Leanna, rather than turn around to look at Golfang. He heard the orc's voice ring out through the hall.

"It will be as you command, Baron Carth."

A fierce thrill of elation surged through Zachareth. He struggled to keep his expression controlled, at the same time catching the fury in Leanna's eyes. Much had rested on this moment. Even after being turned away with Mikael, he had held out the hope that Golfang's true loyalties were still with him. If the captain of the guard supported him, the guard supported him, and if they did, then he had Castle Talon. All that remained was to face down Leanna's wrath.

"This will not help your reputation when the barons sit to decide your fate," she said. "This doesn't need to happen."

"Leave, and it won't," Zachareth said. "Recognize the mercy I am showing you. All I wish for right now is to end your corrupting existence."

To his surprise, Leanna laughed. The sound brought back a flurry of bitter childhood memories.

"You have certainly grown in size and stature, little Zachareth," she said. "And I see you have a few runic trinkets now as well. I hope you did not pay too dearly for them in body or in soul. Even so, I would like to see you try to end me."

Zachareth's hand dropped to Razorsong's hilt. He felt the runestone's biting desire to be drawn, to cut and cleave. It sang with his own anger. Control, he told himself. She wanted him to lose himself, to prove that he was, at heart, still the scared, frustrated youth she had once manipulated.

He refused to obey her anymore.

"One way or another, you will leave this castle, and you will leave this barony," he said.

"You have no proof," Leanna started to say.

"I have lived with the proof almost since my birth," Zachareth snarled, indignation finally causing his controlled tone to unravel. "I have watched, day by day, year by year, as you poisoned my father against me. You made him believe my mother's death was my fault, that I was disobedient and weak. That I was unfit to inherit his duties or his privileges. He gave me nothing because of you."

"He tried to make you a good youth in the vain hope that you would grow up to be a good ruler," Leanna hissed. "I am responsible for none of what you have just described. You were an indolent, arrogant, brattish child who delighted in tormenting everyone with your antics, from the stable hands to Zelmar. You drove him to the brink of despair. Even on his deathbed he vexed himself over the path you had chosen. That was why he finally admitted the truth, that you are not your mother's son. Carthridge slips ever further into crisis while you have been playing with pathetic runemagic. We now stand on the brink of invasion, and suddenly you return, imagining yourself fit to lead us through this. Your childish idiocy will be the undoing of this barony and the death of us all."

"You are bold to speak of the threat of invasion," Zachareth said, his voice continuing to rise as ever-greater fury gripped him. "Did I not speak of the dangers posed by the Mistlands years ago? Do not take me for a fool, not anymore! I know you are in league with the darkness growing there. With Waiqar. Did you despair when your death cult assassins and your summoned spirit failed to kill me?"

He saw her eyes widen in shock and, for a moment, he almost found himself believing she really wasn't behind the cult.

"That is outrageous," she shouted. "I have never made an attempt on your life! I have no idea what you are talking about. Death cults? Spirits? You are mad, Zachareth Carth."

"So I imagined it all, and Mikael of Cailn likewise?" Zachareth demanded, moving forward to plant a foot on the dais, his rage now driving out all other thoughts. "If you did not send the dead to steal my soul, then who did? Who outside these walls knew that I had been to Castle Talon that day and was on the road south again? It can only have been someone here."

"I told you, I know nothing of what you speak," Leanna said, seeming to regain a measure of control as she held her staff with both hands, looking down on Zachareth. "It is not my duty to talk you through your fevered imaginings."

"My lord," called Golfang's voice. Zachareth turned sharply to see the orc entering, followed by two other guards. He was carrying a heavy-looking tome in his hands.

"We came across this," he declared as he approached the dais. "It was not even hidden."

Golfang handed the book to Zachareth. He opened it and, after a few pages, felt a sickening sensation of disgust. The text was in one of the Latari dialects, unreadable, but the diagrams, sketches, and scrawlings that accompanied the words were vile. Dissected bodies, skulls, cadavers, notes that looked to have been written in blood. The book reeked of necromancy.

"Here is proof of your corruption, sorceress," Zachareth said, his voice cracking with the strength of his emotion, the sheer anger. He slammed the book shut and gave it back to Golfang. "As soon as the snow eases, burn this in the courtyard."

"I have never seen that text before in my life," Leanna said shrilly. There was a note of panic in her voice now. "This is all trickery! I am being framed!"

"You are being exposed for what you truly are," Zachareth snapped savagely, stepping fully up onto the dais before Leanna. "A serpent coiling around the heart of this court. A queen of lies, a deceiver, and a debased servant of Waiqar."

Leanna stared at him for a moment, her hawk eyes holding his own. Then she abruptly brought her staff up and uttered a single word.

Zachareth felt the power of the magic immediately. It struck him like a gale, threatening to throw him back to the hall's floor. Tiny scratch marks appeared all over his armor as it took the brunt of the sorcerous blast. Ordinarily, the invisible blade wind would have shredded him and ripped the flesh from his bones.

But all it could do was scratch. The runic lines marking his armor surged with light as the Turning's Bane ignited, the shard channeling the magical surge into its nullifying core. Zachareth grunted with the effort of staying upright in the face of the blast, but it could do nothing more threatening.

He saw a moment of pure shock in Leanna's eyes.

Then Razorsong was in his fist and swinging.

Zachareth felt no resistance. Leanna's head flew from her shoulders in a gout of crimson. Her body stood upright for a moment as her staff clattered to the floor, before slumping back grotesquely into the throne behind her, blood painting it as her head rolled down the dais steps. Her face remained frozen in shock.

Total silence gripped the hall. Zachareth stared at what he had done. He was panting. The runes on his arms and on his armor were glowing fiercely.

He had done it. In the end, it had all happened so fast.

On impulse, he reached out and hauled the body off the throne, letting it fall. Then, Razorsong still in one fist, he turned and sat, ignoring the blood that dripped onto him. He glared out at the assembly, the heat of his wrath giving way to that stolid determination that had driven him for so long. He said nothing.

Golfang was the first to speak.

"On your knees for Baron Zachareth of Carthridge," he barked, his voice ringing from the timber rafters. There was a rustling of cloth and a scrape of armor as those present knelt.

Zachareth looked out over them with a sense of fierce exultation. He had rehearsed words for such a moment, but they all fled. He realized they didn't matter anyway. Carthridge was his.

"This is the beginning of the end," he said. "The beginning of the end for this barony's weakness, for its vulnerability, for its refusal to acknowledge the danger it is in. I am here to ensure that the dark days ahead do not overtake us. I will give Carthridge back its pride and then its power. That is the one promise I make to you as your baron."

He let the words sink in before continuing.

"Golfang, add the sorceress's remains to the pyre, along with her staff. Make sure all are reduced to ash. Ragasta, Amalie–"

He turned his gaze to the two advisors at the side of the throne. Both knelt, their eyes averted.

"I do not know what part you played here," Zachareth said. "Whether you served willingly or out of fear or were enthralled by some dark spell. I will discover the truth by your actions henceforth. Is that understood?"

"Yes, lord," both said in unison.

"Amalie, send messengers to the merchant quarters of Greyhaven, Strangehaven, and Frostgate. Tell them Baron Zachareth has something of great value he wishes to auction and if they wish to participate in the sale, they should be here by the last Moonday."

"Yes, lord," Amalie said, her eyes still not meeting his.

"Ragasta," he said. "Send word to every noble and Carth family member in the barony. Tell them they are to make for Castle Talon for the first Fireday of next month. Tell them their baron calls upon them. Tell them that we are at war."

News arrived in Zorgas via an unusual method – a raven. It seemed as though sending a soul was too dangerous a task to be undertaken now at Castle Talon.

The pale king read the attached scroll by the white, shifting light of the wraiths that circled slowly about the hall's rotting rafters. The words sent icy, bitter anger coursing through him.

He took a moment to control his temper, reread what had been sent, then snatched down one of the wraiths with a gesture and sent it screaming through the stronghold's night-shrouded depths, searching for the one who could yet make things right.

He should have anticipated this, he thought, chiding himself. Rumors had been spreading for months about the strange actions of the heir to Carthridge. Contacts in Greyhaven claimed he had fallen out of favor with the university after conducting unusual – and apparently successful – rune-related experiments on himself. Seemingly he had even traveled to Nerekhall and had been aligning himself with various petty cults and troublemakers. It certainly wasn't the path the pale king had anticipated for him.

And now this. Word from Castle Talon stating that the boy – now a man – had returned and slain the Latari who had been governing the barony since his father's death. The pale king's servant within the citadel had acted impulsively, had called upon the death cult they had been painstakingly building within the barony to strike. They had failed, and it was mere fortune that, in his righteous fury, the new baron had cut down the wrong person. Now he seemed intent on raising Carthridge from its uneasy slumber. And that the pale king could not allow.

Slow, steady footsteps and the scrape of plate mail announced the arrival of the one he had summoned. A mighty figure entered the drafty hall, the flickering, near-aquatic light of the captive spirits above glimmering over his heavy armor and making his bones gleam. He approached the throne with implacable steps and knelt, metal scraping on stone.

"Arise, my friend," the pale king commanded, looking into the purple balefires that burned in the great reanimate's eye sockets. "Once more I have need of you."

"What is it you command, my lord?" rasped the figure's voice. His fleshless skull did not move as he spoke, the words seeming to creep from the hall's darkest recesses. His name was Ardus Ix'Erebus, and he was the pale king's most trusted lieutenant.

"Matters do not progress as they should in Carthridge," the pale king stated, holding forth the scroll. Ardus took it as he continued. "The old baron's son has assumed his father's mantle and seems far too eager to rule as he should. That cannot be allowed, not if the reports about his attitude toward our goals are to be believed. He has already grown too strong. There is a danger now that he might prove to be a powerful adversary. I want you to raise the border cohort of the Host of Crows."

"The seeding and the binding rites are still being undertaken, lord," Ardus said. "The legion is not yet fully embedded."

"Then accelerate the rites," Waiqar snapped, leaning forward in his throne. "See to it personally. Before Snowmelt is ended, I want Castle Talon sacked and the howling soul of Zachareth Carth brought here before me!"

CHAPTER TWENTY-FOUR

The garret was empty.

Zachareth stood in the middle of it, trying to remember where every book in every untidy stack had lain. There was nothing now. Even the table and lectern had been removed. All that remained were the floorboards, thick with dust, and the rafters, draped with cobwebs.

A powerful sorrow gripped him. Despite all that he had learned, despite the power he now wielded, he felt remorse at the fact that he had left. Had Leanna done all this before Bernard had left for Greyhaven? Zachareth had abandoned him, and he had suffered.

He paced the small space, forced to stoop slightly where once he could walk upright. His footsteps sounded, slow and heavy, on the wooden boards.

The waiting was making him melancholy, he decided. The plan he had been pondering for years was finally in motion, but the first few weeks in particular were going to be painfully slow. The fact that they were vital made it even harder to maintain his calm. He wanted desperately to be active, to ride forth and handle every matter himself, but he knew he could not. For now, he had to bide his time.

There was a knock at the door. For the briefest moment, he was a child again, hoping desperately it wasn't Golfang coming with a summons from his father.

"Enter," he called.

A guard – Melvain, he seemed to remember – poked her head in.

"Apologies for disturbing you, lord," she said, glancing uncertainly around the empty attic. "You have a visitor."

"If it's one of my cousins, tell them–" Zachareth began to say before a familiar voice interrupted him.

"Sadly, I come from much less exalted stock, Baron Carth."

Melvain made way for the man who had followed her up the tower stairs. It was Morrow, smiling and clad in his russet robes. Zachareth felt a stab of annoyance. He dismissed the guard.

"I told you not to come here in person," he said to the runemaster. He had no intention of allowing the leader of Silver Horizon into his new powerbase so easily, and he had even less of a desire to let those he was rallying to his standard know of the runemaster's shadowy assistance.

"Don't worry, I don't intend to stay," Morrow replied, pacing casually past Zachareth to stand by the garret's tiny window. "But there are things I wish to impress that shouldn't be left to letters alone. And besides, I have had no word from you since the Temple of the Four Storms. I wished to know if it was true."

"If what was true?" Zachareth asked. Morrow looked at him, framed by the window's light.

"If Zachareth Carth had returned to Castle Talon upon an arcane steed and cut the Latari sorceress Leanna's head from her shoulders," he said. "That's the story that has spread around Greyhaven, anyway."

"Leanna is dead," Zachareth said bluntly.

"And the great and the good of Carthridge have been ordered to assemble here to swear their oaths of allegiance to Baron Zachareth," Morrow surmised, looking once more out the window. "What I find strange is the large number of merchants who seem to have taken an interest in your barony's politics. Are you demanding oaths from them too?"

"They are here to bid," Zachareth said.

"On what?"

"Say what you came here to say, Morrow. I am a busy man."

Morrow looked as though he was going to point out that he'd found Zachareth alone in an empty room but wisely thought better of it. Zachareth had deliberately avoided contacting him since raising Back-breaker. He was already deeply enough indebted to Silver Horizon without inviting them into what he hoped would form the inner circle of his rule. He didn't wholly trust Morrow, and he had decided to view the organization as a problem to be solved. It was not, however, one he intended to deal with just yet. There were more pressing matters.

"Did you find incontrovertible proof that Leanna was in league with the undead?" Morrow asked directly.

"Yes," Zachareth replied. "I searched her chambers as you suggested before I left the Temple of the Four Storms. She had a necromantic tome and more besides. Scrolls, etchings, unclean markings."

"And it has all since been destroyed?"

"Of course," Zachareth said, looking at him sharply, trying to gauge if there was an insinuation in his voice.

"It would be remiss of me if I did not make sure," Morrow said. "I've told you before, Silver Horizon exists to help combat the spread of undeath. It's heartening news that

Leanna was so overconfident in displaying her loyalties and likewise that there was a worthy basis for her death. That will not cause an issue when the other barons ratify your rule."

"Right now the attitudes of the other barons are the least of my concerns," Zachareth said.

"Even when it comes to Cailn and Rhynn?"

"Cailn has already sent word congratulating me on my ascension and have pledged military aid."

"And Baron Greigory?"

"You are not part of my council, Morrow," Zachareth said. "If that is the price of your assistance then so be it, but you do not have a home at Castle Talon yet. We will discuss it in the future."

"Do not fear, I did not ride north to remind you of your debt to us, baron," Morrow said. "I came to advise you regarding Leanna, though that is already dealt with. I came also to remind you of the Key."

It took Zachareth a moment to realize what the runemaster meant.

"You still have it?" Morrow asked.

"I do," Zachareth admitted. He'd locked the Black Key at the bottom of his trunk in his newly reacquired bedchamber above the great hall. He was still afraid of the potential of its corrosive influence, but in the month since Morrow had first left it with him his outright disgust had faded somewhat. He had sensed no overt evil about it. In fact, in the brief moments he had grasped it in his palm he had felt no trace of magical potential at all. That in itself left him with lingering doubts.

"You are preparing for war, and that is well, for it is surely coming," Morrow said. "From what I have seen and from what I sense, you are ready to go to the lengths required to defeat the approaching darkness. In doing so, do not neglect the Black Key."

"You haven't truly told me what its purpose is," Zachareth said. "I do not even know how to manipulate it."

"When the time comes, you will know," Morrow said.

"You speak as though it's inevitable."

"I am facing reality, Zachareth. This fight will be a desperate one. I am offering all the help I can."

Zachareth thought for a moment, wondering why Morrow was so eager to remind him of the runestone's importance.

"You said it summons spirits from another reality. Not the Ynfernael, though."

"No, the Black Plane of the Aenlong."

"And what do these spirits do?"

"They will destroy your enemies."

"That makes them dangerous. Spirits demand a boon in return. What will they want of me?"

"Of you, nothing," Morrow said, his smile for once nowhere to be seen. "I do not deny it is a weapon of last resort, but it is a weapon all the same. When it seems all else is lost, do not hesitate."

Zachareth still did not like Morrow's suggestions, his apparent certainty that the Black Key would be used at some point. It seemed clear that if he did unleash whatever arcane powers slumbered within, things would not be the same again after. And if he wasn't to pay the price, then who would?

"I will keep it in mind," he told Morrow. The runemaster nodded.

"Then, with your permission, I will go to the castle kitchens and take lunch, then be on my way. I'm sure you don't want to have an unknown sorcerer present in the castle when your nobles assemble. I have no wish to undermine you."

"If matters go well here and in the north, I will write to you before the last Runeday," Zachareth said.

"And if they do not?"

"Then you have a choice. Flee further south or prepare Greyhaven for siege. The dead are coming."

The snow had settled, deep and firm, by the time the last of Carthridge's nobility arrived at Castle Talon. Zachareth assembled them in the great hall that evening. The hearth had been lit, though it was not blazing. A chill pervaded the hall, accompanied by shadows that seemed to prowl beneath the tapestries and hang heavy and flickering about the rafters.

The tables and chairs had been laid out for a banquet, but there was little mirth evident among the guests as they arrived and took their seats. The famous Carth silverware was nowhere to be seen – instead the spaces were set with simple wooden bowls and spoons, horn cups, and dull, common knives. There were no candles to add luster to the scene. A sense of nervousness and uncertainty pervaded the room.

Zachareth could sense it. He realized, to his own private surprise, that he was enjoying himself. Nobody but he knew what to expect. That was a new form of power he had not properly experienced before.

He stood and cleared his throat for silence. He alone occupied the high table upon its wooden dais. The only other presence was Golfang, standing fully armored just behind and to the right of his throne. All eyes were on him as he spoke.

"Welcome, my friends and family," Zachareth said, his lone voice filling the hall. "Cousins, uncles, and aunts, and those nobles bound by loyalty to House Carth if not yet by blood. It is good to see you all once again in this hall, even if the times are not as auspicious as we all might like."

There were a few nods, but most of the hall's visitors were still guarded. Zachareth could understand why. Where had any of them been when Leanna had reigned from Castle Talon? None had sought Zachareth out while he had sheltered at Rhynn, and none had publicly challenged Carthridge's usurpation. Here they all were, though, friends and family indeed. Would any of them speak against him now?

"You came here doubtless anticipating a feast," he said. "Dressed in your finery and looking forward to venison and soft cheeses, duck eggs and fresh greens. But we have none of that here."

He smacked his palm on the table twice. Servants began to enter, carrying wooden boards bearing the evening's meal. Muttering broke out around the tables as it became clear just what was being served up.

"Coarse porridge, thin gruel, and gritbread," Zachareth called over the mounting dismay, quietly relishing the looks of shock and outrage spreading around the hall. "That is all the Baron of Carthridge, and likewise his august guests, will eat now, at least for the time being."

"Why?" Marchant, Zachareth's uncle, called out from one of the tables, his face dark with indignation. "Do you seek to mock us, lord?"

"Not at all, dear uncle," Zachareth replied brusquely, waving a hand in Marchant's direction. "I merely seek to educate you regarding the realities we now face. I cannot afford fine foods, and soon, neither will you. As for the silverware, I sold it to a merchant from Tamalir a week ago. He paid a handsome fee."

Several of the ladies present gasped.

"How could you do such a thing?" Marchant exclaimed, outright anger overtaking his indignation. "That plate was priceless. It has belonged to our family for five generations!"

"Six generations now," Zachareth corrected him. "And priceless is much akin to worthless. I have put the money to the best possible use."

He smacked his palm against the table again. All heads in the hall turned as two figures entered, walking with the swagger of born killers. One was a human man, rangy, with a lean, dangerous face and pale eyes. The other was an orc woman, tall in stature and broad-shouldered. Both bore a patina of arms and armor – the man had a longsword strapped across his back and wore a hauberk and leather vambraces with a ratty fur mantle about his shoulders. The woman had a chainmail jerkin that reached below her knees and carried a spear in one fist with long knives crossed over her waist. Both wore long braids down their backs, interwoven with white feathers tipped with red.

There were more gasps as the dangerous-looking pair strode down the hall's central aisle and took the two empty seats at the high table to Zachareth's left.

"These are my guests, Amit and Drenga," Zachareth said, looking from one shocked face to another, daring any of them to hold his gaze for longer than a moment. "They are the commanders of the mercenary war party known as the Red Spears. They are in my pay and have sworn oaths of loyalty until next Greentide."

"This is what the Carth silver has bought?" Marchant demanded. "A group of vagabonds who will take their leave in a few months?"

"Fortunately for you, uncle, the Red Spears are far more effective than mere vagabonds,'" Zachareth said, trying to keep his composure in the face of Marchant's obtuseness. "Their presence is necessary, largely because none of you are capable of raising your own retinues."

There were protests at that, but Zachareth ignored them.

"I do not blame most of you," he said. "Carthridge has suffered years of misrule. Your coffers are empty. I know this. That is why I am going to fill them. And for that, I need the likes of Amit and Drenga. Soon I march with them for the Carthmounts and Maxwell's Mine."

Voices rose in surprise and protest. Zachareth allowed them to wash over him before glancing briefly at Golfang.

"Silence!" the captain of the guard roared. His titanic voice brought an immediate, shocked stillness to the hall. Zachareth smiled at the assembly, but his tone remained stern. He had not summoned any of them to debate his course of action. He merely intended to inform them.

"The silver mines of the Carthmounts have yielded not an ounce of wealth for this barony for years now. They languish under the grip of petty bandits. I am going there, and I am going to show them Carthridge will no longer tolerate their presence. After that, the mines will yield their wealth once more. And when they do, we will raise the greatest host Carthridge has seen for generations."

"And to what purpose?" Marchant dared demand.

"Have I imagined the dead walking abroad within our borders?" Zachareth replied, his voice taking on a sharper edge. He was tired of Marchant's reticence. "Do you think the flight of the common folk, the repeated failures of the harvests, and the dark omens that stalk the norths of Terrinoth are mere exaggerations and fireside stories? Do any here not double-check that the doors to their chambers are bolted at night?"

Their silence was answer enough. Zachareth looked at Marchant as he spoke.

"The dead are coming for us all, uncle. I am going to meet them, but if you do not have the stomach for that, the courage for it, then you will not sup at my table. You are no longer welcome at Castle Talon."

Marchant looked outraged, but as he cast around for support none would meet his eye. He began to realize that he had made a mistake, but it seemed his pride was stronger than his reason. He stood slowly, along with his wife, the scrape of their chairs across the flagstones painfully loud.

"I will not forget this," he said before turning and striding out.

"I hope no one here does," Zachareth said, glaring down the hall as the doors slammed behind him. "Does anyone else wish to join him?"

It seemed that no one did. Zachareth took a slow, quiet breath, ordering his mind as he took in the fact that his gamble was working. He certainly had their attention.

"You have chosen to stay, and that is well," he said, moderating his tone. "For if we are to survive what is coming, I will have need of all of you. Carthridge requires leadership and not from me alone."

He gestured at one of his cousins, seated near the back of the hall.

"Aldren, am I not right in saying that despite the hardships of recent times, you continue to afford improvements to your holdings?"

"I suppose, lord," Aldren answered slowly, clearly fearing that he was about to be chastised.

"My advisors speak of your prudence and skill with coin," Zachareth said. "From henceforth, I am making you treasurer to this barony. You will be responsible for setting up and auditing taxation and income across Carthridge as a central authority. I will no longer leave it to a few petty scribes."

"Thank you, lord," Aldren said, appearing too shocked to give a more comprehensive answer. Zachareth looked across at the other table.

"Uncle Welmark and Lady Gwendolyn," he said, identifying two of the older nobles present. "If memory serves, you were the last among us to lead a sizable host in defense of this barony when you routed the beastmen that had been raiding along the Pilgrim's Trail. You are the most experienced warriors Carthridge has at its disposal."

"That may well be true, lord," Lady Gwendolyn answered guardedly.

"That being the case, I am appointing you to oversee the muster that I will be calling up next month," Zachareth said. "It will be your duty to ensure that each noble provides a sizable retinue and that they are properly equipped. Once the muster is assembled in full, you will see them trained and ready for battle. You may appoint captains and logisticians at your own discretion. Now, where is cousin Selcarth?"

"Here, lord," Lady Selcarth said from close to the hearth, her willingness to call attention to herself giving Zachareth some hope that what he was saying was meeting the right response.

"I'm afraid I must ask much of you, my lady," he said as he looked at her past the other guests. "You have many weeks of traveling ahead. The rest of Terrinoth must know what is happening here in the north. Messages have been sent, but I believe the personal presence of a Carth would help to focus attention. You have always been an able speaker and a skilled negotiator. I would ask that you put those talents to their best use in service to the barony. Ride to each of the strongholds of Terrinoth in turn, tell them that the dead are on the march and ask them to send aid. Our survival may well depend on you."

"I will do so with pride, lord," Lady Selcarth said, her expression fierce as she took in the size of the task he was giving her.

"I have more roles for many of you, each vital in its own way," Zachareth said, addressing the hall more generally. "Those who I have spoken to should meet with me tomorrow morning, and I will give them more specifics. I was not exaggerating when I said that all will have to play their part. It has been far too long since we as a family, as the rulers of a barony, acted together in concert. When we finally do, I believe we will achieve the greatness we all know Carthridge is capable of. We will not only survive the coming night. We will flourish with the dawn."

"Well said, Baron Zachareth," Aldren called out. There was a surge of agreement, and the banging of hands against tables, ringing about the rafters.

"Now, let us eat before this humble fare gets any colder," Zachareth said, forcing himself not to dwell on the burning sense of triumph he felt, the renewal of his hope and determination. "This may be the last night we all spend under one roof for a very long time."

CHAPTER TWENTY-FIVE

"Do you think they'll surrender?" Amit asked, peering down the craggy slope toward the yawning bore of the mine.

"I hope so," Zachareth said. He felt Amit look at him.

"Don't want a bloodbath on your conscience?" the lean mercenary captain asked. Zachareth didn't respond.

"Why not?" Amit pressed. "You've paid us the first portion of coin. You're within your rights to demand we go down there and put every last one of them to the sword, regardless of how many of us die to their fortifications and their traps."

"Would you obey if I gave such an order?" Zachareth asked, turning to meet Amit's eyes. The man smirked as dangerous and unfriendly as any of his other expressions.

"You doubt our professionalism."

"On the contrary," Zachareth said, looking back toward the mine. "I intend to test it to its limit."

"That sounds suitably ominous," said Drenga from Zachareth's other side. In the five days since marching from Castle Talon with the Red Spears, he'd found himself growing fond of the pair. They were hard-edged and open. Between them, they were just about able to muster a sense of humor as well. After feeling as though, as their employer, he should maintain a degree of reserve, he had quickly found himself warming himself each night by their campfire and listening to the stories they told of the war party's adventures. From raids across the Ru Steppes to ambushes in the Aymhelin, it certainly seemed as though he had spent his money well by hiring them.

The mercenary band as a whole were as fearsome seeming as their leaders. Most were humans, but there were a few orcs, dwarfs, and a single, silent elf. They were as ragged, lean and hungry looking as a pack of stray hounds, and they made Zachareth feel welcome. At first, he'd doubted the sincerity of their comradeship, but on the second night, Drenga had allayed his self-doubts.

"You came with us without your fancy guards," she'd said. "Just you and us. So you trust our oaths. Apart from that, your sword looks keen, and Amit tells me those are runemarks on your arms. You're young, and you could use a bit more meat on your bones, but you've got the makings of a warrior. That's what we respect."

Zachareth had done his best not to let on how much the words from the orc woman meant. The past month had been a whirlwind. Between summoning the nobles and acquainting himself with the day-to-day expectations of his role, he had hardly had time to even consider the plan he'd put into motion. Already he felt the pressure that had slowly worn down his father over the years. It didn't matter that he'd ordered Carthridge onto a war footing, peasants still needed boundary disputes resolved, the winter taxes and highway tithes needed to be properly accounted for, and merchants needed to be pursued for their trade fees. In the midst of it all, Zachareth had found himself forced to maintain a stern, silent front, the austerity of leadership. He missed the life he had slipped into in Greyhaven where he'd been just another student, untroubled by airs and reputation, with no requirement to make decisions that affected lives day in and day out.

In that sense, it was a relief to depart from Castle Talon. He had certainly never had personal dealings with a band of war-scarred, mismatched rogues like the Red Spears. It was a welcome change to the petty concerns of farmers or the guarded disdain of nobles.

"Movement," Amit said, pointing to the northern side of the vertical mine shaft. Zachareth spotted what the mercenary had already seen. A figure had climbed to the surface and stepped out onto the rocky slope. Given the distance, it was difficult to be sure, but it looked like a woman, and she appeared to be unarmed.

"Seems they want to talk," Zachareth said. "That's a start."

He unbuckled Razorsong from around his waist and handed the sword, complete with scabbard and belt, to Drenga.

"Don't even think about going anywhere with it," he said.

"Don't worry," the orc said. "I don't fancy having you hound me to the ends of Mennera if I did. Besides, swords are stupid weapons. A spear is both cheaper and more effective."

Zachareth refused to rise to the bait. It seemed that after a pause to look up at the mercenary war party lining the cliffs overlooking the bore, the lone figure had started to trudge around toward an unoccupied stony bluff overhanging the mine's eastern side.

That was the agreed sign. The Red Spears had arrived in the vicinity of Maxwell's Mine that morning. Zachareth had half expected the bandits controlling it to resist their approach in the narrow valleys and foothills that wended their way to the roots of the Carthmounts. It seemed they had grown overconfident in their control of the mountains, though. The Red Spears had marched hard and fast, and by the time the bandits' idle lookouts had spotted them, all they could do was retreat to the mine itself, a great, vertical shaft that plunged like a spear wound into the flank of one of the jagged mountaintops.

Amit had gone to the edge of the mine and called down, telling those sheltering within that if they wished to parley for their lives, they should send someone to the rocky bluffs overlooking the shaft, unarmed. They had been waiting an hour, but now it seemed as though the thieves had finally chosen their leader.

"Wait here, and do nothing, no matter what you see," Zachareth told Drenga and Amit. The former gave him a tusked smile.

"Our favorite way of earning our pay," she said. Amit let out a short yap of laughter.

Unarmed, Zachareth began to ascend the slope, circling up and around toward the bluffs to meet with the bandit's emissary. Despite being alone, he felt confident and strong. It was good to be up among the Carthmounts. He had only been to the mountain range once, as a small child, when Zelmar had still cared enough to bother to inspect the mines in person. He remembered little besides snow flurries and soaring, saw-toothed peaks.

He was glad to find that age and experience hadn't dulled the sight of them. If anything, they seemed even more grand and imposing, rows of white-capped sentinels that ranked away from him into the blue distance. The air was cold and clear, and if he paused and looked southeast, he could pick up the far-off glimmer of Korrina's Tears, leading to a tiny blotch that represented Greyhaven's sprawl.

The bandit had reached the crest of the crags, mounting its summit.

Zachareth went slowly. His lungs and legs were starting to burn from the ascent, and he didn't want to arrive before her panting and sweating. Not that it would make a difference to what was about to happen. He reached the foot of the bluffs but didn't attempt to climb the last dozen yards to the mound of rock the bandit had occupied.

"I am Zachareth," he told her.

"I am Klava," the woman replied. She was wearing a long, battered-looking leather hauberk, and her black hair, shot through with white, was piled high on her crown. She had a scar disfiguring her left cheek. Zachareth put her at about forty years of age. She certainly had the appearance of one who knew how to lead.

"You are the master of the bandits in these hills?" he asked her.

"Bandits we may be, but we have no masters," Klava responded. "I was chosen to speak with you."

"Then I have a simple message for you," Zachareth said. "You will leave the mine immediately, go from this barony, and not return."

"And what do we get for doing so?" Klava asked.

"Nothing."

"That's not how negotiations work."

Zachareth offered her a smile as cold as the deep snows that lay piled about.

"I'm not negotiating."

A thought and motion followed. It wasn't his own. Klava

cried out, first in surprise, then in fear as the rocks she was standing atop shifted. She tried to jump down, but a great, unyielding fist wrapped around her throat, holding her fast and cutting off her horror.

Back-breaker rose up from where Zachareth had ordered it to conceal itself, shaking its elemental stone body free of the rocks and snow. Klava kicked her legs and clawed uselessly at its grip, her eyes wide with fear.

"You should have just gone," Zachareth told her, feeling nothing but dispassion. "You stole from my father, and you have been stealing from me. In your arrogance, you thought Carthridge would never challenge you. Well, Carthridge is here now."

He reached out with his mind once more, imprinting it upon Back-breaker's blank consciousness.

"Send her back to her people," he told the animus.

The thing's blocklike head grated as it turned. Then, with a crunch, it rose up on its haunches, twisted its broad shoulders, and launched Klava into the air. Finally released, she screamed as she arced out over the edge of the bluffs and down toward the gaping pit of the mine. She just missed its edge, plummeting down out of sight, all the way into its depths. Her scream faded to nothing, lost to the cold mountain wind.

"Good shot," Zachareth told Back-breaker, the great beast crunching in an ungainly fashion down to his side.

That would send a clearer message than any negotiation ever could.

The rest of the bandits surrendered. They traipsed from the mine's tunnels and were seized and disarmed by the

Red Spears, who descended to greet them. Amit led the mercenaries while Drenga stayed with Zachareth on the bluffs overlooking the scene.

"Well, that could have gone much worse," the orc said as they watched the last of the prisoners being manhandled up into the cold sunlight. "I must remember that trick next time I find myself in ownership of an animus."

Back-breaker made a grating sound. Zachareth merely grunted.

"I want you to kill them all," he told Drenga. To her credit, the orc didn't look surprised at the instruction.

"Didn't you promise them their lives if they came up without a fight?" she asked.

"Would it trouble you if I had?" Zachareth asked.

"Not especially," Drenga admitted. "Though it can be bad for business if the Red Spears gain a reputation as oath breakers."

"No oaths were made," Zachareth said. "I want to send a message. There are other bandits in these mountains."

"They may resist all the harder if they think you're not taking prisoners," Drenga pointed out.

"Or they'll leave while they still can," Zachareth replied. "They are thieves here seeking easy profit. I do not think they will risk their lives for it."

"Very well. I'll tell Amit," Drenga said and began to descend the slope.

Zachareth considered what he'd just ordered. He was glad to realize it gave him no pleasure. There was an intoxicating element to the power he now wielded, though. He tried to reassure himself that he wasn't acting on impulse. Lives would be saved in the long run. Besides, if the next part of the plan was to be put into action, he'd need to be certain of the loyalty of the Red Spears and confident that they knew he wasn't to be trifled with.

The next stage was about to begin.

Five days passed. The Red Spears remained encamped in Maxwell's Mine, occupying the dugouts the bandits had once inhabited. Zachareth permitted the wealth they had been amassing to be distributed among the mercenaries, making each of them wealthy overnight. Amit and Drenga wanted to know why they didn't move on to the other, smaller workings up amongst the central peaks, but Zachareth refused to elaborate on their inaction.

On the fifth day, Gemil arrived. He greeted Zachareth gruffly, then descended into the mine while the baron waited with Amit and Drenga.

"You want to find out if it's still feasible?" Amit asked as they stood at the opening to the primary shaft, cloaks and pelts drawn close against the chill that pervaded the dank, dark corridors.

"I am," Zachareth confirmed. He had sent word to Greyhaven before setting out from Castle Talon. He had feared, given the disgrace of his departure from the university, that he wouldn't be able to tempt Gemil away from the lecture halls. He had written first to Morrow, who had confirmed that the grizzled Dunwarr had indeed once been a master prospector and that he might be open to the possibility of a part-time return to the bowels of Mennera. Academia, it seemed, had grown stale for the dwarf.

After what felt like an age, Gemil returned, clambering stoutly up out of the main shaft.

"Seems you're right," he said, addressing Zachareth as

though he was still one of his wayward pupils and didn't have the very power of a runestone seared into his skin. "At least one of the seams is still producing. It'll take time to be certain about how much is left, but going on instinct, I'd say you've got a few years of prospecting ahead of you."

"Dunwarr instincts are why I asked you here," Zachareth said. "And also why I'd like you to remain, at least for a while, and oversee operations. I need this mine to become productive fast. I'm willing to pay whatever price you care to set."

"We'll see about that," Gemil said. "But before you get carried away, have you considered the fact that, fine a miner as I am, I can't run this place with just my own two hands. There are a few good lads I know who can be here at short notice, but they'd be my overseers and engineers. Who's going to be doing the grubbing?"

"Two of them are standing right here," Zachareth said. He tried not to feel too much amusement as he watched Amit and Drenga's expressions turn from confusion to anger.

"The Red Spears don't grub," Amit started to say.

"We've already established that the Red Spears will do whatever I tell them to for the duration of their oaths," Zachareth said, heading off the protests he knew were coming. "I needed warriors. Now I need miners. You need only to be able to swing a pick. Gemil will direct everything else."

"This is an insult," Drenga said, fire in her eyes. "A mercenary's oath does not mean you can simply enslave us."

"It is not meant as an insult," Zachareth replied. "It is simply the reality we all must face. We need this mine to resume supplying silver to the barony immediately. In Gemil, we have the expertise, but until workers can be found, we need the raw muscle. Red Spear can provide that. You can also protect the mine if the other bandit groups decide against leaving the Carthmounts after all. And don't worry, forces from Rhynn are already on the way to liberate the other works."

"You should have mentioned this when you first hired us," Amit said angrily.

"The rest of the party won't be happy," Drenga added. Zachareth held his hands up in a placatory gesture.

"I will of course be increasing your final payment, and I will also allow you to keep a sum of the silver you extract. A fifth sounds more than generous, wouldn't you say? That would make you all wealthy. And it will only be for a month until suitable laborers can be found."

"You're paying us to protect and work your mine," Amit said. "Isn't that what the bandits were doing initially? Didn't seem to work out too well in the long run."

"They took advantage of Zelmar," Zachareth said. "But I am not him. You wouldn't take advantage of me, would you, Amit?"

Now the deaths of the bandit prisoners truly served a purpose. He had known he would have to ask this of the Red Spears. He wanted there to be no doubt about his power, his resolve, or what he would do to those who resisted him.

"You should be thanking me," he told them. "Carthridge is at war. The Mistlands are stirring, and I've just given you a duty that puts you at the other end of the barony while making you all rich. In exchange, you just have to swap your swords and spears for picks and shovels for a month."

"We need to discuss this," Drenga said, exchanging a look with Amit.

"Of course," Zachareth said. "Take your time."

"You trust them?" Gemil asked bluntly after the pair had withdrawn from the shaft entrance.

"I trust them to know what awaits them should they betray me," Zachareth said. "I will send for two guards from Castle Talon to act as your permanent escort, should you need them."

Gemil scoffed. "I've had worse jobs and more reluctant students than this rabble, boy. I'll be fine."

"With them, how long until you have your first catch?"

"Everything is still in place from the last delving operation," Gemil said. "So two weeks for a small portion if I work them hard."

"Then I will return with an escort in two weeks," Zachareth said.

CHAPTER TWENTY-SIX

Mirefield was no more. Skerrif discovered as much as he walked his horse into a bog. At first, he thought he had taken a wrong turn, until the mist lifted enough to see humped shapes just ahead.

He edged his mount on, peering through the fog, until he realized what he was looking at.

Houses. It was Mirefield, the same humble village he had encountered with Zachareth the last time he had ridden to the borders of the Thirteenth Barony before leaving for Greyhaven.

The Mistlands had expanded since then. The filthy swamp had crept into the abandoned village, festering beneath the ever-present fog. Now the walls were half-submerged, thatched roofs sloping at strange angles or completely collapsed as the homesteads and barns sank into the ooze.

One day, Skerrif realized, there would be no evidence that Mirefield had ever even existed.

The fear that had been plaguing him since leaving Castle Talon redoubled. Why had he come here? The baron had called for volunteers to ride north and east to establish a proper series of watches over the border. Impulsively – like a fool – he had stepped forward.

He felt as though he had never been the same since the ambush on Captain Travas's host and the subsequent journey to Mirefield with the baron's son. He rarely slept well. Memories of dancing, twitching bones never seemed to leave him. A part of him had felt that if he faced them again, if he sought them out and overcame their horror, he would know peace.

He was regretting that belief as he rode on past the old, collapsing remnants of the village. He wanted to turn, to go back, but he knew he couldn't. He had a duty now to set foot in the Mistlands proper and find out what foulness was brewing there. The baron was counting on all the outriders he had sent forth. When the dead marched, he had to know.

"Kellos preserve me," he murmured as he pressed on. The mist parted enough for him to get a glimpse of the landmark he'd been aiming for, the hillock that lay beyond Mirefield. That, at least, hadn't collapsed or slipped into the bog.

He rode up it, patting his mount's neck in encouragement, trying to seem confident for her. The mist seemed to prowl and creep around them like a predator stalking them. His breath billowed in the cold, seemingly intent on adding to the fog. It was painfully quiet, only the soft thump of hooves against the turf of the slope helping convince Skerrif that he still existed, that there was still a world beyond the few dozen yards he could see.

The crest appeared suddenly. Beyond it was a sea of coiling, twisting gray. He halted, leaning low in the saddle and murmuring to his mare. The temptation was to go no further, to tell himself he had done his duty now and ride for home.

Somewhere down there were the dead, in amongst the filth, waiting for him.

But he needed to see them. He was certain that if he went back now, his terrors would only multiply. As he tried to find the courage to go a little farther, a sudden swooshing sound close to his head made him jump. He looked around, startled, just in time to see a black shape disappearing into the mist overhead. As it went, it let out an abrasive cawing sound before the nothingness swallowed it up.

Skerrif laughed as he realized he'd been surprised by a crow. Some baron's guard he was, being caught out by a lone avian.

He urged his mount down from the mound to the edge of the bog. Unlike last time, the fog showed no sign of lifting, but as he went, he heard a sound above the motions of the horse. More cawing. He caught flickers of movement above, a flock of crows circling through the miasma.

The foreboding he'd felt earlier gripped him once again. It only grew worse when he realized there was more than a mere flock of crows in the mist.

He could see figures standing knee-deep in the muck. They were perfectly still, but there was no mistaking their gaunt, ragged shapes. The dead had arisen.

Skerrif came to a halt, a chill running down his spine as he looked out over the standing corpses. They were arrayed in ranks and files, the precision almost as eerie as their complete stillness and silence.

Compulsively, Skerrif snatched the Hand of Kellos amulet he wore around his neck over his breastplate. A horrifying curiosity clashed with the fear and revulsion he felt at the motionless host before him. Were they aware of him? How far into the mist did their files extend? Why weren't they reacting to his presence?

His mount wouldn't step any further into the marsh, but Skerrif found himself unable to turn back. He dismounted with a splash and tied his reins to the bent boughs of a long-dead tree, standing crooked near the foot of the mound. Then, damning his own foolishness, he stepped out into the mire.

The crows were still calling. The bog popped and oozed quietly around him. It was bitterly cold. The dead stood just ahead, as unresponsive as if they'd been laid out for burial. He waded slowly toward them, struggling in the watery mud, starting to sweat into his leathers. Why in the name of all that was good and sacred was he doing this? It was because he had to confront them, he decided. He needed to see one of them up close, look into its rancid sockets, meet it without turning back at the first opportunity.

"Still, it's damned stupid," he panted under his breath, finding a small patch of semihard ground that he used to close the last dozen yards to the front rank of the resurrected host.

The thing directly ahead of him might once have been one of the Mirefield villagers, though it was now impossible to be sure. It was caked from skull to boot in the mud of the Mistlands. Skerrif realized that it was still dripping from its body, slow and heavy, as though it had only recently adopted the rigid stance it now held. Besides the muck and some rotting scraps of indecipherable clothing, it was all bones. Its skull was exposed, the jaw hanging slack at a slight angle. There was nothing in its eyes, no balefire, just a rancid slurry of muck and decayed flesh. Those on either side of it and behind weren't much different, all of them filthy and rotten. They stank.

"Not so fearsome," Skerrif whispered. He was almost close

enough to touch the nearest when he caught sight of one of the crows circling overhead diving down to alight on the corpse's shoulder. It cawed indignantly as it looked at Skerrif with beady black eyes, then clacked its wicked beak against the side of the thing's skull, pecking at it.

Skerrif was almost amused by the creature's fearlessness, but a sickly crunch cut his nervous mirth short. The corpse in front had just clenched its slack jaw and turned its head so it was looking directly at him.

Skerrif froze. It wasn't just the one before him that had moved. All of those he could see, left, right, and beyond, had turned their decomposing heads to face him. None were looking directly ahead anymore.

"Great Kellos," Skerrif stammered, stumbling back. None of the figures moved any further. None of them made a sound. The crow ruffled its feathers and let out its rasping cry.

You're being a fool, Skerrif told himself, trying to find the courage to unfreeze his limbs. Finally, he managed to turn himself around.

Panting and stumbling in the mud, with the grating laughter of the crow flock ringing in his ears, Skerrif ran for his life.

Zachareth looked back up from the map, his voice tense.

"You're absolutely certain?"

"Yes, lord," Skerrif replied. The baronial guardsman had returned to Castle Talon less than an hour earlier, still befouled with the dirt of the Mistlands and obviously still struggling with what he had encountered. Even days later, the fear was still in his eyes. He'd reported immediately to Zachareth, who in turn had ordered a meeting with Welmark, Gwendolyn, and Golfang in the garret.

Zachareth had converted it into his permanent council chamber. While formal matters were conducted in the great hall, when he had to speak privately with trusted advisors or nobles, he brought them to the top of the north tower. A table and chairs had been set in the center of the small room, and the dust and cobwebs cleared away.

Zachareth had spread his maps of Carthridge across the table and told Skerrif to make sure the village he had visited was Mirefield.

"It was, lord," Skerrif repeated. "I recognized it. It was the place we went to together, the place where you say the undead were turned back in battle once before. They remain there still."

"How many?"

"I could not be sure because of the mist," Skerrif admitted, looking apologetic. "But there were certainly many. Hundreds at least."

Zachareth had no doubt he was telling the truth. He had the same look of fierce determination Zachareth himself had felt when he had recognized the threat the Mistlands posed. The dead were no longer just stirring. They were awake. The knowledge gave Zachareth a sense of certainty. All he had been doing so far was justified. He had made the right decisions, and now he had to stand firm and continue to make them.

"Mirefield makes sense as a staging point for them," Welmark said, drawing one of the maps across the table and tapping it. "They could strike south, cut the barony in half, even lay siege to Greyhaven. Alternatively, if they move west and secure a crossing over the Korrina they could be at these gates in a week."

"Three or four days," Zachareth corrected. "Once they

march, they won't need to stop. Nor do they need a crossing to pass Korrina's Tears."

"They hold the strategic advantage," Gwendolyn mused. "We're going to have to march to meet them, aren't we?"

The question hung heavy in the cold air. Zachareth had been thinking the same since Skerrif had delivered his report. If they didn't face them at Mirefield, the dead could choose their target, and by the time the host mustering at Castle Talon reacted, it would likely be too late to intercept them.

A month and a half had passed since the liberation of Maxwell's Mine. Zachareth had been satisfied with its productivity, and the sight of its silver traveling abroad in the barony had been a huge relief. It had helped to bolster belief in his cause as well. Assuming control of the barony was one thing, but now there were tangible results for others to put their belief in. And few results garnered stronger belief than silver.

The host had been raised. The Silver Banner now flew from the highest tower of Castle Talon, while below, day by day, more retinues arrived. The Tullens, the Blacktalons, the Rencarths and more had brought over a hundred soldiers-at-arms each, accompanied by hundreds more levy spearmen and archers. The camp, sprung up around the base of the castle crag, had been growing for the past week. Now, however, it seemed they could wait for it to grow no longer.

"The snows won't melt for two more weeks at least," Welmark said. "More likely a month."

"Supplies won't be an issue if we go in the next day or two," Zachareth pointed out. "We can engage and destroy the main body of Waiqar's host before we run out of hardtack and salted meat."

"What if the weather worsens?" Welmark pointed out. "We might become stuck on the east bank of the Korrina in a blizzard."

"As I said, that won't stop the dead when they march," Zachareth said. "We have to strike before they do. It's something we must risk."

He noted that none of them had questioned his mention of Waiqar. That in itself was heartening. He no longer felt like a fool when he spoke of the dreaded necromancer. There was an acceptance of the threat they now faced – he believed many had harbored fears about Waiqar before him. He had simply been the first one bold, or arrogant, enough to speak of the danger publicly. He had been right all along. That reassured him that the path he was choosing was the correct one. He had been right before, and he now trusted himself to be right again.

"How soon can we break camp?" he asked Golfang.

"Tomorrow if the instructions are issued before nightfall," the captain of the guard responded without hesitation.

Zachareth was about to tell him to do as much when a faint sound caught his attention. He raised a finger for silence, listening.

The sound reached him again, drifting up languidly through the cold air to the tower's pinnacle. It was a horn, sounding the summons.

Zachareth exchanged a glance with the rest of the room.

"Pray that is what I think it is," he said, moving toward the door and clapping Skerrif on the shoulder on the way past. "You did well to bring us this information. Go and wash, eat and rest."

Skerrif thanked him, but Zachareth was already hurrying down the stairs.

• • •

The camp at the base of the castle rock was a sprawl of canvas and linen tents, cooking pits, latrine rows, and makeshift stables, demarcated by the fluttering heraldic pendants and banners of the different Carthridge nobles. Zachareth hurried through it on foot, giving only passing salutations to those who noticed him. Much of the camp was turning out of their tents and shelters in response to the horn notes still ringing clear through the air.

Zachareth reached the camp's edge, a gaggle of sutlers, merchants, and partially armed and armored levies scrambling to make way for him. He'd already spotted the banner over their heads. It filled him with renewed hope and determination.

A host was marching into the camp. At the front rode two dozen or more horsemen, well armed and armored with a mixture of plate and chain mail. The foremost had a tabard bearing the same device as the one floating from the pennant that streamed overhead. It was the black raven of Cailn.

Zachareth moved to block the procession's route, his hands on his hips. The lead rider, features obscured by his helm, came to a halt and raised a fist to signal the column to do likewise. He dismounted, a squire riding alongside snatching the reins. Once down, he pulled up the pointed snout of his visor.

"You haven't left without me, then?" Mikael demanded with a grin.

Zachareth wrapped his arms around the heir to the Barony of Cailn and gripped him in a ferocious bear hug. He hadn't realized until that very moment just how much his arrival meant. It was an instant of relief amidst the strain that had been steadily building as forces assembled around and before Castle Talon. Just like that, their numbers had almost doubled.

"Easy, or you'll dent my armor," Mikael said, patting Zachareth's back. "All that rune strength. You're like an ox!"

Zachareth released him and stepped back, feeling briefly embarrassed at having given the future baron such a greeting before his retainers.

"I didn't think you were going to arrive in time," he said. "We're marching tomorrow. I've just come from a council of war."

"Have the dead started their invasion?" Mikael asked, his levity vanishing.

"Not yet, but I believe we've discovered where they are marshaling, just beyond a village called Mirefield. We've decided to strike while we're still able. We cannot keep this host together and fed for long in winter. Does Baron Wilem not ride with you?"

"Father is sick," Mikael said apologetically. "A winter ague. I come with his blessing and authority. My little cousin Gilliam is ruling until father recovers or I return."

"I pray he is given both of those eventualities," Zachareth said. "Can your forces march again tomorrow? On foot with a full host, Mirefield is a week's journey."

"We can march," Mikael said, a steely note in his voice. "As long as we can resupply here tonight. Tell me though, has Rhynn joined us?"

Mikael had clearly noted that there were no oaken standards amidst the camp or flying from the ramparts above. Zachareth had been worrying about Greigory's absence, but at least Cailn's arrival would help offset it.

"My last message from Arhynn arrived four days ago," he told Mikael. "Greigory is mustering the host, but he is still contending with the Rhynn council of nobles. They do everything there by vote, and it takes time. Hopefully he is now underway. I have already sent a raven telling him we are marching from Castle Talon and to try to meet us on the road to Mirefield."

"Then we shall have to trust in his speed," Mikael said. "And his hunger for a fight. Speaking of hunger, I'm famished. I hope you've got one of your famous Carthridge porridge and stew feasts prepared for me. You can tell me how you dealt with Leanna while we eat. Rumor has it you cut her head off."

Mikael clapped Zachareth on the back and moved off the track, signaling for his host to carry on and enter the camp. Zachareth caught himself smiling. After weeks of painstaking uncertainty, the road ahead was now clear and firm.

They would march.

CHAPTER TWENTY-SEVEN

Zachareth and the hosts of Carthridge and Cailn found the dead waiting for them just beyond the Bogmound. He experienced a strange thrill, at odds with the impending bloodshed, as he took to the hillock astride Back-breaker and watched while the mist receded.

Skerrif's description had been correct. An undead legion stood arrayed across from the Bogmound in ranks and files beneath another hill. The formation was densest atop the promontory, and as he watched the skeins of fog drift away the breeze picked up and toyed with the array of raggedy pennants and banners, moldering and grave-rotted, that hung above the skeletal host. A great mass of crows took off from amongst them, rising in a cawing flock to circle above the hilltop and its jagged crown of tarnished spears and bared skulls.

"It is truly an army," Mikael said at Zachareth's side, fear in his voice. "May all the gods preserve us."

Zachareth said nothing back. He felt the same fear but still that fierce exhilaration. He realized that Rufus Carth must have witnessed the same sight all those centuries before. This was his destiny, of that much he was certain.

"Cailn will form the vanguard on the right," he said to Mikael, then looked at Gwendolyn at his other side. Despite Welmark's protestations, he had ordered him to remain at Castle Talon with a small garrison force. If the battle went ill, he was to hold Carthridge's seat of power until the bitter end. Lady Gwendolyn had accompanied the main host, and Zachareth had instructed her that she was to take over if he fell.

"My lady, you will take the rearguard on the left," he said. "The central battle will be mine. Prepare your retinues for an immediate attack."

"Attack?" Gwendolyn asked. "Lord, with respect, both sides have the high ground. We would be surrendering our advantage while playing to theirs."

"You are not fighting the beastmen again today, lady," Zachareth said. "These reanimates have likely been standing in formation like this for months if not years. We could be here for weeks waiting for them to attack, and our supplies will last a matter of days. We have to attack them. If we are fortunate, they may not yet be fully animated. We can cut them down before the one who raised them is ready to unleash them. The spells that bind them will not be able to endure a direct assault."

"Has there been any word from Rhynn?" Mikael asked.

"Not since crossing Korrina's Tears," Zachareth said. A rider, muddy and exhausted, had reached the camp with confirmation that Greigory's host was on the march and had diverted to Mirefield, but there had been no further contact. For all Zachareth knew, they could be only hours away, or days. Regardless, he had to press on. He couldn't let their tardiness delay his own plans, or they would be risking total disaster.

"We'll have to dismount," Gwendolyn said grimly, looking

down over the marshland. "Horses will get bogged down too easily. Cavalry will be useless."

"Leave the horses here with the squires," Zachareth said. "When we advance, keep your battle together. Intersperse the soldiers-at-arms with the levies. Go slow, and watch for my signal. Whoever is puppeting these corpses, they stand upon that hill. I'm going to kill them permanently."

"Don't you think they'll be expecting that?" Gwendolyn pointed out, sounding exasperated. "I mean you no insult, lord, but you have never fought in a battle before, much less led a host."

"I have already fought this battle many times," Zachareth responded brusquely, tired of Gwendolyn's caution. "My ancestors were victorious here, and we will be too."

Of course, Rufus Carth had indeed held the Bogmound against the attacks of the undead rather than going on the offensive, but Zachareth wasn't going to admit that. He feared that the necromantic power that sustained the unliving host was growing more and more powerful. They had already had so long to prepare and, unlike a mortal army, they suffered none of the ill effects of campaigning in winter. He was being brash, he knew, but they truly could not wait.

"I will go and raise Cailn's banners," Mikael said. "And watch for your signal."

He held his hand out and grasped Zachareth's, then turned toward his battle.

Zachareth had read that the waiting was the worst part. He hadn't really considered the truth of such a claim until that moment. Everything felt horribly calm and poised, and none more so than the army of reanimates before them. The mist was beginning to creep back in again, reducing the far mound to a vague outline.

He found himself wondering if he should have given some sort of oration to his men. That was what the great leaders in the stories did, wasn't it? As a child, he had memorized Rufus's speech before the battle of the Bogmound. He'd fantasized about refighting that clash. The fact that it was now happening seemed totally surreal. He wondered if he gave the speech now, whether anyone would recognize its origin. He also wondered whether Rufus had actually said the same words recorded by Malrond the Younger. Probably not, he realized.

"What were your thoughts when I first rode up to the gate at Castle Talon when Leanna barred my entry?" he asked Golfang, seeking to distract himself from the strain of waiting. It was a relief to have the stoic captain back at his side. He'd given him the duty of carrying the Silver Banner, a privilege the captain of the guard had tried to reject. Zachareth had insisted.

"I was worried you'd try to break down that gate with your fists," Golfang said, patting Back-breaker's shoulder with his free hand. Zachareth could feel an almost unspoken attachment between the two since they had first encountered each other. It amused him – he hadn't known animus were capable of feeling respect.

"Would you have stopped me if I'd done that?" he pressed. "Would you have killed me?"

"I would have killed anyone that tried to harm you."

"Well, you'll get plenty of opportunity for that today," Zachareth said. He felt suddenly nervous, afraid even. The thrill from before had slowly sloughed off, eroded by the threat of what was about to happen. It still felt unreal.

"Cailn's banners are up, lord," Golfang said quietly. The

captain of the guard was right. The black raven was now fluttering over the mass of Cailn soldiery to the right of the Bogmound, just visible through the fog. They were ready.

Zachareth hesitated for a second, then spoke, forcing himself to be loud and clear.

"Herald, sound the advance!"

"Stay together," Marwand called, shouting over the scraping of armor, the rasping of breath, and the disgusting wet noises made as the host forged through the frigid slurry of the mire.

Skerrif realized he was close to breaking rank and forced himself to catch up with Marwand and the other member of the baronial guard to his right, Mord. It was tough going. Wading through the muck had been difficult the last time, but it seemed nearly impossible now that he was fully armored and at the forefront of a mass of warriors. His limbs were already aching and his lungs burning, and they were barely two hundred paces out beyond the hill.

He strove to keep going, looking down at the marsh more than he did ahead at what awaited them. The dead were where he had seen them before, still waiting, still silent, like some sort of dreadful mirror image of the force now approaching. The fear was almost more than Skerrif could endure, but he forced himself to keep pushing through the mud.

It was bitterly cold. He was shaking. He tried not to think about where he was, what was coming. A voice – Lady Gwendolyn's he thought – rang out. It was indistinct in the drifting fog, but the reactions of those around him were clear enough. The line came to a shuddering, panting halt.

"Are you all right?" Marwand asked, glancing at him and noticing how pale he was. He just managed to nod, jaw clenched.

"Stay strong for the levies," Marwand said, leaning in close. "If they break, we're all dead."

While half of the baronial guard had remained with Zachareth in the central battle, the rest had been dispatched to bolster the retinues with Lady Gwendolyn on the left flank. While the core of her force was built from experienced and well-equipped soldiers, many were little better than commoners with spears, shields, and simple leather hauberks. Some didn't even have helmets. The guards had been interspersed among them to strengthen the line. Right now, despite the press of bodies around him, it didn't seem very strong to Skerrif.

A horn sounded, its notes taken up and repeated to the left and right. There was a ripple of movement, and Skerrif struggled to one side to make way for a file of archers that hurried through from the rear ranks. They began to spread out in front of the paused formation, advancing into range of the undead host.

"Now we'll see just how dead they really are," Mord murmured.

The mixed force of crossbowmen from Castle Talon's garrison and the retinues and archer levies from the barony's towns and villages began to loose their arrows and quarrels, the zipping sound of fletching audible as they whipped away through the mist. Skerrif peered ahead and caught a ripple of small purple lights, followed by the clack and thump of the missiles striking bones and rancid cloth. He realized that every hit was accompanied by a flare of balefire. With the archers in the way, though, it was difficult to make out whether the bodies were actually dropping.

Skerrif didn't have to wait long to discover if the attack would draw a response. There was a long, harsh horn call that seemed to emanate from the mist itself all around them. The cawing of the flock of crows circling the far hillock rose to a fever pitch. Skerrif glanced at Marwand and noted she probably looked just as pale and wide-eyed as he did. Memories of the death of Captain Travas came flooding back. He knew what was about to happen.

One of the crossbowmen ahead of the front line dropped abruptly into the mud, clutching his shoulder. Something was protruding from it – a projectile but no ordinary arrow. The front ranks of Gwendolyn's battle watched in horror as the man screamed and clutched at himself, writhing in the mire. His skin began to slough off, blotches of discoloration spreading across his face as he attempted to drag himself back into the formation, floundering. Those nearest scrambled away from him, risking breaking ranks before the unfortunate went still, sinking turgidly into the mire.

Skerrif could recall all too well the projectiles loosed by the reanimate archers who had ambushed them years before. Their bows had unleashed not arrows, but long, sharpened shards of bone, ensorcelled with foul magics. He had watched as those struck by them began to rot away, their bodies decomposing even as they still lived, becoming festering wrecks in a matter of seconds.

"Kellos be with us all," he muttered as he saw the fog twitched by hundreds of descending shards. They lanced down into the bog or struck home into the archers and crossbowmen, sending men reeling and staggering. Their screams turned quickly to choking as they gagged on their own decomposing throat matter, but they were soon joined by more as a second wave of shards fell.

The archery duel didn't last long. The Carthridge forces

began to give ground beneath the horrifying deluge, first in ones and twos and then in a general flight back toward the reassuring bulk of the main battle.

"Rally behind us," Marwand snarled as they fled past. "Everyone else, hold firm!"

"Shields up," someone else shouted urgently. Skerrif raised his just before he caught the hissing sound of incoming missiles. A heartbeat later and he felt a thudding impact and noticed the wicked tip of a bone shard protruding through the wooden boards just above his forearm. He crouched a little lower and smacked his visor down. He tried not to listen to the screams that rose up as some of the projectiles found flesh.

It felt as though they endured beneath that unnatural, terrible hail for hours. He took another hit to the shield and saw a third splinter plow into the mud around his shins, slowly sinking out of sight. He looked left and right at Marwand and Mord, likewise crouched behind their protection, expressions grim. So the host waited, in the cold and the muck, knowing that those who tried to run were more likely to be hit.

Somehow, it was still preferable to what came next. Skerrif finally noted that the deadly rain seemed to have stopped. He dared lower his shield for a moment and caught the doleful pounding of drums, accompanied by the rattle and scrape of thousands upon thousands of cadavers as they moved in unison.

The skeletal legion had started to advance.

CHAPTER TWENTY-EIGHT

Mikael took the rusting axe head to his shield and swung over-arm with his other hand, bringing his mace crashing down into the pitted helmet of the grinning corpse attempting to carve him open. The bare-toothed leer came apart as the skull shattered, purple fire flaring briefly as the necromantic magics binding the reanimate unraveled and the remains collapsed.

"The heads," the heir to the Barony of Cailn shouted. "Break the heads!"

That seemed to be the only sure way of killing the horrors. A wedge of skeletal warriors had crashed into the Cailn host, marching implacably through the freezing mire until the front ranks collided. Against the advice of his baronial guard, Mikael had insisted on meeting them head-on, his black raven standard at the fore. The first sight of the jerky, walking corpses had filled him with such fear he'd found himself rooted to the spot, but the desperate necessity of action had finally overcome the terror.

Another of the undead came at him, jamming a spear toward his belly. Both of them were constricted by the crushing press of the melee, but Mikael was able to get his shield down in time.

The spear's tip punched through with fearsome force, driven he knew not by sinews, but by the dark magics puppeting the accursed host. He swung his mace for the skeleton's face, teeth and dirt flying, the stink of the marsh depths choking Mikael's nose.

The reanimate disintegrated, but its spear remained, weighing down Mikael's shield and too firmly stuck to be easily dislodged. He stumbled back as yet another corpse came at him, creating a break in the line that was instantly filled by one of his guards thrusting past.

"Lord, are you wounded?" his bannerman, Rolla, demanded, grasping his shoulder in the press. Mikael just shook his head and beat his mace against the shaft of the spear until it splintered, just below the head, leaving only the metal wedged into the plumage of the raven crest on his shield.

"Are we holding?" he snarled at Rolla, snapping up his visor and dragging in a breath of corpse-stinking air.

"It seems so, lord," the bannerman replied. "The levies have stood their ground on either side, but Fortuna only knows about the Carthridge battles. The cursed fog is descending again."

Mikael looked toward the furious clash just a few yards in front of him, seeking a space for him to reenter the fray. Now that he'd had a chance to think, part of him didn't want to, but he overcame that cowardice with a grimace. He had been a poor student from what he knew many considered to be a poor barony. Damned if he was going to be a poor warrior too.

One of his men – he didn't get a chance to see who – reeled back, a sword buried in his side. Blood sprang, bright red, from the wound. Mikael drove himself into the gap, mace swinging.

"For Cailn!"

•••

Back-breaker was a frenzy of destruction. In the first moments of the melee, Zachareth hardly got a chance to even swing Razorsong. The animus ran the risk of sinking into the mire if it stayed stationary, but its strength allowed it to overcome the cloying muck, and its motions were relentless. The baronial guard that had stayed with Zachareth left a wide gap at the center of their formation as the construct swept and swung its great forearms at the oncoming undead and lunged forward with its rocklike, tusked head.

It seemed at first that nothing could stand before it. Zachareth felt exhilaration as bones splintered and shields shattered while swords, spears, and axes sparked and struck harmlessly off its stone hide. Any of the undead that made it past the creature's arms, shoulders and head met Razorsong. Zachareth hardly felt any resistance to each blow, the sword swung with such strength and its edge so keen that it bisected ribcages and sliced skulls in half without slowing down.

For a while Zachareth lost himself in the killing. Finally, Back-breaker had broken and trampled and crushed so many reanimates into the filth that it had succeeded in clearing a space directly ahead of itself. Zachareth used the moment to cast his eye about, trying to make out what was happening across the line.

The undead legion was throwing itself against the Carthridge battle, but the ranks seemed to be holding firm. The baronial guard on either side hadn't conceded an inch of muck. The Silver Banner was still flying high in Golfang's fist.

The fate of the left and right flanks was less clear. They had been reduced to indistinct masses in the fog. It felt like three separate clashes rather than one. Not knowing how they fared caused Zachareth's doubts to redouble. What if the other battles had been routed? What if they were being surrounded, cut off, doomed to a last, desperate stand in the icy mud?

"Lord, look ahead," Golfang called over the hammering of weapons and shields and the cries of the living. Zachareth turned his gaze from the flanks. At first, he thought the captain of the guard was calling his attention to a cohort of mud-caked, grinning skeletons marching in lockstep to fill the gap he'd plowed in their lines. He then understood that Golfang had been directing his attention beyond them, at the hill overlooking the slaughter where the moldering banners of the undead clustered closest. A purple light had started to suffuse the fog there, a sickly emanative that Zachareth now recognized as evidence of necromantic magic.

This was only the beginning, he realized. There was worse coming.

"Hold fast, sons and daughters of Carthridge," he bellowed and urged Back-breaker forward.

The thrust of Skerrif's shield threw the reanimate down. He stood above it as it twitched and attempted to rise and brought his boot slamming down on its skull. He felt bone fracture, and the hideous purple deadlights in its sockets went out.

"Back to the mire, you undead filth," he snarled, bringing his shield up again in time to take an axe blow to the upper rim. It wedged fast and he dragged it out of the way and stabbed with his sword. The weapon clattered and jarred into the thing's rib cage but showed no sign of slowing it as it managed to free its axe, two-handed.

It beat against his shield, then managed to jar a blow off his helmet. He struggled to disentangle his sword, expecting the death blow to follow, but all he heard instead was the now-familiar crunch of fracturing bones.

Marwand had driven past him and brought the axe-wielding undead down with a blow from her warhammer. She fell back in alongside Skerrif, realizing there were momentarily no more foes to break.

"Thank you," Skerrif managed to pant, tipping up his visor and dragging down air.

"Not so bad once it starts properly, eh?" Marwand replied from behind her own helm.

She was right. Skerrif's horror had turned into grim delight as they had met the undead charge. Every swing of his sword was a venting of years of nightmares and waking terrors, a purging of his fears and vengeance for those who had fallen before. Sword to sword, the dead were not so terrible.

He was about to say as much to Marwand when he felt something tugging at his ankle. He instinctively tried to pull himself free but found himself stuck fast. He looked down, expecting to find his boot entangled amidst the bones of the reanimate he'd brought down. Instead, with a jolt of pure fear, he saw that a skeletal hand, encased in dirt, had risen out of the marsh and clamped around his ankle.

More followed. A body began to drag itself up from where it had lain beneath the surface, so caked in black muck that it was completely unidentifiable, the ooze drooling off it. Skerrif cried and lashed out with his other foot, almost losing his balance as he stamped down repeatedly on the thing's muck-encrusted skull. Finally he felt it give way, its hold over his ankle loosening enough to allow him to rip himself away.

It wasn't just directly beneath him that a body had tried to rise up. Shouts of alarm rippled across the line as all around the mire stirred and bubbled, rancid heads and bony shoulders hauling themselves free of their swampy graves, limbs clawing and tangling at warriors already battling for their lives.

"There are more dead," Marwand exclaimed in horror. "They've been beneath us this whole time. This is their trap."

A howl went up, sending a chill through Mikael.

The screams followed from off to the right. He pulled free from the front line, one of his guards taking his place as he tried to get a view of what was happening on the end of the Cailn battleline. He could hear snarling and barking sounds as though a pack of hounds were assailing his soldiers in the mist. He quickly realized it was something far worse.

Shapes came loping from the mist, bestial forms that bounded with unnatural energy through the bog, splattering themselves with its muck. At a glance, they looked like huge wolves, but even the dirt matting them could not disguise their horrifying condition. Their skulls were skeletal and their pelts mangy and rotten with ugly deadlights playing and winking in their eye sockets. Mikael recognized them from the stories of his childhood, from the old fireside tales used to make sure children stayed in their beds at night and travelers didn't stray too far from the road. They sent a chill through him.

"Barghests," went up the desperate cry as more of the fell undead hounds emerged from the fog. "Watch the rear!"

"Rear ranks to about face," Mikael snapped at the horn blower standing beside his bannerman, rousing himself from the fear that had momentarily paralyzed him. The urgent notes pealed out, but he could see in some places that it was already too late. The lead barghests had fallen on the unsuspecting back echelons, bearing down Cailn soldiers-at-arms into the cloying muck where it was difficult for them to rise, then savaging them with long claws and talons. Their screams were chilling.

"They must've gotten around the flank," Rolla said, gripping the raven standard tighter. Mikael looked toward the left, but the main battle under Zachareth was almost impossible to see now in the mist. They were in danger of becoming completely cut off and surrounded.

"We have to push toward the Carthridge standards," Mikael said. "And stay together, or they'll pick us off one by one. Sound the rallying call."

The dead were beneath them and had been all along. Zachareth realized that and knew this was probably where whoever commanded the undead host had wanted them. The bodies already raised before the Bogmound had been the bait. He felt like a fool for not spotting the danger. He had assumed the bodies that had stood waiting for them were the dead of the original battle, but they were not, at least not all of them. Now the fallen from the first battle of the Bogmound were wreaking their vengeance.

The rising had thrown the battle's formation into disarray. Ranks had become fragmented as Zachareth's company was forced to hack at bodies grasping at them in their midst. The levies had started to visibly waver, their cohesion rapidly disintegrating. What was worse, there were barghests loose within the marsh. He could hear their howls.

The mist had grown almost impenetrable. He had no idea anymore what had become of Gwendolyn's and Mikael's forces. They were at risk of being overrun.

And in the middle of it all, Zachareth was angry. He had

been a fool, and people were dying as a consequence. The clash, which had seemed hopeful mere moments before, now hung in the balance.

He could see only one clear course, and it was ahead. It felt fitting. In all the stories, the champion sought out the master of the undying host and, at the point of decision, slew them, turning the tide of the battle. It was how Rufus had done it. It would be how he did it. Mistakes be damned. He would triumph, or he would perish. Either way, he was going up the hill.

"Follow me," he roared into the fog, raising Razorsong's tarnished steel. "Follow me, to death or victory!"

Skerrif stumbled but managed to right himself in time to hack down the skeleton clawing at him with a flurry of heavy, exhausted blows. His body was aching, the effort of fighting in the mud almost more than he could bear.

Marwand was behind him, guarding his back. The formation had completely collapsed, reduced to pockets of the living, still resisting the rising tide of undeath. At some point, they'd lost sight of Mord.

"Lady Gwendolyn's banner is gone," Marwand panted. "Did you see it fall?"

Skerrif twisted to look about but could find no sign of the rallying standard. Had it gone down, or was the fog just too thick now?

"I don't know," he managed to respond before another reanimate was on him.

He was going to die. They couldn't keep this up. He managed to drive the skeleton into the mud and splinter its skull with his shield. The wooden boards felt like a deadweight now, his sword like a lodestone. His limbs were shaking. He could barely breathe.

He heard Marwand gasp with pain behind him and turned to see her stumbling in the mud. A shard of bone was protruding from her shoulder. She stared at it, then at Skerrif, both knowing what it meant. Then she bent over and began to scream.

Skerrif tried to reach for her as more of the projectiles fell around them, but he caught the sound of splashing mud and felt a great weight slam into his side. He was flung over and momentarily submerged, choking on bitter, cold water. He managed to surface, spitting and gagging, and was confronted by a horrific visage that bore him back into the mire. A great beast had brought him down. It was doglike, half its skull bared and its massive fangs already drooling with blood. It stank of rotten flesh and wet fur and offal. Its eyes burned with foul magic.

A part of Skerrif was almost glad it was over.

CHAPTER TWENTY-NINE

Back-breaker faltered. The hill's slope was a ramp of slick mud, and still the dead were clawing up from it. There had been no such mount opposite the Bogmound, not in *The Canticle of Rufus the Bold*. Zachareth realized that it was possible the protrusion had been raised up since and was composed entirely of a vast mound of bodies.

The Carthridge host assaulted the corpse hill, following their baron. The guard led the way, a solid wedge of mud-drenched steel, the Silver Banner above them. There was no way now but onwards, taking the foul slope a step at a time, limbs blazing with exhaustion, shields up, swords, axes, maces, and pole arms hacking, again and again and again. It was a hellish ascent, but the crest was now only just ahead.

Then Zachareth felt the last of Back-breaker's momentum giving out. The animus could find no more purchase on the slick slope. The reanimates were everywhere, clawing at it, jamming their rusted weapons into its stony joints and cracks, hauling it down through sheer weight of numbers. The mud undulated as yet more dragged themselves up like vile, horrifying plants budding up from where they had been seeded.

Zachareth sensed a rare flicker of independent thought from the animus, raw frustration that it could no longer obey the commands it had been given. Without hesitating he threw his leg over and dropped down to its side, scything down several reanimates that lunged jerkily toward him with a single, ferocious stroke of Razorsong.

They couldn't stop here. Not now.

The dead fell like wheat before his longsword. There was no need for finesse, for parry and counterthrust, or to adopt the guards Golfang or Greigory had carefully taught him. The runes gave him the strength and speed to obliterate whole ranks of skeletons before they could land a blow. He felt invincible, and as he waded toward the crest he ignored Golfang's warning, the orc calling that he was too far ahead.

He couldn't pause. There was no time to regroup. The reanimates here weren't mud-caked, he had realized. They hadn't risen up from the bog. They had marched here from somewhere else, clad in heavy, rusting armor, their leering skulls hidden by great helms or snouted visors.

They were the bodyguards of the one who had raised this host. He was close.

Zachareth's feet found level ground. He'd reached the summit. His heart was racing, his lungs burning. The dead were all around him, but ahead they parted, stepping aside with the chilling, wordless synchronicity of puppets jerked on invisible strings.

At last, he was face-to-face with the one who commanded the undying host. He had hoped it would be Waiqar but had known in his heart that the chances were slim. The crows that still flocked and cawed overhead had given him a clue.

A massive, skeletal figure advanced through the serried

ranks of its guards, armed in heavy old plate mail, a wicked-looking axe in each fist. Its eyes blazed with purple death fire. Despite himself, Zachareth felt a moment of utter terror as the thing bore down on him.

"Another Carth whelp, come to die," rasped an icy voice, coming not just from the undead champion but from all the walking corpses around him.

"Ardus Ix'Erebus," Zachareth said, finding his courage and raising his sword.

"You know me, then," Ardus said as he halted before the Baron of Carthridge.

"I know my ancestors defeated you," Zachareth said defiantly, drawing on the stories of his childhood to strengthen his resolve. Rufus had faced down this very foe and triumphed. He would do the same.

"You are a fool if you think that," Ardus said. "But I knew that already. You have led your host mindlessly into a slaughter. I had thought today I might be tested, but there has been no hint of strategy. All you could think to do was to seek me out. I am... disappointed."

"Then let me end that disappointment, craven undead," Zachareth snarled, stung by the undeniable truth in Ardus's words. He struck.

Ardus made no move to parry, and he felt an upsurge of vicious delight as he anticipated Razorsong cleaving down through the skeleton's pauldron. Instead, the impossibly keen edge of the sword rebounded from Ardus's shoulder with a ringing clang and a flare of purple light, numbing Zachareth's hand and almost making him lose his footing.

The crows seemed to laugh, a chorus of croaks. Ardus's skeletal grin remained fixed.

"You have trusted your petty runemagic thus far, whelp," came the deathly voice. "But it is nothing before the power of true sorcery. Of necromancy. Let me show you."

Ardus attacked. Zachareth knocked aside the first axe stroke but barely got to the second as it slashed in at his torso. The weapon jarred a glancing blow off his breastplate, the head pulsing purple for a moment while the marks of the Turning's Bane began to glow in response, warding away the foul arcana.

Zachareth tried to repost, but the other axe was already back, coming in a downward stroke set to split him from the shoulder like a log of wood. He stepped back, struggling in the mud, the axe missing him so narrowly it left a tiny nick in his breastplate as it passed downward.

Now was a chance for a counter. He lunged with Razorsong, roaring as he drove with all his strength at Ardus's midriff, the bands on his arms blazing. The undead warrior twisted so the strike wasn't clean, but it should still have been enough to shatter ribs. Instead, once again, the sword merely glanced to the side. Zachareth realized he had barely scraped the ancient plate.

Axe blows rained back down again. Ardus was not swift like Greigory, but his style of fighting was powerful and relentless. He gave little care to defense, seemingly confident in his own invulnerability. His twin axes struck with shuddering power, jarring Razorsong and biting deep into Zachareth's armor whenever they broke through. The downward strikes in particular had the force to cut him from head to groin. He knew that if one landed, it was over.

He managed to stab into the reanimate several times, and at one point even drove Ardus back a few paces using the wide, sweeping strokes he had seen Greigory employ. The respite lasted only a few seconds. Ardus resumed his assault, balefire flickering, body, arms, and armor riven with vile magics. Zachareth parried as best he could, falling into his opponent's rhythm. When an opening appeared, he lunged again, this time for the skull.

The mud beneath him gave way. He slipped, the blow going wide. His heart seemed to stop as he righted himself and realized his guard was completely open. He expected a final, terrible blow, pain and then oblivion, but instead he found himself looking back up at Ardus. The hulking skeleton hadn't moved.

"You toy with me," Zachareth snarled, feeling a toxic, burning rush of shame and anger.

"It has been centuries since I last taught a mortal fool like you his place in the world," Ardus replied. "I shall ask my lord to make a gift of your bones, that I might add you to my retinue. The body of Rufus's scion will serve me for eternity."

Roaring, Zachareth attacked. He swung Razorsong in a series of hacking blows, all poise and finesse gone, fury making the runes in his sword, armor, and arms blaze brilliantly in the fog. Ardus parried with the hafts of his axes, but Zachareth felt the sword's edge bite into them now. He beat down the guard and struck one, two, three titanic blows against Ardus's armor. The third and final one crunched through the shoulder. Zachareth felt bone snap and give way.

Remembering the dangers of getting his blade caught, he twisted and tore Razorsong free, his muscles aching with the effort. Ardus stood unbowed, a rent running almost to the abdomen. Purple smoke coiled slowly from what, in any mortal opponent, would have been a fatal wound.

"Pathetic," Ardus's voice hissed. "I will make your servants suffer for that."

"Zachareth," shouted someone behind him. He stepped back from Ardus and risked a glance. It was Golfang. The orc, the Silver Banner still in one fist, had almost hacked his way to his side. The baronial guard was strung out with him, struggling desperately against the final, densest formation of reanimates. Golfang hewed down a skeleton with a mighty swing of his falchion before pointing with the broad-bladed weapon off to the right.

"Cailn is with us," he bellowed over the chaos of the desperate melee.

Zachareth saw that he was correct. Further along the slope, another wedge of men-at-arms and baronial guard were hacking their way into Ardus's reserve. The black raven of Cailn flew above them, and Zachareth spotted Mikael at the forefront, swinging a mace like a man possessed. The sight of his friend gave him a surge of hope. He wasn't alone. Carthridge wasn't alone.

Even as the warriors of Cailn pressed on however, the ground around them was splitting open as more bodies forced their way up. It was as though they were fighting the slope itself. As he watched, the raven banner faltered, dragged down in the midst of the fighting.

"They will be too late," Ardus taunted as the spear tip of the Cailn assault began to disintegrate, Mikael isolated and almost alone. "I will drown the last survivors of your host in a tide of mud and corpses. You have been outfought tactically, and now you have been outfought in single combat as well. Submit, and end this childish defiance."

Zachareth knew the deathless champion was right. He could not win. He had gambled everything on a frontal assault, and it had failed. And yet, there was still one weapon not yet employed, one he had pushed to the back of his mind again and again, but which now stood stark and alone, the last slender thread supporting his hopes.

He had no other choice. For Carthridge, a sacrifice would be made. He was willing to pay.

"You wanted real magic, powerful magic," Zachareth snarled. "Then witness this."

He reached into the pouch at his side, closed his eyes, and grasped the Black Key. As he drew it out, he ran his thumb over its knotted surface.

The reaction was instantaneous. A pain, more searing than anything he had experienced before, shot through his body. He cried out, eyes snapping open, sword slipping from his grasp. He had dropped the Black Key as well and stood transfixed as he saw it fly into the muck a few yards in front of Ardus.

Even as it tumbled, it ignited. A lance of pure and utter darkness shot skyward from the runestone, no wider than Razorsong's blade, but totally impenetrable. It beamed away into the fog, accompanied by a keening noise that Zachareth realized was a terrible, unearthly scream.

The pain in his body seemed to coalesce in his skull. He collapsed to his knees in the mud, clutching his head in both hands, the agony momentarily driving out all other thoughts.

The slender pillar of darkness before him started to bleed out into the world. Shadows billowed and coiled down its length, and Zachareth heard whispering and laughing, playing counterpoint to the terrible wail that made his ears ache and his skull feel as though it was slowly, slowly fracturing into a thousand pieces.

The shadows began to assume shapes. There were incorporeal

talons, and wicked, barbed tails, and, worst of all, faces. Each
was leering and bestial, and they dragged themselves from the
pillar of darkness like drowning men returning to shore. The
first to assume partial shape seemed to scent the air, and its
scream joined the wider, aching, keening noise as it swooped
down in a billow of black smoke.

Zachareth could only stare as the freed spirit surged into
the ranks of the reanimates directly to his left. Its body may
still have seemed incomplete, but the effect of it was anything
but. Bones flew through the air as it splintered dozens of
skeletons with a single swoop, and purple energy blazed as
the necromantic magic binding the bodies was dissolved by
something even more potent.

Sensing the delights that awaited them, the other spirits that
had been forming around the pillar darted down with a howl.
They fell all around Zachareth, their shadow claws raking and
splintering and shattering.

A flock of the creatures struck at Ardus. Unlike the
raised minions, the champion of undeath fought back. The
necromantic magics surged, and briefly, the dark spirits –
demons, Zachareth realized – were driven back.

The defiance didn't last long. The creatures lashed out with
renewed ferocity, more surging from the darkness unleashed
by the Back Key to strike from every side. The light of Ardus's
balefires began to flicker and weaken, and Zachareth saw
scratches, first a few, then dozens, then hundreds, appearing
on the warrior's heavy armor. Little by little, the demons were
carving Ardus apart.

Despite the agony, a sense of giddy elation gripped
Zachareth. It did not last long. He heard screams beyond the
wailing of the Key and its cursed spirits.

The pain in his skull had dissipated enough for him to lower his hands and look around. He saw that, to his revulsion, the Ynfernael monsters weren't only attacking the undead. Some were ripping into the baronial guards of Carthridge and Cailn. The effects of their terrible forms were even more marked as they found living beings to cull. Blood bloomed, a crimson addition to the surrounding mist, armor no protection against wicked, insubstantial talons and fangs. He saw his warriors falling, their very souls torn apart and feasted on, the spirits like wild animals gorging on marrow from cracked bones.

"No," Zachareth bellowed, trying to rise, trying to overcome the pain and the shock. "Not them! You do not take them!"

But the demons weren't listening or did not care. He saw them sweeping around Golfang, the captain of the guard turning at bay, the Silver Banner seeming to gleam above him. He saw one demon fall upon Mikael, maw distended grotesquely as it shrieked with slaughter-lust. Blood flashed, and Mikael stumbled and fell. Zachareth stared in horror, despair replacing the vicious delight he had felt as the demons had decimated the undead. He felt sick with sorrow and shame, disgusted with what was happening around him.

This was the price Morrow had hinted at, he realized. This was the damnation that had claimed him after all his efforts to avoid it or delay it. The Black Realm unleashed. His allies betrayed, his friends butchered.

And yet, this was the only way. Even amidst the horror he felt, the revulsion, he knew it to be true. In a sense, that was the worst realization of all. Without the power of the Ynfernael rune, it would already have been all over. And in that certainty, there were the first seeds of comfort, of reassurance. What else could he have done?

Somehow, Ardus had not yet been destroyed. The magics that bound him were strong, and they blazed with purple luminescence as they battled with the attacking spirits. His bones were starting to disintegrate, and his armor had been lacerated to pieces, but still he made one last lunge through the demonic storm. His bony fist clamped around Zachareth's throat, and everything changed.

He found himself elsewhere. He was alone, in a hall or the ruins of a hall. The marshland, the slaughter, the demons, they were all gone. Even Ardus was nowhere to be seen. His only companion was a man, sitting on a tarnished throne, gazing down at him. He was tall and painfully gaunt, in a regal sort of way, with pallid flesh and pale eyes. His expression was one of chilling disdain.

Zachareth knew who he was instinctively. The fire that had burned within him before rekindled. Briefly, all the horror of what he had unleashed was forgotten.

"Waiqar," he snarled.

"How perceptive you are, Zachareth Carth," the man on the throne said without even the coldest hint of humor.

"You dare show yourself to me in person?" Zachareth demanded. He tried to take a step forward, tried to raise his sword from the dirt, but found he could not. He experienced a moment of gut-wrenching helplessness.

"Do not try to strike me down, Baron Carth," Waiqar said in a lazy tone. "You cannot, for you are not truly here. Believe me, if you were, I would rend you to pieces, body and soul."

"What trickery is this?" Zachareth snapped.

"Dear Ardus is sending you a final message from me," Waiqar said. "Since he has been unable to defeat you, and since you have played your hand and foolishly sold your soul to the darkness,

I thought I would indulge myself by making you an offer."

"I will not join you," Zachareth said, rage burning in every word. Waiqar laughed.

"You would be surprised how many times I have heard that before, only to take oaths of fealty all the same. You are in a particular predicament, Zachareth. You must now see that you have been misled by those you trusted. The Ynfernael has wormed its way into your bones. It has taken advantage of your pride and your determination. Soon you will be nothing more than a slave to demons. Today has made sure of that."

"Rather that than the eternal curse of undeath," Zachareth declared, trying not to even consider the possibility that the Ynfernael had already claimed him, body and soul.

"Is that really what your life has become then?" Waiqar asked. "The lesser of two evils?"

"Your evil is final and eternal," Zachareth said. "I will master the power I have been given. Carthridge will be no one's slave. Under my rule it will become the strongest barony in Terrinoth. Your schemes will never threaten it again."

"You are either deluded or already possessed," Waiqar said. "You are a boastful fool. The Ynfernael may have saved you today, but one way or another, your soul is forfeit."

Zachareth could hear the keening sound now, the terrible shrieking of the dark spirits of the Aenlong unleashed. The hall around him seemed to be flickering and coming apart like a dream being stirred to wakefulness. Waiqar alone remained constant on his ancient throne, his gaze piercing.

"Our time is at an end, but I will see you again, Zachareth," the great necromancer said. He tried to answer, but the shrieking was too much, making him hiss and clutch at his ears in pain.

He realized he could move again. He was still on his knees in amongst the carnage, a billowing cloud of darkness surrounding him. His consciousness returned to his body, but there was no trace of Ardus Ix'Erebus save for the bruises around Zachareth's neck and the echo of mocking laughter from Waiqar's cursed lieutenant.

Zachareth straightened and stood, the despair he had felt before lost its edge. A grim, renewed certainty filled him. Waiqar truly did live, and it was the necromancer's fault he had been forced to use the Black Key, to unleash the horrors of the Ynfernael. It was all Waiqar's doing. He had killed Mikael and all the others, not Zachareth.

The threat to Carthridge was greater than ever. He knew he couldn't falter now. He had to rise up. He had to master the fate that had befallen him and seek vengeance for those who were lost.

The darkness of the Black Key had blanketed the battlefield. The demonic souls were still rending and tearing apart friend and foe alike. Zachareth grasped Razorsong and raised it and threw himself through the mud and bodies where the tainted runestone had fallen. It lay in the mire, pulsating with energy, the blackness still surging up and out of it in a great, billowing, shrieking cloud.

Zachareth remembered the Ironbound and the Whisperer in Nerekhall. He remembered how the construct had struck and broken the tainted shard into pieces. He raised Razorsong and brought it slashing down.

It jarred back from the stone with a crack. Immediately, pain stabbed through his skull as though he had been the one struck. He cried out, then gritted his teeth and swung again.

It was agony. The darkness broiling up from the stone

twisted and howled. The pain in Zachareth's head worsened. His vision began to blink and gray out. Everything else around faded into oblivion until all he could hear was the screeching, and all he could feel was the terrible pounding in his skull, the bubbling, acidic vileness of the Ynfernael made manifest.

His sight was failing. He could feel blood on his lips, in his mouth, warm and bitter. The pain in his head was too much.

He screamed, venting the last of his strength into a final, downward stab. The tip of Razorsong, impossibly keen, struck the heart of the darkness squarely, plunging through the shadowy matter still surging through the accursed portal.

The pain suffused him entirely, locking his jaw and shutting down every thought, all except the realization that the howling had stopped and he was falling.

After that, there was nothing.

CHAPTER THIRTY

Unyielding, rough textured stone woke him.

Zachareth moaned, trying to roll away from it as it pressed against his throbbing skull. There was a grinding sound and a low, hollow chuckle.

Slowly, his thoughts returned. His skull ached terribly. He could still taste blood. He opened one eye, flinching at the light, then the other, and beheld stone given life.

Back-breaker had been nudging him with its boulder head. The great animus was scarred and dripping with muck, but it was still imbued with the essence of life.

Nor was it the only being watching over him. A burly figure stood blocking the weak sunlight filtering through the dissipating mist. A brilliant standard rippled behind him. Zachareth squinted and managed to raise himself into a sitting position, pulling himself free from the cold, cloying mud with difficulty.

"Still alive then, pup?" Golfang asked.

Zachareth wasn't sure. He took the orc's outstretched hand and struggled to his feet, moaning at the aches running through him. Back-breaker backed off a few paces, joints grating.

He looked around as the exact memories of what had transpired came flooding back. All around him was a scene of silent devastation. Piles of broken skeletal remains were interspersed with the bodies of Carthridge's and Cailn's fallen warriors, intermingled in a final, lasting death. The mist was slowly starting to clear, and a chill breeze was tugging at the trampled marsh grass and twitching at the ragged banners that littered the battlefield.

He could find no trace of anything living. It seemed as though only he and Golfang had survived, along with Backbreaker.

"You're unharmed?" he asked, looking at the captain of the guard. The massive orc shrugged.

"It'll take more than a few demons to end me."

Zachareth suspected it had more to do with the Silver Banner, which he had planted in the bloodstained mud of the hilltop a few yards away. He hadn't been aware of its magical properties, but he remembered the light that had shone from it as the spirits freed by the Black Key had attacked.

He looked through the mud, seeking any sign of the cursed runeshard.

"You destroyed it," Golfang said, seeming to sense his thoughts. A sickening feeling began to settle in the pit of Zachareth's stomach as he contemplated just what had happened. He remembered how the cursed creatures had decimated friend and foe alike.

"Mikael," he said as he recalled seeing the heir of Cailn fall before one of the shadow horrors. He stumbled through the wreckage until he found the raven standard.

Mikael lay nearby. Zachareth knelt and lifted him in his arms, pulling him from the muck.

He was dead. His eyes were closed, his youthful face pale and strangely peaceful. A brutal wound had been torn across his chest, his blood mixing with the muck around him.

"Gods forgive me," Zachareth murmured, closing his eyes and bowing his head. He felt an abrupt, profound sense of loneliness, an abject desolation more potent than even shame or sorrow. He was responsible for this. He had caused the deaths of his friends, his own warriors, of those loyal to him, who had followed him up the corpse hill into the jaws of a living nightmare.

He heard Golfang approach and opened his eyes, angrily cuffing away tears. He looked up at the orc.

"What have I done?" he asked him.

"Won," Golfang said simply.

"At what cost?"

"That's not for me to say, lord."

Zachareth looked out over the bleak vista, still cradling Mikael.

"I unleashed this," he said. "I killed them all."

"I will not pretend to know what bargains you have struck, lord," Golfang said. "All I'm sure of is that those who lie here now would have died regardless of the magics you unleashed. At least this way their bodies will not be defiled with the curse of undeath. Your powers have stopped a terrible fate from befalling Carthridge."

"This power, it is not one a mortal should wield," Zachareth said.

"All your life you have sought power," Golfang said. "To be master of your own destiny. Do you feel now that you have any more control of your fate than you did before all this?"

The orc's question was genuine. Zachareth stared blankly

over the cold, quiet desolation. Had it truly been for nothing?

No, he tried to tell himself. Waiqar had returned. He knew that now for certain. The fears he had harbored for years had been correct. If he had not done all that he had, Carthridge would surely have fallen.

"Right now, strength is all that matters," he said as he recalled the taunting of the great necromancer, sitting safe in his moldering hall. Zachareth had beaten him. Was that not worth any price? Carefully, he laid Mikael down and stood. Golfang nodded.

"If that is so, then you had best find your strength once more, pup," he said, looking past Zachareth, down the mound. "Because they will want to know what happened here."

Zachareth didn't understand what he meant at first until he followed his gaze back across the devastation toward the Bogmound. There were figures there, he realized, ones not yet utterly befouled and filthy from the desperate battle in the marsh. They had dismounted from their horses and were crossing the battlefield toward the hillock that Zachareth had captured.

One of them was carrying a pennant bearing the Grandmother Oak of Rhynn.

Zachareth felt both relief and trepidation. Greigory was here. The victory was secured, but how much had the Baron of Rhynn witnessed? Sudden shame gripped him. Could he really explain what had happened to his old friend? Could he really admit to having used dark magics, even in the cause of righteousness?

He found Razorsong in the mud and sheathed the wicked blade as Greigory and his entourage climbed the mound. The baron had his helmet off, and his face was full of concern as he reached Zachareth and, to his surprise, threw his arms around him.

"Thank all the gods you still live," he said, breathless from wading through the bog and up the slope. "I could not have endured if my lateness had led to your demise."

"Well met, Greigory," Zachareth said, returning the embrace, forcing his tone to stay measured. He tried not to let the relief he felt show too clearly. It seemed as though the forces of Rhynn had not arrived in time to see the terrible power of the Black Key, only its aftereffects.

"The main body of my host is a half hour's march away," Greigory said, breaking the hug. "We have chirurgeons who can assist with the wounded."

Zachareth thanked him, suddenly too exhausted to do anything else as Greigory noticed the body of Mikael.

"That will strike his father hard," he said, his voice hollow. "Such terrible slaughter. What fell magics were unleashed here? We heard the howling and saw dark flashes on the horizon as we approached. I have never felt greater dread."

Zachareth found himself lost for words. How could he articulate what he had done? That he had made a pact, albeit by slow degrees, with a cult of the Ynfernael? That he had unleashed demons on his allies? The shame almost made him blurt out what had happened.

"The magics of the undead were strong," Golfang said just as he began to speak. "We were fortunate to triumph."

"But the dead are defeated?" Greigory asked.

"No," Zachareth said, mastering himself as he considered the further struggles that lay ahead. Revealing the truth now would serve no good purpose. It was something he was going to have to bear or risk disaster in the battles to come.

He knew he could never speak of it. It had to remain a secret forever. "Waiqar showed himself to me. He has returned, as I feared, but he was not present here, not in person. He sits in some crumbling citadel. Doubtless he is already laying fresh plans."

"You saw him?" Gregory wondered, but though it was a question there was no accusation in his tone, no hint that he thought his old friend mistaken.

"Yes, through his magics," Zachareth replied. "We have dealt him a blow here today, but it will only have checked him, not stopped him. We need to warn the rest of Terrinoth."

This was only the beginning, he told himself. He would lead not only Carthridge out of darkness but all of Terrinoth. That was the only way to guarantee Waiqar's defeat and to make the deaths of Mikael and all the others truly worthwhile. One kingdom, united in defiance of the curse of undeath. And if not, he would not trouble himself when the darkness encroached upon their borders.

"We will warn them," Gregory said, putting a hand on Zachareth's shoulder. "But whether they will take heed is another matter."

"Then Terrinoth be damned," Zachareth said fiercely. "Our baronies are all that matter, Gregory. If others will not stand by our side, then Rhynn and Carthridge will have to be enough. I will never rest in the defense of our homes. I will rally the people, see the silver mines back to full productivity, secure the harvests, and rebuild this host, greater than before. Never again will my people live in fear of what stalks them from the mist. Never again will the armies of death threaten our borders. I will bring safety and security back to Terrinoth, whether the other baronies will it or not."

"Zachareth the Great they'll call you if all that comes to pass," Greigory said with the hint of a smile, clearly recalling the boy he'd scrapped with in a castle courtyard all those years before.

"Maybe so," he replied, holding Greigory's gaze. "But it will be enough that I am Baron Zachareth."

ACKNOWLEDGMENTS

A huge thanks to all of the Aconyte team, especially my editor Lottie, without whom this book truly wouldn't have been written. Thanks also due to Katrina and the team over at FFG for continuing to not only build amazing worlds but let me play in them as well!

ABOUT THE AUTHOR

ROBBIE MacNIVEN is a Highlands-native History graduate from the University of Edinburgh. He is the author of several novels and many short stories for the *New York Times*-bestselling *Warhammer 40,000 Age of Sigmar* universe, and the narrative for HiRez Studio's *Smite Blitz RPG*. Outside of writing his hobbies include historical re-enacting and making eight-hour round trips every second weekend to watch Rangers FC.

robbiemacniven.wordpress.com
twitter.com/robbiemacniven

DESCENT
LEGENDS OF THE DARK

A handful of heroes stand between a monstrous horde and the destruction of the mystical heart of Terrinoth!

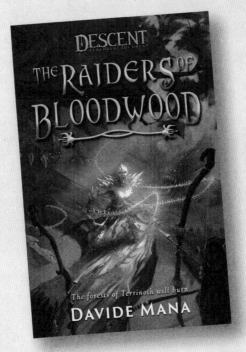

The invasion of Terrinoth has begun. Brutal Uthuk Y'llan hordes swarm across the land, ravaging everything in their path. A great champion has arisen in the Darklands: Beastmaster Th'Uk Tar, bent on destroying the wild and mystical Bloodwood as his first step in conquering the great forests of the Aymhelin and annihilating the elves who call it home.
If the Amyhelin burns, so will Terrinoth…

DESCENT
LEGENDS OF THE DARK

*Epic fantasy of heroes and monsters in
the perilous realms of Terrinoth.*

*Legends unite to uncover treachery and dark sorcery,
defeat the darkness, and save the realm, yet adventure
comes at a high price in this astonishing world.*

Legend of the Five Rings™

Brave warriors defend the empire from demonic threats, while battle and political intrigue divide the Great Clans.

EVAN DICKEN

MARIE BRENNAN

DAVID ANNANDALE

Follow dilettante detective, Daidoji Shin as he solves murders and mysteries amid the machinations of the Clans.

JOSH REYNOLDS

JOSH REYNOLDS

JOSH REYNOLDS

The Great Clan novellas of Rokugan return, collected in omnibus editions for the first time, with brand new tales of the Lion and Crane Clans.

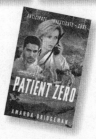

WORLD EXPANDING FICTION

Do you have them all?

ARKHAM HORROR
- ☐ *Wrath of N'kai* by Josh Reynolds
- ☐ *The Last Ritual* by S A Sidor
- ☐ *Mask of Silver* by Rosemary Jones
- ☐ *Litany of Dreams* by Ari Marmell
- ☐ *The Devourer Below* ed Charlotte Llewelyn-Wells
- ☐ *Dark Origins, The Collected Novellas Vol 1*
- ☐ *Cult of the Spider Queen* by S A Sidor
- ☐ *The Deadly Grimoire* by Rosemary Jones
- ☐ *Grim Investigations, The Collected Novellas Vol 2*
- ☐ *In the Coils of the Labyrinth* by David Annandale
  (coming soon)

DESCENT
- ☐ *The Doom of Fallowhearth* by Robbie MacNiven
- ☐ *The Shield of Daqan* by David Guymer
- ☐ *The Gates of Thelgrim* by Robbie MacNiven
- ☑ *Zachareth* by Robbie MacNiven
- ☐ *The Raiders of Bloodwood* by Davide Mana *(coming soon)*

KEYFORGE
- ☐ *Tales from the Crucible* ed Charlotte Llewelyn-Wells
- ☐ *The Qubit Zirconium* by M Darusha Wehm

LEGEND OF THE FIVE RINGS
- ☐ *Curse of Honor* by David Annandale
- ☐ *Poison River* by Josh Reynolds
- ☐ *The Night Parade of 100 Demons* by Marie Brennan
- ☐ *Death's Kiss* by Josh Reynolds
- ☐ *The Great Clans of Rokugan, The Collected Novellas Vol 1*
- ☐ *To Chart the Clouds* by Evan Dicken
- ☐ *The Great Clans of Rokugan, The Collected Novellas Vol 2*
  (coming soon)
- ☐ *The Flower Path* by Josh Reynolds *(coming soon)*

PANDEMIC
- ☐ *Patient Zero* by Amanda Bridgeman

TERRAFORMING MARS
- ☐ *In the Shadow of Deimos* by Jane Killick
- ☐ *Edge of Catastrophe* by Jane Killick *(coming soon)*

TWILIGHT IMPERIUM
- ☐ *The Fractured Void* by Tim Pratt
- ☐ *The Necropolis Empire* by Tim Pratt
- ☐ *The Veiled Masters* by Tim Pratt *(coming soon)*

ZOMBICIDE
- ☐ *Last Resort* by Josh Reynolds
- ☐ *Planet Havoc* by Tim Waggoner
- ☐ *Age of the Undead* by C L Werner *(coming soon)*